"The author skilfully interweaves fact an[fiction in an] engaging narrative. The novel's strengths l[ie in the] [person]al stories and human frailties behind the [p]olit[ical figures] and in its portrayal of the courage and re[sili]ence [of the family,] notably his wife Clarinda."

~ **Harriet Elvin,**
Chief Executive Officer at
Cultural Facilities Corporation Canberra

"A compelling family saga - telling, like never before, the story of one of Australia's most extraordinary families."

~ **Professor Tim Bonyhady,**
Author of *Good Living Street:*
The Fortunes of my Viennese Family

"This is an Australian story about love and loss. It is the story of the author's ancestry, but it speaks to us all. Every Australian should read it."

~ **Kay Whitney,**
Access and Learning,
Canberra Museum and Gallery

Clarinda and Henry

Catherine Blake

First Published in Australia by Aurora House
www.aurorahouse.com.au

This edition published 2018
Copyright @ Catherine Blake 2018
Typesetting: Allen Smalley
Cover design: Kay Whitney and Luke Harris

ISBN number: 978-0-6481112-8-3 (paperback)

National Library of Australia Cataloguing in Publication entry:

 A catalogue record for this
book is available from the
National Library of Australia

Distributed by:

Ingram Content:
https://www.ingramcontent.com/
Australia: phone +613 9765 4800 | email lsiaustralia@ingramcontent.com
Milton Keynes UK: phone +44 (0)845 121 4567 | email enquiries@ingramcontent.com
La Vergne, TN USA: phone 1-800-509-4156 | email inquiry@lightningsource.com

Gardners UK:
https://www.gardners.com/
phone +44 (0)1323 521555 | email: sales@gardners.com

Bertrams UK:
https://www.bertrams.com/BertWeb/index.jsp
phone +44 (0)1603 648400 | email sales@bertrams.com

For Simon, Stephanie, Eleanor and Joshua

Acknowledgments

I would like to thank my family – Simon, Stephanie, Eleanor and Joshua – for their amazing support and encouragement to take a year away from my teaching career to focus entirely on this novel. And, of course, I must thank my dog, Boof, for always being there when I needed an exercise break!

Thank you also to my publisher, Linda Lycett, and her wonderful staff at Aurora House, in particular her senior editor, Sarah Vogler, and to Rosemary Peers from Lynx Publishing for the original edit of the text.

I would also like to thank Ian Thom – also one of Clarinda and Henry's great-great grandchildren, and Menie's great-grandson – for his corrections and detailed comments on facts within the book, and also my friend Kay Whitney for her overwhelming support and enthusiasm for this project and the fabulous photograph on the cover.

I am also deeply grateful to my second grade teacher, Mrs Clear at Eastwood Public School in Sydney back in 1973, for planting the initial seed that I should, one day, become a writer. Teachers can make a difference. I have endeavoured to locate the whereabouts of Mrs Clear or her relatives, so if you are out there reading this, please get in touch with me through my publisher.

There are also many friends who read all or part of this book and encouraged me hugely to keep going. They include Bette Triglone, Alison Sweeney, Melissa Kretchmer, Philip Habel, Lauren French, Julia Ison, Andrew Boukaseff, Renee Ferris, Heidi Akister, Chris Dacey and Cathy Piani. And yes, Lauren, I will include a character based on you in my next book!

Contents

Men rule in commerce, in the market, and in the state; but women form the men who are so to govern, and thus become the real, albeit the silent, governors of the whole affairs of human society.

~ **Henry Parkes**, the *Empire*,
26th of January, 1853

Prologue

(On board the *Strathfieldsaye*, off the coast of
New South Wales, 23rd of July, 1839)

Clarinda clutched the hand of one of the women with her in the ship's hold as it lurched over another swell. Her head lolled back in agony with the motion and she expelled a guttural, animal groan.

"Go fetch the surgeon will you, Mary?" she heard one of the voices say from within her delirium of pain. "He be in his cabin or on deck with some of the other gentlemen, I expect. 'Tis late but we need to find Mr Allan. Go fetch him, Mary. Quick now!"

There were muffled whispers and sighs from the women around her and Clarinda clawed at the hand she held and begged, "Is anything wrong? Is the baby all right? Oh please, please, is anything wrong? Please don't let anything be wrong!"

"Now, now! 'Twill be all fine, Clarinda. All fine. The baby will be here soon."

"Please, oh please, dear Lord, may this baby live!" Clarinda moaned before another contraction ripped through her, consuming her with pain.

When the pain eased she breathed with shallow relief. "Dear Lord, may this one live. Please may this one be a healthy baby." The women gathered around her all added their own silent prayers to hers.

Mary, meanwhile, had climbed the ladder from the hold and run towards the raised poop deck nearby. She strained her head from below to see if any of the cabin passengers were there in the dark of the night, or whether all were in bed so that she might venture up unseen to knock at the surgeon's door. She heard deep, animated chatter from the far end of the deck and called up to the voices, "Hello? Excuse me? Is anyone there?"

A shadowed face appeared at the rail. "Are you calling to me, by any chance?" the man asked in mock surprise.

Mary gritted her teeth. She had been a dairymaid in her home town of Cork and had always resented the haughtiness of those who thought themselves above her. But she knew that for Clarinda Parkes's sake, she must swallow her pride now and not react with her accustomed sharpness. "My most sincere apologies, sir," she said. "'Tis a passenger having her baby, sir. We need the surgeon. We in steerage be needing Mr Allan most urgent."

The man guffawed and turned to another hidden from Mary's view. "Do you hear that, Adams? Mr Allan is needed for a child birthing – urgently apparently."

Mary heard the other laugh heartily and another face peered over the deck rail towards her.

"He's indisposed, I believe, my dear," the second man called. "Celebrating our reaching the coast of New South Wales. In his cups, you know, as is often the case with Mr Allan."

Even in the dark, Mary could see the two men's delighted smirks before the first man said, "We could throw him down to you, perhaps, if you're desperate?"

Mary bit her lip hard. She knew the ship's surgeon would be useless if he was as inebriated as he had been on the two other occasions of childbirth during the voyage. The women had had no choice but to band together and deliver the babies themselves. But this was a different case. It looked as though the baby was positioned the wrong way and the women had not been able to turn it. "Could I... do you think, sirs..." she hesitated. "Could I just talk to the surgeon, please? Just a quick word."

"Have it your way then, my dear," said the first man, and the two disappeared briefly only to return with the surgeon hanging between them, his arms draped around their necks, his head lolling to the side and his eyes fluttering. The first man slapped the surgeon playfully across the face. "Someone to see you, Charles. Someone from steerage with an important job for you, it seems," he said.

Mr Charles Allan attempted to stand upright as he gazed down at Mary, his eyes rolling. "What-is-it?" he slurred.

Mary swallowed hard. "Sir, 'tis one of the steerage passengers. She be in her hour. She be in her hour and be not so well, sir. The baby be turned, we women think. He be turned most unnatural like, sir. We've tried to move him ourselves."

The surgeon groaned and the two men on either side chuckled.

"Please, sir," Mary continued firmly above their laughter. "Please can you not come down to help?"

The surgeon groaned once more. "Oh, she's in good hands," he said in a stumbling voice. "You womenfolk have delivered other babies on this voyage without my help. She's in good..." But before he could finish his excuse, a spasm overtook him and he retched violently. The other men laughed.

As Mary stumbled back towards the opening to the hold she noticed a tall, gangly figure ahead. She swallowed hard again when she realised it was Henry Parkes in his heavy, fraying coat, peering over the rail at the darkened cliffs of their new home. He was waiting for her, and even in the dark she could see the intensity of his blue eyes.

"'Ow is she, Mary?" he asked in his deep, commanding voice.

"Oh, Henry, she be doing just fine now," Mary lied, and averted her own gaze from his questioning one. "Baby'll be coming along soon. I best be down there now. We be fetching you first thing." She pushed past him and walked hurriedly towards the hole that led down to the women's hold.

The stifling, dank air of the hold took Mary's breath again as she raced through the narrow alley of bunkbeds towards the gathering of oil lamps and women at the far end. There were impatient sighs from some of the other women lying awkwardly in their narrow beds, and a few irritable yells of "Get that damn baby out, would ya!" and "Can't a soul get no bloody sleep round 'ere!"

A hand reached out to Mary as she passed one of the lower bunks and Sarah Crump, holding her own baby within the tangle of blankets, asked in a whisper, "Is all well, Mary? Will Clarinda be born of this baby soon? It's been all night, poor thing. I'm praying it's born before the dawn."

"Let's pray so, Sarah," Mary whispered back. "Let's pray she be holding her baby with you along with the first light. 'Tis never for certain, is it? Be in the hands of God, it be. In the hands of God." Mary crossed herself and squeezed Sarah's outstretched hand before continuing on.

There, still crouched on the bare boards, Clarinda wailed, her hair lank from sweat, her lip bleeding from where she had bitten it hard during one of her agonies.

"He be not coming, the surgeon," Mary whispered to the others. "He be in his cups again."

There were huffs and rolled eyes amongst them.

"We know he's no help when he's had too many gins," said one woman.

"Did you tell him the baby's turned, Mary?" asked another. "Did you tell him it's not like the other two we got out?"

"Yes, I did. I told Mr Allan all that."

For Clarinda, the conversation went unheard, unknown, so intense was her suffering now. Instead, the unceasing, unbearable waves of her contractions were all that she was.

Henry heard Clarinda's scream from the dark hold below as dawn was beginning to light the unfamiliar cliffs. The scream was followed by another and another with barely a breath drawn between. He looked towards the strange pattern of the southern stars and prayed to the God he questioned unceasingly, for there was nothing else he could do.

Clarinda's screams stopped and she began to pant heavily with the relentless need to bear down. One of the women yelled, "Come on now! Come on! It be 'appening. It be 'appening whether for good or nought. It be 'appening now I reckon. God bless your soul, Clarinda, and the baby's. God bless your souls."

And with this the woman placed her hand on the warm, moist scalp of the infant as it entered the world.

Clarinda heard the angel cry, a loud, insistent cry that she had not heard from her other two blessed children who lay in the earth in Birmingham. She heard the sighs of the women around her as the infant's shoulders were manoeuvred out of her, followed by the arms, body and legs. Finally she felt the warm, wet body of a child laid upon her breast. One last push ended with the squelched thud of the placenta as it hit the hold's floor.

"Oh, Clarinda. It's a wee baby girl," Mary whispered to her. "Ah, she be beautiful."

Clarinda clutched the precious baby to her breast and wept. She wept with relief for a healthy baby at last. And she wept for her home in Birmingham, and for the loss of her father's love and for her two other babies who had died. And she wept with fear and uncertainty for the life ahead of her; the new life she would share now with Henry in the strange town of Sydney.

Her tears fell like a baptism on the baby's fair head.

PART I

Birmingham

ONE

The first thing Henry knew of her was her voice. Soft, measured, melodious. He heard it clearly from the shop as he sat in the workroom behind. It was a voice you could drift away upon – *like a soothing lullaby*, he thought. He could use this in one of his poems.

"What I need is a sort of button, I suppose," the voice said. "Not a set, just the one, with this design upon it. Do you think it could be done?"

Henry got up from his lathe where he was turning ivory into a candlestick and peered through the curtains towards the shop. Mr Holding was examining a picture on the counter before him with his eyeglass wedged in place and there, leaning over the picture with him, was a woman whose clear, cream face and rosebud lips made Henry think of one of the porcelain dolls he had once seen Lord Leigh's youngest daughter playing with in the gardens of the Stoneleigh estate.

"Mm," Mr Holding was mumbling. "Most intricate. A lot of detail to it. Could be a difficult project. Henry? Henry?"

Henry rubbed the ivory dust from his hands before drawing the curtain and entering the shop. *She's a beauty*, he thought, a beauty in a way his sisters were not. Her brown hair waved around her face and her eyes were the pale blue of a forget-me-not.

"Yes, Mr 'olding?" he said, unusually self-conscious of his rough Midlands accent before this woman.

"Miss...ah...Miss..." Mr Holding indicated towards her.

"Miss Varney," she offered.

3

"Ah yes, Miss Varney is asking if this picture could be carved. I believe you could do it, couldn't you, Henry? A detailed drawing, but one I believe you could carve deftly. You can see the lines are delicate around the face and..."

Henry stole a glance towards Miss Varney as Mr Holding talked and, noticing a resemblance to the picture, looked from one to the other. Miss Varney smiled shyly towards him.

"My mother, you see. It's a picture of her," she explained. "Like a cameo, I suppose, is what I want."

"Why, she is very beautiful, your mother," Henry offered, still looking towards Miss Varney.

"Ah yes, she was," Miss Varney's eyes lowered. "She died some time ago when I was quite young. That's why I decided to have this made. I want to always have her image before me."

Henry mumbled his apologies for her loss.

"Anyway, do you think it could be done?"

"Yes, Miss Varney. Could be done. I'll put my best into this one. Could be done for certain."

She smiled briefly towards him and Henry was struck once more by her beauty. He could gaze into those eyes for an eternity, he thought as a deep blush spread across her cheeks.

Mr Holding coughed to gain their attention. "You're Robert Varney's daughter, aren't you? The whipmaker down the road here on Moseley Street?"

"Yes, I am indeed. But..." she hesitated. "But I have a little saved. I would like to pay for this myself and not involve Father."

"That will be fine," Mr Holding agreed as he jotted notes alongside the picture.

"Well, thank you," said Miss Varney, glancing again at Henry, but directing her words mainly towards the older man. "I'll be around in a while to see how it is going, Mr Holding."

4

Henry refused to end his involvement in the conversation. "I'll be onto it quickly, Miss Varney," he said. "Won't be more than a few days, I think. Give me maybe two days for it." He dipped his head to her.

Her eyes remained lowered as she replied, "Thank you. Yes. I'll visit again in two days then." She gathered her purse from the counter.

"Nice meeting you, Miss Varney," Henry called, just before the bell rang on the swinging door behind her.

"Bit smitten? Hey, Henry?" Mr Holding asked, chuckling.

Henry flushed slightly at the friendly taunt. "Be getting back to it then," he mumbled and, embarrassed, left the picture of the deceased Mrs Varney on the counter as he returned to the workroom.

That night, as Henry sat around the hearth with his family, his thoughts of the fascinating Miss Varney were regularly interrupted.

"You be going to that Union meeting this Friday eve?" his brother George asked him.

"Yes, for certain," stated Henry.

"I'll be there with you, too," said James.

"Good, good. You brothers got to stick together on the politic side, I feel," said Mam, as she worried over her darning by the low candlelight.

"We're making a difference, 'enry," continued George. "The Birming'am Union's making a real difference to the working man's life 'ere in Britain."

"Yes," said Henry simply. He would normally have continued the conversation with fervent remarks on the need for universal suffrage and equal parliamentary representation, but tonight he was distracted. George continued undeterred.

"We made the difference at that meeting last year on New'all 'ill," he said. "If it wasn't for that, and for all the people coming from towns around, the Reform Act would never 'ave been passed back in London. Mr Grey would never 'ave come back as prime minister and that Tory buffoon, Wellington, been pushed out."

Sarah paused at her reading then and looked towards her brothers. "Was the Reform Act enough, though?" she asked. "I've been reading 'ow more needs to be done to ensure equality."

Henry pulled himself out of his reverie.

"Yes," he said. "'Tis good that we now 'ave Birming'am represented in parliament by Mr Attwood and Mr Scholefield. At least we, and so many other growing towns like us, 'ave some representation. But it 'asn't made a massive difference to our daily lives yet, 'as it?"

"No," said James. "We still can't vote ourselves. Not you, 'enry, or you, George, or even Da over there." He looked towards the sleeping figure of their father, sitting in the corner with his pipe hanging from his mouth. "'Tis only the rich that can vote still, not us working men. It's not right!"

"Yes, James, all men should 'ave the vote," said Sarah, and their other sisters, Maria and Eliza, looked up from their needlework and nodded in agreement.

Little Tom pulled on Maria's apron. "Am I a working man, Auntie Maria?" he asked. They all laughed.

"You will be one day, for sure," said Henry. "Unless the world changes and all men become equal, Tom, you'll 'ave no choice but to be a working man like your poor Da was before 'e died, and the rest of us."

As Henry lay in bed alongside young Tom later that night, he found he could not sleep. His mind was whirling with thoughts of Miss Varney. He wondered if she thought him too rough and coarse a man. He wondered how he had never seen her before, and how he could see her again after she had collected the cameo. But this was not all that he thought of. He thought of her fine, long-fingered hands and the shape of her under her modest dress – the small, slight waist and the rise of her breasts. And he thought of the low, burning ache he had felt at her glance. He felt this now with a terrible longing.

Clarinda Varney did not think herself beautiful. When she was younger, she had been an ungainly, angular girl with pimples and fingernails bitten to the quick. Although she had memories of her late mother, also named Clarinda, telling her she was pretty, the young Clarinda had known the face in the mirror was not particularly attractive, not like that of her fair, green-eyed friend Isabella Parry.

As she grew older, Clarinda's skin cleared, her body became more rounded and womanly and her striking blue eyes shone from their bed of thick, dark lashes against her pale skin. This was the beauty that Henry Parkes had admired. But because her stepmother had always commented rudely on her features, Clarinda had never changed her initial opinion about her appearance. Ann Varney would make remarks such as, "Your nose reminds me of a mole's nose, Clarinda," and, "Such a shame you didn't inherit your mother's defined cheekbones." Not that Ann Varney was particularly good-looking, but she was a master at self-deception when confronted by any faults regarding herself.

And so, as Clarinda crossed the street, running to avoid a rattling carriage, and strode down the path towards her home several blocks away, she found herself flushed and excited at the thought of the young man's intense, honest gaze. While she knew her father would never approve of an ivory turner as a suitor for his daughter, she felt an unfamiliar, guilty thrill. Thoughts of the tall, handsome man remained with her as she skipped up her rose-lined path and through the austere, white front door, before hanging her bonnet and coat in the hallway. Wilbur came scuffling towards her on little brown paws and jumped on her, whimpering until she picked him up and nuzzled him affectionately.

Ann Varney appeared from the parlour, small, dark and sullen. "Where have you been, Clarinda?" she demanded in a superior tone. "I need you to help Betty beat the rug from the drawing room. Isabella Parry is upstairs waiting for you in your room, so I suppose it must wait."

"Yes, Stepmamma," Clarinda said as she went up the stairs still holding Wilbur to her chest.

"Don't be too long at your idle chatter, Clarinda," Ann Varney called after her. "You've been out so long and I need that rug beaten."

Inside Clarinda's bedroom, Isabella sat on the wicker chair flicking through a fashion paper. "Hello there," she said in her cheery, light voice, looking towards Clarinda as the door opened.

"Isabella! I didn't know you planned to visit today. How long have you been waiting?"

"*Ever* so long," Isabella complained, but Clarinda scoffed at her.

"I've only been down the road and back. Everyone seems to think I've been away from the house for ages."

"I know," laughed Isabella. "Your stepmother was complaining that she needs you to beat the rugs or some such task."

Clarinda rolled her eyes and sighed. "I know, she's already told me – before I was barely through the door. There's always some housekeeper's task Stepmamma wants me to do."

Clarinda and Isabella had known each other for as long as they could remember. They had grown close when Robert Varney had engaged a tutor to instruct Clarinda soon after her eleventh birthday, and Benjamin Parry had asked if his own daughter could join her for the lessons. And so, Clarinda and Isabella had met daily in the Varneys' drawing room with the severe Miss Picton.

Isabella, unlike Clarinda, had not been at all afraid of this strict, unsmiling lady and would poke fun at her when the girls were alone.

"Did you see her pick her nose with her handkerchief, Clarinda, when we were supposed to have our heads down at our writing? It was dis*gusting!*" Isabella said one time, giggling.

"You shouldn't be talking of unladylike things like that, Isabella!" But Clarinda laughed along despite herself.

"Well *she* shouldn't be picking her nose, should she?"

Sometimes Isabella would copy Miss Picton's lisping voice or imitate her walk with her bottom sticking out and her nose in the air. "It's like she's a pigeon!" she'd exclaim. "We should call her Miss Pigeon!"

Not only had they chattered and laughed and, on Clarinda's instigation, discussed Bible passages, but Isabella had been there for Clarinda when her mother had died of influenza and she had fallen into a dark, unrelenting melancholia. Isabella had also been there for Clarinda when her father had married Ann Fleming soon after her mother's death and the conflict between Clarinda and her stepmother had begun.

"I should call you Cinderella, Clarinda," Isabella had half jested. "Like in *Grimm's Fairy Tales*. Poor you with your evil stepmother."

It was only Isabella who Clarinda told of the cruelty of Ann Varney. When they were younger, these brutalities would make them both cry. Clarinda told her friend of the beatings across the back of the legs her father gave her with a strap upon her stepmother's request, who would insist he punish her for any minor slight or disobedience. She told her of Ann Varney's taunts, how she admonished her if she found her crying for her mother and how, when no one was looking, she would pinch Clarinda cruelly on the bottom or the arm for no apparent reason. And they would agree that the jest of Cinderella was not entirely untrue.

"My poor, poor Cinderella," Isabella would comfort as she stroked Clarinda's hair.

When they tried to fathom the reasons for her stepmother's persecution, Clarinda and Isabella agreed she must have some peculiarity of personality. She appeared to possess a lack of perspective or reality. It was as if Ann Varney convinced herself things were a certain way and that made it so. It seemed she had decided Clarinda was a worthless, troublesome girl and so, without any evidence to show, in her view it was the case.

It was in the spirit of this firm friendship that Clarinda, after discussing some of the plates in the fashion paper, told Isabella about the cameo of her mother she'd commissioned and the attractive man she had met in the shop.

Isabella squealed with delight and put her hand to her mouth. "But he's an *ivory* turner, Clarinda!" she exclaimed. "You can't be falling in love with an ivory turner, you know. Your father and stepmother would never allow it, nor your brother!"

"I know, I know," Clarinda laughed. "I'm not in love, of course. It is just that he was *ever* so handsome and he kept staring at me with his beautiful almond-shaped eyes."

The two girls giggled.

"And, you know what else?" Clarinda continued. "Not only is he an apprenticed ivory turner, he has a Coventry accent. Father would be *most* disapproving indeed!"

There was a sharp rap at the door and Ann Varney stepped in without waiting for a response. "Isabella, you must go now. Clarinda has chores to do," she said.

The two friends hugged affectionately and Isabella left with Ann Varney following her down the stairs. Clarinda changed her shoes and tied her apron, moving with sharp, quick jerks and muttering under her breath angrily, "I'm not a child! I'm twenty years old! I'm not your servant! You are nothing like my own sweet mother! You are horrid! Horrid! I wish you'd fall down a well!"

Clarinda sighed, bit her lip and reached for her Bible, clutching it to her chest as she closed her eyes tightly and took two deep breaths. "Dear Lord," she said softly. "Please give me the patience and the willingness to bear this cross you have given me. And please help Stepmamma and Father to be kinder. I know mine is a small cross to bear, really, Dear Lord, and I thank you for all my other countless blessings. Amen."

Clarinda found the maid in the sweltering kitchen scouring a pot with water she had boiled over the fire. Betty was younger than Clarinda. The daughter of a blacksmith, she had taken up service to help support her ever-growing family. The thought suddenly struck Clarinda as she watched the girl's quick, deft movements that Betty was the breed of girl a man such as the handsome Henry Parkes should court. Certainly not someone like herself. She laughed at her foolish imaginings of having a connection with the man. But still... the thought was there.

"Betty," she said, and the girl turned abruptly, her sleeves rolled to her elbows and her face red and moist from her labouring. She smiled a flash of crooked teeth.

"Miss Varney? What you be doing down here in this heat?"

"Stepmamma has a task for us both," Clarinda announced. "We're to beat the rug from the parlour."

Betty raised her eyebrows. "You know, Miss Varney," she said and looked over her shoulder as if someone might be listening, "no disrespect intended, but truly, Mr and Mrs Varney should be paying you a wage with all you do. If they're going to treat you like a maid, they should pay you something, too."

Clarinda laughed lightly. This sentiment was not far from her own thoughts but she knew she could not let their maid know of her feelings towards her own father and the woman he had married.

"Oh, Betty," she said, smiling. "You know all the advantages I get being the daughter of an established whipmaker. Of course I should help around the house. Don't be silly thinking I should need a wage."

"'Spose you're right, Miss Varney," Betty agreed reluctantly as they left the stifling kitchen to attend to the rug.

Later that night, after supper had been served, Clarinda escaped the brooding atmosphere of the lounge room where her brother, John, was playing with a pack of cards and her stepmother clunked at the pianoforte while her father grunted over a newspaper. She recalled Betty's words and mulled over the injustice of her situation and the hopelessness and helplessness of it all. And as she fretted, the image of Henry Parkes with his rough workman's hands and unkempt, curling hair niggled in the recesses of her mind so that when Clarinda fell into a fitful, heavy sleep, her dreams were haunted by him.

Two

enry's parents, Thomas and Martha Parkes, had never learnt to read or write having had no education or other opportunity to learn such skills. But from an early age, Martha's children knew she was an intelligent woman. She would often tell them stories of her past as young Martha Faulconbridge when she had been a lady's maid to Miss Hamilton in Coventry.

Miss Hamilton had been confined to a chair on wheels due to a childhood illness that had left her unable to walk. Consequently, Martha's duties had included companionship. During the long hours Martha had spent sitting with the invalid, undertaking tasks such as massaging her limp feet or plaiting her hair, Miss Hamilton had read to her. It was then, over the four years of her service, that Martha had listened eagerly, enthralled, to plays such as *The Alchemist* by Ben Jonson or those of Shakespeare, and novels such as *Robinson Crusoe* by the great Daniel Defoe.

So when it had come to idling through the long, dark, evening hours with her own children, Martha had recounted the stories she'd been read many years earlier. She'd retell these stories and plays in detail, reciting whole tracts of *Robinson Crusoe* – her favourite – word for word.

One night, after James had found a battered copy of the novel at the library, the family had sat around the hearth and James had read the opening chapter to them. As he'd read, Mam had begun to say the words along with him, as if they'd been imprinted in her mind.

13

"'Tis nothing," Mam laughed, dismissing her family's astonishment and praise at her ability to recite the novel. "Just got a good ear, that's all. I 'ear it, I remember it, nothing more."

And so, it was not overly surprising when young Henry began to demonstrate a remarkable talent for his letters. Sarah, fourteen years his senior, was his main tutor over the years, having attended the Stoneleigh village school for most of her youth before she and her siblings were sent out to regular work because of Da's troubles. Together she and Henry read the novels of Sir Walter Scott and the plays of Shakespeare. Henry loved the poets best though: Byron, Moore, Shelley, Campbell and Leigh Hunt. Like his mother, he could remember whole tracts of these poems and of Shakespeare. Sometimes in the evenings, he would recite them to the family in his Midlands accent.

It was through these readings and retellings of literature that Henry developed an idealistic, romantic side to his personality, so that when he met Miss Varney – a beautiful, winsome creature – he was easily swept up in the desperation of love.

On the morning that Miss Varney was to return to the shop, Henry was distracted and edgy as he turned the pedal of his lathe with his foot and carved the shape and pattern of a decorative door handle. He had completed the cameo of Mrs Varney the day before so that it would be ready whenever Miss Varney should visit the shop.

John Holding wandered into the workroom to watch Henry at his task. "Doing a solid job there, Henry," he said. "You've certainly moved on from your earlier days of turning, when you could only make simple buttons and cotton reels."

"Thank you, Mr 'olding." Henry didn't look up from his work.

"Expect that pretty Miss Varney will be visiting us for her purchase sometime today," ventured Mr Holding, positioning his eyepiece to take a closer look at the door handle forming on the lathe.

Henry paused momentarily at the mention of her name. "Yes," he said simply.

"I hear she's a regular at the Carr's Lane Chapel," Mr Holding offered. "You're not religious yourself, Henry, are you? I don't often hear of you going to church or chapel."

"Sometimes I do, Mr 'olding. Not often, not regular or anything."

"Perhaps you should begin to become a regular at Carr's Lane. I'd say you'd get better acquainted with Miss Varney if you did."

As Mr Holding opened the curtain to return to the shop he winked at Henry. Henry stopped his work and stared after him, grinning.

When he heard the bell ring in the shop and her beautiful, mellow voice, Henry did not hesitate to leave his lathe and join Miss Varney and Mr Holding. He felt a stirring deep within as soon as he saw her and she smiled towards him shyly.

"I 'ear you're a regular at Carr's Lane, Miss Varney," he said as she examined the cameo. "I've got a mind to be more often at chapel myself."

She made no comment but glanced at him.

"I believe," he continued without hesitation, "that the renowned Reverend John Angell James leads you all there. I've 'eard 'im before – a passionate man in 'is sermons for sure."

Still she said nothing, but Henry was undeterred.

"Perhaps I could walk with you there this Sunday," he suggested. "I live 'ere on Moseley Street, too, you see – at my parents' 'ouse, Thomas and Martha Parkes."

Clarinda still did not speak. She was feeling a strange lightness, almost as though she was not really standing there before this forthright man, but she gathered herself together and with uncharacteristic boldness replied, "Would you also like to join me, Mr Parkes, on my visit to Yardley early on Sunday morning before chapel, to teach at the Sunday School there? It is a walk of four miles, but a few of us are doing some considerable good and providing religious tracts to the parents of the children we teach as well. We are in need of more hands to assist."

And so, on the following Sunday, as the sun was rising, Henry met Clarinda at her front gate to walk the country lanes together to Yardley. And their courtship began.

Robert Varney was unaware of his daughter's young suitor for some time. He and Mrs Varney attended the less evangelical Lombard Street Chapel and so did not come across Clarinda and Henry together at Sunday service. It was not until the young couple had been courting for several months that Clarinda's brother, John, saw her with Henry walking arm in arm along a wooded lane and alerted Mr Varney to his daughter's alliance. That afternoon, when Clarinda returned from a walk with Isabella through the Spring Gardens, she was confronted by Ann Varney as soon as she arrived home.

"Your father and I wish to speak to you, Clarinda," her stepmother said in a peremptory tone as Clarinda unbuttoned her coat. "In the parlour if you please. Immediately."

A dizziness came over Clarinda and she grasped at the hatstand beside her before following Ann Varney into the parlour. Her father sat in the high-backed armchair facing the doorway with the red damask curtains drawn behind him, his long, black-bearded face glowering. Clarinda knew this look and bowed her head to avoid his glare and clutched her shaking hands.

"I have heard some most disturbing news," he began. "I have heard that you have been seeing a young man behind our backs, Clarinda."

She swallowed hard and met his gaze. "You refer to Mr Henry Parkes, I believe, Father."

"I do indeed!" His voice rose and his words were clipped.

"Yes, Father. Yes, Stepmamma. Henry Parkes has been courting me. He loves me and I love him."

Ann Varney scoffed, "You don't know the first *thing* about love."

Mr Varney rose from the chair and strode towards her, his hand raised as if to strike her. Clarinda flinched away from him but he lowered his hand and bellowed, "How dare you! How dare you do this behind my back! And an apprenticed ivory turner. A lowly ivory turner and *my* daughter! I forbid it, Clarinda! You are still not of age! You are still under my authority! I am a respectable businessman in this town. You are the daughter of a master of a reputable business. This man is beneath you. I forbid you to see him again!"

Clarinda's eyes had lowered again during her father's tirade. She was visibly shaking now and tears pricked at her eyes. Her thoughts were a whirlwind of anger and distress. She loved Henry Parkes. He was her hope and her everything and she would not give him up. He was her future and her escape. But she felt frustrated and powerless before her father. With a sob of anguish, she hurried past her stepmother and ran from the room and up to her bedroom, throwing herself on the bed.

Back in the parlour, Ann Varney rolled her eyes at this childish display of suffering.

"You must keep a closer eye on her, Ann," Robert Varney said with rage still evident in his brusque voice. "She has always been too wilful and independent. I blame her mother, God bless her soul. She was always too easy on Clarinda."

"Yes," Ann agreed. "I believe that must have been the case, to have created such a silly, disobedient, thoughtless girl. She needs to realise her duty is to you, Robert. As your daughter, she must abide by your rules and guidance."

"That is as it should be, Ann, indeed."

"We must have her married soon to a respectable businessman like yourself."

"Yes, I have been thinking along those lines. Someone like James Kemp, perhaps, or that fellow John is friendly with... Samuel Reynolds."

"Yes, indeed," Ann approved. "Some strong man who will temper her independent ways and insist on her obeying common rules of propriety."

The next day, Isabella came to visit Clarinda and was surprised by her friend's red-rimmed, puffy eyes.

"What on earth is wrong, Clarinda?" she declared as she flopped down beside her on the unmade bed.

"Father has forbidden me to see Henry. Forbidden me!" Isabella put her arm around her friend's shoulder. "I don't know what to do. I'm not twenty-one until July, so I have to obey him. I can't bear not to see Henry until then, Isabella. I can't bear it!"

"Oh, Clarinda," Isabella said. "I knew this would happen. Don't you remember, I told you your father would never allow you to be courted by a simple ivory turner."

"He's not simple!" Clarinda snapped. "He's so smart and eloquent, even though he has barely been to school. And he's going to those lectures at the Birmingham Mechanics' Institute most nights, too. Henry has a mind greater than my father's, I believe. Who is my *father* to judge him!"

"Oh, Clarinda. Whether he is smart or not is not the point for your father, I suppose. Oh poor, poor Clarinda."

Clarinda sobbed into Isabella's shoulder until Isabella's sleeve was damp and creased. Suddenly, Clarinda looked up wildly. "You could get a note to Henry, couldn't you, Isabella? You could take it to Mr Holding's shop, couldn't you? Stepmamma is keeping such a close eye on me. Please, Isabella!" And of course, her friend agreed.

The letter read:

Dear, Dear Henry,

Father has discovered us. He has forbidden me to see you. He is such a proud, self-righteous man, as I have told you before, and he disapproves of your trade. Which is ridiculous, for he began as a tradesman himself. Henry, it is five months until I am of age. I am forced to obey him. Dear Henry, how are we still to meet? I cannot bear not to see you. What should we do? There must be a way. Please write to me through Isabella. I know you will find a way.

Yours truly,
Clarinda

But Henry did not find a way. Clarinda was restricted to the house and only left it when her brother could chaperone her. Even on her walks with Isabella, John accompanied them. And so, for those five long months, the only correspondence between Henry and Clarinda was by letter delivered by the faithful Isabella.

Friday, 16th May, 1834

My Dearest Clarinda,

I thought of you throughout my day at Mr Holding's. I have been carving a set of pipes for a bagpipe. It is very intricate, precise work but, as you know, I do love the challenge and the variety. I notice the smell of the ivory each day now that you have pointed it out to me. As you said, Clarinda, it is just like singed hair.

Sarah sends her love. She is sitting by my side now reading a novel by Jane Austen which she borrowed from the library. I am so pleased you and Sarah are fond of one another. As you know, she is very dear to me, as are you, darling.

I have been to another lecture at the Birmingham Mechanics' Institute, this time on the subject of Economics. It was fascinating but I fear I have no mind for numbers. The lecturer, a Mr Graham, was startling in his arithmetic.

My dearest, darling Clarinda, how I miss your lovely face. When I think of you, Lord Byron's poem comes to mind, 'She Walks in Beauty':

She walks in beauty, like the night

Of cloudless climes and starry skies;

And all that's best of dark and bright

Meet in her aspect and her eyes;

Thus mellowed to that tender light

Which heaven to gaudy day denies.

And so, sweet Clarinda, I will dream of gazing into your perfect eyes and long for the day when I can once more behold you.

Yours always,
Henry

Monday, 19th May, 1834

Dear Henry,

My days are long and dreary. How I miss you. I have been attending Carr's Lane Chapel but John chaperones me to ensure I do not meet with you. I am sorry my father has insisted you no longer attend, for I believe you were beginning to grow in your religious conviction and education. However, I know you understand that your appearance there would only make things even more difficult and strained for me at home. I long for my birthday when I am no longer considered a child in the eyes of the law. Of course, Father and my stepmother will still attempt to stop our courtship when this time comes. Oh, Henry, there must be something we can do!

My loneliness without you is relieved only by Wilbur and, of course, Isabella. I sit for hours with Wilbur on my lap, tickling his little, furry ears. He is such a comfort. Isabella speaks most highly of you, Henry. She had not been convinced of the reasons for my devotion to you until our constant exchange of letters over the last months and her consequent meetings with you. She agrees you are a wise, intelligent and humorous fellow, as I know you to be, dear Henry. Write again soon. Your letters are a relief to me, for I do fear you will forget me. Please do not forget your love.

Yours truly,
Clarinda

Friday, 23rd May, 1834

My Dearest Clarinda,

Be assured I have not and will not forget you, my love. Your fears are unfounded. I am pleased Isabella is proving to be such a loyal friend and I am flattered by her impression of me as you related. I wait with anticipation for her visits to the shop for then I hear of you, my darling.

I have been thinking lately of your father's disapproval of me. I wonder, would he have disapproved so fiercely if my family had remained as tenants to Lord Leigh on the farm in Stoneleigh. Of course, you and I might never have met, but I would not have been reduced to a trade if not for my father's troubles.

I feel I should tell you in more detail the cause of these troubles and what came to pass so that you can marry me knowing all. I hope you will still consider me worthy of your love once you have heard this in full. So, my darling, my confession begins...

Our family had been tenants at Stoneleigh for generations and we expected my eldest brother, Thomas, to inherit the tenancy one day and continue on there. Due to the wars with France, the price we received for our harvests had increased remarkably and continued to increase, even though Napoleon was defeated in the year of my birth. It seemed this growth would continue and so my father decided to lease extra farming land nearby. This decision proved disastrous. When I was just eight years old the prices began to drop considerably. Lord Leigh refused to drop the rent on our farm lands and so we became destitute.

The years after this were the unhappiest of my childhood. We moved to Glamorganshire for about two years. Then we travelled to Gloucester where Da attempted to start a shop and, at such a young age, I began work as a reaper for a farmer. When the harvest was finished, I found work, first making ropes for a mere pittance and then on roadworks. This was difficult and tiring work. I had to crush stones from dawn till dusk with barely a break. Can you imagine, dear Clarinda, your Henry as a lad, toiling so desperately? I remember days when I barely ate and still had to find the energy to work so hard. To me those days seemed endless.

Da's shop failed and he decided we should return to the Warwickshire area. My father still had debts there so we moved to a hovel some distance from our previous home to avoid discovery but, of course, one of his debtors in Coventry, Mr Gilbert, found out Da had returned and he was arrested and thrown into debtors' prison.

Perhaps this is not a tale you should relate to your own father, Clarinda, for I fear he would frown upon our union even more severely if he knew my father had spent more than a year in prison.

And so, the end of my sad story...Mam had a brother in Birmingham and so she, myself, my brothers George and James and my sisters all moved to Birmingham. Thomas had already married and moved to Pontypool but he had died of influenza after his wife had left him with his son, so we took in his son, young Tom – only a baby then – to care for, too. I worked at first in the brickworks here digging clay. I was beaten unconscious with a crowbar *by the manager, Wilson, and Mam insisted I leave his employment. Then I was fortunate to be apprenticed to Mr Holding at the age of eleven. Da joined us in Birmingham when he was finally released from prison and, as you know, has worked as a gardener for some of the landed gentry around here ever since.*

So, my dear, dear Clarinda, do you still want this humble man? My origins were solid, but misfortune has indeed brought a decline in the standing of myself and my family. Am I still worthy of your love? I pray you continue to believe so, my dearest, darling Clarinda.

Yours forever,
Henry

Tuesday, 27th May, 1834

My Darling Henry,

Do not fear, your family's and your own suffering only serve to make me esteem you more, if that were indeed possible. I wept when I read of your slaving from such a young age. You are an amazing man to have overcome such trials and to have maintained a confidence and assuredness within. And, of course, I am always aware of the little schooling you received due to these misfortunes, and yet you are so learned and hold such discerning views on a variety of subjects. Henry, you are indeed a brilliant man.

My own silly sufferings at the hands of my stepmother and, at times, my father, are overshadowed by the real hardships you and your family have been through. You are more than worthy of my love.

Yours,
Clarinda

Clarinda and Henry

Tuesday, 3rd June, 1834

Dearest Clarinda,

I will be forever grateful for your love. Perhaps this time apart is giving us the chance to reflect on the extent of this love between us and to truly realise its value.

You talked in your last letter of me 'slaving' from a young age and, indeed, it was a form of slavery. Have I told you of the time I saw the brilliant orator and abolitionist George Thompson? It was at a meeting of the Birmingham Political Union and he, a thin man with a long nose and over-sized ears, was nonetheless eloquent in the anti-slavery debate.

The Slavery Abolition Act was passed last year but I do not believe all forms have been abolished completely in Britain. Is it not terrible, my dear Clarinda, that across Britain there are workhouses where children are forced to work in appalling conditions due to poverty, much the same as I was? The Anti-Slavery Society, which Mr Thompson represents, believes slavery is a crime before God. He argued that transportation of criminals to penal colonies such as New South Wales and Norfolk Island is itself a form of slavery. Would you not agree, Clarinda? It is a subject I feel most passionately about and one that touches me deeply due to my own experiences at the hands of hard masters.

These convicts are not all hardened criminals. Did you know the Swing Riots offenders were largely transported to the colonies? These were farm labourers who were simply protesting the use of machines. There were many working men from Dorset, Oxfordshire, Shropshire, Kent, Essex, Surrey and Norfolk who were convicted of machine breaking and transported. They were men who were trying to make a living and found conditions desperate. They were transported to the other side of the world to work in hard labour for protesting for their rights and their need for support.

And then there are all those struggling men and women who stole something basic, like a loaf of bread to keep themselves and their families alive, who found themselves transported. This is definitely a form of slavery, is it not? Sydney Town in New South Wales is spoken of as a place of hardened criminals and prostitutes, but I do not believe it can be so, any more than London, or even perhaps Birmingham these days where the working man feels growing desperation. I do feel strongly about the rights of working men and the need for universal suffrage in order to address the inequalities in Britain. I want you, my dearest Clarinda, to understand how important this is to me so that you can understand me better.

So another day and another passes until we meet again, my dearest. Do not think me unseemly when I profess that I long to hold you and to feel your sweet head resting upon my chest once more. How I miss our long walks together to the Sunday School in Yardley. I love you.

Yours,
Henry

Friday, 6th June, 1834

To my dear Henry,

I do so love to hear your views on the current world. There is so much you have seen and know. Are you still taking the Latin classes under the tutelage of Mr Toulmin Smith? I do admire you for your desire to learn, darling Henry. I would love to hear more of the lectures you are attending and any other great orators you have seen, for these are part of what have shaped you, my dear Henry.

Isabella told me you have grown something of a beard of late. She thinks it is most distinguished but I am not convinced I should find it pleasing, for then I could not gaze upon your whole dear face, Henry.

My work at the Sunday School continues. The children there are so receptive. Do you remember young Catherine James? She was asking of you last Sunday. I do feel she admires you greatly, Henry – as a child, of course. Isabella and I have been on some beautiful walks, always with John. I wish you could join us but it is only a little while longer until I am of age. We visited Vauxhall Gardens yesterday where we heard the Grenadier Guards' military band. It was very rhythmic and Isabella kept marching on the spot in jest and I was quite overcome with fits of laughter. She is incorrigible at times.

Yes, another day and another and one day soon we shall be together once more, my darling Henry. I miss you.

Yours forever,
Clarinda

Wednesday, 11th June, 1834

Dearest Clarinda,

How is my dear? After your last letter I shaved off my beard. Do not laugh. I do not wish to displease my love, so upon reading of your disapproval, I immediately applied the clippers! Can you doubt my love after such an act?

I met your brother by accident on Bradford Street just yesterday. He knew me it seemed, for although no words were exchanged, not only did he scowl towards me but he shouldered me roughly and unnecessarily as we passed. Do not be concerned though, Clarinda, I was not badly hurt. And do not speak of this to your brother, for it is but a slight and we should still hope for a reconciliation with your family in the future.

My Latin classes are continuing at the Birmingham Mechanics' Institute and I have attended lectures in arithmetic, writing, and music at the time of Queen Elizabeth, which included performances on the pianoforte. I found this lecture most peculiar.

But if you are wanting to know of the events that have shaped me most extremely, I should relate to you my attendance at that auspicious meeting of the Birmingham Political Union on the 7th of May, 1832, of which you would have heard, of course, for it was the climax that ensured the Reform Act was eventually passed.

Are you aware, dear Clarinda, of how important that Act is? Before it, many large cities full of working class people, including Birmingham, had no representation in parliament, while many small Tory boroughs with only a few rich inhabitants held several seats in London. There is still more to be done for all men to gain the vote, however, and I believe passionately in this right. Lord Grey's Reform Act did extend the franchise but only to those possessing property worth £10, so that most working class people are still not allowed to vote. The 1832 Act was an important beginning but there is still much to be done.

Let me tell you of my memories of that famous night on Newhall Hill, here in the heart of Birmingham. I had already attended many peaceful rallies during those 'Days of May', as they are now called, but the 7th of May was the most stirring and significant. There were some 250,000 people there, many having come from towns around, all waving flags and banners and cheering for our common cause. Can you imagine, dear Clarinda, the thrill of being one amongst thousands of voices singing in unison the Union hymn: 'By union, justice, reason, law, we claim the birthright of our sires!'?

And there were numerous speeches, of which Thomas Attwood's call for the petition to the House of Lords to pass the Bill was perhaps the most stirring. I have heard him speak many times, of course, but never with such passion and fervour. It was difficult to hear all that was said with so many there, but a bugle was used to quiet the masses and the feeling of solidarity and comradeship made the exact words used to some extent unimportant.

As you can no doubt tell, Clarinda, from what I have related, this was an event that was vital to the shaping of your Henry. I regret the Union has been disbanded, for there is still much to be done for the working man.

But now, let me speak of my love for you. I have composed a poem to you, dear Clarinda, and I humbly enclose my poor refrain:

Oh! 'Tis not that thy form is fair,
    Thy every motion light and grace;
'Tis not the glory of thy hair—
    'Tis not the sunshine of thy face.

The spell that hold me, fond and true,
    Is that dear self unspeakable—
That something which is always you—
    In simplest acts most beautiful.

What is it, love?—I cannot tell!
    Those honey'd lips, those passion'd eyes,
I kiss because I know so well
    The heart that to my heart replies.

And so, my darling, goodnight.

Yours forever,
Henry

Saturday, 14th June, 1834

My darling Henry,

Your poem is truly wonderful. It could have been written by Shelley or perhaps Thomas Campbell, so eloquent are your words. Your brilliance thrills me, dear Henry. And your passion for all men to be treated equally is admirable. I do wish I could have been there with you on the sloping reaches of Newhall Hill.

The day of my coming of age is drawing closer. I do wonder what you think should be done at that time, for I fear it might be difficult to continue our courtship while I still live under my father's roof and am dependent on him. Please tell me what you think we should do. It is a matter of constant worry for I do so love you.

Yours forever,
Clarinda

Tuesday, 17th June, 1834

My dear Clarinda,

How is my darling? I, too, have been reflecting on what should be done when you come of age next month.

My first thoughts are, of course, that we should be wed immediately. There are, however, some obstacles to this. Firstly, I will not attain the age of twenty-one for another two years and while this is not a legal requirement, it is nevertheless the custom that both parties should have reached their majority. The other concern is that I will not be able to support you properly until my apprenticeship is complete when I plan to start a business of my own.

One solution would be for us to become engaged. An engagement is a promise to wed and is almost as unbreakable as a contract. It would, no doubt, be difficult for you to be engaged to me while you remained under your father's roof, but I do not believe he would be justified in insisting you break our betrothal. This would be even more shameful to him than your marrying an ivory turner, I would think, once he learned we were already engaged. It is against custom that I should not ask his permission first but, in the circumstances, this would be impossible.

Let me begin again, dear Clarinda. We have talked of marriage but there has been no formal proposal and acceptance. If I could, I would, on bended knee, ask for your hand in marriage. But alas, my request must be on paper instead, and so I apologise for its unromantic form. Clarinda, darling Clarinda, will you marry me? Will you consent to call me your betrothed from the day of your birthday when you come of age? I wait, with only slight anxiety, for your reply.

Your hopeful suitor,
Henry

Thursday, 19th June, 1834

Dear, Dear Henry,

Yes! Yes! And again, yes! I consent to your proposal. Henry Parkes, I agree to be your loving wife. Oh yes, my dearest.

Your soon-to-be betrothed,
Clarinda

THREE

When Clarinda told her father and stepmother of her engagement to Henry Parkes the day after her twenty-first birthday, she expected an angry reaction. But the reality was still a wrenching shock to her.

"You have disobeyed me, Clarinda! I forbade you to see that man," her father yelled, his face so close to hers his spit landed on her upper lip.

"And I have done as you asked. I have not seen Henry until yesterday when I came of age," Clarinda said.

"Your dear mother would have been disgusted at your behaviour. I cannot believe that a daughter of mine would act in such a way! I am your *father!*"

"And I have obeyed you always until now, Father. But I love Henry Parkes and I *will* marry him. I am of age now. I can decide my future for myself. It is my life and I will follow my heart."

"Your *heart?*" Ann Varney interrupted. "You will follow your heart, you say, stupid girl as you are, and you will find yourself destitute. What do you imagine your life will be like, Clarinda? Do you expect Henry Parkes to achieve anything like your father has? For I sincerely doubt it!"

"Henry has a wage. And when he finishes his apprenticeship he will begin his own business. You do not know him. He will be a successful man one day. He is a wonderful man!" Clarinda struggled to keep her voice level.

"An *ivory turner?*" Robert Varney said in a patronising tone. "You will live as the wife of an *ivory turner?*"

"You, yourself, Father, was once only an apprenticed whipmaker," Clarinda snapped back. "You were, back then, only Henry's equal."

Robert Varney thrust his arm back in anger and slapped Clarinda across the face. She gasped and held her hand to her stinging cheek.

"Very well!" her father said, holding himself tall. "If you will marry this man whom I forbade you to see, you are on your own, Clarinda! I will not turn you out onto the streets, but I will not treat you as a daughter of mine, either."

"She could move into the room beside the kitchen, Robert," Ann Varney said with barely disguised delight. "She could work alongside Betty as a servant."

Robert Varney did not respond immediately. He rubbed his brow and shook his head for a time, glaring at the ground.

"Yes. Perhaps you are right, Ann," he said eventually, his voice shaking with emotion. "We will move your bed into the area off the kitchen, Clarinda. If you are to marry Henry Parkes you will need to get used to a less comfortable life. I may once have been a lowly apprentice, as you have pointed out, but I have raised myself to a position of master and businessman. And I worked tirelessly so that you, my daughter, and John could live lives of privilege. I never expected you to throw that back in my face."

"I have not intended to disrespect you, Father," Clarinda replied, maintaining her steady voice. "I have appreciated all that you have done for me and I love and esteem you. But I *will* marry Henry Parkes." She turned and walked towards the kitchen.

Later, John found her there crying into Betty's shoulder.

"Oh, John," she said immediately and flung herself on him. "I love Henry. I truly do. I love Father, too, but I cannot give Henry up for him."

John patted her shoulder uncertainly. "I expect we will not have much to do with each other from now on, Clarinda. I am sorry for that."

"And I am, too, John. You have always been my dear older brother."

"But I cannot be as a brother to you from now on if you are to marry Henry Parkes. Father is right. He is not good enough for you. You will live a life of poverty with him."

Clarinda's sobs halted abruptly as she stared at her brother. "You will not support me in this, John?" she asked in disbelief.

"No, Clarinda. I cannot support you in disobeying Father. I am sorry, but you are a woman and therefore of lesser understanding and intelligence, and Father has your best interests at heart. You should not go against him."

Clarinda, speechless, watched as her brother left her there in the kitchen with Betty.

Clarinda spent over a year living beside the kitchen in her father's house, treated with icy disdain. She toiled every day, except Sundays, cooking and scrubbing in the kitchen and polishing the furniture or mopping floors. But the evenings were her own and she was no longer chaperoned by her brother.

On evenings when Henry was not at classes or lectures at the Mechanics' Institute, he and Clarinda would stroll together, arm in arm, with Wilbur trotting along beside them, to the Parkes's family home within the narrow brick row of terraced houses. Clarinda was shy around his family at first. She was not used to their heartfelt discussions of politics or literature, or their light, playful banter. But sitting on a stool beside Henry long into the evening with Wilbur sleeping in her lap, Clarinda came to grow comfortable and at ease.

It was Sarah Parkes who found the bedsit in Cheapside. They all agreed Clarinda should move out of her father's house as soon as a suitable place was available, and that Henry would help pay the rent with his meagre apprentice's wage. Clarinda placed flyers in shop windows and glued them to lamp posts around Birmingham, advertising her skills as a seamstress, and soon the regular orders for dresses and gowns kept her busy throughout each day and helped pay for the room.

It was an unusually sweltering, steamy day in July, 1836 when Henry Parkes and Clarinda Varney were married at St Bartholomew's Anglican Church in Edgbaston, Birmingham. Even in the cooler air of the high-ceilinged stone building, Clarinda felt flushed in the eggshell blue satin dress she had made for the occasion with its low-waisted bodice and puffed gigot sleeves. Henry wiped sweat from his brow and loosened the cravat he had borrowed from a neighbour as the minister pronounced them man and wife and the church verger, the only witness, shook his hand heartily.

"Well, Mrs Parkes, no one can stop us now," Henry exclaimed, sweeping the borrowed top hat from his head and bending to kiss her fully. Clarinda laughed as his lips left hers.

"No husband," she said proudly. "Not even my father can stop us now."

Clarinda reached for Henry's arm and the young couple strode through the empty church and into the heat of the garden for the few miles walk back to the bedsit in Cheapside. Henry was aware of each touch and movement of her as they walked, his every nerve-ending heightened by the expectation of what they would now do there in that room. He had waited so long and his adoration of Clarinda had made the wait agonising. The most he had seen, touched and kissed of her hidden body were her soft nipples, and even this, Clarinda had later said, made her feel ashamed because they were not yet married in the eyes of God. But now, she was his, wholly, totally his.

But he was uneasy, too. He did not know how his chaste wife would respond now that the moment he had longed for was almost here. He knew her to be passionate, for she had often struggled to withdraw from their ever-closer embraces over the two years of their engagement, but he worried that now the time was upon them, her Christian sensitivities would restrict her fervour.

But Clarinda had longed for him as much as he for her and so, as soon as they had climbed the stairs to the cramped room, she closed the window to shut out the clatter of carriages and the call of voices from the street below. Without a word, Henry began to fumble with the buttons on her dress and once this was discarded, she stepped immediately out of her undergarments. He kissed her ardently and ran his rough hands over her as she felt for the buttons on his trousers, and it was then that he knew his passion would be returned.

The young couple continued to spend their days apart, yearning for the evenings when they could be alone together. There, in the stuffy, confined room in Cheapside, with only Wilbur to disturb them, they made love each night with growing intensity. For Clarinda, it was as though she was a different person altogether, with her newfound senses tingling and alive and visceral. And Henry was more to her than she could have imagined, raw and real in his strong physicality. There was no sin in this innate, divine act of coupling, she believed, and she gave herself to Henry completely.

Their infatuation ensured their visits to the Parkes's family home became irregular and less frequent than his sisters would have wished, as did Henry's attendances at classes and lectures at the Mechanics' Institute. Thomas and Martha were understanding of their son's absence.

"They be in their first flush," Thomas would say in an undertone to Martha and chuckle. "Just like we be all those years ago, 'ey? 'E be a young strapping lad with lusty needs. Good on 'em, I say." And Martha would tut-tut at him with feigned disapproval.

Sarah, on the other hand, missed her youngest brother greatly. She was now in her thirties, unmarried and still living with her parents. She worked as a stay-maker, which was tedious, strenuous work and Henry had been the light in her dull life throughout the years.

When she was still a young girl, Sarah had accepted that her life could not be as important as her brothers' might be and so, with a fiery, ambitious, parental-type love, she had made it her mission to make Henry a great man and, indeed, she thought he still would be one day. Her pride in her youngest brother was like a physical ache. But she also knew he must forge his own life now. And so, with humility and acceptance, she did not complain to her parents of his absences as Maria and Eliza did, or to Henry when he did visit. But still Sarah missed Henry overwhelmingly.

When Clarinda realised one day in August that she was pregnant, she felt excitement tinged with a slight regret that her time alone with Henry would end. She told Isabella of her suspicions one Sunday. Autumn seemed to have come early that year and they strolled together around the outskirts of Spring Gardens where the leaves were a glory of orange, red and ochre.

"I've missed my courses, Isabella," she said bluntly. "And I've been sick and queasy for most of each day, especially when I haven't eaten for a while."

Isabella squeezed her friend's hand tightly. "It does sound like it, Clarinda. Oh, how wonderful! You'll be a mother!"

"It is quite wonderful, isn't it?" she agreed but bit her lip.

Isabella knew Clarinda too well to not sense her unease. "Tell me, Clarinda," she insisted. "You're worried about something."

"Yes," Clarinda admitted. "I do worry, though, that Henry and I are still in that tiny bedsit. I cannot imagine a baby sharing that space with us. But we can't afford anything else yet, especially with the cost of a baby as well. And Henry is thinking of starting his own business, which will use up the small amount we've saved."

They walked in silence for a while, the only sound the leaves crunching beneath their boots.

"Could you ask your father for a loan?" Isabella ventured after a time.

Clarinda was quick to reply. "That would be impossible. Father has not spoken to me since I moved into the bedsit. He has not even acknowledged our marriage. I think I am dead to him." Tears welled in her eyes.

"I'm sure it's not as bad as that, Clarinda. Your father will come around. Perhaps I could speak to John. I do feel I'd have an influence because I think he's quite partial to me," Isabella giggled. "He seems to have been ever since he had to chaperone us all those times before you were engaged."

Clarinda smiled and wiped away her tears. "Yes, he is the one from my family who I feel loves me the best, too. We were close growing up. Perhaps John could be persuaded to talk to Father."

"Especially if I told him you were with child, Clarinda! Surely a grandchild would soften your father's attitude."

"I would hope so," Clarinda said doubtfully. "He is such a stubborn man and Stepmamma goads him into believing Henry and I are partners with the devil himself!"

"I know, Clarinda. I feel for you and Henry. But I could talk to John if you like."

"I'll think on it, Isabella. Not yet, we'll see perhaps if news of the baby is enough to bring Father round."

That night as they sat by the guttering candlelight, Clarinda told Henry of the baby. She could not see his expression clearly but she heard his sharp intake of breath as he moved her from his arms and jumped up from their tattered settee. For a moment, she thought he was disappointed, but then he pulled her up by the hands and hugged her firmly.

"Oh, Clarinda, Clarinda!" he said and swung her around lightly by the waist. "A child, our own child. Oh, my darling, a baby already!"

Clarinda smiled at him knowingly. "It's not surprising, really, Henry. It was sure to happen with your constant demands."

He slapped her lightly on the bottom and laughed. "*My* demands indeed. I don't 'ear you complaining, young lady." He grabbed her around the waist again and pulled her onto the bed.

"It must 'ave 'appened almost our first time," he whispered into her neck as he gave her soft kisses there. "We were meant to be together, weren't we, my darling? A baby on the way already. Do I need to be careful with you now?"

She shook her head and wrapped a leg around his waist. "No, Henry – only a little careful perhaps."

Thomas Campbell Parkes was born on the 18th of April, 1837 in the bedsit at Cheapside in Birmingham. Henry was at work and Clarinda was alone when the waves of urgent, insistent contractions came over her. She yelled desperately down the stairs to Mrs Chapman, the landlady, who came at a run and, before the doctor or a midwife could be called, the baby was born.

From his first breath, Thomas was a sickly, pallid, wan child. But in Clarinda's eyes he was perfect. This tiny person was the miraculous creation of her and Henry's love, with his petite, clutching fingers, the sparse auburn down on his precious head and the almond-shaped eyes like his father's. She fretted over Thomas's soft, pathetic mewls and held him to her for hours trying to coax him to suckle more strenuously.

"He doesn't cry as much as I'd expect," she'd said to Henry when he'd first held his fragile son. "He doesn't seem to cry like other babies, either. It's more like a whimpering, don't you think?"

It was Martha who persuaded Henry to call for the doctor. She had borne eight children of her own and even though only one had died in infancy, she could tell this little baby was not the sturdy, thriving boy that he should be. The doctor confirmed her fears. Unless the baby drank more breast milk and showed more vigour, there was grave concern he would not survive long.

On his family's insistence, Henry moved Clarinda and baby Thomas with him into Martha and Thomas's room in the Parkes's three-roomed terrace. From there, each morning as he left for work, Henry would kiss his wife and gaze upon his son, wondering if this would be the last time he'd see him alive. Isabella came to visit each day and helped Clarinda and the Parkes women care for the tiny infant.

One evening, Martha whispered to Thomas with tears in her eyes, "I think you should go for the reverend, Thomas. I do think that baby needs baptising soon. 'E's not long for this world, I feel. Go fetch the reverend before it's too late. Go now. 'Twould be a wonder if baby Thomas made it through the night."

And she was right. Thomas Campbell Parkes died during the early hours of the morning on the 5th of May as he lay in Clarinda's arms, newly baptised and only seventeen days old.

FOUR

Clarinda fell into a deep melancholia, much like she'd suffered after her mother's death. Thomas was buried in the cemetery at St Philip's where Clarinda's mother was buried. The Parkes family came to mourn with them along with Isabella and Clarinda's brother, John. As the coffin was lowered into the ground, Clarinda wailed and tried to throw herself into the small, desolate hole, but Henry held her back.

Day after day she sat in their bedsit with Wilbur whimpering at her feet, humming or singing a lullaby and rocking incessantly as she had with Thomas in her arms when he was still alive.

Lullaby and good night, with roses bedight,
With lilies o'er spread is baby's wee bed,
Lay thee down now and rest, may thy slumber be blessed.
Lay thee down now and rest, may thy slumber be blessed.

Henry found her rocking and singing in this way one evening when he returned from work. She was sitting in the dark without a candle and, although it was too warm for a fire, there was a chill in the air from the open window.

"Clarinda, my darling." He knelt in front of her and pulled her to him. "You cannot go on like this. 'Ave you eaten? 'Ave you seen anyone today? My love, my love. We can get through this. There will be another baby, and another."

41

Tears trickled silently down her cheeks as he spoke. "I am trying, Henry. I do try. But I cannot bear it! I cannot bear to think of Thomas cold and alone in that grave." Her tears turned into sobs.

When her cries lessened, he said, "'Ave you seen Isabella at all, my darling? Or Sarah?"

"They come around, yes, Henry. Your family are so kind. But I don't want to talk to anyone. What is there to talk about now that we have lost Thomas?"

"There is so much to talk of, my dear. There'll be other children. And I'll be finished my apprenticeship soon, Clarinda. We can start planning for my business. And there are books you can read. You love to read. It'd take your mind away from the sorrow."

Gradually, Isabella drew Clarinda away from the bedsit during the day. First on short walks around the streets of Cheapside and sometimes to the Parkes's home, and eventually on longer walks along the country lanes. Isabella spoke of the sights around them, such as the tall alder bushes which refused to turn from green in the early autumn, the colourful hedgerows of crab apple, or the lone nightingale that had not yet left for warmer climates. She encouraged Clarinda to listen to the whistling songs of the birds and to play conkers with her with the horse chestnut seeds as they had done when they were younger.

Over the weeks, the colour began to return to Clarinda's cheeks and an occasional smile trembled at her lips. She began to listen more attentively to Henry's readings of bits from the newspapers that might interest her. He was particularly excited at the reestablishment of the Birmingham Political Union, which had been disbanded in 1834 when it was thought its work was finished.

"Do you remember, Clarinda, that stirring piece I read to you from the *Journal* back in '35 encouraging the Union to reform? 'Awake, Arise, and Put Forth Thy Strength! Why slumberest thou while the

TORIES, the deadly enemies of REFORM, are in the field?'" As he repeated the words from memory, Henry punched the air for emphasis. "These calls from the working-class men 'ave inspired the leaders of the Union – Attwood, Salt, Douglas, and the others – to move for more change. The Reform Act was a first step, but it 'as not been enough."

And when Henry returned to their bedsit with his friend John Hornblower on the evening of the 19th of June after a mass meeting of the Union, they talked long into the night about the changes needed.

"We are now demanding 'ousehold suffrage, which would mean I could vote once we've lived 'ere for three years, Clarinda," he told her excitedly. "And abolishing the property qualifications for those who sit in parliament so that common men could become members."

Henry's enthusiasm was infectious and it, along with her walks with Isabella, helped to lift Clarinda's dark mood little by little.

She also began regular walks with Wilbur to meet the older Thomas Parkes at his garden plot. His was one of twenty small plots in an area not far from their home, which were leased out to Birmingham inhabitants so they could grow their own vegetables. Thomas missed the farming life from before his harsh time in prison and, even though he was employed regularly to attend to the gardens of wealthy Birmingham residents, he took great pride in his own little plot. Here he grew beans in the summer, pumpkin, carrots and turnips over the autumn and winter, and snap peas and rhubarb in spring. It was another way he could provide for his family as he aged.

Clarinda helped him to dig and plant and, if rain had been scarce, to water the plants. She found this basic, simple work cathartic; it gave her a feeling of rejuvenation to see the young plants pushing their way through the soil and to harvest the ripened vegetables for their supper. Sometimes she and Thomas would sit on a stool nearby and talk about the vegetables or the weather or of his life growing up on the farm at

Stoneleigh. Clarinda found his honest, simple talk in sharp contrast to her own father's, and Thomas seemed to understand that she didn't want to talk about herself as all she would be able to speak of was her anguish over the death of her son.

In time, their friendship became so easy and relaxed that they could sit comfortably for an hour or more without speaking while Thomas hummed and puffed on his pipe and Clarinda petted Wilbur in her lap. And she began to call him Father.

One evening in late June, Henry came home shouting and waving a copy of the *Birmingham Journal*. Clarinda was so startled she spilt some of the soup from the spoon she was using to stir broth over the fire.

"Clarinda, the King is dead!" Henry was choked with emotion. "King William 'as died. 'Is niece, Princess Victoria, is to become Queen! At only eighteen and unmarried!"

"I didn't think you favoured King William, Henry – or the monarchy at all," Clarinda said as she wiped the soup that had spilt onto her apron. "And King William was against the abolition of slavery and the Reform Act, wasn't he?"

"Yes, yes!" he laughed impatiently. "'E was still the King, I suppose. And it is a momentous day, don't you see? We must drink a toast to our new Queen, to Princess Victoria – Queen Victoria!"

Henry rarely drank liquor but he had brought home a bottle of dark beer and he poured them each a glass. The strong ale made Clarinda feel light and buoyant and, after a second glass Henry kissed her fully as he had not dared while she was still deeply grieving.

"Oh, Clarinda." From the candle that flickered beside them she could see the raw look in his eyes. "Could I make love to you again, dear Clarinda? Could we try to make a new life again?"

She did not answer immediately but took the pot of soup from the fire and drew him to the bed. "Yes, Henry. Yes, I think it is time."

Later as they lay naked in bed, Clarinda asked, "Will Princess Victoria be a better monarch, do you think, Henry?"

"I think she will be," he said as he stroked her head where it rested on his shoulder. "She will be less tyrannical than most other monarchs before 'er, I imagine. She is a young and pure woman."

"Will she support the working man's cause, do you think?" Clarinda asked.

"As I 'ave said before, Clarinda," Henry raised himself to lean on his elbow and look down on her, "the Conservatives think our constitution makes life in Britain fair for all, because we 'ave the three forms of government combined. We 'ave the monarch, the lords and the commons. But until the 'ouse of Commons is elected by all people, and not just the elite, there is no fairness or democracy in the system."

"Do you think we should have a monarch, Henry? You don't believe in revolution like in France, do you?"

"No, not at this stage at least," he replied without hesitation. "Revolution would be extreme. I do think, as Thomas Paine argues in *The Rights of Man*, that 'uman rights are a result of nature and that a government that doesn't protect the rights of all men, deserve and justify a revolution against them in some circumstances. But I 'ope a peaceful means of gaining equality is still possible."

"So should we have a monarch? Should Princess Victoria be made Queen?"

"It is a complicated matter, Clarinda. I think if the monarch's and the people's rights and interests are united, then we should 'ave a monarch. The aristocracy is a different thing entirely, though."

Clarinda raised herself up against the bedhead so that they sat level as he spoke.

"The aristocracy," he continued, "are mainly a corrupt 'ereditary fallacy. There should be no title or greater rights for men due to their birth alone."

45

"But isn't that how a monarch becomes King or Queen?"

Henry laughed. "So many questions, Clarinda. It's complicated, and sometimes it's 'ard to explain. But surely Princess Victoria's youth and purity will ensure she is a great monarch who will support the rights of all men."

On the 4th of July, Henry was given time off work during the middle of the day by Mr Holding so he could walk with Clarinda to James Bridge and watch the first steam train to travel between Manchester and Birmingham on the Grand Junction Railway line.

There was a crowd of people on the bridge and the excitement reminded Henry of the fervour of a Union meeting. He jostled through the crowd with Clarinda behind him and managed to find a spot where they could see the shining metal tracks of the James Bridge Station below.

A man beside them said to another, "It'll only take nine hours to travel between Liverpool and London! It's a miracle!"

They first heard the strident puff of the engine in the distance and birds took flight as the whistle blasted and the dark form of the locomotive hurtled towards them. They had never seen anything move so fast. It chugged rapidly towards the cheering crowd and Clarinda clutched Henry's hand as the engine pelted nearer and nearer to the bridge. The whistle sounded again and they covered their ears before the engine and eight polished carriages rushed helter-skelter beneath them.

"What a sight to be'old!" Henry said in Clarinda's ear. "What more will man invent? It's a wonder!"

As Clarinda's spirits began to lift, John Hornblower visited them in the evenings more regularly. He was an apprenticed printer whom Henry had met through lectures at the Mechanics' Institute and Union meetings.

"John's rather an odd combination, Henry," Clarinda said after she first met him. "So serious in his politics and yet so comical in his appearance – with his balding head and his red beard flourishing luxuriously from his chin."

"I know 'ow you feel about beards," Henry laughed.

Clarinda sat on the settee beside Henry most nights, listening to the men's discussions about politics, the state of the economy, literature and the wonder of the steam engine, and it helped to distract her from her grief, particularly over the long, dark, haunted evenings.

"The amendment to the Poor Law has not made things any better," John said in his gravelly voice one night as they sat around the low fire. "Those workhouses are like prisons. There's an attitude that it's the poor fellows' own fault. That it's their fault they're paupers. That they are just lazy and hopeless – even the children."

"Yes, 'opeless they be," agreed Henry. "'Opeless because of bad fortune and the government's attitude, I think. There but for the grace of God go I."

"Yes, Yes. That goes for me, too."

"And yet you plan to brave it in London when your apprenticeship is finished, John? I 'ear things are much worse there."

"No, Henry, I don't believe they are worse. While it is growing and developing here in Birmingham with all the new factories, I want to start over, you know. I'll try my luck in London, for sure."

"When do you think of going, John?" asked Clarinda, pausing from darning one of Henry's few shirts.

"Soon as my apprenticeship is done, come October, I think."

Clarinda glanced nervously at Henry. He had spoken at times of the possibility of their moving to London one day, but the thought of the upheaval this would cause to their lives made her apprehensive. And, of course, she would never want to move so far from Isabella.

"The masters at those work'ouses can sell the bodies of anyone who dies there, too," continued Henry.

"Oh, how awful!" Clarinda cried. "Who would buy such a thing?"

"Doctors and 'ospitals, I suppose, Clarinda," explained Henry. "That's 'ow they find out 'ow our bodies work – by studying real bodies."

"How would those poor souls enter Heaven then? That is a terrible thing!" Her mind returned to her dear, darling Thomas and she heard no more of the men's chatter that night.

On another of John's visits, the conversation was of the young, up-and-coming writer Charles Dickens.

"I've finished reading all of 'is series called *The Pickwick Papers* that appeared in *The Spectator* in London," Henry said. "There's copies at the Institute's library. It'll 'elp the working man's cause if some of the elite get to reading it, that's if they 'ave any 'eart or sympathy at all."

"I'd like to read that sometime, Henry," Clarinda said, pouring more tea for herself from the kettle that simmered on the hearth.

"I could try to borrow the copies for you. A few at a time, maybe."

"I hear there's a new series that Dickens has written called *Oliver Twist*," said John. "All about a poor young boy in and out of workhouses and the like. It's about time someone in the literary world started to state it as it really is here in England for the common man."

"That's right, John. 'E's the first novelist I've read who shows man cannot always act on 'igher principles." Henry sat straighter in his chair. "Sometimes circumstances force a person to act against their morals and beliefs. Like the political activists and the desperate poor who end up convicts across the ocean. I do not think criminals are born criminals. It is the unfairness of the world we live in that makes them offend."

John nodded into his beer.

"Henry has enlightened me greatly on the world, you know, John," Clarinda said. "There is so much I did not know or understand until Henry informed me. I'm very blessed to be married to a man such as him, don't you think?"

John cuffed Henry on the shoulder.

"I think he's the lucky one, to have such an understanding and intelligent woman as his wife," he said. "Not all of your sex are as receptive to our radical ideas."

The talk inevitably turned to politics and the economy and Clarinda began to lean sleepily against Henry's shoulder.

"When will they get rid of these damned Corn Laws?" John said. "What with the prices so high, it's creating the poverty we talk of."

"Yes," agreed Henry. "Though it 'elps the English farmer, just not the working man in the big cities. What's needed is to keep the import duties 'igh but then to keep the taxes and prices low for English produce, and not these exorbitant prices we all are 'aving to pay."

"It's all very confusing," interrupted Clarinda at this point, sitting up and looking towards Henry. "It seems like a balancing act of sorts."

"Yes, Clarinda, my love, that's exactly what it is. A balance is needed so everyone is treated fairly."

"Yes indeed," agreed John. "Instead of it all being tipped one way."

Henry's apprenticeship was to finish at the end of July and, although Mr Holding was keen to keep him on in his employ, Henry had ambitions for his own business.

"I need to strike out on my own," he'd told John one evening as they walked through the dirty streets to the bedsit. "You know what I mean, don't you, John? I want to be independent. I don't want to work for another and I *definitely* don't want to work in some monstrous factory. I just need the finance, that's all. Not much, just enough for my own lathe and a few materials and the rent on a shop."

Henry did not speak to Clarinda directly about this because he was afraid of the impact his worries would have on her already delicate emotional state. But Clarinda was a practical woman and not unaware of their financial situation. She spoke to Isabella of her concerns often.

"You know, Clarinda, as I've said before, you need your father's help in this," Isabella said on one of their many walks. "I could speak to your brother. Surely a loan could be arranged."

"Father has still not spoken to me, not even after Thomas died! I don't think there is a possibility of his helping us in this."

"Well, perhaps John has something saved. He has an interest in your father's business, too. Perhaps I could ask him without your father's involvement."

And so, unknown to Henry, Isabella arranged for Clarinda to meet her brother at a coffee house in a suburb of Birmingham that Mr Varney was unlikely to visit. Clarinda felt a pang of regret as she watched John approaching the door. She saw him so rarely now.

"You look well," John said as he kissed her lightly on the cheek. They sat at a corner table away from the window and ordered two coffees.

"How have you fared since your loss, Clarinda? You have been in my thoughts, you know. I am so sorry."

"Thank you, John. It is something I find difficult to talk about. The pain is beyond words." She lowered her eyes to the table. "You don't realise how much I appreciated your coming to Thomas's funeral."

He reached across the table and held her hand. They had not held hands since they were young and Clarinda felt the tears pricking again.

"How is Father and Stepmamma?" she asked.

"Well enough. I do think Father, despite his severe attitude, misses you terribly. He still loves you, you know."

"He hasn't spoken to me since I moved out."

"Yes. He is a proud man."

They sat in silence for a moment before Clarinda asked, "And how is the business going? And how is dear Betty?"

"I don't really know much about Betty. She keeps the house well and Stepmamma keeps her on her toes."

"And what of you, John? Are you happy still working for Father and living in his house under his rule?"

He withdrew his hand from hers. "Clarinda, I am my own man. Business is good and I will move out of our family home when I marry."

"Is there anyone you are thinking of?" she blurted out, immediately regretting the question for John flinched and a frown furrowed his brow.

"That is not something I wish to discuss with you, Clarinda. Now, Isabella Parry has told me of your need for a loan? Or, should I say, Henry's need? I am not surprised he cannot manage his affairs without your intervention."

Clarinda bit her lip to stifle the urge to snap back in Henry's defence. "He manages fine, John," she said calmly instead. "I haven't told him of our meeting today. He knows nothing of this. I ask for your help as my brother. It would not need to be much, I don't think."

"How much would it be?"

"I know Henry will need to buy a lathe. I would say no more than ten pounds."

John grunted. "This is why Father was against your marriage to Henry Parkes, you do know that, Clarinda, don't you? Henry Parkes will bring you down. He is not good enough for you."

This time she opened her mouth to argue, but John raised his hand to warn her against it and she swallowed her words.

"I will arrange a bank draft for that amount. This is because of my love for you, Clarinda, and not due to any wish to help Henry Parkes personally. Do not speak of this to Father."

"I would not have the opportunity to, John, as you know." Her tone softened. "Thank you, John. You do know I love Henry dearly. I didn't intend to create this conflict. But I love him so much." Despite her efforts, tears began to fall now. These seemed to affect John for he spoke in a calmer voice.

"Clarinda, I know this rift was not intended. You are still my dear sister and I wish things could be different."

"Oh, thank you, John! Thank you!" She reached for his hand again and he took hers willingly and squeezed it firmly.

That evening, Clarinda fretted over how to tell Henry of the loan. She knew he was as proud as her brother and father. She cooked Henry's favourite meal of rabbit stew with dumplings and waited anxiously for his return.

"You asked *what*, Clarinda?" was his first reaction to her news, and he threw his arms in the air. "You know I don't need your family's charity! I can do this without their 'elp!"

It was the first time he had raised his voice to her and Clarinda bit her lip and did not answer while he muttered angrily, pulling off his boots. They were both silent while Clarinda served him a large bowl of the steaming stew and took a seat beside him on the settee.

"Your family already think I am worthless," he said between mouthfuls. "This will only reassure them of the fact. Why didn't you talk to me about this first?"

"Because I knew that you wouldn't want me to ask them for help," she said simply. "And it is only John who knows. Father will find out nothing of this."

"That's not the point! You know it's not, Clarinda. Your family are the *last* people on earth I would 'ave wanted to raise this with."

"They are still my family, Henry." She continued to appear calm despite her feelings of frustration towards him at his manly pride. "It will get you started and then you can pay John back as the business grows. They have done little enough for us. I don't think this is a lot to expect."

Henry snorted and continued slurping his supper. When he had finished and she had taken his bowl and placed it in the bucket, he came over to her and hugged her from behind.

"I'm sorry for yelling, Clarinda," he said and she turned around to face him. "I know you were trying to 'elp. It's just that I want to stand as a man on my own two feet."

"I know, Henry," she said and kissed him lightly on the lips. "You are a wonderful man. This loan does not make any difference to that. Think of what you've had to endure in comparison to my family. John has had education and luxury and a business to go into all his life. You lost the stability of your farm when you were so young. And it is my *brother* we are relying on, not my father. My family owes me this at least for all the slaving I did after we were engaged. There is justice in this, Henry. It is what you and I deserve."

And so, the loan was accepted. Henry bought a spare, second-hand lathe from Mr Holding and rented a shop on Bradford Street where he would not be in direct competition with his old master. He had a sign made to hang out the front of the shop that read, *H. Parkes, Ivory and Bone Turner*. He felt proud and greatly optimistic for the future now that he was starting out on his own. He would become as important a businessman as Robert Varney one day. He was determined.

In September, Clarinda realised she was pregnant again. She did not tell anyone for several days. She felt a dread within her and a confusion of emotions. She so wanted another child, but could another child even come close to replacing her precious Thomas? And she feared that complete, overwhelming love for a child which left her so vulnerable. Another baby could also be ripped away from her as cruelly and easily as Thomas had been. She could not bear the utter desolation of the loss of another child.

Once again, she told Isabella first. She began crying before the news was fully out and Isabella understood Clarinda's distress without the need for explanation.

"The chances of another sickly child are so unlikely, Clarinda," she comforted. "This is a good thing. You and Henry can start again. Don't fret. This will be a healthy child, I just know it."

And, of course, Henry was ecstatic when he heard the news.

"This will be a new beginning for us, Clarinda," he assured her. "Me with the business and another baby on the way. We can really start again now. Next year will be a wonderful year, you'll see."

FIVE

Before he finished his apprenticeship, unknown to his master or to Henry, John Hornblower spent several evenings printing pamphlets that contained some of Henry's poems so they could be distributed about the town. When he gave the dozen copies to Henry one night at their bedsit, Henry shook his hand heartily.

"'Ave you seen, Clarinda?" He turned to where she sat at the table stringing the beans for their supper. "My poems are published! John 'as published my poems!"

Clarinda jumped up from the table and wiped her hands roughly on her apron before hugging John and kissing him on his whiskery cheek. John blushed from his cheeks to his balding head.

"Oh, John!" Clarinda exclaimed, reaching for one of the pamphlets. "And his poem, 'To Clarinda' is the first. You've made a real poet of him, John!"

Henry recited some of the stanzas to them:

"Thou art the bloom, I am the leaf,
And love the light we yield."

On the October evening after John's departure for London, Clarinda was aware of Henry's restlessness and kept quiet for a time as he read the latest copy of the *Birmingham Journal*. She had begun knitting a baby's jacket from the wool John had bought her as a farewell gift. Henry glanced at the light brown stitches on the needle.

"'Twas a generous gift from John," he said. "Would 'ave cost a bit for someone about to start out on 'is own in London."

"Yes, it was very kind of him. I had mentioned to him how I wanted some wool but that we couldn't afford it at the moment."

Henry huffed and ran a hand through his hair.

"Clarinda, I don't want you to fret too much. Just that everyone's struggling, it seems. Things aren't looking really rosy for the winter. And I suppose if others are struggling, they're not likely to buy fans and trinkets and the like from me. Can be 'ard in the turning business. There's only so many buttons and cotton reels people need. And there's a fair few other ivory turner businesses 'ere in Birming'am now, I suppose. I do wonder if we'd be better living somewhere else."

Clarinda did not want to encourage his thoughts of moving from Birmingham, particularly on the very day John Hornblower had left for London. They sat in silence again for a time, the only sounds the heavy breathing of Wilbur from where he lay at Clarinda's feet and the rhythmic clicking of her needles.

"I went for a walk with Isabella today," she said after a time. "It's getting cold. We went to the Bull Ring to have a look at the shops. I haven't been there for ages."

"I don't know if I like you walking around there on your own with Isabella, my love," Henry said.

"It was fine, but I do know what you mean. Birmingham is getting so crowded and they're putting up more of those back-to-back rows of houses like your parents' but even smaller, it seems. And some of the children around are so destitute and dirty. We saw a dog fight on one corner with a crowd of men, and even some young boys, cheering and goading the poor animals on."

"It's getting rougher in some of the areas you used to wander. I don't think you and Isabella should go to the Bull Ring again without me."

"I suppose you are right, Henry. Some of the paving is very worn now, too, so it is hard to walk easily without tripping. And the noise of the hammering and the engines everywhere is becoming overwhelming. I expect it'd be even worse in London."

This last remark hung in the air for a moment before Henry said, "Best if you stick to the lanes outside the centre of town from now on, my darling, or the parks. You 'aven't been to the Botanical Gardens for a time, 'ave you?"

"No, I suppose I haven't. Do you know why?" She looked up from her knitting with a glint in her eye.

"No. Do tell. I can see you 'ave something of interest to tell me, you cheeky one."

"Because Isabella has been frequenting there with a gentleman friend," she said, "and I'd be in the way!"

"As she indeed! Anyone I'd know?"

Clarinda hesitated. "Probably not, Henry," she said uncertainly. "He's a friend of her family's and mine, you know. One of the, as you would say, hoi polloi."

"Ah," he nodded. "Not a Union member, I gather then."

Henry continued to attend the meetings of the reformed Birmingham Political Union throughout the late autumn and the harsh winter. The Union membership was growing as the economic situation grew worse and Henry proudly wore the Union badge he had made on the lathe in John Holding's shop some years earlier. The streets of Birmingham seemed to be filling with homeless people braving the cold. Even with the town's huge Lichfield Street workhouse, which housed over one thousand people – including children – there were beggars on many street corners. Henry thought himself fortunate to still have a home, no matter how small.

Henry borrowed copies of *The Spectator* from the Mechanics' Institute library and read the serialised chapters of Charles Dickens's *Oliver Twist* to Clarinda in the evenings as the baby's jacket grew on her needles.

"'The parish authorities,'" he read in a sarcastic tone, "'magnanimously and 'umanely resolved that Oliver should be 'farmed', or, in other words, that 'e should be despatched to a branch-work'ouse some three miles off, where twenty or thirty other juvenile offenders against the poor law rolled about the floor all day, without the inconvenience of too much food, or too much clothing, under the parental superintendence of an elderly female who received the culprits at and for the consideration of sevenpence-'alfpenny per small 'ead per week.'"

Henry paused and whistled. "'E really can write, can't 'e, this Dickens fellow. I think 'e's only around our age. 'E sure does say it as it is."

"It is very moving, Henry. It worries me somehow. I'd hate for a child of ours to end up in a situation like that." Clarinda instinctively put her hand on her growing stomach.

"We'll not get as down-and-out as that, my darling. I wouldn't let us get as low as that," he said, but he did not mention that he had already considered closing his shop if things did not improve.

On Christmas morning, Clarinda woke to find a note from Henry on the bed beside her saying he'd gone to gather holly and ivy to take to dinner with his family. They couldn't afford much else to celebrate. She pulled back the blankets and gathered a shawl to wrap around her as she poked at the fire. The baby was stirring, like a butterfly dancing inside her, and she sat for a minute holding her hands to her growing form and said a silent prayer for him. She heard footsteps bounding up the stairs before the door was flung open.

"Merry Christmas, my darling." Henry was bundled in his coat with his hat pulled low over his ears and his arms full of branches of holly and tendrils of ivy.

"I went to the 'ill to get these," he said as he piled them on their one small table and pulled off his coat. "My it's chilly out!"

He came over to the fire and kissed her.

"Merry Christmas, Henry," she laughed. "You're in good spirits this morning."

"Of course I'm in good spirits – not every day I get to spend with my beautiful wife, now."

They walked through the icy streets with Wilbur by their side and Henry's arms full again with the holly and ivy. Their breath was foggy in the freezing air.

"Merry Christmas to you," they mumbled to each person they passed. "God bless you."

Inside the Parkes's home, the fire was roaring and the room was filled with the mouth-watering smell of roasting goose.

"Merry Christmas!" There were hugs and kisses all round and Maria helped Clarinda out of her coat and insisted she sit on the chair usually reserved for Henry.

"You can sit on the stool by her feet, 'enry, as she's expecting a baby and all," Maria said.

Sarah, Eliza, George and Tom helped Henry to hang the holly and ivy about the room.

"It looks so merry!" said James's wife, Mary Ann, clapping her hands from where she sat beside Clarinda. "Look, Georgie, Will." She bent towards her young sons who sat on the floor by her feet, sucking on peppermint lolly treats. "It's like we are in a garden."

"Where's the mistletoe then?" asked Thomas. "'Enry and Clarinda, and James and Mary Ann should be sitting under some mistletoe, I think! Like all young lovers."

"No need for mistletoe for me to kiss my darling wife!" exclaimed Henry and dropped the ivy he held before striding directly to her side to bend and kiss the blushing Clarinda.

"Enough of that now," laughed Martha.

They ate roast goose and potatoes with gravy and turnips from Thomas's garden plot, followed by plum pudding which had steamed over the fire for hours. They drank canary wine and toasted Queen Victoria.

"I think that was the happiest Christmas I've ever had," said Clarinda to Henry as they walked back home that evening through the shadows cast by the oil lamps. "I really feel like I'm one of your family. They are so dear to me – every one of them."

"I know, Clarinda. And you to them. They love you as one of their own, I feel. Yes, it 'as been a wonderful Christmas."

The January of 1838 was a bitterly cold month. Martha complained it was the coldest she had ever known and Thomas was concerned the intense frosts would ruin the harvest from his garden plot. A letter arrived one day on the Royal Mail Train from John Hornblower, and Henry, eager for news from London, was only slightly reluctant to pay the penny for its delivery. Fortunately, John had written in small, squashed writing to ensure the delivery price would only be for the one page.

Friday, 12th January, 1838

Dear Henry,

I wish you and Clarinda the best for the New Year and hope you are both well. My time in London has been more than eventful as one would expect in such an industrious city. I have begun work as a printer on 'The Village Magazine' and the pay, while more than I received in Birmingham, is only just sufficient to cover my costs here in London. I have found lodgings with a Mr Stentake, tailor, at Red Lion Court, Charter House Lane and the landlady provides a simple but adequate meal for myself and the three other lodgers. One of these is an Irishman called Patrick Callaghan who has told me of the extreme poverty in his homeland at present and the harsh infringement of civil liberties due to the Irish Coercion Bill which, as you are aware, disallows large gatherings of people. Patrick, the first Roman Catholic I have ever befriended, has introduced me to the London Working Men's Association of which I have become a member. They have a similar agenda to the Birmingham Union, although there is more talk of rioting and forcing action through direct means.

I witnessed a terrible fire here just two nights past, which destroyed the Royal Exchange. It was quite a sight to behold and I, along with hundreds of other London inhabitants, crowded the bridges over the River Thames to behold the frightening event. There were some hundred firemen and around twenty-five fire engines there by the time I arrived but, due to the extreme cold, the hoses were frozen for a time so that no water could be applied to the roaring blaze. It burned all through the night and into the following day and I returned to my lodgings while it was still ferocious. I heard the most remarkable stories the next day of how the bells of the Clock Tower, before it burned to the ground, began to chime the tune of 'There's Nae Luck About the House' for a full five minutes and that, early in the morning, a bag of around twenty sovereigns was blown from a window of the Exchange by the force of the inferno to be gathered up by the excited crowd below. Some said the fire was even more extreme than that of 1834, which destroyed most of Westminster House.

Please give my regards to Clarinda and I hope she is comfortable at present in her condition.

Yours sincerely,
John Hornblower

Thursday, 8th March, 1838

Dear John,

I was gratified to receive your letter of the 12th of January and I, too, wish you the best for the New Year. Clarinda is faring well and is continuing limited work as a seamstress. I am pleased that you are settled in London and your firsthand account of the fire at the Exchange was of great interest to me. When you next write, I would greatly appreciate a summary of your expenses in London, for I still do not discount the possibility of joining you there if it would prove financially beneficial. My business is not thriving at present but I still hold hopes of a recovery.

I have heard much of the London Working Men's Association of late as Thomas Attwood has been speaking of a meeting of minds between the London group and our Union. You would, I expect, have heard of the National Petition drafted by Douglas earlier this year which, apart from our other demands, includes the extension of voting rights to universal suffrage so that all men, without any property qualifications, would have the right to vote. This is something which we must all work towards together and if you have any influence in this regard in London, it could prove invaluable.

I heard a fiery speech recently at the Bull Ring by a man named Fergus O'Connor. He advocates for direct action and rioting in order to achieve our aims. This forceful approach, I feel, is opposed to the peaceful means by which the Birmingham Political Union proposes to ensure further reform. It is concerning that your London Association seems to be of a similar view to O'Connor and some others here in Birmingham, such as Bronterre O'Brien. I do wonder if O'Connor and O'Brien's Catholicism and the harsh conditions in Ireland influence them to pursue more violent means than necessary.

Catherine Blake

I wish you continued luck and success in your new life.

Yours faithfully,
Henry Parkes

Friday, 8th June, 1838

Dear Henry,

I was pleased to hear news of the Birmingham Political Union adopting the Charter of the London Working Men's Association. The meeting held here on Glasgow Green on the 21st of May to launch the Charter was as moving as any I have attended on Newhall Hill in Birmingham. The Charter, along with the National Petition and our solidarity, is expected to force great change. There is talk of a Convention to be held here in London and of our joint action being referred to as the Chartist Movement. These are indeed great times for the working man and I am confident that Britain will become a land of equality and liberty at last due to our actions and those of all other Chartists.

There is great excitement in London at present with the preparations for the Coronation of Queen Victoria to be held later this month in Westminster Abbey. The railway has again been extended with the opening of Paddington Station this week and talk of it being extended even further. I am sure that you have also heard tell of the transatlantic crossings by paddle steamer in April, first between Cork and New York in eighteen days and then from Avonmouth to New York in just fifteen days. We are indeed living in exciting times.

I hope Clarinda is well and that your business is improving. I have heard a new postal system is to be introduced whereby payment for a letter will be made by the sender and not the recipient. I hope this shall not complicate or interfere with our future correspondence.

Yours faithfully,
John Hornblower

Clarinda and Henry

Friday, 22nd June, 1838

Dear John,

I write to give you some lines I have composed only yesterday on the advent of Queen Victoria's coronation.

Stanza

High-destined daughter of our country, thou,

Who sitt'st on England's throne in beauty's morning!

God pour his richest blessings round thee now:

And may the eyes that watch the glory's dawning,

With hearts right glad and loyal, proudly scorning

All that dare hostile to Victoria be,

Daily behold new light they name adorning!

So may'st thou trust thy people's love for thee,

Queen of this mighty land, Protectress of the Free!

I forward this to you in hope that you might be able to print it in your paper.

Yours faithfully,
Henry Parkes

As the baby grew heavier, Clarinda was reluctant to go on long walks with Isabella. Not only was she uncomfortable and anxious to be near her home when the labour started but she also began to feel more vulnerable in the streets of Birmingham. The increasing number of pick-pockets and beggars and the growing filth and noise of the town were disconcerting and heightened her protective feelings towards her unborn baby. And so Isabella came regularly to the bedsit in Cheapside to visit Clarinda instead. On one of these visits, on a Saturday afternoon in late June when Henry was still at his shop on Bradford Street, Isabella and Clarinda were sitting side by side on the settee enjoying the summer sun streaming through the open window.

"I still can't quite believe I am engaged to be married!" Isabella said excitedly. "Henry must meet Lionel after the baby is born. As we are such great friends, our husbands must be, too."

"Yes, Isabella, they must. I hope Henry is not too proud, though. It will be difficult when Lionel is a friend of my brother's and the animosity is still so great there. But you are right, for *our* sakes they must be friends. I am so happy for you. He is a wonderful man and he adores you."

"I know he does." Isabella giggled and Clarinda was laughing along with her when she abruptly stopped and stood up, clutching at her skirt and gathering it around her.

"What has happened?" Isabella asked in alarm at her friend's strange behaviour.

Clarinda began to run to the door with her skirt still bunched, calling behind her, "My waters have broken, Isabella! I must get to the lavatory downstairs quickly. Call for Mrs Chapman and the midwife. The baby is coming!"

Isabella sat startled for a moment, looking at the trail of liquid Clarinda had left behind her on the carpet and the puddle that had soaked into the settee. She composed herself and picked up Wilbur to stop him from sniffing at the strange liquid before running with him after Clarinda downstairs.

Henry and the midwife were summoned by Mrs Chapman's boy as she and Isabella helped Clarinda upstairs to the bedsit once her waters had stopped flowing and the contractions had begun. For Isabella, this scene of a real childbirth was overwhelming and she was relieved when the midwife arrived and Clarinda told her she should leave.

"I'll be fine now, Isabella," Clarinda said. "Don't fret. It'll be over soon."

Isabella kissed Clarinda on her already damp forehead and left the room. Henry was outside on the landing, leaning against the rail.

"'Ow she be?" he asked Isabella urgently, his Midlands accent becoming more evident in his anxiety.

"I don't know, Henry. The midwife is taking care of her now. She said all is fine so I suppose we just wait now. Do you want me to wait here with you?"

"No," Henry responded immediately and more brusquely than he had meant. "I'm best on my own, thanks, Isabella. You go on 'ome. Thanks for 'aving me sent for. I'll send word when all is fine."

The labour was longer than the previous one and Henry waited fretfully on the landing deep into the night, listening to Clarinda's screams. He was hungry, tired and thirsty when the midwife finally came to him.

"The babby be a girl," she said as he stood on the landing trying to see into the room around her solid figure. "I'm sorry to say it, sir. The babby doesn't seem too healthy. She's very small and frail. Would you like me to go for the doctor?"

Henry was unable to speak for a moment. It was as though he was choking with the familiar grief and shock at the news.

"Yes," he said eventually. "Go for the doctor. Thank you. Go quickly then."

In the room, Clarinda lay on the bed, her hair a mess of curls upon the pillow and her face pale and ashen in the candlelight. In her arms was the baby. Even smaller than Thomas had been, the tiny creature did not open her eyes but cried feebly and her breath was ragged.

"Henry," Clarinda said weakly. "Henry, it's happening again." But she did not cry. Her voice did not waiver and she reached for his hand as though she was comforting him.

"I think we need the reverend, Henry. Not a doctor. We need to have the baby baptised. Go and get the reverend. I can already feel her slipping away."

And so, as before, Henry and Clarinda's baby died soon after a baptism performed in a rush in the night in their little bedsit in Cheapside. Clarinda Martha Parkes was born at around 10 o'clock at night on Saturday, the 23rd of June, 1838, and died in the early hours of the morning on Sunday, the 24th of June.

Six

Clarinda did not cry. She felt numb and empty. She continued her usual occupations of sewing, cleaning and cooking. She even went on walks with Isabella and trips to the garden plot with Thomas. She talked rarely on these outings, only in answer to questions. It was as though she was merely going through the motions of living.

"She's mourning deeply, I believe," Martha said to Henry when he came to visit the family on his own one Sunday. He was desperate and confused about the change in Clarinda. Martha held his hand and he cried as she had not seen him do since he was a boy.

"This will pass, 'enry. It's 'er way of coping. I think 'er pain is just too much for 'er to bear. She's shutting it out some'ow."

"But I can't even talk to 'er. It's like she's not even there, Mam. And I am grieving too. She's my wife. I need my wife."

"Give 'er time, 'enry. It's different for a woman. She'll be 'er own self in time. I do remember the sorrow I felt when our first 'enry died. It took a lot to get over. The loss of one child is so 'ard, but the loss of two in such a short time..."

"I know, I do know. I feel it, too. But it's like she's pushing me away and I need 'er, especially now. I'm mourning our babies, too."

He sobbed and Martha pulled his head to her chest and rocked him back and forth as though he was her baby still.

Isabella did not know how to help Clarinda. She regularly suggested walks and tried to awaken the old Clarinda by chatting endlessly about everyday things or the sights around them, as she had done when Clarinda had been grieving for Thomas. But Clarinda just nodded and agreed or smiled woodenly at her friend's efforts. Eventually, Isabella decided the only course was to attempt to force Clarinda to express her grief openly. *Surely*, she thought, *it was better for Clarinda to admit her pain than to continue in this pretence.*

They were strolling together through Spring Gardens on a cool August morning when Isabella first broached the babies' deaths directly with her friend.

"You have had a terrible loss, Clarinda. First Thomas and then Clarinda, your two little babies. It must be so hard to bear."

Clarinda did not blink.

"What was little Clarinda like? I never saw her. Did she look most like you or Henry? How did it feel to hold her in your arms? Do you miss holding her, and Thomas? I remember how it felt to hold Thomas. And he smelt like warm milk. Was Clarinda the same?" It was cruel, she knew, these words she was firing at her friend, and Isabella had a lump in her throat as she waited for Clarinda to respond.

Clarinda coughed slightly before simply saying, "These cool mornings are lovely, aren't they, Isabella?"

Isabella nodded and the two continued their walk in silence.

One day in late September, Clarinda sat with Wilbur at her feet on the bench near the garden plot and watched the elderly Thomas as he dug a furrow for the carrot seeds. She had not offered to help and he had not requested it. Thomas hummed and whistled to himself to cover her silence.

There was a strong, blustery wind that day and Thomas's shirt was buffeted as he worked. When he had finished planting the seeds and had covered them with the earth he had dug, he stood upright awkwardly and rubbed at his sore, rheumatic shoulder before bending to pick up the watering can. It was with this action that Thomas let out a sudden, sharp yelp like a dog in pain. Clarinda jumped abruptly to her feet as he collapsed to his knees with a thud and clutched at his chest. She ran to him and knelt with her skirt in the clods of dirt, holding him upright by the shoulders.

"Father, are you all right? What has happened? Where does it hurt?" she asked anxiously. It was the most words she had uttered in one breath for months.

The older man licked his lips and with effort said, "Get me 'ome, Clarinda. Get me 'ome. I think I need my bed."

"Let me get you to the bench first, Father. And fetch you some water from the well."

"Yes," he agreed and staggered to his feet, leaning against her heavily with his arm about her thin shoulders.

They hobbled awkwardly to the bench on which Thomas lay full length and breathed deeply.

"I'll be all right now, pet," he said. "'Twas just a turn of some sort."

"I'll just fetch the water first," she said.

Clarinda went to the plot to get the watering can and as she hurried to the well nearby, the tears suddenly, unexpectedly, began to fall at last. It was as though a dam had been broken by the shock of Thomas's collapse. A great torrent of tears dropped heavily onto the ground before her as she ran, and sploshed into the well as she reached for the bucket, so that when she returned to Thomas on the bench, her face was a crumpled mess of grief and agony. Thomas sat up when he saw her and she fell against his shoulder and sobbed and sobbed for all she had lost.

"There, there, my pet," he said, patting her gently, ignoring the throbbing pain in his chest. "There, there, Clarinda. Let it all out, my darling. Let it all out."

When Clarinda had got him home, Martha, in her fuss over Thomas, did not immediately notice the change in her.

"He just yelled out and collapsed," Clarinda explained as she helped Martha take off his boots.

"I'll be all right now then," Thomas said as they half-carried him to the bed. "'Tis just some silly turn I 'ad. 'Twill be fine with a bit of rest."

"Shall I go and fetch the doctor?" Clarinda asked.

"Yes, do," said Martha, tucking the sheets in around Thomas. But then she paused and turned to smile in recognition of the old Clarinda, whose face was red and her eyes still puffy from the tears she'd shed at last. Martha reached her hand out to clasp Clarinda's.

"'Twill be all right now, Clarinda. All will be right now," she said soothingly.

It was Thomas's heart, Mr Porter said after he had examined his reluctant patient. What Thomas needed was rest. No strenuous exercise or stress. The garden plot would have to be tended by another for a while. And with this new responsibility and purpose, Clarinda seemed to wake from her reverie. Each day following Thomas's collapse, she would visit the garden plot with Wilbur in tow and water the seeds Thomas had planted. As the seedlings began to grow, her spirits gradually lifted.

She visited the Parkes's home each day as well. It was as though Clarinda's maternal instincts were now centred on the old man. She had Henry borrow again the copies of *The Spectator* that held the serialised *Oliver Twist* and she read the tale to Thomas as he lay in bed or with his feet up on a stool in his armchair by the fire. She made him cups of tea and warm, healthy broths to assist his recovery. And she spoke openly of her grief to Martha as the two women sat sewing or chopping up vegetables while Thomas snored fitfully. But she still rarely cried. It was as though she had grown a hardness – a shell around her that kept her protected.

For Henry, it seemed his wife had returned to him, but with a slight difference. If he had had to explain the change in her, he would not have known how to put it into words, but he knew a subtle one had occurred. It was as though she was more isolated from him, as though she did not need him as she had before. There was a strength in her that had not been there previously. He was uneasy about the change.

Henry sat at his lathe in the quiet of the shop on Bradford Street each day. He could no longer afford ivory and so fashioned his trinkets only from bone which he collected from a local slaughterhouse. He pushed the pedal of the lathe with his foot to turn the bone and shaped it with his tools like a potter with clay. He made simple cotton reels and candlesticks, and more complex and detailed items like pipes and lidded boxes. It was intricate work but he had a natural talent for pattern, shape and symmetry. As he worked, his thoughts often drifted.

He wondered if this was all there was to be for him in this life. Was he to struggle on like his parents and eventually reach old age, battered and broken, living off a meagre wage, uncertain how to survive in the future when his body and ability to work gave way? Thomas and Martha had children who could support them as they aged, but would he and Clarinda have any children who survived? And would he want his children to grow up in such a desperate, hopeless world? The rights of the working man in England would improve eventually, he felt certain, but would it make a difference in his lifetime? Would he end up in a workhouse like so many others? And Clarinda? Was Robert Varney right to think he was not good enough for his daughter?

It was inevitably at this thought that Henry's natural pride and self-belief kicked in. He, Henry Parkes, would prove Robert Varney wrong. He would be someone of importance one day. He would succeed beyond Robert Varney's, or indeed anyone's, expectations.

But then the cycle of worrying would begin anew. He already had debts, including the rent on the shop. How could he rise from his depressed state in Birmingham? How could he stop their descent into poverty? Was London a place where he could succeed? Or would he find his lot in London as bad, if not worse, than here? And could he move so far from his family and leave his parents and his sisters to struggle on without him? They had his other brothers, George and James, but would he be deserting them all if he moved away? And, if he were to move to London, why not even further away to America or perhaps even Australia? Would the distance make any difference if it meant they were, in any case, apart?

And then his thoughts would settle for a time on what he had heard of these distant lands. There was much talk of the opportunities available in America and the reports in the newspapers were of acres of farmland, including tobacco plantations and cattle ranches. But he would need the money to pay for his and Clarinda's passage if they were to move there, whereas the government offered free passage to Australia for skilled workmen. He would not even need to find money for food during the months on board ship.

But then he would think of the distance. What would it mean to live on the other side of the globe? It was such a long way from everything he treasured, loved and knew in this world. Would he and Clarinda be enough for each other in such an alien, isolated world? And would their situation be improved at all anyway, even if they were to rip themselves completely from this life they knew?

Henry was hounded by these thoughts throughout the months following baby Clarinda's death. He wrote to John Hornblower about his worries, but John, having no appreciation for the emotional pull of Henry's family, did not hesitate to express the opinion that, of course Henry should move to London and, if need be, to America or Australia. But it wasn't until after Thomas's collapse, as Clarinda began to lift from her melancholia, that Henry spoke to his sister, Sarah, about the possibility of moving from Birmingham.

"I can't keep the shop going, Sarah. I keep making the goods, but no one is buying. I 'ave 'ole days without a customer even entering the shop. It's 'opeless. I'm already behind on the rent and I can't see things changing soon."

"What do you think you'll do, 'enry? There must be a way." Sarah and Henry were alone, walking along Edgbaston Street. Signs of the economic downturn were everywhere: shop fronts boarded up, beggars huddled with empty caps on the ground in front of them, refuse piled high on street corners.

"I think there is only one option, Sarah, and it distresses me greatly." He sensed the sudden tension of her body beside him.

"I feel I know what you are about to say, dear 'enry."

"Oh, Sarah, you know that, if I could, I would always remain near to you and Mam and Da and Eliza and Maria and young Thomas. But I 'ave a wife to think of now, and 'opefully children before too long."

"I know," Sarah said calmly and reached for his hand. "You need to move away from Birming'am, 'enry. You need to start afresh. You 'ave always 'ad such potential. Even as a young lad I knew you would one day be a great man. You won't be if you stay 'ere though. It'll only continue to drag you down if you stay in Birming'am."

Henry felt relief and a guilty excitement rush over him. "I knew you'd understand, Sarah. And George and James are both 'ere and not suffering in their trades as I am. I won't be leaving you all completely destitute. And if I stayed, you would only end up supporting me and Clarinda along with Mam and Da."

"Yes, 'enry. It's all right. You don't need to explain further. Where do you think of going?"

"Well, London, of course, as a start at least. While it is expensive, there are sure to be more opportunities there."

"Yes." She nodded slowly, staring at her feet. "And if you cannot find work in London?" She looked at him imploringly now.

"Well, I suppose we'd 'ave to go further." He swallowed hard. "I suppose America or maybe even as far as Australia."

They were silent for a time.

"Australia is a long way, 'enry," she said simply.

"Yes, it is. But there are great opportunities in the town of Sydney. I could earn some money and then bring you and the others out to join us. Even my brothers should be thinking of such a move. It would not mean we would be apart forever, dear Sarah. I would make sure of that."

She nodded slowly again.

"Well, London it will be," she said and smiled towards him. "'Ave you talked to Clarinda?"

"No," he said. "Only that it might be an option. I wanted to tell you first. I will talk to 'er tonight. I don't think she will be too distressed to move to London. She will miss Isabella, of course, but she 'as no real ties to 'er own family now."

"Be careful there, 'enry. I believe she still loves 'er family despite all that 'as 'appened. She may not be as amenable to the idea as you think."

But Clarinda had been expecting the news. Once more, in her own practical way, she had been aware of the hopelessness of Henry continuing on with the shop in Birmingham. Even during the months of her bitterest grieving when she had appeared apart from the world, she had been aware of all that was going on around her. And the fact of her babies' deaths and the sorrow she felt made her feel less connected to her home and its surrounds. No matter where she was or what she did, the reality of their deaths was everything now.

She would miss Isabella and John and the familiar parks and places, and even her father would seem more absent from her in London, but what did any of that matter now? Nothing would change the reality of her babies' deaths. And so, Clarinda smiled at Henry as he told her of his plans.

"It will really be a new beginning, Clarinda. We'll be able to forge a real life for ourselves. I think we should get tickets on the steam train to London when we go. We'll leave Birming'am with a real sense of the possibilities of the future. It will be you and me together, Clarinda, and that's all that is important now."

He did not tell her of his thoughts of America or Australia, fearing if she thought they might leave their home country completely, she would refuse to leave Birmingham at all. So, for now, he kept these thoughts from her.

PART II

London

SEVEN

Clarinda and Henry left Birmingham as second-class passengers on a steam train bound for London on Friday, the 23rd of November, 1838. They had sent most of their belongings ahead by steam wagon the day before, including Henry's lathe and tools.

On the morning they were to leave, they made a last visit to the Parkes's home. All the family were crowded into the room they called the lounge, even though it had once served as Henry, George and young Tom's bedroom. Present were James and Mary Ann with young Georgie and Will, Maria, Eliza, Sarah, George and Tom, and the elderly Martha and Thomas Parkes. It was an overwhelming scene. Clarinda could barely see the faces before her through her thick veil of tears. Henry shook both of his brothers' hands firmly and gazed into their faces as though he should memorise every mark and line. Clarinda kissed each cheek as it was offered to her and squeezed her precious Wilbur until he yelped before handing him to young Tom.

"Look after him, Tom," she said. "We'll send for him when we are able."

The older Thomas Parkes was still too ill to stand for long and so had settled into the armchair by the fire. Clarinda went to him. "Oh, Father," she said, choking on her tears. "You have been so good to me. You have been such a kind, dear father to me these last few years."

"There, there, pet. We'll see each other again. You'll be able to visit from London, I'm sure. And Clarinda, I know your own father will be grieving for you today."

She smiled through her tears. "I hope so. I do hope he feels at least a pinch of regret. He has not visited me to say goodbye, you know, as my brother did."

"Yes, pet, I know. I do indeed. 'E be a stubborn man."

Sarah was calm in her forced, composed way. Later that night she would shed a storm of tears into her pillow and feel that her heart had truly broken. But for now, she was self-sacrificing – the rock for her distraught sisters and mother to lean on.

Martha clutched her son's bent form to her with unknown strength. "Oh, 'enry! 'enry! My darling boy! God keep you both! God keep you both, my dears! Oh, 'enry! 'enry!"

He had to tear himself away from her.

"I will see you again, Mam. I will. I will visit and maybe, when Da is better, you can visit us in London. We can show you all the sights there. It will be such an adventure. 'Tis not as far away as it used to be, not now with the steam trains and all."

But, really, Henry knew he might never see any of his family again. He knew London, no matter how far away it seemed, might be only the first step on a journey to the other side of the world. His tears began to stream as he held Clarinda's hand and turned at the door of his family's home to wave his other hand high in the air and call, "God bless you all! God willing we'll meet again!"

Isabella came to the station to see them off. She was crying even before she saw them approach. They each held a large bag and Henry had a blanket under one arm, for the journey was sure to be cold as second-class carriages had no glass in their windows.

"Your brother said he had seen you, Clarinda. I am so glad he said goodbye. Lionel sends his best, of course. Oh, Henry! Clarinda! I will miss you so." She clutched them both to her tiny frame.

Clarinda had not thought it possible she could shed any more tears that day, but they came in a torrent again.

"Isabella! I am so sorry we will miss your wedding. We do wish you all the best in your marriage to Lionel. You have been like a sister to me. You must visit us in London. You must visit us often!"

"Yes, Clarinda. I will! I will!"

The train's whistle hooted rudely then and the steam spread along the station from the coal-fed engine.

"We must go," Henry said and moved Clarinda gently away from Isabella's arms.

"God bless you, Clarinda! God bless you, Henry! I will miss you!" Isabella called as they stepped up and into the already crowded compartment.

Within minutes, with Isabella waving her hand wildly towards their window, the train began to chuff slowly and rhythmically away from the station.

Henry held Clarinda's hand firmly. "A new beginning, my darling," he said as she wiped her tears with her other hand. "A new beginning it will be. You and I, we'll make it big now, just wait and see, my darling."

They both watched silently as the familiar hills and church steeples of Birmingham passed by their open window, and dirty, roughly dressed boys waved to them and cheered. Henry and Clarinda rocked back and forth, the wind in their faces, and watched together as the world moved faster than they had ever seen it move, whizzing past them as the steam train hurtled along the tracks, quicker and quicker, every second dragging them further and further away from their home in Birmingham.

Clarinda's tears fell heavily as she thought of her mother's grave and the two small graves of her babies with their simple headstones that would remain there in Birmingham. She had gone to visit them the day before and had sat on the cold, bare earth of the graveyard for hours saying a final goodbye to her mother and her two dear children, and she felt a terrible wrench now, as though she had been punched in the chest, as the train moved her away from them forever.

The journey, which Henry had anticipated with feelings of both nervousness and excitement, proved exhausting. About half an hour after the train left Birmingham, a storm hit and rain and then hail fell through the window directly onto them. Other passengers huddled together, sitting on the floor in the aisle between the two rows of seats to stay as far away as they could from the unrelenting rain. There was only room in the narrow aisle for a few and so Henry and Clarinda clutched one another on their wooden bench seat, perched as far from the window as they could.

Despite Henry's attempts to shelter her with his broad shoulders, they were both soon damp and shivering and Clarinda's teeth chattered uncontrollably. The only break from the torrent was when the train entered the occasional tunnel along the way. One of these was at least two miles long and lasted for a glorious five minutes, but then they were out into the rain again. It became a monotonous agony, sitting there with every part of them cold and wet throughout the long afternoon.

They had looked forward to seeing the sights of Coventry when they passed, but all they could see, due to the rising ground around the track, was a jumble of shack-like houses and a few church steeples and tall chimneys poking above the rise. From there, the rain was so heavy they could barely make out any of the passing towns or sights. It wasn't until the train reached Primrose Hill on the outskirts of London that the weather cleared and they looked out, still shivering, on a crescent moon lighting its bed of clouds. They arrived in London soon after, wet and cold as they stepped off the steam train and onto Euston Station in the dead of night with the London fog thick all around.

"This 'as not been the beginning we 'ad 'oped for, Clarinda," Henry said, hugging her to him protectively in the hustle of the crowd. "But it'll get better once we 'ave somewhere to sleep and, in the morning, things will seem brighter."

She smiled at him as they pushed through the throng of people towards the gates, dragging their bags behind them.

"Yes, Henry," she said. "We have each other. That's what matters. And as you said, it's a new beginning for us in London."

Sunday, 26th November, 1838

My Dear Sarah,

By the time you receive this letter I hope my father will have got the better of the severe illness which he suffered under when we left Birmingham and, together with my poor dear mother and you all, be better in health and spirits than I can hope for. As we did not get lodgings till late yesterday, I hope you will excuse my not writing before today. I shall now endeavour to tell you all that has passed since we parted.

The train which we came up by left Birmingham about one o'clock, and for the first fifty miles of the journey the rain and wind beat through the nothing but naked windows of our carriage with such bitterness that I began to think we should surely be the subject of a tale in the Penny Storyteller, entitled 'The Weather Slain'. The day cleared up as it died away, and the ghost of a devil that dragged us along tore out from Primrose Hill with the bright crescent moon above us in a calm and beautiful sky. In half an hour afterwards we were in London.

I enquired of one of the company's porters where we could get lodged for the night, and he directed me to a coffee house just outside the gates, and offered to carry our baggage there; but when we got to the gates the sentinel would not let him go out. That the fellow knew well enough, so I was obliged to have another carry it the other six yards. A double expense to begin with!

The next day I saw John Hornblower. He could do nothing for the first two or three hours but tell me how glad he was to see me, and stuff me and Clarinda with good things, and he then took me through the streets till late to show me the fine places. All the time Clarinda was waiting at the coffee house. Eventually, he got us a very comfortable lodging at a respectable house in Hatton Garden. We have a furnished room on the fourth floor, for six shillings per week, with a good-sized dressing closet, where we keep our bread, cheese and coals, and find our own linen and crockery.

Staying at the coffee house was very expensive, but I was afraid of going to strange lodgings, and am glad I did not. We have spent about twenty-four shillings since we arrived in London, though we have been as careful as we could.

I can say nothing of how we are likely to succeed at present, but I am in good spirits. We were both so ill the first night after we got in that we could not get an hour's sleep, but now feel much better.

Your affectionate brother,
Henry Parkes
Give my best love to my mother and father.

The room they rented was the windowless garret of a terrace house belonging to two elderly sisters, Misses Constance and Hilda Irvine. It was at one end of Hatton Garden while the other end was busy with an array of shops, including chemists and druggists, jewellers, wine merchants, tailors, hatters, tobacconists and, of course, several taverns.

But the garret was clean and, because the roof immediately above them was tiled, it didn't let in drafts of winter air. There was a small hearth that aired adequately through its close chimney. Having no window it was, however, dark and a little gloomy, and candles in London were almost double the price of those in Birmingham. But Henry and Clarinda tried to make the most of their little room in London.

At first, they only had the items they had carried with them in their luggage on the steam train from Birmingham. Their other belongings, including Henry's lathe and tools, were held at the wagoner's office until they could pay for their release. The unusual expense of the tickets for the steam train, their first lodgings in the coffee house and having to pay the six shillings for their room in advance, had left them with barely enough money to pay for bread and milk.

"I'll sell some of the trinkets I brought with me, Clarinda," Henry said on their first night in the garret as they lay in one another's arms on the hard bed. "I'll set off first thing in the morning and go amongst the shops and see if I can sell any so we can get the money for our other luggage. Once I 'ave the lathe, I'll be able to set up properly, I think."

Clarinda was quiet for a while as he stroked her hair. Eventually she said, "Where could you set up your lathe, though? This room is so small. Shouldn't you look for other work first?"

"Perhaps you are right. I will do both, I suppose, try to sell some of my bone turnings and ask for work around. Something's sure to come up."

Henry set off the next day through the dirty fog and cold of the London winter, asking at shops and factories for work and trying to sell his bone creations or gain commissions for items to be made. Clarinda sat in the garret with no view of her new city. She was afraid to venture out on her own. Thoughts of the alien world of London overwhelmed her.

She knew that she should make herself busy in some way to stop herself from falling into a deep despondency, but she seemed to lack the will and energy. Instead, Clarinda sat all day in the wicker chair, alone with her thoughts and worries, listening to the creaks of movement from the Irvine sisters and their maid in the rooms below, and the wailing and hissing of their numerous cats.

Eventually, when the few hours of daylight had long passed, Clarinda heard Henry's footfall on the steps and the hatch door open. He climbed into their loft and Clarinda jumped up and ran to hug him.

"Clarinda? Is everything all right?" Henry asked, loosening her tight grip on his shoulders.

"Yes, Henry. All is fine. I'm just so happy to see you. I have missed you terribly today. Tell me all that has happened?"

They sat on the two wicker chairs across from each other, knee to knee and hand in hand. He told her of how he had trudged through the cobbled lanes and streets, asking at every place he came to if they had work and trying to sell his goods. He'd had some luck at the hatter on their street, a Mr Thomas Rich, who'd ordered a dozen hatpins to be turned by Henry. But, sadly, until he could pay for the release of his lathe and tools, he could not even begin this work.

He had bought some milk, a small amount of tea and half a loaf of bread for their supper with some of their few remaining shillings and, while they ate, Clarinda listened to his chatter and felt her dark mood lift.

"The water 'ere is disgusting, I think," Henry mumbled as he chewed on the hardened loaf. "'Ave you noticed its yellow colour, as though it 'as come straight from the Thames without being cleaned at all? I don't think we should drink it without boiling it to get all the impurities out first. Everything is very expensive, too. John 'ornblower 'ad warned us of this, of course. Potatoes are around one shilling per pound, and this milk was the cheapest I could find at four shillings per quart. We are going to 'ave to be frugal till I find work."

"I do wonder, Henry, if we should have stayed in Birmingham," Clarinda said. "I worry things won't be any better here."

He sighed. "We 'ave to give it a try – just for a bit at least."

"Yes, you're right. We have only just arrived in London. It must get better. I have been quite miserable today, you know," she admitted.

"Oh, my darling, I'm sorry for that." He squeezed her hand. "What 'ave you done all day?"

"Nothing," she answered bluntly. "Nothing but sit here and mope, I suppose. I'm afraid to go out on my own."

"Yes, you must be careful. It's a very big city. But you can't sit up 'ere on your own every day. I'll tell you what, I'll go with you tomorrow to see the great Bucking'am Palace, if you like. We can go in the afternoon, after I've looked for work again. It's not far from 'ere. Queen Victoria's the first monarch to make it 'er official home, you know, which is why it is now called a palace and not just Bucking'am 'ouse as it used to be. We might even see the Queen!"

"Yes, that would be wonderful, Henry. I would feel quite all right out there with you beside me, I think. It is a little daunting. But I do want to see some of the sights."

"We'll make an excursion of it," he said and leaned over to kiss her.

The sun peered through the sulphurous fog the following afternoon when Henry and Clarinda set out on their walk to Buckingham Palace. Clarinda had to stop several times with a fit of coughing from the foul air of the factories and countless smoking chimneys along the way. But although a little anxious, she was thrilled to be on an outing in this great city with Henry by her side. She held his hand tightly.

Henry was aware of her uncertainty and tried to coax her from it by pointing out some of the sights. As they walked along Clerkenwell Road and passed its shop-fronted square, he said, "Remember *Oliver Twist*, Clarinda? It was in the square 'ere that the Artful Dodger and Charley Bates were supposed to 'ave pickpocketed the watch from the gentleman who later takes in Oliver. I can just imagine it, can't you? It seems so real now seeing the place."

There was a throng of people in the square and Clarinda stared at the faces warily to see if any looked like the type who could be an Artful Dodger or a Fagin.

As they came onto Oxford Street she felt even more unsafe and uncomfortable. There were regular shops such as drapers and furniture stores and the occasional shoe shiner, but also a group of brazen ladies in low-cut, colourful dresses, with overly rouged cheeks and lips. One of them winked at Henry as they passed and called out, "Hey, m' covey!" before blowing him a kiss. Henry half-smiled.

"Was that a prostitute?" Clarinda was shocked.

"Don't fret, Clarinda. There are prostitutes in Birming'am, too, you know. Just not always so obvious."

"Oh," was all she could say, pondering.

In one open square there was a crowd laughing hilariously at the antics of a Punch and Judy performance – a show Henry had heard of but never seen. They stood and watched briefly.

"It's quite barbaric, really," commented Henry, "to laugh so much at the poor woman being beaten. Quite like the spectacle of a 'anging, I suppose. People enjoying others' suffering."

"Were shows like this in Birmingham, too?" asked Clarinda.

Henry sniggered. "Probably, my dear. Just not around where we'd usually go, I suppose."

They walked under the sheltered colonnade along Regent Street, past fine columned buildings and onto Piccadilly Circus – an expansive, circular boulevard, with carriages racing past to roll on in a myriad of directions. And then on into St James Park.

"We're almost there, Clarinda. Just at the end of this park, I believe."

The park was crowded with people so it was difficult to see ahead. Some were sitting on benches under trees and others attempting to stroll through the busy throng, holding parasols and bamboo canes. There were many police officers and soldiers with bayonets moving people on and questioning those they thought suspicious. Henry was pushed on the shoulder lightly by one police officer and he almost tripped Clarinda in the movement.

"It's nothing like our parks in Birmingham," Clarinda whispered in Henry's ear. "You can barely see the beauty with so many people, and all these cannons everywhere. I'd much prefer a quiet country lane or Spring Gardens back home."

"But look at the swans," Henry tried to cajole her, "and all the other water-fowl there on the lake. They are a sight to be'old."

"What is that strange bird?" exclaimed Clarinda, pointing to an awkward white bird flying above them with a huge wingspan and a yellow, bucket-like beak.

"I think it's called a pelican, darling. I read that a pair were given to one of our Kings as a gift from the Russians 'undreds of years ago and their numbers in London 'ave grown incredibly since."

She watched the remarkable bird in awe and thought how much more Henry knew of the world than her.

And then they were there, standing on the paved square before Buckingham Palace. It was an imposing building, symmetrical in its numerous columns and countless windows, with the Union Jack flying full-mast from the central rising roof. In front of the marble arch entrance were two sentry boxes where unsmiling guards stood in high black busbies and red jackets with polished gold buttons, each holding their bayonet firmly.

"To think that Queen Victoria is probably in there, somewhere," said Henry.

"Yes," agreed Clarinda. "But with so many people milling about her home, she must be quite put off. I wouldn't want to live in a place like this."

He laughed and pecked her on the cheek. "I guess you're right, my darling. Much better to be you and I living in a garret on 'atton Garden than the Queen of England in 'er splendid palace!"

EIGHT

Clarinda realised she was pregnant again one morning in December. She felt a confusion of emotions at the familiar nausea, which was accentuated by the empty, flat feeling of too little food. When she told Henry of the baby, his smile was forced.

"I knew there'd be another soon, my darling," he said. "You must rest yourself. This one will be all right, I feel."

But really, they both worried for a baby born into their troubles.

The bleakness of the weather matched their moods. Henry wrote home to ask for a loan as he had still not found work and they were near to starving. Sarah sent them enough to pay for the release of their other luggage, including Henry's lathe, so that he could now complete the few commissions he had gained in London. Clarinda helped boil the bones over the fire in their little room while Henry turned the hatpins and some buttons for a draper. But they had barely enough to pay for their rent, let alone food.

"It's getting desperate," Henry said one afternoon when he returned to their room after having again spent hours searching for work.

"It is, Henry. I'm not sure we can keep on like this for much longer. I never imagined we'd be reduced to this. I'm even starting to think we might have to go to a workhouse."

She had expected Henry to be shocked at the suggestion but he simply nodded his head and his easy agreement made her even more distressed.

"I don't know how I could ever live in a place like that either, Henry. A workhouse barely feeds you enough to keep you going at the pace the work demands, anyway. You have said so yourself. And what would become of our child?"

Both their minds turned immediately to the fictional Oliver Twist but neither spoke of this horrible comparison. They were silent for a time. There was one possible solution that Henry dwelled on now: free passage to Australia, but he wondered how to broach the subject with Clarinda.

But talk of the workhouse that night quickened his boldness and, in a rush, he mumbled his thoughts, not daring to look at Clarinda as he spoke, instead focusing on his own clenched hands. "I 'ave been thinking for a while that maybe we should leave England altogether, Clarinda."

She gasped and stared at his bowed head with wild, questioning eyes.

"Leave England? Is that what you said? I had not even considered that, Henry! Where could we possibly go? And wouldn't we starve, in any case?"

He raised his eyes to her and held her hand tightly as he spoke to her slowly, as though he were explaining a lesson to a child. "We would still 'ave each other, Clarinda, no matter where we went, and that's what's important. America is an option, of course, and the steam paddle boats to New York are becoming quite regular, but we'd 'ave to find the money for our fares. And New York is a big city, too, so I don't know if we'd live any better there than London. The other possibility is the land they call Australia."

Again she gasped. "Australia is on the other side of the world, Henry! It's such a long way away! We'd be turning our backs on all we know!"

He crouched by her feet, gazing up into her eyes. "Our passage would be free if I was accepted for my skills," he said. "We would be fed every day of the entire journey without cost. It would save us from starving. And there are great reports coming from the town of Sydney. I was reading a brochure only today all about it. It is a wonderful place. The colony of New South Wales is three times the size of England, Scotland, Ireland and Wales put together. The soil there produces almost anything – pomegranates, oranges, lemons, figs. Land can be bought for seven pounds an acre in some towns and for five shillings per acre in others. Think of it, Clarinda. We could buy an acre of land for less than we pay for rent 'ere each week."

She nodded. It was a lot to take in but, with her practical nature, she could see the sense in what he was saying.

"And, Clarinda," he said, "the climate is the 'ealthiest in the world. We would raise our family in a warm, sunny land and our children would be less likely to be sick there."

She nodded again, looking thoughtfully into his steady, blue eyes.

"You seem quite decided on this, Henry."

"I can see no alternative," he said.

Henry began to visit the Government Emigration Office daily, but getting a free passage on a ship was not as simple as he'd thought. There were hundreds of other men lining up each day along the steep stone steps that led to the offices, and out into the street. Every hour spent there waiting in the slow-moving queue was an hour Henry might have spent trying to get work.

He became even more discouraged when Mr Marshall, the shipping agent, told him that an ivory turner was not as much in demand in the colony as carpenters, masons or smiths. For Henry to gain passage, Mr Marshall said, he would have to produce remarkable certificates of good character. It was yet another blow. But Henry was determined not to go under.

Clarinda and Henry

Thursday, 6th December, 1838

My Dear Sister,

My expectations of London have met with disappointment in nearly every particular and so my thoughts have returned to emigration. The information which we have obtained since we have been here respecting Australia has determined both Clarinda and myself to make up our minds to emigrate to a land that holds out prospects bright and cheering to unhappy Englishmen, though at a distance of 16,000 miles.

I have been to the Government Emigration Office to ascertain what assistance they afford to mechanics wishing to emigrate, and we can have a free passage, being young and having no children. The first chartered ship, I believe, will sail in March, and that vessel, I trust, will convey us safe to Sydney.

In the meantime we have much to do, and I must necessarily trouble you not a little. You have been so kind to me, and have sacrificed so much for my welfare, that I am ashamed to ask you for further assistance; but I hope a time will come when I shall have it in my power to prove my gratitude.

In the first place to procure a free passage, I must have certificates that state I am of good character. Would Maria obtain such testaments from Rev. George Cheatle, minister of Lombard Street Chapel, as a certificate must be signed by a clergyman and he is the only person of that class who can know anything of me; and from Mr B. Hudson, bookseller, Bull Street; Mr R. Matthison, stationer, Edgbaston Street; Mr Pickard, ironmonger, Bull Street; Mr Porter, surgeon, Bromsgrove Street; Mr Wright, thread manufacturer, Bromsgrove Street; and my old master, Mr J. Holding. This last certificate is of particular importance and tell Mr Holding that he must state my skills at ivory and bone turning to be exceptional, as it seems those in my trade do not gain passage as easily as other mechanics.

For Clarinda, we must also have signatures. Could Maria obtain these from Mr J. Hardy, paper manufacturer, Great Hampton Row; Rev. G. Cheatle, Lombard Street; and Mr Derrington, missionary, Garrison Lane.

As we shall be about four months on our voyage, and as there is no washing allowed on board, we must have at least fifteen changes of clothing each, be they ever so poor ones. Therefore, the next thing I want is, if Eliza or Mam can find time, and are able to do so, for them to make some of these garments for us, as fast as possible and Clarinda will make some more.

I hope Mam and Da are well – and Eliza, Maria and young Tom. Give our love to all. I am very glad the dog gets on so well, and hope you will be able to keep him as a playfellow for Tom. I am very sorry to hear they are going to take away my father's garden now that he cannot keep it up, but I wish he was going with me to Australia, and he could then buy a five-shilling acre of land and make another. And I would come and fetch my mother, too, and she should have a dairy, for cows are only four pounds each, the very best.

Your affectionate brother,
Henry Parkes

One day as Henry was out looking for work, he was drawn to the gallows outside Newgate Prison by a throng of people yelling and cheering. A young, lanky man was being marched by guards across the courtyard where people jostled to catch sight of him, and some reached out to touch his hand for good luck. Henry watched as the condemned man grinned towards his audience and gave a slight bow of his head in acknowledgement. It was almost as much of a false entertainment as the hangings Henry had heard of years ago when prisoners were paraded along the streets in a cart to Tyburn Gallows.

He wondered if this man was a victim of his circumstances and the need to survive, as so many criminals were. He asked a hawker who was selling roasted nuts from a cart nearby, "What's 'e convicted of?"

"He murdered the maid at the house where he was footman. Too heinous a crime for transportation. First swinging for over a year here at Newgate," the hawker answered.

Henry watched as the man mumbled the hanging psalm in chorus with the strong voice of the clergyman, "Behold I was brought forth in iniquity, and in sin did my mother conceive me." He was led up the stairs to the gallows and, with a swiftness that startled Henry, the burly hangman pulled a white hood over the man's head and put the noose around his neck.

How would this young man feel, Henry thought, *to never see the world again? Perhaps the slavery of transportation was preferable to death.* Before Henry could clarify his thoughts further, the trapdoor the man stood on dropped. His feet kicked and twitched violently for a moment, and the mask about the man's head seemed to be sucked in to where his mouth would have been, before a great rush of urine trickled down his leg and dripped onto the stones of the courtyard.

Henry felt as though the world had stopped around him. He stared at the spot where the urine puddled. And then the noise of cheering and the sobs of a few people around him brought him back to reality. His shock was relieved only slightly by the knowledge that the man had taken another's life and not hung for a property crime committed for survival.

Throughout December, Clarinda continued to spend her days alone in their little garret room conserving her energy for the baby. Henry worried over her listlessness and tried to force on her the bigger portion of their meagre meals.

"You're the one who must go out in the cold, Henry. You need the energy, too. I don't know how I would survive if anything happened to you."

"You'd probably fare much better, Clarinda, for you could return to your father and not be shackled to such a sad and sorry wretch as me."

This was not entirely jest, as they both knew, but Henry's self-belief despite their current hardships was still strong.

"I have been thinking of my father, Henry," Clarinda said at the mention of him. "I will probably never see him again." She began to cry soundlessly.

"Oh, Clarinda. 'E was so unkind to you. We 'ave each other now. We will get through this." Henry hugged her close.

"I think I must write to him, though. Surely he will answer when he knows I am to be on the other side of the globe."

"Yes. I'm sure 'e will, darling."

Clarinda did write to her father, a simple letter stating that she and Henry were to leave England and that she esteemed her father and wished she could hear from him before she left.

He never replied.

It was at Christmas that Henry and Clarinda reached their lowest. They had eaten nothing for the previous two days but a few slices of stale bread. That Christmas Day morning, they sat in their wicker chairs and listened despairingly to the clank of pots from the maid downstairs as she prepared Christmas dinner for the Irvine sisters. It was the delicious smell of the goose as it roasted that undid Clarinda.

"Could we just ask for a morsel, do you think, Henry? I know you do not want to be indebted to our landladies, but just a morsel, surely."

"I don't think they would give us any, Clarinda. And what would I say to them? That they 'ave beggars lodging in their garret? They'd just as likely kick us out into the street."

But Clarinda was desperate with hunger. "I will ask, Henry, although they barely acknowledge me. I'll tell them we are starving!" She had never shouted at Henry before, but her voice suddenly rose and she began to scream. "I am starving, Henry. If I don't get some proper food, I think I might die! And if I don't eat, the baby will never survive! I cannot bear to lose another child. I need food! I'd do *anything* for food!"

Henry was shocked at her sudden outburst, and shamed. "All right, Clarinda," he said in a soft, soothing voice. "Calm down, calm down. You're right. We need food, especially with the baby. If anyone is to ask the old crones, it will be me. But let's wait until we know they 'ave already eaten and then we can ask for some leftovers, or maybe just wish them Merry Christmas and they might offer us some without us 'aving to beg."

"All right, Henry." Clarinda's voice was strained but she no longer yelled. "But I do need to eat something. I can't go on like this. And the baby will surely die if I don't get some food soon."

"Yes, darling. I'm sorry things are so desperate."

Later, when they thought the ladies had finished their meal, and with some holly Henry had gathered as an offering, they both climbed down from the garret and made their way to the dining room on the second floor. Henry knocked on the door before walking in with Clarinda on his arm, both smiling falsely, and with Henry waving the holly in the air.

"Miss Irvine. Miss Irvine," he said and bowed gallantly to each of the surprised ladies who still sat at the dining table. Clarinda noticed anxiously that the dishes had been cleared. "We do not wish to intrude but we would like to wish the compliments of the season to two such charming women and 'ope to cheer your 'ome with this small gift of 'olly."

It was said eloquently, with only a hint of his Midlands accent, and the Irvine sisters both blushed.

"Ah, thank you indeed," said Miss Constance Irvine, glancing at her sister uncertainly. "We will have the maid place the holly on the table, perhaps, and Merry Christmas to you, Mr Parkes, and your wife."

There was an awkward pause before the maid came into the room carrying a huge plum pudding. Clarinda felt dizzy at the sight of it and her breath quickened.

"Well, ah..." Miss Hilda Irvine hesitated. "Would you like to, ah, partake of some pudding, and maybe a little wine as well?"

Clarinda almost swooned.

"We do not want to put you to any trouble," said Henry. "But perhaps a small piece for us both. It looks so delicious."

And when it was served at last, Clarinda had to stop herself from stuffing the whole piece into her mouth at once.

At night now, Clarinda often woke in a fever of panic. Her dreams were always of the baby. She dreamt of it being born in a rush on the burning yellow sands of a beach she had seen in a drawing of Sydney. Or sometimes on the bare ground in a bark hut where she watched on as though she were floating above her labouring self. And in one dream, the baby was born as black as an Aboriginal. Always in these dreams, Clarinda was alone with the baby and her feelings of utter, hopeless abandonment were overwhelming. She woke panting and clutching at her stomach, and only when she felt a light flutter of the baby moving inside was she able to calm herself. She would pray then for its safe delivery and for it to be a baby who would survive.

"Let it live, Dear Lord. Whatever else, please let my baby live," she would whisper. "Please let this one live."

Clarinda received a letter from Isabella Parry, now Mrs Lionel Davenport. She was ashamed that her feelings towards her friend were now tinged with the bitter taste of jealousy, knowing how privileged Isabella's life was in comparison to her own. The life she had led in Birmingham seemed so distant and remote from her current world. Isabella would never understand the desperation of Clarinda's life, would never experience the animal hunger she felt each day, could not even imagine what it was to struggle so completely to survive. Clarinda cried tears of self-pity as she read the letter.

Friday, 4th January, 1839

My dear Clarinda,

I hope you and Henry are well. Your recent news has alarmed me. I had thought London such a distance between us, but Australia is beyond imagining! We must still write to each other regularly even though we will be so far apart. I fear I will never see you again.

My wedding was a rather grand affair. I wish you could have been there. I wore an apricot dress with a lace collar and sleeves, much like the ones you see in the fashion plates of late. I was told by many how the colour accentuated my eyes. Your brother was there, of course, being such a good friend of Lionel's, but we only invited family and a few close friends. I am loving married life. I had not realised how exquisite it would be. I have moved into Lionel's house on Bull Street and we still retain the services of his housekeeper and gardener, Prudie and Cecil Campbell. Sometimes I am at quite a loss to know what to do with myself.

I miss our walks together, but I have begun walking quite regularly with Lily Andrews. The Spring Gardens are rather fine at present despite the winter cold. Lily is a good companion, but nothing on you, dear Clarinda.

Please write soon and send my best to Henry.

Yours affectionately,
Isabella

Sometimes, during her long, quiet days in the garret room, Clarinda could not help wondering if her life would have been happier if she had not fallen in love with Henry Parkes, and in fact had never met the tall, handsome man she'd married. She felt guilty at these thoughts, as though she were betraying Henry. She would chastise herself and remind herself of the wonderful man Henry was and how fortunate she was to be loved by him.

Nevertheless, she found herself wishing things were different. She wished they did not have to leave England, and that she'd live her whole life in Birmingham and never have to face the challenge of a new world. Sometimes these thoughts even drifted to the question of whether she could have loved another man as passionately as she loved Henry. But then she reminded herself that this life was God's will, and she thought again of Henry's brilliance and the successful man he would hopefully become.

She prayed to God to forgive her for her disloyal thoughts. She had sworn she would love Henry and serve him for better or worse, for richer or poorer, in sickness and in health, till death part them. This was her duty now.

She thought also of the conversation she'd had with Sarah Parkes on a walk through the familiar country lanes of Birmingham a few days before their departure last November.

"I'm sure 'enry will be a great man one day," Sarah had said, leaning into Clarinda as she held the crook of her arm. "'E will need your 'elp, though. I have always 'elped 'im, not only in 'is lessons when 'e was young, but in building 'is confidence and belief in 'imself. 'Enry needs this. I think all great men need this reassurance from a woman. 'E needs to be reminded of 'is brilliance to really achieve what I'm sure 'e must. And I won't be there in London to do so."

Clarinda had squeezed her sister-in-law's hand affectionately. "I do know he is a remarkable man, Sarah," she had said. "I will make sure he is reminded of this regularly. I agree with you entirely. Who knows what Henry might do if he truly continues to believe in himself."

"Yes. 'E might be a schoolteacher one day, I feel. Or maybe even a surgeon or a lawyer. 'E 'as always been so clever, like our Mam. We must make sure 'is brilliance isn't wasted."

"Yes, Sarah. We must make sure he reaches his potential. I will do all I can, even though I'm sure my own mind is only feeble in comparison to his."

"You and I both, Clarinda," Sarah had said.

Even though this conversation had happened before Clarinda had known the utter desperation of starvation, she knew it was her duty to stay loyal to Henry still.

Thankfully, Clarinda and Henry's struggle was eased a little after Christmas. Henry gained a few commissions and, after completing these, sold some of his tools so they could buy food. Sarah began to send them an occasional halfpenny when she could. And the Irvine sisters, obviously charmed by Henry on his Christmas visit, asked them sometimes to tea in the evenings. There was usually teacake or buttered scones – and sometimes platters of fruit – and Constance and Hilda Irvine would listen attentively to Henry as he read them his latest poems.

At the end of January, Henry, at last, obtained employment in a large turning business making twine boxes from wood. It was heavy work and he was paid for the number of boxes he made. He could earn up to six or seven shillings if he worked throughout the day. But still he had to take the time to visit the Emigration Office to try to obtain his and Clarinda's passage to Australia.

He had heard, before he got his job, of a ship that was leaving for Sydney just after Christmas, and he had hoped they would get a passage on board – even though it meant they would have to leave in a rush – so desperate were they for food then. Sadly, they were not included in the passenger list, and this happened again with another ship that left at the end of January. The next ship to sail was not to leave until the 26th of March. It seemed such a long time away.

Henry's brother James wrote to him with news from Birmingham, saying that on the 1st of November the previous year, Birmingham had at last become a Municipal Borough. This meant, Henry knew, that it had its first elected town council to work alongside the Tory-dominated Street Commissioners and Parish Board. William Scholefield, a member of the Birmingham Union, had been elected as mayor.

The Street Commissioners are making the Council's work impossible, James wrote. *They've stopped the Council from meeting in the Town Hall, even though it was built from the funds from our rates and so is publicly owned. And the Parish Board has been refusing to hand over any newly collected rates to the Council, claiming it is an illegal body until it has been incorporated for three years. We in the Union are outraged, as I am sure you will be, Henry. The Council's first plan was to build a constabulary, as Birmingham is becoming increasingly dangerous because of the number of beggars and desperate thieves about, but the Council cannot obtain the money to create it.*

While this report was something that would have fired Henry's political fervour even a few months before, he felt so removed from his old life in Birmingham that he read the news with only feelings of mild annoyance and concern for his family there. His entire focus, these days, was on making enough money so he and Clarinda could eat, and on obtaining a passage to Australia. The rights of the working man in Britain would not be his concern anymore. His life would now be bound up in the rights of New South Welshmen.

Henry leaped down the steep steps of the Emigration Office two at a time, smiling broadly and barely able to contain his urge to laugh out loud. It was confirmed. He and Clarinda were included on the *Strathfieldsaye*'s passenger list, which was to sail from Gravesend to Port

Jackson, Sydney, on the 26th of March, which was in less than three weeks' time.

Other men who were queued on the cold, stone steps or leaning against the wooden railing turned towards Henry as he bounded past them and one man called after him, "Good luck to ya, matey! Good luck to ya!"

Henry ran nonstop along the dirty streets to the house in Hatton Garden, up its numerous stairs to the garret's hatch and pushed open its wooden door with such force it fell noisily against the floorboards. Clarinda jumped up from the wicker chair in surprise as he stumbled into the room yelling, "We're going on the twenty-sixth, Clarinda! We've got a berth on board! We're going to sail on the twenty-sixth of this month!" He ran to her and danced her around in a circle.

Clarinda did not know whether to laugh or cry in that instant. They had been hoping for this news but its reality was momentous.

"Please stop, Henry! Stop!" she said and he ceased twirling her. Clarinda caught her breath, smoothing down her skirt with shaking hands.

"I thought you'd be excited?" Henry said, disappointment clear in his voice.

"I am. Oh, I am, Henry. It's just that... that... it's a little overwhelming, I suppose, now that it really *is* going to happen."

"It's the best thing that could 'appen! We're really going to start afresh again now. It'll be a wonderful new beginning this time. I'm sure of it!"

"I know you're right, Henry. I think it's just the uncertainty that worries me a little. And the baby. It means the baby will definitely be born either on board ship or in a strange land. It will never see England. It'll not be truly English, you know."

"The baby will be a New South Welshman – and lucky to be one, too." He paused then and pulled her down gently into her chair as he sat beside her. "I do understand your worries, Clarinda. I'm sorry you'll 'ave to go through the child birthing in some foreign land. But you'll see, it'll be for the best. And this little one," he patted the growing swell of her stomach, "will be 'ealthy and 'appy, I feel sure." He leaned towards her and kissed her.

Soon after the news of their sailing, Henry had a poem published in the newly formed London newspaper *The Charter*. It was several stanzas long and entitled 'Poverty'. He read it aloud to Clarinda and, as he did, she thought again of how much this intelligent man might achieve if he was given the right opportunities.

"You are such a capable, brilliant man, Henry – to have poems published in a London paper is proof indeed. You must take the newspaper to Australia with us. The poem is sure to be published there, too. It is very moving. You might even become a famous Australian poet!"

They received letters from the Parkes family before they left and Thomas sent them a pound and some garden seeds to take with them. Henry's letters home became increasingly plaintive as the reality of perhaps never seeing his family again sunk in.

How I will miss my beloved Father and Mother, he wrote to Sarah. *A father and mother bowed down with years of affliction, and steeped in poverty and wretchedness. The very thought seems to make me unhappy forever when I know that half the circumference of the globe will shortly lie between us.*

Clarinda's thoughts were also often of her family during this time. When she was alone during the day she wept for their loss, for they were truly lost to her now. She knew she would probably never see them again – not her father or her brother, and she even regretted not seeing her stepmother. It was so final. Almost as though they were dead and buried along with her mother.

Clarinda thought of her farewell to her brother when he came to visit her in the bedsit in Birmingham and how John had hugged her close. But of course, this memory made her dwell with bitterness on her father's refusal to see or speak to her since the day she had first moved from his house. The cruellest thought of all was that he had not even replied to her letter when she'd told him of their travelling to Australia and knew he'd probably never see his daughter again – it was a painful blow. She wondered if he had ever really loved her at all.

And so, when a letter arrived for her from Sarah Parkes containing a sovereign from Robert Varney, Clarinda felt some of the sorrow lift. He had, at least, acknowledged her existence. He may not love her enough to write to her, but at least he recognised he still had a daughter.

I went to visit Robert Varney, Sarah wrote. *I knew how much you grieved his dismissal of you. He was loath to see me, of course, as the sister of Henry Parkes, but I would not be moved from his parlour. I badgered him on his duty to you. I told him it was a sin not to acknowledge you when you were to move to the other side of the world. Ann Varney argued with me and said the most terrible things. I cannot imagine what your life was like with such a woman – I think she is quite deranged. Eventually I persuaded your father to send you this sovereign and, while he gave no words to accompany it, I do believe his sending it is heartfelt.*

It was a small token, but it was something. *I must harden my heart now*, Clarinda thought, even as the tears fell heavily onto Sarah's letter, smudging the ink. She must try to forget her father's rejection of her. She had married Henry Parkes for love and had thereby lost the love of her father. There was nothing she could do to alter this now. She would sail to the other side of the world and begin a new life, and she must try to forget Robert Varney. She must try to leave the pain of him behind.

Clarinda spent her final weeks in London busily sewing clothes from cloth Sarah had sent. She tried to focus her thoughts on the task at hand

and on the growing baby inside her. It was too daunting to dwell on the journey they were about to take and the overwhelming thought of leaving England forever. But these thoughts niggled in the recesses of her mind as she sat for hours sewing undergarments, shifts and shirts in plain white cloth.

Henry continued to work at the turning factory most days, but his hours there were reduced because of his preparations for their journey. He reluctantly sold his lathe and the remainder of his tools, for he could not take them on board and they needed the money. He arranged tickets on a paddle steamer to take them to Gravesend in time for their departure on the *Strathfieldsaye*.

A week before they were to sail, Henry dragged their boxes of luggage by rope through the streets of London to the dock on the Thames where the *Strathfieldsaye* waited. Soon it would leave for Gravesend where Henry and Clarinda, and most of the other passengers, were to board. His first sight of the ship was of its white sails billowing like wings above the rooves of the buildings around the dock. Then, as he rounded the bend in the road that led down to the river, he saw the hull of the *Strathfieldsaye* floating in the dark waters of the Thames.

"You should 'ave seen it," he said to Clarinda that night as they sat by the waning candle. "I've never seen a sailing ship, except in pictures, you know. It was a great thing to see. It 'ad three masts, each with three sails and other smaller, triangular sails about. The body of it 'ad only a few windows – port'oles, aren't they called? They 'ad shutters over them, no doubt to keep the water and the weather out. There were other rooms, I think, in the back part of it with port'oles, too, which'll be the cabins for the paying passengers, I expect. It was a monster of a thing, Clarinda, all rocking and swaying and the sound of the water slapping against its sides. To think it'll be our 'ome for months and take us across three oceans!"

"It frightens me, Henry. The thought of just the wooden ship beneath us and the sea all around," she admitted.

"Yes, it's not something to think on too much, Clarinda. Lots of people 'ave done it before us. We'll get used to it after a few days, I expect."

Neither of them spoke directly about their fears of storms and shipwreck – and even the possibility of piracy.

John Hornblower came to visit Clarinda and Henry one evening. They had not seen him for some time and he had shaved his beard so that he was now bald on both head and chin.

"It must be cold in the winter, John, with not an 'air on your 'ead," Henry laughed as he offered him the ale he'd bought for the occasion with some of their last coins. Henry was too proud to tell John how destitute they were, although signs of it were all about the garret room.

"We've packed all our belongings, you see, John," Henry explained. "They're all on the ship now as it makes its way to Gravesend where we'll meet it on Tuesday morning."

"Such an adventure!" John remarked. "I wish I was coming along with you both. I thought I was the brave one coming to London ahead of you, but that's nothing like Australia on the other side of the world!"

"It does scare me a little, John," Clarinda said. "But as Henry says, many have done the same before us."

"Yes, yes," John said and took a sip of his beer before saying, "Have you heard then, Henry, about our doings in the London Working Men's Association?"

Henry nodded quietly at this inevitable change of conversation to politics. It was not something he had thought of often since their time in London and he felt a tinge of guilt for his lack of involvement.

"I went to the National Chartist Convention that was held here in London last month," John continued. "Lots of the Birmingham members were there. I was a little surprised you didn't join us, Henry."

"There've been other more personal things on my mind, John. We've 'ad some difficult times."

There was an uncomfortable silence.

"Well, I suppose you won't have unjust laws in New South Wales, like we have here, Henry," John said after a time. "The conservatives won't have had a chance to get their talons into such a new colony."

"Well, yes, that is true," said Henry. "But remember New South Wales is still under British rule. The governor is the direct representative of the British Government."

"But surely the power of the elite cannot be anything in comparison to what it is here," John said. "I cannot imagine there is much of an elite class in a place populated mainly by convicts and ex-convicts."

"That is one thing that worries me, John," Clarinda interrupted. "That we will be living in a place full of criminals."

"I 'ave talked to you about this before, Clarinda," Henry said, his annoyance evident in his voice. "Most of the people transported were working men objecting to the abuses of the British Government, or people who stole to stay alive because of their extreme poverty. They became criminals by necessity. We 'ave known 'ow desperate a person can become and what it is like to starve." Henry glanced at John, realising he'd betrayed the extreme circumstances he and Clarinda had been living under.

"I am sorry it has been as hard as that, Henry," John said. "I hadn't realised how much you have struggled in London."

As John left, he and Henry hugged each other heartily.

"'Till we meet again, Henry and Clarinda," John said as he stood on the steps leading from the garret. "Good luck to you both. I hope you find New South Wales a place you can thrive!"

PART III

On Board the Strathfieldsaye

NINE

It was the first time either Clarinda or Henry had ever been on board a boat. They walked to the quay through the busy streets, each carrying the bag they had arrived with in London only four months earlier. The paddle steamer was already smoking from its two great funnels as they clambered uncertainly along the gangplank. Henry found seats beside a window where they could look out on the sights of London, the dome of St Paul's Cathedral glittering in the sunlight.

"I'm feeling quite excited," Clarinda said. "I'm a little nervous, of course, but it will be such an adventure."

"I'm so glad you're feeling that way, Clarinda. We must be 'opeful and positive now. I feel certain this will be a good move – I feel it in my bones, as Da would say."

She squeezed his hand as the gangplank was drawn in and the wheels of the steamer began to turn with great sloshing sounds from the water moving through them.

"Good riddance to London!" Henry exclaimed.

"Yes, I don't mind that I'll probably never see London again," Clarinda said. "This city hasn't been good to us at all."

Henry tucked the rug he carried around their shoulders as the wind tore through the open window.

"We'll be able to tell our children all about this trip, Clarinda, and 'ow we braved the oceans to make their 'ome in Australia."

The steamer took just under three hours to arrive at Gravesend. They could see the swelling sails of the *Strathfieldsaye* as the grey town came into view. Clarinda felt a sense of unreality as they disembarked and walked along the bustling port towards the great ship. *This will be the last time I walk on English soil*, she thought, and the last time she would walk on land before she and Henry arrived in Sydney.

"That must be where we go," Henry said, dragging her towards a small line of people. "That man 'as the uniform of the Emigration Officers. I think this is where we board."

He reached into his pocket for their folded ticket.

"Why are there so few people in the queue, Henry?" asked Clarinda.

"Lots of others would 'ave boarded already," he explained. "The people who stayed overnight at the Emigration Depot are probably already on the ship."

Henry handed the ticket to the officer who wrote their names in a fine hand on the passenger list and indicated they should board a small rowboat which would take them to the ship. The other people in the queue before them sat uncomfortably in the boat, huddled together, hugging their bags to their chests and pulling shawls and coats about their shoulders.

"Well, this is it, my darling," said Henry cheerfully. "We're on our way!"

Their living quarters on board the ship were a bitter disappointment. They had not expected to be separated, having heard of other ships that had a married couples' area away from the single men and single women's. But the *Strathfieldsaye*, an old convict ship, had one great area in the hold divided by a partition with male passengers at the front of the ship and females at the back.

"I'll meet you on deck when we're settled," said Henry, kissing Clarinda quickly as they were directed to two separate hatch doors.

Clarinda bit her lip hard as she climbed down the wooden ladder, trying to stop the tears from falling, but the sight before her as she entered the female hold made it difficult not to cry... It was like one giant mass of bodies crushed together. Women were sitting on narrow beds, with some swinging their legs from top bunks and others half-reclining with their stockinged legs showing. A few were crying into their straw mattresses and some were cradling young children. The beds were arranged in two rows of bunks all along the walls around a long wooden table with bench seats on either side. Some women sat there, playing cards and chatting.

Clarinda ran her eyes anxiously along the rows of bunks to find a bed that wasn't taken. A young, dark-haired woman at the far end of the room sitting on one of the upper beds, waved to her. Clarinda made her way towards the woman, looking about her as she went.

"Hi ya," said the dark-haired woman in a lilting accent Clarinda had never heard before. "I'm Mary. Mary Reardon. There's a spare bed next to me, if you like." She patted the space beside her – it was really all part of the same bed, just separated by a low partition.

"Thank you. I'm Clarinda Parkes. It's all very close down here, isn't it?"

"It is indeed, Clarinda. Can I call you Clarinda?"

"Of course, if I can call you Mary."

"Never been called anything else," she said and laughed. "I was a milkmaid back home in Cork, where I was always just Mary."

Clarinda smiled. "I've been a seamstress of sorts, I suppose. But I've never really held a job."

"Lucky you," said Mary. "I'm getting used to the squash of this place. It was like this in the Emigrant Depot, too. I spent two nights there. Wasn't what I was expecting, though. They should warn us of the conditions before we come on board, I think."

"Yes," agreed Clarinda, putting her bag on the bed beside Mary and climbing up clumsily, using the bed below as a step. "I had thought I'd

117

be with my husband. I didn't know we'd be separated." She sniffed and wiped a tear.

"There're a few others in here bemoaning the same thing. Not me, though. Not got a fella yet."

"Are you going out to Australia all on your own?"

"I am indeed. 'Twas hard saying goodbye to everyone back home in Cork, but things were pretty tough there, and when I got to London, so I figured I'd take the chance."

"You're very brave. I shouldn't complain about being separated from Henry, I suppose. At least I have him on board. I think, if you don't mind, I might go up on deck now to see if I can find him."

"'Course, I'll see you later, Clarinda. Eliza down there'll be getting our supplies for dinner soon."

A ginger, freckled woman who sat on the bunk below smiled up at Clarinda.

"We're in messes of eight women and she's cap'ain for the first week," Mary explained. "You should be in our mess. We've only got six of us so far."

"All right, thank you," said Clarinda and clambered down from the bed.

On deck, Clarinda had to hold her shawl tightly around her to keep it from blowing in the wind. There was no sign of Henry as she walked towards the front of the ship, stepping over ropes and cables, past a tall mast where two sailors were untying ropes high above her, up some narrow steps and onto another larger deck where Henry had disappeared down into the hold.

The ship was swaying slightly and she held onto the rail to steady herself as she stared at the town of Gravesend a mile out. The realisation this ship would be their home for the next few months and that she and Henry would only see each other when on deck was confronting.

"Clarinda! Clarinda!" She turned suddenly at Henry's call as he climbed from the hold. He strode towards her and she rushed into his arms, her head to his chest. "I'm so sorry we aren't together. It wasn't what I'd expected."

"I know, Henry. It's not your fault. There are other husbands and wives separated, too." She looked into his eyes and smiled.

"Are you all right, Clarinda? 'Ave you found a berth?"

"Yes, beside an Irish girl. It's very crowded down there."

"Yes, and all manner of people, it seems. I'm beside some rough fellow from Sussex. 'E swears and spits. I'll be picking up some bad 'abits if I'm not careful." He laughed and she made herself laugh along with him. "We've got to be positive about this," he said. "It won't be forever, and we'll be fed and all. The first mate's been to speak to us men in steerage. 'E said we'd be sailing for Plymouth tomorrow if the winds and the tides are right. 'E said it'd take maybe six or seven days along the English Channel before we set out into the Atlantic. We 'ave to be brave now, Clarinda."

"I know. I will be, Henry. I will be brave."

Henry and Clarinda ate apart in their separate areas of the hold, crowded along the long, central table on the bench seats with the other steerage passengers. Eliza, the woman on the bunk below Clarinda, was responsible – at least for the first week – for gathering the food from the ship's steward, taking it to the cook, delivering it to the others in her mess, and afterwards washing the dishes in the deep buckets of soapy water on the main deck.

"The cook's as black as the ace of spades," Eliza told Mary and Clarinda as she stepped awkwardly over the bench seat to sit opposite them. "His eyes shine so white from his face, but he's a merry old thing, all singing and laughing and 'Yes Ma'am' this and 'Yes Ma'am' that."

They ate beef stew with chunks of bread, washed down with strong black tea. It was the first meat Clarinda had eaten for months and the most delicious meal she'd had since she'd left Birmingham – apart from the occasional cake in the Irvine sisters' dining room.

"We'll have to enjoy this food while we can," said Mary. "We won't always be getting fresh food like this, you know. Not once we're away from land."

"But there's chickens and pigs and all sorts in pens at the far end of the deck. I saw them, and you can't help hearing them, either," said Eliza.

"And smelling them!" the woman sitting beside her said.

"They're not for the likes of us," said Mary. "They'll be for the cabin passengers up on the poop deck and the cap'ain. Not for us steerage passengers."

"Oh," said Eliza, deflated.

But Clarinda was thankful that she was to have any food at all.

That night, as she lay in the narrow bed with Mary close beside her, trying to ignore the unfamiliar rocking of the ship, Clarinda held her rounded stomach and prayed. "Dear Lord," she whispered. "Keep us all safe. All of us on board this ship. And keep my baby well. Please let it live! And thank you for providing us with food and shelter."

Henry lay stiffly in his own bunk, his feet hanging over the edge, with the man beside him snoring in sharp bursts. Despite the discomfort of the bed, his belly was full and he felt a great sense of optimism. For the first time since their arrival in London, Henry felt as though he really could make a great life for himself and Clarinda and their baby. He felt certain they would prosper and thrive in their new home. *The future is mine*, he thought. *This is only the beginning.*

Clarinda was woken by the sound of men's voices up on deck and the sloshing of water, followed by a rhythmic scraping sound. It was so strange being on board a ship, like being in a different country. Even the sounds were a mystery. As she lay there in the dark with the rank smell of Mary's breath blowing over her and the deep, even breaths of sleeping women all around, she realised the scraping sound was a brush on the boards and that some of the sailors must be scrubbing the decks.

There were heavy footsteps directly above her and the muffle of deep voices. She wondered if Henry was awake, too, listening to these unfamiliar sounds and feeling as uneasy as she did.

She lay there, unmoving, holding the lump of her stomach and trying to catch what the sailors called to each other, until Mary suddenly snorted and sat up straight.

"Where the...?" she started to say, looking wildly about her. "Oh," Mary said as she realised where she was. "I was dreaming the strangest dream," she whispered to Clarinda and laughed. "That I was in a great big tub with wheat all about me and being tossed and turned back and forth. But of course, it was only the swaying of the ship that I felt."

Mary lay back down. Even with the partition between them, Clarinda could see her face quite clearly.

"I'm feeling most peculiar," Clarinda said. "I know nothing about what today will be like. I'm quite ignorant of the ways on board a ship."

"You'll get used to it soon enough," said Mary. "As we all will, I reckon. They followed the routine of the ship in the Emigrant Depot, so I've already got an idea how it'll be. A bell will ring soon to get us all up, and we'll be having breakfast down here before the bell rings again to get us all on deck. The cap'ain will tell us what's to happen today, and hopefully we'll set sail for Plymouth. Then it'll just be a case of amusing ourselves somehow. That's going to be the hardest part, I reckon, filling each day with nothing much to do."

"Yes," said Clarinda. "I've been quite used to that lately, though." She thought of her endless days stuck in the garret in Hatton Garden, and how she'd learnt to be quiet, still and self-contained.

"I hope you don't mind me asking," Mary said, "but are you having a baby? I've noticed you have a look about ya."

Clarinda laughed. "Yes, I am having a baby. It's not that obvious yet, I don't think, because I've been eating so little until now. It's been about five months, though."

"Oh," said Mary, nodding thoughtfully. "Might be born here on this ship then. I noticed two other women looking pregnant, too – one of them's further down over there."

Clarinda looked across hopefully to where Mary pointed at a lower bunk close to the hatch where a fair head appeared above the blanket. She had hoped she would not be entirely alone in her pregnancy.

"I expect the ship's surgeon'll help with the birthing," said Mary. "I've helped my Mam with lots of hers, though, so I'll be able to help if it comes to it."

Just then a loud, pealing bell sounded and the women around them began to stir.

"I wonder what's for breakfast," said Clarinda, her stomach rumbling in anticipation.

Later, after Henry and Clarinda had met on the quarter deck above the women's hold, the captain addressed the throng of passengers, talking through a speaking-trumpet and standing on a raised platform on the cabin passengers' poop deck. He introduced the ship's surgeon, Mr Allan, and the first mate, and he told the passengers they would sail for Plymouth in a few hours. There was a buzz of excitement at the news.

"Let's sit on the deck and watch the preparations," Henry said to Clarinda. He found them a seat on a barrel on the main deck. It was a blustery day and the sailors were busy all around, some swaying high above on the rigging footropes, unfurling the sails. Henry pointed to one of these figures, precariously perched on the footrope, his shirt billowing about him and his head bare.

"I spoke to that sailor this morning," Henry shouted in order to be heard over the noise of the whipping sails. "'E's a ship's apprentice, a young lad named Jimmy, barely sixteen years old. Said 'e was from Deal, so used to the ways of boats. Said 'e'd been on boats all his life, fishing since 'e was a boy."

"There's so little I know about boats and ships, Henry," said Clarinda.

"Me, too, Clarinda, and yet we're going to be on board this one for months to come. I'm going to make it my project to find out more about the ship – what the masts are called and 'ow they navigate and all. It'll be quite fascinating."

Clarinda smiled. "You always have such a thirst for knowledge, Henry. It is so admirable."

The anchor was raised mid-morning and the sails flapped and billowed loudly as they caught the strong wind; then the ship began to move away from Gravesend. Henry and Clarinda had to stand on the barrel to see over the sides of the bulwarks. Henry held Clarinda around the waist with one arm and with the other held onto a rope to steady them against the tacking of the boat along the Channel. They could see rugged cliffs leading down to narrow, flat beaches with brown sands, and little villages with stone buildings.

Henry was the captain of his mess for that week so he left Clarinda on deck early to collect the rations and take them to the cook. After both had eaten, and Henry had washed the dishes for himself and the seven other men in his mess, they met again on deck just as the ship passed a peninsula with low buildings and a church built of stone with a flint roof, its windows winking in the sunlight. The ship moved further from the shore and they could see the small wooden vessel and the glow of the lightship that marked the Nore: a large and treacherous sandbank where the River Thames meets the North Sea of the Atlantic.

"There's been lots of ships grounded and wrecked 'ere," Henry told Clarinda. "That's why the captain's taking us the long way around, I expect."

Not long after there was a town with a pier with metal railings that stretched far out into the water and they could see people in groups, like tiny dolls, walking along it with umbrellas and hooped skirts. The wind was ebbing now and there were shouts and calls from the sailors as some climbed the masts again to reef in the sails, and with a clanging rush of the chain and a deep thud, the anchor was released and the ship came to rest.

"Why have we stopped now?" asked Clarinda.

"I don't know, my dear. Maybe it's too dangerous to sail through these waters as the night comes on. We'll 'ave to wait and see, and trust the captain on this."

That night it was too cold to stay on deck for long, so Clarinda and Henry retired to their separate holds. Henry lay on his bed, listening to the yells and guffaws of a group of men as they played cards at the central table. They were betting low stakes but Henry, being so poor and never having gambled before, didn't join them but scribbled silently in his notebook instead.

He had spoken to the young sailor Jimmy again in the afternoon and the boy had told him the names of the masts and the sails and other parts of the ship. Henry wrote these now in a list: the staysail, the jib, the fore-and-aft rig, the square rig, the mizzen mast, the main mast, the fore mast and the bowsprit. It was like a new language to him – some words he had heard before but never known what they represented.

He thought of what Jimmy had told him of how it felt to be on one of the riggings high above the ship: "'Tis like you're a bird, lookin' down on the world," Jimmy had said. "And when the wind picks up sometimes and the ship's swayin', you feel like you're flyin' with your shirt blowin' like wings."

"But aren't you afraid up there, Jimmy?" Henry had asked.

"Nah. Just gotta hold on, like. Climbed up there a hundred times and never even slipped. You wrap your toes around the ropes, too – that's why we always climb barefoot. You get used to it after the first few times."

Henry found it hard to imagine becoming accustomed to the height and the danger. He wondered, if his family had been seafaring folk if he might have had to go to sea like Jimmy when his father had run into debt all those years ago, and how different his life would have been.

The next morning as dawn broke, Henry was woken by the clanking of the anchor being raised. He jumped from his bunk and crept to the ladder to climb on deck. The sailors were busy around him again, some scrubbing the deck, others yanking on pulleys and hitching ropes. The captain, a short, stocky man, strode amongst them, giving orders and checking the tautness of ropes. His first mate walked alongside him, tall and lanky, winking at the sailors as they passed, his black tarpaulin hat bobbing. They both nodded towards Henry as they came upon him.

Clarinda joined him on deck again after breakfast.

"Did you sleep, my darling?" he asked after kissing her lightly on the lips, conscious of the eyes of so many other passengers around.

"Yes, the baby didn't stir much. It seems to be soothed by the rocking of the ship. It's not as restless as when we were in London."

Mary Reardon approached them and Clarinda introduced her to Henry.

"I 'ear you're on your own on this ship, Mary," he said. "Let me know if there's any way I can 'elp you – if any of the male passengers bother you or anything."

"Thank ya, Henry. I will indeed. There's a few rough uns about from what I've seen," she said and sat beside them on a piece of sacking.

As the ship moved along steadily and the wind buffeted the sails, Mary told them of her family in Ireland. She was the eldest girl, she said, with an older brother and seven little ones after her. Her father and brother were farmhands on the farm where she had been a milkmaid and between them they kept the family. Her brother was to marry soon and his betrothed would be moving into their two-roomed lodgings with the rest of the family. There was already barely enough room for them all and so Mary had decided she would move to London as Henry and Clarinda had done. After finding it difficult to get work there, she had finally decided on emigrating to Sydney.

"It near broke my heart to leave my family," she said. "I thought at first that I'd be back one day, as London's not too far. Don't know if I will now, though. I'll never see my young brothers and sisters grown. It's such a terrible thought."

This was the first time Clarinda had seen the jolly Mary cry. She put her arm around her and Mary sniffled into her shoulder.

The ship sailed past Margate shortly after the midday meal, just as Henry came back from scrubbing the dishes in the buckets of soapy water at the far end of the main deck. He and Clarinda could see the long, wooden jetty and the high, stone walls around the harbour filled with sail boats and rowboats and its sandy beaches, populated with distant holiday-makers, some splashing in the sea.

"Maybe when we get to Sydney and I earn enough, we'll be able to go on a 'oliday somewhere, Clarinda."

"Where would there be to go on holiday in Australia, though?" she asked.

"I don't know, but I expect there's some nice river spot or beach or something," Henry said.

Just after the ship passed Margate, the weather became cloudy. There was suddenly a squall of wind and a sharp storm of stinging hail began to fall. Henry held his coat above Clarinda as he kissed her goodbye and she and Mary ran to their hold. Mary was laughing at their sudden drenching as the last woman in slammed the hatch door shut and others lit oil lamps about the room.

"That storm came on with barely a warning," Mary said. "I've heard the weather's mighty changeable at sea."

"We're barely at sea yet," said Eliza from her bunk. "If it's so changeable here, imagine what it'll be like when we get out on the ocean."

It rained for the rest of the afternoon and they came to anchor at six o'clock that night just opposite the town of Deal, but the rain kept them from venturing out. It wasn't until the next morning, Good Friday, that they saw the newly constructed pier and the long, flat beach of brown sand surrounded by cottages, with a mass of fishing boats dragged up onto the sand and tied to poles. All the passengers and crew were summoned on deck by the bell for a church service to mark Good Friday. Many of them were Roman Catholic, but the captain, being Protestant, conducted a service from a Church of England prayer book followed by the Litany.

When the service had finished, Clarinda said to Henry, "You know, I've never even properly met a Roman Catholic before, let alone an Irishman, but they're just the same as us, really, aren't they? Mary's such a lovely person. I can't understand the enmity some feel towards others who are different in some way. We are all people. All of us on this boat are as mortal as each other. Religion shouldn't make a difference to how we treat one another."

They travelled on a good wind that day and, although there was little sunshine, it was comfortable sitting on the deck with a shawl or a coat for protection. The coastline from Deal to Dover was spectacular, with high, jagged cliffs reaching down to the occasional narrow beach of sand

and the waves beating hard against them so that they could hear their distant crash. But none of the other sights, Clarinda and Henry agreed, were as magnificent as the headlands of Dover. The chalk cliffs stretched for miles to the jutting point called Shakespeare's Cliff and they could see Dover Castle with its numerous stone turrets rising high above.

"Look, the coast of France!" someone yelled from the other side of the deck and the passengers swarmed to the one side to see the ominous, dark stretch of land in the distance.

"It's so close," Clarinda remarked, surprised.

"This is the narrowest part of the English Channel," said Henry. "I think it's only about twenty miles across. Can you imagine 'ow frightening it would 'ave been to live in Dover during the French Wars with the French coastline so near?"

They tacked through the Channel throughout the night and by the morning they were off the Isle of Wight. The swell was the biggest they'd had and many passengers were sick, some vomiting overboard or even directly onto the deck so that the ship's apprentices had to mop the mess up and splash it overboard. The movement made Henry feel unwell, so he returned to his bed soon after breakfast, while Clarinda sat on deck with Mary and Eliza throughout most of the day as the ship rode the huge waves. She loved the ship's rise and fall, as though she were being rocked in a massive cradle. The novelty of it made her spirited and exalted despite Henry's illness.

"I hated being on this ship at first, you know, but I find that I love the sea!" she called to Mary and Eliza as another great wave splashed against the ship with a thud and the spray nearly wet them from where they sat on sacking on the hard deck. "Isn't it exciting! The smell of the salt in the air and the wind through your hair. I never thought I'd think this, but I like it even better than a walk through a wooded lane back home. It's so beautiful and immense!"

Clarinda did not see Henry again that day and the ship tacked about all night and came to anchor at Plymouth Sound early the following morning.

The ship's first day in Plymouth Sound was Easter Sunday and again the captain led a service directly from a prayer book and all on board attended, no matter their denomination. They remained anchored off the shore of Plymouth for more than a week, waiting for the final passengers to board and the remaining provisions to be loaded.

It was a tedious time while they waited to set sail, but they got used to the routine of life on board the near-stationary ship. Some passengers who could afford the fare, rowed in small boats to the town to break the monotony of the days idling offshore and to walk on dry land and English soil once more. But most, like Henry and Clarinda, remained on board.

It was soon after they arrived in Plymouth Sound that one fellow, whose bunk was near to Henry's, disappeared from the ship, leaving all his clothes and belongings behind. There was speculation as to whether he had escaped the uncomfortable conditions on the *Strathfieldsaye* or whether he had somehow fallen overboard. A group of sailors set out briefly in a rowboat to see if a body could be recovered, but none was found and the captain auctioned off the missing man's clothes and belongings to the other passengers.

Life on board the ship proved too hard for some. Three single men in steerage decided to give up their free passage to Australia and disembarked in Plymouth. Before they sailed, the shipping agent's clerk brought a last bag of letters on board. These included letters from Isabella and each of Henry's sisters. Sarah also sent them another sovereign.

Henry replied briefly:

Plymouth Sound
Sunday, 7th April, 1839

My Beloved Sister,

It rejoices Clarinda and me to learn that all of you are still well in health. Thank you for the money. I was very glad of it as I had only three halfpence when I received it, and no more. We fare very well on board the 'Strathfield-saye', considering all things, but the steerage of an emigrant ship is a most miserably uncomfortable place. I am more solitary and companionless than I ever was in all my life in this crowd of human beings. Some of them are of the most indecent and brutish description. My hopes of ultimate success are as good as ever, which is worth enduring the disagreeableness of the next four months.

They talk of our going direct to Sydney, and not touching anywhere, so I expect you will not hear from me again until we are safely in New South Wales. Until then, from the lines of Campbell:

'Our march is on the mountain wave,

Our home is on the deep.'

Our united love to Da, Mam, and all of you. Give Clarinda's love to her father and brother, if you ever see them. You should look out for the news from sea, to learn whether we arrive safely. And should we never meet again in this world, may we meet in a better one, and should you never hear from me again, may God reward you for all you have done for me. Farewell, my dear, dear sister. Farewell to you all.

Your affectionate brother,
Henry Parkes

Eventually, on the 8th of April, the ship was attached to a steamer that tugged them out to the open ocean. Clarinda and Henry stood together on deck with the other passengers, straining to see the shore of England for what would probably be the last time. Some of the passengers linked arms and sang *Auld Lang Syne*. Clarinda cried openly, watching Plymouth's Mount Edgcumbe fade into the mass of distant land that was England. Henry hugged her close to him and felt his own tears prick.

The ship moved on and away from the disappearing shore and eventually the steamer left them with a mighty toot of its horn. At last, the *Strathfieldsaye* had begun its long journey to New South Wales.

Clarinda kept a diary from their first week at sea. It described the weather, the other passengers and the meals. The cook's galley was opposite the forecastle where the sailors slept, and when it was her turn as captain of her mess, Clarinda took the provisions collected from the ship's steward in a net bag and hung it from the next hook in line for the cook to prepare. The cook's assistant handed her two kettles, one full of strong tea and the other of weak coffee, which she delivered to the other members of her mess in the women's hold before returning to collect the food.

She watched as the cook stirred huge pots of rice or pease pudding over the iron galley stove or ground the part-dried potato, baked it in the oven, mixed it with hot water in a tin dish and left it covered to steam briefly before mashing it with a little butter to make a type of mashed potato. The ship's baker reached with his shovel into another oven with its cast-iron doors to produce loaves of fresh, aromatic bread for each mess, and the cook's assistant sliced the salted beef or pork. After her months of hunger, the regular meals were a blessing and a relief to Clarinda, and she began to put on weight and to feel the baby moving about inside her more vigorously.

She and Henry met daily on the main deck before and after the midday meal. There were always lots of other passengers around, chatting, reading, knitting or playing cards, and they longed for the chance to be alone.

"I miss just having you about, Henry," Clarinda said one afternoon when they met on deck. "We can never find anywhere to be alone. I've made friends with people I would never have expected to, though. Like Mary and Eliza."

"I think I'm missing you more than you are me, though, Clarinda. I can't relate to some of these rough, rude fellows. David Chapman and 'is Sussex mates are quite barbaric. There's no shame in the men's 'old at all."

He reached for her hand then and looked into her eyes intently.

"And I'm missing 'olding you, Clarinda," he whispered. "I'd so like to spend a night with you alone. It's almost as though we are engaged again and we 'ave to wait to be properly together as man and wife. That's the greatest agony of this journey for me."

"I do miss being in your arms, too, Henry, but with the baby and all, it's probably for the best. Still, I wish we could find somewhere to be alone."

Unlike the cabin passengers, there was no chance of privacy for those in steerage on a free passage.

The weather during the first weeks was fine and windy most days and the sails were rarely furled even during the night as they bounded the waves of the Atlantic Ocean towards Africa. They saw albatross gliding on massive wings and occasionally dipping the tip of a wing into the water and Henry recited Coleridge's *The Rime of the Ancient Mariner*:

"At length did cross an Albatross,

Through the fog it came.

As if it 'ad been a Christian soul,

We 'ailed it in God's name."

A shoal of porpoises followed the ship one day, diving in and out of the waves with their slippery bodies shining. A sailor fastened a harpoon and attempted to spear one, but the porpoises' movements were unpredictable and he missed each time.

"I'm glad he didn't kill one," Mary said as they watched the porpoises moving fluidly away from the ship. "They've probably never even seen a human before. They wouldn't know the danger of us."

"Yes," agreed Clarinda. "They seem so free and wild. I couldn't bear to see one skinned and chopped up into steaks just to fill the sailors' stomachs."

Another time they saw the great spurts of water from a pod of whales at some distance and the vague dark shapes of them as they neared the surface. It was a wonder to see real ocean animals that they had only ever seen in pictures.

Another ship was sighted about two weeks after they had left the coast of England. The captain called for the flags and the first mate hauled a range of them of different colours and design while the captain used his telescope to see the other ship's flags. This lowering and raising of flags continued for some time until the other ship was too distant and the first mate got on the trumpet to tell those on deck the news they had deciphered.

"That ship was the *Glenbervie,* on its return trip from Sydney," the first mate announced, "bringing goods to England from Ceylon. They said they'd had a rough passage around the Cape of Good Hope and had their main mast broken during a storm, but the carpenters had managed to put up a temporary one and they are now doing well."

It was a thrill to hear news of other people, no matter how brief or distant. Henry wondered at the flag signals. He asked Jimmy, the young ship's apprentice, who explained as best he could. "Seeing's I can't read or write," he said, "I'm probably not the one for you to ask. But as far as I know, each flag stands for a letter and so they use them to spell out words. 'Tis a complex business."

Sometimes Henry brought on deck his copies of *The Works of Shakespeare* and *Things as They Are; or The Adventures of Caleb Williams* by William Godwin, and read passages aloud to Clarinda. After a time, some of the other passengers began to gather around him, sitting cross-legged or with legs splayed on the wooden boards to hear him read or recite his own poetry or those of other famous poets such as Shelley or Byron. Many of these passengers couldn't read or write themselves and Henry's 'Reading Group', as Clarinda called it, became a regular occurrence before the midday meal each day.

On nights that were not too windy, Henry and Clarinda would meet on deck. This was their greatest opportunity for intimacy, hidden in the dark shadows of the night. They were never completely alone, though, with other passengers and sailors milling about. But they would kiss deeply and Henry would feel the soft press of Clarinda and the hardness of the baby inside her and return to bed with feelings of unease and longing.

TEN

larinda woke as she fell hard onto her side on the bare boards, hitting her head on Eliza's mattress below as she went. There was a deafening roar and a pounding of waves and the screams of other women around her. The ship was at a strange angle, with the front of the women's hold raised above her and the vague form of bags and other loose items sliding towards her in the darkness.

The ship suddenly hurled forward with a bang like a cannonball and Clarinda's side of the hold was raised into the air abruptly and she began to slide fast on her bottom towards the petition board at the other end, her nightshirt bunching around her protruding waist. She raised her arms to defend herself from the blow of the wall, but before she reached it, the ship tipped the other way again like a mighty see-saw and she screamed just as two hands from one of the lower bunks grabbed her and held her tight as she hung dizzily, almost in mid-air.

Clarinda managed to pull herself upright and awkwardly fell on top of the woman who held her just as a mass of water came sloshing down the hatch and foamed about the floor.

A sailor, unrecognisable due to the dark and his drenching, appeared at the hatch opening holding a swaying oil lamp and yelled above the wind and the crashing waves, "Tie yourselves to your beds and close any shutters!" He slammed the hatch door and the women looked wildly about them for something to attach themselves with to the bed railings.

The woman on the narrow bed with Clarinda wrapped the blanket around them and tied it tightly to the bedpost that reached up to the bunk above.

"Are you okay?" she shouted above the noise. "Are you hurt?"

Clarinda rubbed the hip she had fallen on. "Only a little," she shouted back as more oil lamps were lit about them to reveal strained, dishevelled faces. "I hope my baby's all right."

Other women interrupted their talk with screams and yells as the ship tossed violently this way and that.

"I'm pregnant, too," the woman said and Clarinda remembered then that Mary had pointed this same woman out to her before.

"I haven't said thank you for helping me," Clarinda said. "Thank you."

Anything loose was still sliding about the floor as Clarinda had been, or sloshing in the water that had entered the hold.

"I didn't know if I'd be strong enough to hold you."

"Well, you were. Thank you so much."

"Do you think we're going to die?" the woman asked.

"No, no," Clarinda answered uncertainly. "The captain will have it under control. I'm sure he's been through lots of storms."

But then, as a wave thudded like a clap of thunder against the ship, another woman yelled, "We're going to sink! We're doomed! We'll be a wreck!"

Others about them started to cry and wail more loudly, with some vomiting onto the floor or on their beds.

Clarinda clutched the hand of the woman beside her and began to recite a Psalm. "They cry unto the Lord in their trouble," she said in a shaking voice. "And He bringeth them out of their distress. He maketh the storm a calm – so that the waves thereof are still – then are they glad because they are quiet, so He bringeth them into their desired haven."

Another woman called out as she finished, "He who holdeth the winds in his fists and the waters in the hollow of his hand, save us!"

And then another began to say the Lord's Prayer and Clarinda and others joined in a chorus of raised, desperate voices that could barely be heard above the storm.

Their prayers continued for a time, until tired voices dropped out as the tempest raged on and on unceasingly. Clarinda continued to pray silently. The fierce rise and fall of the ship seemed unending, and she wondered if she would ever see Henry again or if they would both die in this nightmare.

She imagined herself amid the mountainous waves, the water filling her and smashing her angrily like a ragdoll, and she wondered what her last thought might be as she drowned. She tightened her grip on the hand of the woman beside her, feeling the heat of another person, perhaps the last human she would know and touch.

The ship's tumultuous dance continued on into the night and the women's sobs and cries abated as they became strangely resigned to the continual fury of the ocean. It was as though they were stuck forever in this hell.

But then, gradually, after agonising, sleepless hours, the pounding of the waves became less violent and the roaring of the wind faded and they could hear the comforting yells of the sailors and the smack of ropes on the deck above, while the ship still heaved but with a gentler rocking. Many of the women began to cry and laugh hysterically with relief.

"I think our prayers have saved us," the woman beside Clarinda said and they hugged each other tightly, laughing.

"It's so strange, I don't even know your name," the woman said.

"Clarinda. Clarinda Parkes."

"I'm Sarah Crump. My husband's in the men's hold. I thought I'd never see him again."

"That was what I feared also," said Clarinda. "And our babies. I thought they'd never see the light of day."

A sailor opened the hatch to reveal a ray of dim light.

"We're through the worst," he yelled down to them. "But there's still a mighty swell, so keep yourselves down here and tied to the beds. We'll let you know when it's safe to come on deck."

"Hallelujah!" yelled the woman who had shouted they were doomed all those long hours before. "God be praised! We're saved!"

It was several hours later, when the rocking of the ship had subsided, that a tired and haggard-looking sailor opened the hatch fully and climbed down the ladder with a shallow bucket.

"You are all safe to move about now, ladies," he said and began bailing the water from the hold's floor with the bucket and passing it to another sailor on deck who hurled it over the ship's side. "Best to hold on as you go, though. Still a bit of a swell."

Sarah untied the blanket that held her and Clarinda and they queued to leave the dark, damp hold. Clarinda searched anxiously for Henry amongst the mass of weary faces and raced to him when she saw his tousled hair and strained face above the men around him.

"Henry! Oh, Henry. I thought we'd never see each other again!"

"My darling," he said and bent to bury his head in her shoulder. "My darling Clarinda. I am so, so 'appy to see you! I thought this ship was going to be our grave." He began to sob.

"Oh, Henry, don't cry! You rarely cry! We are saved! All is fine!"

She cradled his head in her arms. It was strange for her to be the one comforting him. Henry tried to laugh.

"What a night!" he said through his tears. "What a damned night! I never want to go through anything like that again!"

"But we *did* get through it, Henry," she said. "The Lord saved us. We are saved."

The storm had created havoc on deck with ropes, torn canvas and pots and pans from the cook's galley scattered about. The carcass of an albatross lay battered on the quarter deck just outside the women's hold. The cook and his assistant were complaining loudly about a barrel of flour that had smashed open, causing most of its contents to be swept into the ocean or mixed with the seawater still on deck.

Some of the livestock had drowned and others were dead from the wet and cold. A lifeboat had been swept away, along with the ropes that had tied it, and the main sail had been torn to ribbons. Some of the sailors were busy high on the swaying mast replacing the sail while others were mopping the water that still swished about on deck.

Jimmy came past Henry and Clarinda carrying one end of a ripped sail and Henry called to him as he went. "Mighty rough storm, 'ey, Jimmy?"

"Yes," the young lad said. "The roughest I've been in. Never seen waves so big – double the height of the masts some were. I thought we were goners for sure."

"Was anyone injured?" Henry called after him.

"Yes. One of the sailors, Bill Bailey. Got knocked over by a loose mast. He's with the surgeon now."

By late afternoon, most of the damage had been repaired and the mess cleaned. Henry helped some of the male steerage passengers bring their sodden mattresses and blankets on deck to dry. Their hold had been flooded by a wave that had smashed through the hatch. Fortunately, Henry's bed was dry.

"Do you think we'll have to go through a storm like that again?" Clarinda asked Mary and Eliza as they watched the men lugging the mattresses.

"I hope not, Clarinda, but there's still a mighty long way for us to go," said Mary.

"And I hear the worst is usually around the Cape of Good Hope," said Eliza. "The cape of Africa, that is."

"Strange it's called the Cape of Good Hope," said Mary.

"I suppose all you can do is hope!" replied Eliza. They laughed uncomfortably.

In the evening, the ship's bell was rung five times to gather everyone on deck for a service of thanksgiving for bringing them safely through the storm. A Union Jack was placed on cushions to serve as the pulpit and the bare heads of all on board bowed as the captain read the service.

The days began to blend into one another and Clarinda wrote in her diary regularly so she could keep track of the date. She felt happier than she had for a long time. She loved the ocean, despite its dangers. She loved its immensity and its changing moods and the feeling of rocking beneath her. The lonely days spent starving in the garret room in London seemed a long time ago. She enjoyed the company of the other women around her, especially Mary and Eliza – and her new friend Sarah. She had never had much to do with working class women before, but she found her new friends were honest and open in the way Betty, the maid at her father's house, had been. There were no pretences or expectations of how she should be.

She noticed Henry kept himself apart from the others around him – except for his 'Reading Group'. He seemed to prefer the company of the young ship's apprentice Jimmy to that of the other passengers. Clarinda thought this was possibly because of what he learnt about the ship from the lad. Henry's mind was always active, always searching for knowledge.

Clarinda and Henry had their first taste of fish several days after the storm. The sailors had caught bonitos using hooks with strips of canvas attached, greasy with fat. The fish were caught by the dozens, silver and shining as they slid about the deck where they were hurled. The cook fried them up and each passenger who was there on deck had a taste.

"It's an unusual flavour," Clarinda said, sitting on a barrel alongside Henry. "Like nothing I've tasted before."

"I expect we'll eat a lot of fish in Sydney, as it's beside the water," Henry said. "I like the taste. It's firmer meat than I expected but I like 'ow it flakes in your mouth."

"There are a lot of new things we'll have to get used to, Henry, aren't there?"

"Yes, my darling. Eating fish is just one of many."

As they approached the tropics, the ship began to move more rapidly with the drive of the trade winds. The sails whipped and the ropes clanged against the masts. The salt air took their breath away as they sat on deck with their hair blown about. A man who worked as a shoemaker used his scissors to set up as a barber one morning when the wind had died down slightly. Henry had his hair trimmed roughly so that it curled at strange angles about his face and the clippings blew about the ship and off into the ocean. Clarinda imagined Henry's hair floating past fish and sharks and over the oceans to the shores of England.

It was difficult to move about the deck with the force of the winds and many people fell over when a blast hit hard. One man fell down the open hatch of the men's hold from on deck and broke his arm. And one day, when Clarinda and Mary were taking a walk around the main deck, Mary fell into a bucket of water being used by a sailor. Clarinda couldn't help laughing at the comical figure of Mary, with her stockinged legs sticking up in the air and her bottom stuck in the bucket.

"Help me, Clarinda!" Mary yelled indignantly as the sailor, grinning widely, grabbed her under the arms and heaved her upright. "Oh, and I'm wet and all!" she exclaimed.

"You all right, Miss?" the sailor asked, still smirking.

"Yes, yes." Mary blushed. "Thank ya. I'll be fine now."

"I'm sorry, Mary," said Clarinda as they hurried away from the man. "I'm sorry I laughed. You just looked so funny. I'm sorry. I shouldn't have laughed!"

They both laughed heartily later when they told the story to Eliza – once Mary had changed from her sodden skirt.

"I'm that embarrassed," said Mary as she, Clarinda and Eliza sat on their bed. "That sailor must've seen most of my legs and all. I feel quite ashamed! He was the tall sailor with the tattoo of a mermaid on his arm and the strong, broad shoulders, ya know?"

"Taken a bit of a fancy to him, have you?" asked Eliza.

"I had until now," said Mary. "Too embarrassed to even look at him again now that he's seen me with my bum in a bucket!"

There were often flying fish dancing across the waves on gossamer wings now, so close to the ship they could have been caught easily with a net, but no one tried.

"We sailors don't kill flyin' fish," Jimmy explained to Henry. "They're thought to be the souls of dead sailors, so it's bad luck to kill 'em."

One day a shark was baited with a piece of salted pork on a hook. When three sailors hurled it on deck Henry and other passengers ran from its gnashing teeth as it slid about with its tail thrashing. Then the sailors stabbed it hard with a knife and its cold eyes glazed over, no longer staring menacingly at Henry. The sailors cut it into steaks on the deck and the blood was washed overboard before the cook fried it up. Henry had a piece and found it tasted like chicken. He would never have imagined eating shark meat during his life in England.

The weather grew hotter, the winds dropped and daylight broke and ended earlier. The boxes and luggage from the deep hold, where they had been kept since they were loaded in London, were brought up on deck. Clarinda replaced the clean sets of underclothes in their boxes with the ones she and Henry had been wearing and rotating for the previous two months. Some of the sailors stripped down to their trousers and jumped overboard to swim in the calmer water and escape the heat.

"Oh dear," said Mary, blushing. "There's that sailor who helped me out of the bucket, Clarinda, swimming way out. Look at the muscles on him."

Clarinda giggled and squeezed Mary's hand. "He is very handsome," she said.

As the weather grew hotter, the pitch on the deck began to melt and flow about. The men started to go barefoot in the mornings and evenings, but not during the middle of the day when the wooden boards of the deck and the melted pitch burned their feet fiercely. The passengers and sailors bathed more regularly in barrels of seawater collected using a steam pump, with the women modestly sheltered by a great sail that the sailors hitched for the purpose.

Often the passengers would be surprised by a sudden torrent of heavy rain, thunder and lightning, but then, just as suddenly, the sky would clear and the bright, hot sun would again beat down on them mercilessly.

And then there were sultry days when there was not a breath of wind or a ripple on the ocean so that the ship barely moved and the sea shone with a strange phosphorescence as though lit from beneath.

The reality that they were to land in Sydney Cove in only a few weeks or – depending on their progress – months, hit Clarinda around this time. Until this point, she hadn't allowed herself to dwell on what her actual life in Sydney might be like. Their arrival had seemed a long way off, but now the time was approaching more rapidly than she wished.

"Do you ever wonder what Sydney will be like?" she asked Mary as they sat in the shade of a sail one hot afternoon, shifting slightly every now and then to avoid the dark pitch that oozed towards them.

"I think about Sydney all the time. I'm excited to get there," Mary replied.

"I suppose I am, too," Clarinda said uncertainly. "Although I love being on board the ship. Sometimes I think I'd like the ship to never actually arrive in Sydney."

"That would only happen if we were shipwrecked!" Mary was horrified. "We have to land somewhere."

"You're right. But I'd like it best if that somewhere was Plymouth. It will be such a different life in New South Wales, I expect."

"A better life, I think, Clarinda. We won't have to starve like we both did when we were in London."

One day the bell was rung unexpectedly and a sailor high in the rigging shouted, "Land ahoy!"

Henry was already on deck but Clarinda, Mary and Eliza quickly climbed the ladder from their hold to see a rocky outcrop of islands on the horizon with a halo of misty salt air. They could see the green hue of vegetation and the white foam of the ocean as it beat against the rocks.

"It's Cape Verde, I think," Jimmy told them. "Off the coast of Africa."

It was their first sight of land since they had left England all those months earlier.

The sunsets and sunrises in the tropics were spectacular. They glowed as though the sky was burning, with deep crimson, russet orange and hues of vibrant purple. Henry and Clarinda would sit in each other's arms on deck as the cool of evening approached and marvel at the sight.

"It's like nothing I've ever seen before," Henry said.

"Yes," agreed Clarinda. "God truly is marvellous to create such a thing."

It was during their time in the tropics that one of the few children on board became sick. The cause was unknown, but the boy began to sweat with fever during the night and the surgeon was called. The boy and his mother shared a bunk close to Clarinda's and she watched as the poor mother clutched the whimpering child to her with his burning red cheeks and his limp and listless body. She thought of her own two babies and of the unbearable ache she still felt at their loss.

During her fitful sleep that night, Clarinda could hear the boy's whimpering gradually cease and his breath become ragged and hoarse like an old man's. When she woke in the morning, he lay white and cold in his mother's arms as she rocked him back and forth.

Mary whispered to Clarinda, "I think the poor, wee soul's dead."

Clarinda got down from her bed and went to the woman. "There now," she said gently. "I think he's passed. I think your boy has gone to a better place."

The woman did not make a sound, but continued to rock and stroke the boy's head.

"Would you like me to try to find your husband? What is your husband's name?"

"'Tis the same as my boy's," the woman said gruffly. "Thomas. 'Tis Thomas Higginbottom." She flinched as she said it, the same name as the dead boy in her arms.

Clarinda pulled a wrap around her nightshirt and went on deck to find the sailor who had kept the night watch so he could go into the men's hold to tell the father the terrible news.

A funeral was held on deck that afternoon. The boy's body was sewn into a canvas while the mother wailed and the father stared at the horizon with heavy eyes. Henry held Clarinda's hand tightly as they stood amongst the congregation of passengers and remembered their suffering at the funerals of their own dear children.

"We, therefore," said the captain, "commit this body to the deep, to be turned into corruption."

The bell tolled as the body was lifted overboard by two sailors and they heard the splash of it as it landed in the ocean. At this, the mother fell onto her knees and the father crouched beside her and held her to him, sobbing.

"Oh, how awful," whispered Clarinda to Henry, her tears falling heavily. "To bury your child at sea. To know his body will never be home." She thought with slight gratitude then that at least her own Thomas and Clarinda were buried at home in Birmingham.

Clarinda was becoming ungainly in her pregnancy. It became awkward for her to climb up and down from her top bunk and her narrow bed became impossible to lie in comfortably. If she lay flat, the weight of the baby was on her and if she lay on her side, it was difficult not to fall from the bed. She decided the only way she could sleep comfortably and safely was on the hold's floor with her blanket under her so that she could spread out on her side. Sarah Crump, who was further on in her pregnancy than Clarinda, decided to do the same at her end of the hold.

Some other women complained. "There's no room for us to walk about with you lot on the floor," one woman said. "We'll be tripping over you in the night if we're not careful."

Clarinda and Sarah ignored these comments.

As the ship approached the Equator, the sun began to beat down directly overhead at midday so that no shadow was cast. A sailor played a trick on David Chapman – Henry's bunkmate.

"If you're brave enough," the sailor said to the man, "you can climb partway up the mizzen mast to see the equatorial line."

David Chapman, not wanting to appear cowardly, followed the sailor up the mast warily, placing his foot on each rope as the sailor's foot left it, and when they had reached a height to see clearly across the ocean, the sailor passed him a telescope to look through.

"D'you see it? D'you see the line on the ocean?" the sailor yelled so that all below on deck could hear.

"Yes, I do! 'Tis amazin'! There's actually a line!" David Chapman shouted.

It was only when they had clambered down to the deck that the sailor cuffed the man on the shoulder and guffawed heartily. "It's no real line, mate," he said, and he waved the telescope about so all could see where he had tied a string across the bottom so that it appeared as a line when looking through the glass.

Henry and those about him laughed and David Chapman blushed and laughed along with them. "I's only joking," he said. "I knew it wasn't a real line in the ocean or nothin'. Just playin' along with the joke, I was."

There was a great celebration among the sailors when they crossed the Equator. Henry and Clarinda joined the crowd assembled on deck to watch. An older, grey-haired sailor was dressed up with a crown and held an ordinary fork in his hand, sitting on a throne made from a chair covered with gold cloth.

"I am Neptune!" he called to those on deck in a deep, booming voice. "I am Neptune, God of the Ocean! Come forth any sailor who has never before crossed the Equatorial line!"

The other sailors applauded loudly as three of them came forward to be blindfolded. A spare sail was filled with seawater from the barrel that was used for bathing and each of the three sailors was nudged forward to stand before Neptune.

"What are your names?" he asked them, and as they opened their mouths to answer, three other sailors stepped towards them with brushes covered in tar and pushed these roughly into their mouths. The blindfolded sailors spat and retched as the crowd cheered and Clarinda giggled in surprise.

"How bizarre!" she said to Henry. "Those poor fellows eating a mouthful of tar!"

"It's a tradition, Clarinda. It's what all sailors do when they cross the line for the first time. It is quite barbaric, though."

Then each of the three sailors was individually shaved with a wooden razor and when this was completed, they were pushed backwards into the sail of seawater. When each emerged from their dunking, they pulled off the blindfolds and cheered along with the crowd, before the captain handed them a cup of rum.

"It's time for the music!" yelled Neptune and two sailors rolled a barrel of rum from the cook's galley while another began to play a fiddle.

"This could get a bit rough," said Henry as he and Clarinda watched the sailors begin to drink and dance about the deck. "It might be better if you were down in your 'old, Clarinda. They'll all be drunk and rowdy soon enough."

Throughout the afternoon, Clarinda sat at the long table in the stifling hold with Mary and most of the other women, many fanning themselves with whatever they could find, while they listened to the thuds from the dancing above and the hooting of the sailors.

"This is ridiculous," one woman said after a while. "It's so damned hot down here and they're having so much fun up *there*. We haven't heard any of the women who are with the sailors complaining or anything. I'm going to go up and join them. Anyone else brave enough to come with me?"

There were muffled exchanges and some tut-tutting before three other women, giggling, stood up from the table to join the woman and climb up from the hold to the whoops of appreciative sailors on deck.

Clarinda did not know if Henry was amongst the group of partying sailors and passengers, but she suspected he had returned to his own hold soon after the merriment began and so she was reluctant to escape the heat and go on deck. Mary, however, needed to be persuaded not to join the other rebellious ladies.

"You'd put yourself in danger, Mary," Clarinda said to her from her seat beside her on the bench.

"Yes, they're all drunk and not themselves, Mary," Sarah Crump agreed. "It's not the thing to do. Leave the sailors to their carousing."

"But it's so *hot* down here! And it sounds like they're having a right old time up on deck. Won't you come with me, Eliza?" she urged. "Who knows, we might even find ourselves a fella each!"

Eliza laughed. "I'm not planning to get myself hitched to some sailor who's always at sea, Mary. I know you're all goggle-eyed for that mermaid-tattooed fellow, but you can't go throwing yourself at him."

Mary rolled her eyes. "You lot are no fun," she said, scowling. "And I wouldn't go throwing myself at anyone!"

"Mary, be sensible," Clarinda said, patting her hand. "It would not be the right thing to do. You heard how the sailors cheered when the other women went up. They're clearly drunk and it would seem loose for you to join them."

"Yes, Mary," agreed Eliza, "and I'm sure we won't be stuck down here for much longer. They'll all be passed out before too long, I expect."

Mary rolled her eyes again but laughed lightly. "I suppose you're all right. I'm just *so* hot!"

"I know. We all are," said Clarinda as Mary huffed and laid her head on the table.

Eventually, as the evening set in, a sailor came to the hatch and called down to them, "Come on deck for the burning, ladies."

149

Mary jumped to her feet. "You're coming up now, you lot, aren't ya?" she asked the whole table of women. "I can't hear any music any more, or any hollering. I don't think there's any danger now."

"All right," Clarinda said reluctantly. "*If* we all go together and see if the male passengers are up there, too." She looked at the other women for their ascent.

"Yes," said Sarah. "I suppose we could at least take a look now."

Mary went up the ladder first and nodded down to the others. "Even Henry's up here, Clarinda. And your husband, Sarah," she said.

Clarinda was relieved. "All right, Mary. We should be fine then."

On deck, the music and dancing had stopped and the sailors were sprawled all over the deck. The ship's surgeon, Mr Allan, was heaving over the rail and soon collapsed onto the boards.

"He's a one, the surgeon!" said Mary. "Always in his cups, he is. Surprising it's even allowed, him being responsible for us all."

Henry came to Clarinda immediately. "What a racket they've made all afternoon," he said. "And look, there's young Jimmy over there, passed out from the drink."

Clarinda turned to see the lad lying on the sail that had held the seawater for the ritual dunking, his eyes lolling back into his head and a line of saliva winding down his chin grotesquely.

"It's a fast life at sea, I suppose," Henry said. "'E's young to be getting drunk along with these other 'ardened sailors, though."

"Yes, he's just a baby," Clarinda said.

"I suppose you 'ave to grow up fast as a sailor. They like their drink. The poor lad doesn't 'ave much choice."

A barrel of tar was rolled off the ship then and a torch lit from the galley hearth and hurled over the side onto the floating barrel. It immediately burst alight and they watched as it glowed and floated away from the ship.

It was a beautiful evening and the stars were bright. Henry and Clarinda sat with Mary and Eliza, watching as sailors dragged themselves off to their beds in the forecastle and the sailor with the mermaid tattoo helped Jimmy to his feet. The first mate roused the surgeon who staggered towards his cabin on the poop deck. Most of the passengers sat on deck, having spent the day in the hold as the sailors partied. There was a cool breeze after the hot day and few wanted to venture back to the stifling atmosphere of the holds.

"It's like a different world in these parts, isn't it?" said Clarinda, leaning against Henry's chest to look up at the night sky. "I feel, sometimes, as though I'm in a different world altogether from the world that holds England."

"Yes. When I think of everyone back 'ome, Da and Mam and Sarah and all, I can't really imagine them continuing on with their lives in Birming'am," agreed Henry. "It's almost as though their lives must 'ave frozen in time. I can't imagine Sarah taking 'erself off to 'er work each day or little Tom growing and learning and changing."

"Yes, he'll have grown into a man if we ever do make it back to England to see him."

They were silent for a moment, deep in thought, before Henry said, "I still 'ave 'opes that some of them will follow us out to New South Wales when they 'ear of the life we've got. If Da and Mam could cope with ship life, I'm sure they'd 'ave a better life and live longer if they came out to us."

"It's a long way to go, though, Henry. And they are already ageing."

"I'd like some of my family to come out, too," said Mary who was sitting beside them. "Life in Ireland is so mighty hard. And I'd like to think I'll see some of my kin again."

The stars shone down on them like so many winking eyes as they thought of their homes, and Clarinda wondered what her father and John were doing at that moment, and whether they ever thought of her.

Suddenly, Eliza was at her shoulder, nudging her urgently. "It's Sarah," she said. "She's having the baby. I went down to the hold to get my shawl and she's been down there on her own for a bit with the pains coming on."

Mary jumped to her feet. "We should get the surgeon. We should get Mr Allan."

"You saw the state of him," Clarinda said. "He's as drunk as a lord!"

"You're right. There's not much point asking him for help when he's in his cups. Let's get some of the other women to help," said Mary.

"And I'll get the cook to boil some water, if he's not too drunk himself," said Eliza and raced off towards the galley while Clarinda and Mary gathered other women around them.

"I'll let Sarah's 'usband know," Henry called after them as they climbed down into the hold.

Later, Henry sat on his own on the deck, thinking of what opportunities might lie ahead for him. He imagined himself as a renowned businessman in the unsophisticated town of Sydney, with perhaps several ivory shops and men working under him. Once he'd saved enough money working for others, he was determined to succeed in his own business. It had proved not to be possible in England, but in a colony barely fifty years old, populated by so many others who had struggled back home, surely he would become an important man amongst them. He could write home then and tell of his success – the success his sisters and Mam and Da had always expected.

Sarah Crump's baby was born within the hour. He was a fair-haired boy like his mother. Clarinda felt a fierce longing for her babies as she watched Sarah snuggling the infant to her breast. She held her hand to her stomach and prayed quietly again. "Please, Lord. Let this one live. Please may this child survive!" To Sarah she said, "He's a beautiful baby. And he looks healthy and strong. God bless you both, Sarah."

"And let's hope your baby is born as easily, Clarinda," Sarah said to her. "I'll pray that he is as healthy a baby as mine."

ELEVEN

The weather became cold and blustery as they sailed towards the Cape of Good Hope. It was as though they had experienced two distinct seasons within just a few weeks. During the day, strange birds circled the ship, their call like a chattering. The sailors called them cape hens and cape pigeons. Clarinda drew them in her diary. The hens were larger, black with white bills and wings pointing in the shape of an arrow, while the pigeons' stomachs were white and their outstretched wings had grey and white markings, some appearing like spots.

"There're a lot of new things to get used to," Mary said, watching the birds gliding easily on the winds as Clarinda sketched them beside her, holding the paper firmly against the fierce wind. "I expect we will get used to them all soon enough."

"We'll be seeing kangaroos before we know it," Eliza said. "Hopping about like giant rabbits. And the Aboriginals. The first dark-skinned person I ever saw was our cook here."

"It will be very different in Australia, yes. And to think that when it is night in Sydney, it will be daytime back home," said Clarinda, "and the other way around."

"Ah, 'tis most peculiar," said Mary.

One day, a mass of seagulls flew repeatedly around an area of water close to the ship, cawing and squawking, and so Clarinda and Eliza who were together on deck, intently watched the water where they circled. Suddenly they saw the great dark mass of a whale leap from the water and twirl in the air like a giant dancer with its fins spread like wings, scattering the seagulls before crashing in a thunderous slap back into the ocean. A huge spray of water splashed over the ship, which rocked violently as the passengers on the deck gasped.

The great beast lifted one of its fins from the water and waved as if in greeting. Clarinda had tears in her eyes as she watched. To have seen such a creature, who may never have been seen by human eyes before, seeming to communicate with them. Once it had disappeared again, she watched the deep water closely until she saw it abruptly rise once more at some distance and spin in its strange dance before vanishing into the wide ocean.

Clarinda was heavy with the baby now. It moved about inside her urgently in a way neither of her other babies had.

"It's a blessing," Mary said as she watched Clarinda rubbing her stomach where the baby pushed at her as she lay on her make-shift bed on the floor beside their bunk. "It means he'll be a healthy one. He's moving about so much to say he wants to get out into the world."

"I hope he can wait until we're off the ship," Clarinda said. "I'd like us to be in Sydney when the baby comes."

"Never you mind that, now, Clarinda. We managed with Sarah and her baby – and with Edith over there earlier on the trip. And I told you before, I've helped my Mam with lots of her babies. And who knows if I'll be around if ya have the baby in Sydney. I'll have to take some housekeeping job or something as soon as I can when we get there."

"Oh, Mary!" Clarinda cried. "I hope we'll be nearby. I'd hate to be without you when we get to Sydney."

"We'll have to wait and see," Mary said. "We might not have a choice."

The waves became monstrous as they continued towards the Southern Ocean. The rolling and heaving of the ship made it difficult to sleep at night or to move about during the day. Everyone held on to ropes as they walked and tied themselves to their beds at night. Clarinda had to tie herself to Eliza's bunk beside her where she lay on her make-shift bed. At mealtimes they ate with one hand and held their plates with the other to stop them from sliding.

"D'ya think we'll ever be able to stop rocking when we get on dry land?" laughed Mary one day as she, Clarinda and Eliza walked together around the deck, bracing against the wind and the violent swaying of the ship. "I think I'll look like a madwoman for the rest of my days, just rocking back and forth like I'm in a great rocking chair wherever I go."

"Or we might start walking permanently like the sailors," said Eliza. "You know how they walk mostly, with their legs wide apart to steady themselves."

"Yes," said Clarinda. "I suppose some of them do – like they're astride a small horse. I wonder if we've started to do that ourselves without realising it, to balance ourselves with the movement."

"At least, if we have, no one will see it beneath our skirts. It's the men who should be worried," said Mary.

Just then, there was the loud ring of the bell and a din of shouting voices from the other side of the deck. They raced over to the crowd of sailors and passengers leaning over one side of the ship. Henry was there and turned to them. "It's Jimmy," he said. "The ship's apprentice. 'E's fallen from the mast!"

They could see the head and an arm of the lad, waving furiously from the crest of a huge wave. The first mate heaved a buoy far into the water. Clarinda clutched Henry's arm and prayed as she watched. Jimmy reached for the buoy but, just as it came close to his outstretched hand, the wave surged and he disappeared under it.

"Oh no!" cried Clarinda. "Dear Lord, save him!"

Jimmy's hand reappeared and he stretched his face out of the water, spluttering and gasping for breath. The first mate threw another buoy while the first drifted away. Jimmy caught the buoy this time and the first mate began dragging him in, with other sailors grabbing the rope to help.

"Dear Lord, help him!" Clarinda prayed, and others about her began to pray loudly.

Again a great wave swept over Jimmy and he and the buoy disappeared under it. The first mate and the other sailors continued to pull furiously on the rope, arm over arm, dragging Jimmy from the depths.

"Pull, pull!" the first mate called urgently.

Every person on deck stared at the water, waiting anxiously to see Jimmy's head appear in the spot where the taut rope disappeared into the waves, expecting any moment to see him burst from the sea. Suddenly the rope slackened and the sailors holding it fell with a thud onto the hard deck.

"Oh no! 'E's let go!" Henry yelled as the empty buoy appeared splashing through a wave.

The first mate wildly dragged the buoy from the water and threw it back near the spot where Jimmy had last been seen. They watched for the sight of Jimmy's hand reaching for it. The mass of sea below seemed endless as they waited, their eyes strained and searching wildly for a sight of him.

Eventually, with a deep sigh, the first mate turned to them all and said in a cracking voice, "We've lost him. There's no chance he's survived now."

Another sailor pulled at the first mate's sleeve roughly. "He can swim, though, Jimmy. He can swim. He might still be out there where we can't see him. He's a strong swimmer, he is."

"I'm sorry," the first mate said. "There's nothing we can do now. He could be anywhere, even if we tried to turn back. There's nothing we can do."

Henry put his arm around Clarinda as she sobbed.

"Poor lad, poor lad," he repeated over and over as she cried and others wept about them.

A service was held for Jimmy that afternoon. The captain committed the absent body of James Samuel Chippendale to the deep.

That night Henry dreamt that Jimmy was being ripped apart by a great shark. The lad was screaming as the shark's jagged teeth tore into the arm he stretched out to reach for the buoy, and the blood stained the water a deep red. Jimmy's severed head floated up on a wave beside the ship, with Henry staring from the deck into the lifeless eyes. Then the eyes transformed into the eyes of the shark Henry had seen stabbed on deck, and suddenly the shark was beside him again, ripping at his own arm.

Henry woke with a yell. He was sweating and panting heavily and couldn't think where he was for a brief moment, staring up at the roof of the hold, until David Chapman grunted beside him. He remembered, with a shock like a punch to his chest, how the poor lad had disappeared into the waves. He wondered what Jimmy's death had been like, whether he had drowned as soon as he had gone under that wave, or whether he had managed to swim around desperately for a time, searching for the ship and being buffeted by the waves until finally, exhausted and freezing, he could swim no more. He wondered where, in that deep ocean beneath them, Jimmy's body was now.

Henry had never expected to witness such a thing. It was worse than the hanging he had seen in London. Jimmy had simply been doing what his work required. What chance did he have, with no education and his background on boats, but to work at sea?

The feeling on board was morose over the next few days but gradually the shock of the tragic death lessened. Henry was reminded of Jimmy whenever he looked up at the masts or spoke to another sailor, and the memory of his death became mixed with his thoughts of the working man's struggle, so that Jimmy became almost a totem for equality in his mind.

The weather grew colder as they travelled through the swells of the Southern Ocean and the sailors began to watch for the tips of icebergs and smaller, floating ice drifts that could rip apart a ship's hull. It was freezing at night sleeping in the hold, especially for Clarinda who still slept on the floor as the baby grew. She piled bundles of clothes over her to try to keep warm. She was much larger with this pregnancy, and she felt the pressure of the baby on her pelvis as it grew.

The steerage passengers shared two water-closets and Clarinda found herself frequenting them several times each night. They were near the forecastle and she had to wrap herself tightly in her blanket and walk in the cold night from the quarter deck, along the main deck, past the men's hatch entrance and the foremast, to the area alongside the cook's galley. The closets were smelly and putrid, despite their regular covering of chloride and lime by the ship's apprentices, and the soapy, freezing bucket of water outside on the deck that she used to wash her hands had had numerous other dirty hands in it throughout the day.

As she found her sleep disturbed by the cold and the discomfort of the baby, Clarinda began to worry again about their arrival in New South Wales. Most of the voyage on the ship had been a happy time for her and she felt relaxed in its daily routines. It was almost as though this were her home now. And her friends on board were more like family than her own had been, especially Mary.

She longed to be with Henry at night, but this was the only part of arriving in their new home she thought of with pleasure. Everything else was a question. What would it be like? Where would they live? What would she do? Would Henry find work? And the most concerning of all, where would the baby be born, and would it survive? The enormity of these uncertainties made Clarinda bite her lip and bury her face in her blanket with her eyes squeezed shut to stop the tears from coming.

And yet occasionally she felt a glimmer of excitement at the thought that this was a new beginning for her and Henry. She prayed it might be the life that they hoped it would be, for them and for their children.

One day, Clarinda sat with Mary at the long table in the women's hold, her back to the table as her stomach could no longer fit comfortably beneath it.

"Do you think the Aboriginals will be friendly?" Clarinda asked.

"Don't know really. I guess so. We've been there so long now – the British and Irish – they're bound to be living just like us," Mary replied.

"We haven't been there as long as they've lived there, though, Mary," Clarinda said. "I don't expect they will be living like us. I wonder if they are much about town. I don't know a lot about them."

Eliza joined them then, pulling her legs over the bench with a flash of stocking. "I hear they're half naked all the time – the savages," she said.

"Surely not in town!" gasped Clarinda.

"I've heard some of them are. And they never wear shoes," Eliza said, scratching at the welts on her arms where lice had bitten her.

The three women were silent for a while.

"Do you think the convicts will be a problem? Do you think the place will be rough and unseemly?" Clarinda asked eventually. "Henry says it won't be, because most of them committed crimes due to poverty, in order to survive. He says they're mostly decent people like anyone you'd meet in Birmingham. But I'm not so sure. I think I'll feel quite unsafe."

"Yes," agreed Eliza. "I think that sometimes, too."

"It's like in *Oliver Twist* – that series written by Charles Dickens. Have you heard of it?" Clarinda asked. "At the end of the story, the young pickpocket, the Artful Dodger, gets transported for stealing a snuff-box."

"But that's not real. That's a story," said Eliza.

"It can't be too dangerous a place," said Mary. "It's been settled for over fifty years now. And I hear of ex-convicts making it big in Sydney and all."

"Yes," Clarinda said. "Henry always talks of Francis Greenway when I ask him about convicts. He was a man who was transported for forgery and became the government architect in Sydney. Apparently most of the great public buildings there were designed by him. Henry said he died just a few years ago but he's famous in Sydney, and *he* came out as a convict."

"Are there great buildings in Sydney?" asked Eliza.

"I believe so," said Clarinda. "Government House and the like."

"I've never told you this," Mary whispered, "but my uncle was sent out about ten years ago for poaching a few rabbits. 'Twas what everyone about our village did, but he had to go and get himself caught."

Clarinda and Eliza moved their heads closer to hers as she continued.

"He got sent to Van Diemen's Land, and my aunt was going to follow him out when he was freed, but she and her baby died of the smallpox."

"Is he still there?" asked Clarinda.

"Yes, he's still in the colonies somewhere, as far as we at home know. We heard word from him only a few times, 'cause he can't write and he had to get someone else to write the letters for him. The last we heard he'd got his ticket-of-leave and was planning to go to Sydney Town to make it big. He said Sydney was the place to be."

"We'll have to still see each other when we're there," Clarinda said. "I can't imagine being in Sydney without you two."

"We mightn't have a choice, though, Clarinda. It'll depend on where the work is – for Henry, too," Mary said again.

"I suppose. But I do so hope we can still see each other. I don't want to be as alone as I was in London."

"You'll have the baby to care for, too, Clarinda, so you won't be entirely alone," Eliza reassured her.

"I pray so. Oh, I do so hope this baby is all right!" said Clarinda.

It was on Clarinda's birthday that land was sighted again. All of the passengers and sailors crowded on deck to see the rocky outcrop with its mass of green trees. It was the first vegetation they had seen clearly since leaving England. The bell tolled soon after the sighting to gather the passengers for the captain to speak. He told them this was King Island, at the entrance to Bass Strait, which ran between Van Diemen's Land and the mainland of Australia. Everyone cheered at the news. They were off the coast of Australia at last. They had finished their crossing of the open sea.

"We should be in Sydney Cove before we know it!" Henry said excitedly, holding Clarinda's hands. "We 'ave really made it!"

There was a strong headwind that day and the ship tacked backwards and forwards, making little progress. They saw other rocks, some rising only a hundred feet from the water and others rearing thousands of feet into the sky, thick with vegetation. The sailors lowered the anchor that night for the first time since Plymouth and the ship swayed unsteadily in its ocean bed.

In the morning, the wind had died down and the anchor was hauled up as the decks were scrubbed at first light. The progress was still slow but the tacking of the ship was mainly in a forward direction now. Clarinda and Henry sat on deck watching the strange rocks that rose from the water, the white foam crashing about them. And then someone called, "Look, is that land? Is that the mainland?"

Everyone on deck looked from the port side of the ship towards a distant haze on the horizon. As they sailed further, they saw a stretch of it snaking like a great arm towards them.

"It's Wilsons Promontory," a sailor told a man sitting further along the deck, and the news travelled fast amongst the passengers.

"It's our first sighting of mainland Australia, Clarinda!" Henry said, holding her rounded shape against him. "This is our new 'ome!"

Clarinda said nothing. She could not share Henry's enthusiasm. This land and its vegetation were so strange to her. She looked towards it with mounting anxiety.

That night, the ship continued to sail along the coast of New South Wales, and as Henry and Clarinda watched they could see the lights of fires burning on the dark shore. It was strange to think of the Aboriginals camped around these fires, their lives so different from their own. Clarinda was mesmerised by the distant glow and felt an unusual calm come upon her as she stared towards the flickering.

The next day they were close enough to the shore to see inlets of regular yellow sandy beaches, more golden than any they had seen before. The bush was like a thick, green haze of hair stretching beyond the beaches or sprouting awkwardly from jagged cliffs, some almost perpendicular to the sea, others looking like the ruins of a castle in their disorderly jumble, so different from the coast they had seen as they sailed the English Channel. And then they saw dark figures on a beach moving about and some in the water near the shore, like tiny upright ants in their blackness. *They're people, real people,* Clarinda thought. They had legs and arms just like her, and hearts and minds. But they seemed so alien even from this distance.

That evening, as she sat beside Henry and gazed at the glowing stars and the occasional fire on the dark shore, Clarinda felt her first contraction. Henry felt her body tense beside him.

"Are you all right, Clarinda?" he asked anxiously.

"I had so hoped this baby would be born on land," she said softly, breathing deeply. "But I think it's determined to be born on the ocean. Henry, I think it's..." She gasped with the pain of another contraction.

"My darling," said Henry. "It'll be an ocean baby. It'll be a New South Welshman. Be brave, Clarinda."

The baby, Clarinda Sarah Parkes, was born at dawn on the 23rd of July, 1839 on the *Strathfieldsaye*, as it sailed in the Pacific Ocean off the coast of New South Wales. Henry was always to call his daughter his blue-eyed ocean child.

PART IV

Memoir of Menie Thom (Nee Parkes)

TWELVE

I have always been Menie to my family, not Clarinda, to distinguish me from Mamma, after whom I was named. Menie is an odd name, I suppose, but one which apparently most closely resembles my attempts to say my name as a young girl. Sometimes Father would call me his blue-eyed ocean child, for I was born on board a ship as my parents first arrived in this great southern land.

I am writing this memoir to honour my parents now that they have both passed. I grieve for them terribly. Their lives were remarkable, I believe. Not only Father's public life, but also Mamma's quiet, self-sacrificing life – always supporting Father and us children. My father will always be remembered as a politician and, perhaps, as the former editor of the newspaper the *Empire* that once rivalled *The Sydney Morning Herald*. But in writing this memoir, I particularly want Mamma's life to be remembered: Clarinda Parkes, once Clarinda Varney, a woman who suffered greatly and loved greatly and who I will always hold dear. This is her story, and my father's.

One of my earliest memories is of Father arriving home and his tall, bear-like frame looming over me as I ran to him and proudly recited the speech I had been practising with Mamma, which went something like, "Father, take us in a big ship to see my grandfathers, grandmother, uncles and aunties in England. Do please, Father!"

It was probably one of my first perfect sentences and I remember expecting Father to smile and shower me with kisses. How surprised I was then when he ignored me completely and strode past me towards Mamma.

"What 'ave you been teaching the girl?" he asked her crossly, and I thought Mamma might cry as I did then.

But in her usual calm manner, Mamma sat up high in her chair and answered him boldly with words to the effect of, "It is nothing more than Menie should know. I have simply been telling her of her family back in England. It is she who has got it into her young head to ask if she could visit them."

I don't remember what passed between Mamma and Father after this, only that I probably ran to Father, insisting on his usual attention.

We did not know at the time that Father's mother, Martha Parkes, had died a few months earlier. I believe the letter from England telling Father of this terrible event did not arrive until months after her death. I don't remember details of my father's grief, but I'm sure it was great, for after he received the news he often spoke of his Mam with tears in his eyes.

I know that Mamma always missed her home in England. She never returned, although Father did on three occasions. I grew up hearing Mamma talk of the beauty of her home – the neat hedgerows and regimented, green fields, nothing like the disorderly tangle of bush she found in Australia and that I so love.

Mamma would complain of the heat and the harsh sun of New South Wales and try to describe to me the crispness of the air in England, and the smell of honeysuckle and the sweet, juicy taste of wild blackberries.

Poor Mamma, even when Father built Faulconbridge – that stately house in the Blue Mountains with its magnificent views of Sydney across the plains – I don't think she ever truly thought her new home compared to the England of her memories. I often think of what a huge wrench it must have been for her and Father to travel so far to such a different land.

I can remember the Christmas when I was four years old. I know I was this age because my brother Robert had just been born. He was all pink and wrinkly in his perambulator as I walked alongside Mamma to the market place. There was a Christmas tree in the middle of the market with the Union Jack fluttering on top.

"I've heard that the trees they use in England are fir trees, not eucalypts like this one," Mamma told me and squeezed my hand. "I forget sometimes you don't know what a fir tree is, do you, Menie?"

"Is it something beautiful from England?" I asked.

"Oh yes, like the pine trees here, but the *smell* of them! The smell of fir trees would fill the air!" She breathed in through her nose as though she were smelling a rare perfume. "Prince Albert, the Queen's husband, was the one who began this new craze of Christmas trees. It's a tradition from his home in Germany."

"Oh," I said. "Would Prince Albert miss Germany as much as you miss England, Mamma?"

Mamma sighed at my young child's perception. "I suppose he would," she said.

"I'll never leave my home," I said, stamping my foot. "Australia is my home and I will never go anywhere else!"

I know that my parents' first years here were hard. Father had expected to find work and lodgings in Sydney Town on his first day ashore. But Sydney at the time was overrun with emigrants like my parents and so employment and housing were scarce. Every day of that first week, Father left Mamma with me on board the ship and trudged the streets of Sydney searching for work, just as he had done in London the previous year. Eventually, he found a dirty, unfurnished room without a fireplace, despite the cold of winter. Mamma told me how she carried me in her arms for a mile to this unwelcoming room, which became like a prison to her for the next week while Father continued to search for work.

Father always kept a lucky sixpence. It was the first money he earned in Australia during the days when he was searching for work in Sydney and Mamma and I were still on board ship. He would often tell me the story of how he had got it.

"I was getting so desperate, Menie, with you just a babe. Mamma and I 'ad travelled over all those oceans, and yet nothing seemed to be going our way. And then a chance encounter changed our luck. A gentleman in a top 'at and tails rode up through the dusty streets on a fine bay stallion. Seeing me and obviously thinking I looked like a trustworthy fellow, 'e asked me to 'old the 'orse while 'e did some business with a local whipmaker. I thought this particularly ironic, as you know your grandfather – your mother's father – was a whipmaker back in Birming'am and 'ad always disliked me intensely.

"Well, I decided to 'old the 'orse for the gentleman mainly because of this last piece of information, because I thought it showed some kind of providence, and so it did. For when the gentleman returned 'alf an 'our later, 'e threw me this sixpence and said, 'To get you started in this fine land, young man. Good luck to you.' It was the first coin I earned in Australia. I 'ave never spent it, even when things were desperate, and I never will. This is my lucky sixpence."

Father's first job in Australia was as a common labourer at Sir John Jamison's property in Penrith, Regentville, thirty-six miles from Sydney. We lived there in a hut with an old door as a bed and a piece of bark for covers. I am often relieved that I was too young to remember such trials.

My early memories are of a small comfortable home in Domain Terrace in Sydney, where we moved when Father gained employment as a customs officer. One evening, as I sat on his jigging knee, he told me in dramatic terms of how he had caught a smuggler that day, chasing him along the wharf and downing him with his fist.

"Don't tease the poor girl," Mamma laughed as I sat, wide-eyed and hanging on every word from my heroic father.

I still wonder at Mamma's leaving her own father's house shortly after she became engaged. It was such a brave move for a young woman of that era. My mother always proved stronger than she appeared. She told me of my brother and sister who had died before I was born, saying they would have been my big brother and sister, Thomas and Clarinda, and I must always think of them. I have often wondered what it would have been like to be the younger child with older siblings. I once asked Mamma what I would have been named if the other Clarinda had lived.

Mamma had laughed. "Menie, of course!"

I'd persisted. "No, really, what would my proper name have been?"

She had suggested Martha, after Father's mother, or Sarah, his sister. "But definitely not Ann," she had said. "My ghastly stepmother is Ann!"

Mamma had a cameo whose smooth surface I loved to run my fingers over when I was a child. It was carved with a picture of her own mother, and Father had made it for her. My mother and father had met when she commissioned the cameo.

"I think I fell in love with Henry that first day," she told me when I was older. "I had never met a man so determined to get what he wanted."

I giggled. "He wanted you! That's what he wanted!"

Mamma blushed. "Yes, I suppose he did."

I think now how lucky Father was to have married the compassionate, patient, forbearing woman that my mother was. She'd always said he would become a great man one day, and he had. I wonder if he would have achieved so much without her behind him.

Unlike Mamma, I have always loved the Australian landscape. I have known nothing else, of course, but in my mind the England of Mamma's stories seems too tame against the wild beauty of my home. I love to walk in the hush of the bush, the only sounds the snap of twigs and fallen bark beneath my feet and the occasional ring of a bellbird. I love the gnarled confusion of limbs of the eucalypts and the earthy reds and browns of their ragged bark. And then to see the flash of brilliant colour of a parakeet swooping low beside me! Or to hear the sudden raucous screams of a flock of cockatoos as they spread their yellow combs and take to the sky in a sea of white.

I have lived in many Australian towns: Sydney, Penrith, Pambula, Ballan and in Mount Victoria in the Blue Mountains. They have all had their own kind of beauty. I would not want to live anywhere but Australia, even though I have suffered through drought, floods and fire, and I am thankful my parents brought me here. And how proud I will be when my father's dream of a federation of the colonies is achieved. I use the word 'when' with purpose, for it must be so, after all his efforts to create a united Australia.

I am getting ahead of myself. There is so much to relate before I write of this – so many years between. I need to cast my mind back to around 1845. I realise now how young both my parents were at the time, although they seemed old and wise to my six year old mind. Indeed, a photograph I have of Father taken almost nine years later shows a youthful, unlined, unbearded face and dark wavy hair, not the shock of white mane and beard of his later photographs.

My father resigned from his job at the customs office around this time, and set up business as an ivory turner in Kent Street and then in premises at 25 Hunter Street in the centre of Sydney. We lived above the shop and Mamma, Robert and I probably saw more of Father during this time than at any other.

I can remember long, steaming days sitting at Mamma's feet in the dappled light of the shop, playing with the knuckle bones I treasured or the miniature teaset that Father had fashioned for me, while Robert tried to spin his top with his awkward toddler hands. Father would work at his lathe in the room with us, the rhythm of the turning wheel like a melody. If a customer entered, Mamma would talk to them, showing them the brooches, paper knives and chess pieces Father had carved or the exotic fans and fabrics he had imported from Asia. Robert and I would often annoy each other then, and Mamma would have to hush us or call for Father to attend to the customer while she soothed us. I always loved Father's deep, sonorous tones in the quiet of the shop. His voice seemed to fill the room like an echo.

In the evenings, I would sit with Mamma at the low bench in the kitchen and practise my letters while Father sat at the table with a group of like-minded men, some of whom I called 'uncle' because they were so close to Father. One was Charles Harpur, a thin, gaunt man who would let me sit on his knee and pull at his beard when my lessons were finished. He was a poet and I can remember a sonnet he composed for Robert when he was still a captivating baby:

Ay, crow, rogue, crow! Thy little Being thrilling is
Like an embodied carol of a bird!

Uncle Charles was a regular in our kitchen that year, as was William Duncan or Uncle William as I called him – also bearded and with a Scottish brogue that I did not always understand. There were others who came less often, like Henry Halloran and Daniel Deniehy. I would sit at my lessons or on the floor under the table, looking at their great booted feet as they talked of the colony or of poets. I know now that Uncle William was the owner of a newspaper at the time, *The Weekly Register,* and that some of the other men, including my father, would compose poems or editorials for this paper and others such as *The Chronicle*.

"It is through poetry that we will stir the masses into higher thinking," Uncle Charles would pronounce in his reedy voice.

"Through that and education," Uncle William would say. "Without education, there can be no higher thinking amongst the people of New South Wales. There must be equal education for all children."

Father would grunt in agreement. "And then there would be an educated force to stand against the New South Wales neo-aristocracy – the squatters who take tracts of prime land and employ the cheap labour of convicts."

I distinctly remember the time I heard a passionate discussion on the ills of transportation to the colony, for it surprised me when I knew that Father was friends with many ex-convicts who we called emancipists to their faces due to the stigma, and I knew that even Uncle Charles's own parents had been convicts.

"'Ow can New South Wales, or indeed any of the colonies, prosper and grow with shiploads of convicts continuing to arrive on our shores!" my father said. "The felons of England should not continue to be dispatched to a young, developing colony. They are like a canker eating into our very souls. It is disastrous to the social and moral interests of New South Wales."

"Aye," Uncle William said. "Even the emancipists and their children, the generation of native-born Australians, our currency lads and lasses, want the end of transportation. No one should force upon a community a thing from without that they unanimously refuse to receive. It is our natural right!"

I was perplexed at the time as, I realised later, was Mamma. I listened intently to a conversation between her and Father after the men had left.

"I am confused, Henry, at your anti-transportation stance," Mamma said. "I thought you pitied many of the convicts, as people who are forced into crime by the injustice and inequality of the world. People who are forced to steal and commit other crimes in order to survive."

"Yes, Clarinda. That is right. But there 'as to come a point when Britain finds another means of reforming its felons. We cannot continue to be a land of criminals, no matter 'ow petty their crimes or the fact that they 'ave committed them due to poverty. And think of our own children. Would you want Menie to be friends with only convicts and children of convicts?"

"She already plays happily with little Tommy. He is an emancipist's child."

"I know, but our population 'as already grown excessively from when we first came to Sydney, and convicts, who are cheaper labour, will continue to take employment from the native-born Australians like our own Robert, when 'e is grown."

"I suppose you are right. You know so much more about these things than me," Mamma said, but I noticed her frown and that she bit her lip the way she always would when she forced herself to stay silent.

Uncle William left the colony shortly after this discussion. Father told me he had obtained a very important job as sub-collector of customs at Moreton Bay. And Uncle Charles moved back to Jerrys Plains for a time where he lived and worked with his brother on a farm.

Mamma was growing large and heavy with another baby and she often groaned and rubbed her back as she boiled the bones for Father's creations. I do not think my mother had any close friends in Sydney. She devoted her time to Father and us children. Sometimes she talked of a friend from the ship, Mary Reardon, who worked as a housekeeper on a property on the Hawkesbury River, but I never met her. She would also receive letters from England from an old friend, Isabella Davenport. These letters, however, did not seem a pleasure to her, for Mamma would often cry quietly onto their pages.

My sister Mary was born on the 16th of February, 1846. I can remember the day well for I was bundled with little Robert to a neighbour's house, a Miss Pratt, a cantankerous, grumbling woman. She made us sit outside all day in her small plot of garden under the blazing sun with barely a bite to eat and, when Father came to fetch us at last, we were both red and raw with sunburn. But little Mary was a treasure to me. She lay in Mamma's arms like a dark-haired doll. I remember Robert reached to pull at her sparse locks with his chubby hand and I slapped it away hard.

"Ow!" he yelled. "She hit me, Mamma. She hit me!"

"You are a big brother now," Father told him firmly. "You need to 'elp your mother, Robert, and be gentle with your baby sister."

I did not need to be told the same thing, for I immediately took Mary on as my pet. I can remember how I would sit by her basket each day and stroke her hair, singing the lullaby Mamma had sung to me and Robert when we were babies:

Lullaby and good night, with roses bedight,
With lilies o'er spread is baby's wee bed,
Lay thee down now and rest, may thy slumber be blessed
Lay thee down now and rest, may thy slumber be blessed.

When she began to crawl, I would follow Mary around the shop floor, shaking a rattle that Father had made for her and talking to her when she pushed herself up with her podgy arms to sit: "Little Mary, little Mary, what a poppet you are! Does Mary want a kiss? Does Mary want a kiss from her big sister Menie?"

I was asleep in the bed beside Mary that night in December when she died. All three of us children had struggled with a cold and a lingering cough. It had settled on Mary's chest more than Robert's or mine, I suppose, and her cough had become hacking and violent throughout the day. I woke in the morning to find the bed empty and Mamma laying Mary's small body on a white cloth on the kitchen table, watering her baby limbs with heavy tears. My shock was like a weight bearing down on me.

"Your sister has gone to 'eaven, Menie," Father said as he bent from his great height to hug me.

Later that day, when the horror had spread through me, I tried to imagine a winged Mary sitting on a cloud beside the indistinct forms of my other sister and brother who had died.

Thirteen

Mamma was desperately sad after Mary's death. I can remember it was a long time before I saw her kind smile again but, while I was heartbroken, the intricacies of my young child's world soon overcame my sorrow, so that I forgot about my sister's death for whole days at a time.

I had developed a fascination with flowers and would beg to be allowed to walk through the bush in search of rare blooms. There was an older girl, Jane, whose father managed the grand post office near our shop, and whom I worshipped. She was easily persuaded to roam the bushland with me. I would take a cloth bag to put the flowers in and Jane would carry a big stick to kill any snakes we came across. I am surprised now Mamma had allowed these ventures, for she had a morbid fear of snakes and spiders, but I suppose she was so overcome with grief that she didn't think too much about it.

I collected red bottlebrush and waratah, grevillea with their spidery tendrils, delicate, white tea-tree flowers and the hanging, yellow-tipped Christmas bells. I would chatter to Jane as we walked in the shadows of the gums about my imaginings of fairies living in the hollows of trees or in the shells that washed up in the mud at Circular Wharf, later known as Circular Quay.

"You are a peculiar little person, Menie," Jane said to me one time, and I bristled at the remark.

"I am not peculiar at all!"

"I don't mean it in a cruel way. More as a compliment to your individuality."

I tried this new word silently on my lips. "Did you know that my father's a radical?" I said, thinking it had something to do with individuality and other important words like it.

"Yes, I do know, Menie. My father has told me. I don't think my father agrees with all your father's politics, though."

"Well, he should. My father is a very wise man."

Jane laughed. "Of course he is, Menie. All fathers are."

I thought this statement ridiculous. I definitely knew of some fathers who were not wise, like Sam Lynch's father who spent all his evenings drinking at The Whaler's Arms Hotel at The Rocks and had never composed a single line of poetry.

Father's business was doing well, and so we moved into larger premises on Hunter Street with a brass sign hanging from the shop entrance: *Henry Parkes Ivory Manufactory and Toy Warehouse* it read in shiny gold letters. I was particularly pleased with the move for I had a room to myself in the flat upstairs. Robert was a bother to me by then, always running about with a stick shaped like a gun and pretending to shoot with loud explosions as I tried to concentrate on my reading, so I was thrilled to have a space I could retreat to without him.

Mamma was pregnant again and I worried at the strain I saw on her face whenever she put her hand to her expanding stomach. I was almost nine years old and by now had a greater understanding of her troubles. I lay in bed at night thinking how terrible it was for Mamma and Father that only Robert and I had survived of their five children. I decided it was my mission to protect the new baby so that no cold or chill would assail them.

By then there was a new set of men who came to visit Father in the evenings. I did not realise at the time how embroiled Father was becoming in the politics of the colony, and perhaps Mamma did not, either. Chief amongst these men was Jabez King Heydon, an auctioneer on King Street. I did not call him or any of the others uncle because I did not bother with them as I had with Father's friends when I was younger. The other men I remember included the cripple James Wilshire, and Isaac Aaron, whom I believe Father had known from the Union back in Birmingham. I overheard Father telling Mamma about some of the other visitors, like John Dunmore Lang, Angus Mackay and Francis Cunningham. I remember many of these names because so many of them became prominent in public life in Sydney.

The one thing all these men had in common with my father was that they were radicals. They believed in the need for reform to reduce the power of the aristocracy and the squatters, the need for equal distribution of public lands, universal suffrage and public education. I did not understand the import of these phrases at the time, but they began to skip off my young tongue with ease on my walks through the bush with Jane.

I know Father always kept in close contact with his old, radical friend, Charles Harpur, mainly through letters, until the man's sad death in 1868 on his farm in the Eurobodalla Shire. Uncle Charles had accidentally shot and killed one of his sons the year before, and his shock and grief had led to his health failing. He left behind his wife of eighteen years, two remaining sons and two daughters.

There was an old Aboriginal man who used to terrify me as a child. He was known as Rickety Dickie, probably because of the shaky trolley he moved around on, both his legs being paralysed. He would growl at any child that passed him and, if I saw him scooting towards me with surprising speed, I would hide behind the nearest tree or run, panting, into the safety of our shop. When I was older, I realised he was probably in pain and alone in the world, and I felt guilty that I had run from him.

Father said we should feel remorse for the British treatment of the Aboriginals or 'the savages', as some called them. So many of them had died since Captain Cook had landed here. He told me that many of them had died of smallpox introduced by the British. And that in areas like the Hawkesbury, there were still reprisal killings between the British and the Aboriginals. When I was older, I found out about some of the terrible massacres of Aboriginals that had occurred. The year before I was born, about thirty Aboriginal men, women and children were killed at Myall Creek and, later, seven of the perpetrators were hung. It is horrid how cruel men can be to one another.

There were other infamous Aboriginal characters in Sydney when I was growing up. There was Cora Gooseberry and her sons, who sold fish and oysters on the streets. Cora wore a breastplate engraved with fish and her greying, frizzy hair reminded me of the dandelions I would blow on to make a wish.

And there was the tall Mahroot who wore his hair gummed and dreadlocked and lived in a hut beside Bunnerong Creek alongside other huts he had built and leased out to other Aboriginals – some of them from different clans who had moved to Botany Bay. Mahroot, I remember, was often in the company of white men, for he worked as a whaler alongside them and drank with them in the taverns. Other Aboriginals lived around Botany Bay sheltered only by a few pieces of bark balanced against a tree.

I became particularly curious about the Aboriginal women. I had so many questions. I can remember one day waiting on the bridge by the filthy Tank Stream while I watched a girl about my age expertly manoeuvring a bark canoe through the gentle ocean waves, catching fish with a hook and cooking one of them in the canoe on a fire burning on a clay pad. I wondered how she had learnt such skills. After drenching the fire with seawater, she came from the ocean carrying the canoe on her head with the line of fish hanging dripping over her shoulder. I bravely walked to stand in front of her. The girl looked at me without expression as I said, "Excuse me, what is your name?"

"Alinta," she said and didn't return my smile.

"Are you from here?" I pointed to the ocean, thinking it would show that I meant the area we called Sydney Cove.

The girl shook her head as she looked towards where I pointed to the sea. "No, I wasn't born on the water," she said in perfect English. "I am Eora. I was born here. This is my people's land." She swept her hand around to include the expanse of land around us and turned away from me abruptly.

Mary Edith was born on the night of the 3rd of March, 1848. A midwife had been called and, because it was too late to ask a neighbour to look after us, Robert and I lay sleepless in our beds, listening to Mamma's cries and moans. Eventually, I heard a gentle tap on my door and Robert appeared in his nightshirt.

"Menie, can I sleep with you? Please. I hate to hear Mamma screaming so."

I immediately pulled back my covers so he could climb in, relieved by his company. It was perhaps the closest we had ever been, lying there in each other's arms in the dark, listening to the terrible agonies of childbirth.

Mary Edith was a healthy, robust child. I remember thinking she was like an old, knowing soul. Her infant eyes seemed to twinkle with understanding and her cheeks were rosy with good health, which made me fear losing her less. When she could crawl, Mary would scamper so quickly and athletically across the boards of the shop floor that I thought she might escape out the door and into the street if a customer were not to close it.

Soon after Mary's birth, Father's visitors started to leave earlier in the evenings to give him time to write regular newspaper articles. I overheard Father explaining his and his visitors' plans to Mamma as she nursed young Mary in her arms.

"Robert Lowe 'as agreed to stand for us radicals in the seat of Sydney, to try to split the vote between those irascible conservatives William Wentworth and John Lamb. Lowe is no radical 'imself, but 'e is the perfect foil. 'Is eloquence and wit will match any of Wentworth's bluster."

"Is Robert Lowe the albino, Henry?" asked Mamma. "The little, wiry man with white hair? I saw him in the Domain one time and thought he might be blown over by the breeze."

Father laughed. "Yes, that is 'im – 'Pink-Eyed Bob'. Perhaps 'e looks no warrior, my dear, but in matters of turns of phrase and clever jibes, 'e is our man. 'E does not support our principle of universal suffrage, but in all other matters 'e is with us!"

"Will that be enough, Henry?"

"I think so. I do. We do not need to talk of the policies 'e doesn't support, only those that 'e does, and 'e is a known public figure who can stand up to the likes of Wentworth."

It was several days after my ninth birthday when Father charged through the door one evening, waving his hat about his head and racing to Mamma to swing her about the room. I laughed despite my surprise at my father's uncharacteristic behaviour.

"'E won!" he called, laughing. "Lowe won! 'E was only just behind Wentworth! They both 'ave a seat! But 'e beat Lamb. Lowe 'as a seat in the Legislative Council as our representative!"

And then, spying my clapping hands, Father put Mamma down and ran to me, flinging me round and round until I was giddy and breathless. It was a wonderful feeling to be in this great man's arms.

The next night, as my family sat at the kitchen table eating mutton stew, Father read aloud an article he had written in the newspaper *The Atlas*, after the victory.

"That was a day when public virtue sprung up, as from the four winds of 'eaven," he said in solemn tones, "and grew a mighty thing, before the great 'ands suspected even its existence. That was the birthday of Australian Democracy." He thumped the table when he'd finished and I felt a pride for this amazing father of mine such that I had never felt before.

Washday was Wednesday and Father was left to man the shop alone. I would go with Mamma into the yard that we shared with the other shops around us, balancing the washing basket with its bundle of clothes. Robert was always a bother on these days, running about and almost knocking me as I carried the steaming pots of water from the kitchen fire to empty into the huge tub. And when Mary was crawling, there was always the fear of her getting under my feet and tripping me so that I might scald myself or her.

Mamma rigorously scrubbed the clothes on the washboard with the bar of foaming laundry soap. "You are a blessing to me, Menie," she would say, smiling as she wiped the damp hair from her face with the back of her hand. And later I would help her to wring the dripping clothes through the mangle and hang them on the clothesline there.

I remember it was always a problem if it rained on a Wednesday, for every other day was allocated as wash day for another family in our row of shops.

Mamma kept a small garden plot at the back of our shop where she grew kidney potatoes, cauliflower and peas. We also had chooks and it became Robert's job to collect the eggs in the morning and distribute them equally between ourselves and the neighbouring families.

As I grew older, I would go to the marketplace for Mamma each day to get mutton from the butcher or fish from the fishmonger or, if I was brave and they were about, from Cora Gooseberry or one of her sons. I loved these ventures, walking along the winding cobbled streets of Sydney or down the worn paths between the fields to the water and Port Jackson's jagged cliffs. If there weren't other tasks for me at home, I would go first to the Botanic Gardens on the headland or venture into the steep climbs of The Rocks, with its whitewashed cottages and bright geranium bushes.

Other times I would walk through Hyde Park and along Macquarie Street towards the Domain. The buildings there were magnificent. I would stare at the sandstone walls of Hyde Park Barracks, and the less impressive Rum Hospital – later to become The Mint – with its second-storey veranda where sick convicts used to sit in the sun. Then I would pass the grand sandstone buildings of the Sydney Infirmary and Parliament House, and the single-spired St James Church across the road.

The Botanic Gardens was my favourite place, though. I loved the masses of wildflowers there and the spreading canopies of the banyan trees, which were later called Moreton Bay figs. Sometimes I would sit on the carved sandstone of Mrs Macquarie's Chair, looking out onto the harbour and thinking of how the former governor's wife used to sit there and dream of ships sailing from England.

FOURTEEN

Throughout most of our childhoods and into our teenage years, Mamma set each of her children lessons in mathematics, literature, grammar, spelling and all the other areas that Father thought crucial to a solid education. National schools had opened in Fort Street and Crown Street in Sydney, but Father did not think the instruction at these schools was competent or consistent at the time, and so the role of educating us went to Mamma. She could be a hard taskmaster when needed, which was often the case with Robert, but I was a willing and diligent student.

I almost certainly became interested in writing because of Father's influence. He had been a writer ever since I could remember. Many of his poems have been published and he wrote political editorials for a range of newspapers, even for John Fairfax's conservative *The Sydney Morning Herald*. When I was just three years old, Father had a book of verse published called *Stolen Moments*. Some of its poems had been written in Birmingham or on the ship to New South Wales, but many were written during his time in Sydney. My favourite was, of course, the poem he wrote for me: 'To My Daughter'...

Clarinda and Henry

The billows of the huge Pacific,
The mystic winds with music wild,
Thy yearning mother's beatific
And anxious prayer, were all, my child,
To welcome thee to life—
A sunbeam 'mid the tempest's strife!

I have myself had some stories and editorials published over the years under pseudonyms. But I do not believe any of these, or, indeed, any of Father's other writings, were ever as powerful as the speeches that he wrote and presented over the years of his political career. I did not hear many of his performances, but I was the first person he sent a copy of the volume *Speeches, by Henry Parkes* published in 1876. Even now, as I read his speeches, I can imagine my father reciting the words with evocative, varied cadence and inflexions in his booming Midlands accent, dropping his 'h's:

> *I think it must be manifest to all thoughtful men that there are questions projecting themselves upon our attention which cannot be satisfactorily dealt with by any one of the individual Governments. I regard this occasion, therefore, with great interest, because I believe it will inevitably lead to a more permanent federal understanding.*

And then my favourite part of this particular speech in support of federation, in which I'm sure Father spoke with exaggerated drama, eyeing individuals in the audience with a firm gaze:

> *I do not mean to say that when you leave this room tonight you will see a new constellation of six stars in the heavens; I do not startle your imagination by asking you to look for the footprints of six giants in the morning dew, when the night rolls away; but this I feel certain of, that the mother-country will regard this congress of the colonies just in the same light as a father and mother may view the conduct of their children, when they first observe those children beginning to look out for homes and connections for themselves.*

My father was a naturally brilliant man, as he has often told me his mother was before him. It is still amazing to me that he had very little education.

But once again, I am getting ahead of myself, for the time of which I am still writing was before even his first political speech.

One of Father's first speeches was made at a great public meeting at Circular Wharf when the convict ship the *Hashemy* dropped anchor in June 1849. I was almost ten years old and aware of the bustle of the preceding days as Father composed the anti-transportation speech for the merchant John Lamb, whom he had previously opposed and defeated through Robert Lowe. But they were now allies on the issue of stopping the convict ships. We were visited at all hours by various enthusiastic, fiery men such as Mr Lamb and Robert Campbell.

"Even Fairfax in *The 'erald* is claiming a breach of faith by the English parliament under Earl Grey!" Father had exclaimed to Mamma on one of the previous nights. "Our Legislative Council only agreed to accept more convicts, which Grey is calling 'exiles' to try to soften the blow, if an equal number of free immigrants were sent out. The *'ashemy* 'as only convicts!"

I know from Father's reports of the mass meeting that the speakers stood in the rain on an omnibus as a platform and that, at the conclusion, a delegation walked to Government House to present the protest resolutions to Governor FitzRoy.

"But the Domain gates were closed and guarded, barring us from entering. It was outrageous!" Father told us that night. "FitzRoy 'as agreed to only six of us presenting the petition to 'im at a time that suits 'im. Tomorrow at two o'clock!"

The following evening, Father was even more furious when he told us that Governor FitzRoy had spoken to them with disdain and refused to send the convicts back. I sat with Mamma and listened to his tirade in a state of semi-shock. I had known my father was a passionate man, but I had never heard him speak with as much anger as on that night.

Father was part of other protest rallies against transportation and became a leading member of the Anti-Transportation League. He even approached the Chief Justice's wife, Lady Stephen, to ask her to sign a petition from the women of New South Wales to the British Government to plead the case for the end of transportation, which Mamma also signed along with around twelve thousand other women. Eventually, transportation to New South Wales ended in 1852.

My father's political persona was always a mystery to me. I tried to follow his career in parliament as closely as I could, but the ever-increasing hours and days he was away from us over the years fostered an unexpressed resentment within me. Mamma's devotion to Father was definitely tested at times, although she rarely wavered openly except for one time when he was absent for more than a year. But that was later.

One of my favourite memories is of a visit to the Victoria Theatre in Pitt Street with Mamma and Father as a celebration for my tenth birthday. Robert and Mary were to be minded by my older friend Jane. I had never experienced a play or, indeed, any proper outing, and, from Father's reaction, I wondered if he had, either.

I had passed the exterior of this magnificent building on many occasions after it was built the previous year, but it was the interior that still stays bright in my memory. The ceiling was decorated with panels painted in golden geometric figures and filigree and the upper and dress circles swept above us with elaborately painted balconies. I stood in the pit, peeking around the mass of people until the lamps were dimmed and the curtain drawn with a swish and I stared with wide eyes as Shakespeare's *Othello* began. It was a magical few hours as the actors' voices carried towards me and I caught glimpses of lighted faces or flowing robes. Father was ecstatic afterwards as we walked the short distance to our home.

"Desdemona was remarkable, and so beautiful," he said. "'Er face was like an angel's and it was as though she 'ad actually died on stage, don't you think? And the melody of 'er voice as she spoke!"

After that night, I secretly nurtured a dream for many years that I would become an actress and come to play Desdemona in a theatre to a worshipping crowd.

Mamma had another baby on the 14th of December, 1849. Milton was a russet-haired boy with almond-shaped eyes like Father's.

"He reminds me a lot of our first child, Thomas," Mamma confided in me one day as I sat with her in the morning sunshine while Milton slept in his basket beside us. "He had your father's eyes, too, just like Milton."

I did not know what to say to this intimacy, but I remember feeling flushed with pleasure that Mamma would share this with my ten year old self. I knew she would not have shared it with Robert.

As I aged, my relationship with Mamma became more and more one of a close friend. I suppose this was partly due to her loneliness and the fact I was the eldest girl by many years, and as a result of the years that we spent together caring for the younger children. But it was also due to Mamma's sweet personality. She was always a kind, patient, sympathetic woman.

Many years later, when I was first married and moved away to Pambula, I missed her intensely. I missed my father, too, of course, but never with the ardour that I missed Mamma. He was an absent figure for so much of our lives, caught up in his man's world.

I can remember the argument I heard between Mamma and Father soon after Milton was born when I was sitting in my room reading with my door open. Father wanted to expand the business to establish branches of his fine goods in Maitland and Geelong, an area that was soon to become part of the new colony of Victoria.

"I do not think it wise, Henry," Mamma said in a firmer tone than usual. "You will have to borrow to finance these other businesses and you will have no control of them from such a distance."

"Angus McKay 'as already agreed to manage the Geelong store, Clarinda. You must trust me on matters of business. I know things didn't go well when I 'ad the shop in Birming'am, but the business 'ere in Sydney is thriving."

"So let it thrive, Henry. There is no need to build an empire."

There was a pause in the conversation.

"Clarinda," I heard my father say in a steely voice, "you are a woman. You must trust me on this. I will become a great businessman if you will but let me. You cannot 'old me back like this."

Mamma did not reply, and when I came into the kitchen a short time later, I found her alone and sitting in her usual chair, knitting with a fury in her movements that I had not seen before.

"Are you all right, Mamma?" I asked, hugging her skirted legs. "I know you and Father have quarrelled."

She sighed. "He is a great man, your father. I must trust him, he is right. But I worry so. I could not bear for us to be as poor as we once were, particularly now that there is you, Robert, Mary *and* Milton to care for."

My father should have listened to Mamma, and he apologised and said so later, for the branches in Maitland and Geelong, even during their short lives, did not prosper. I do not think Father was ever a good businessman. His mind was too set on higher ambitions and principles to be shackled by the mundane daily matters that an ongoing business required.

It was after the businesses in Maitland and Geelong had closed that Father began to take me on Sunday trips on the harbour to the North

Shore or Pyrmont to collect wildflowers. I still wonder at these trips, for just as they began unexpectedly, they ended suddenly and to my great disappointment.

On the first occasion, Father insisted I come with him to Campbell's Wharf after church and there he hired a small, blue rowboat. I sat in the boat while he rowed it with great vigour across the harbour. Sydney Harbour has always been a beautiful place with its rugged sandstone cliffs and outcrops of bushland growing in parts right to the water's edge, but this was the first time I had seen it from the water. It was a breathtaking sight, with Sydney Town's yellow sandstone buildings and whitewashed cottages, and Government House atop rising ground in the centre with the grasses of the Domain stretching below and around it. I was lulled by the gentle rocking of the boat, the splash of water against its wooden hull and the rhythmic puffing of Father as he rowed.

Eventually, we reached the sandy shore and Father dragged the boat, with me in it, from the water's edge and then gave me his hand to help me from my seat. I wondered then if there ever could be a man as wonderful as him. We walked through the bush and I gathered flannel flowers, Christmas bells and bottlebrush. I even found a rare golden waratah nestled in the fallen bark and undergrowth. A kookaburra cackled from his perch in a stringybark.

Father was always quiet on these trips, watching and following me through the bush until I turned to him, smiling, and showed him my cloth bag was full. And then we would make our way back to the boat and begin our trip home.

These were magical occasions for me. I suspect now that Father wanted to escape from the hustle of the city to ponder on his next ambitious venture. Or perhaps it was simply that he needed time away from the younger children. Milton was always a grizzly baby crying for Mamma and sleeping fitfully.

Poor little Milton. I wonder what he would have become had he lived. I remember those terrible days in late January 1851, when Mamma was pale-faced and red-eyed from her sleepless nights, trying to care for him in his fever. I tried to help as much as I could, cooking dinner and playing with Mary so she would not be a bother to Mamma. But on the night of the nineteenth, I sat with Mamma beside Milton's crib as she cooled his burning brow with a damp cloth and I read pages aloud from the Gospel of John to distract her and pass the long, agonising hours. Suddenly, Mamma gave a sharp gasp and lifted the cloth. I followed her gaze to Milton's grey face, and it was as though she and I held our breaths for an eternity, waiting to hear an intake of breath from the child.

"Oh, Milton! No!" Mamma cried and pulled his limp body to her. I will never forget the look of utter despair on her face as she held him.

When Father came home in the early hours of the morning, Mamma was in an exhausted sleep on the settee beside me while I was wide-eyed and numb, waiting for his return.

"What are you doing up, Menie?" he said when he saw me. "Aven't you slept?"

I choked on the words as I told him. "It's Milton, Father. Milton has died," I said and watched, horrified, as he staggered against a chair nearby and sobbed.

Mamma realised she was pregnant again a few months after Milton's death. She told me before Father.

"Oh, Menie, I don't know whether to laugh or cry, but I think there will be another little Parkes before the year is out," she said and hugged me tightly.

I did not know what to say for I felt a terrible foreboding in my eleven year old soul.

Before the terrible night of Milton's death, Father had begun a new and brave enterprise. He had begun a newspaper, the *Empire*, using the printing shop of a friend to publish the weekly broadsheet.

"It's through the press we can 'ave the greatest impact agitating for change," he told me as we sat around the kitchen table one morning. "There's no truly liberal newspaper in Sydney. We need one."

"But will we ever see you, Father? How will you keep the fancy wares shop going *and* make a newspaper as well?" I asked, and noticed Father glance guiltily towards Mamma.

"We'll probably see Father more," she replied for him. "Once he sets up his own printing shop next door – after the Davidsons have moved out."

I was doubtful. And the night of Milton's death proved my fears were correct. By then Father had decided to make the newspaper into a daily and the first of these was to appear the next morning. As a result, Father had stayed at the printing press until the early hours while I waited to tell him the tragic news.

His late hours were to become a regular occurrence, even when the printing equipment he ordered from England arrived in March and he set up his editorial office in a shed behind our fancy goods shop, and then later in the downstairs rooms of our flat. It was true he was still at home during these long hours, but he was too busy to spend much time with us.

Mamma bore her grief hard once more after losing Milton. I found comfort in young Mary whom I had begun to call Polly. I suppose it is strange we had pet names so different from our real names, me as Menie and Mary as Polly. Her nickname began its life when I called her 'my poppet' and then 'my pocket-poppet', which was followed by my singing her the song 'Poor Polly Pocket'. The name Polly stuck and my sister never hesitated to answer to either this or her Christian name.

During the hot summer of 1851, I would often take Mary with me to the cool of the Botanic Gardens. It was a long walk for her three year old legs so I would carry her most of the journey. Sometimes on the way we'd buy an ice from a street vendor, and on one occasion there was a mechanical pipe organ on George Street playing dance tunes. Mary became mesmerised by a woman and man who waltzed about the street, side stepping the horse-drawn carriages and omnibuses.

When we arrived home from these trips, we would usually find Robert playing cricket on the street with the other local boys. Poor Mamma would be sitting with her Bible in her lap, staring at the wall, her thoughts no doubt on Milton and the other babies she had lost.

"Would you like me to make you a cup of tea, Mamma?" I would say to try and cajole her from her sorrowing, and Mamma would physically flinch as her attention returned to us, before then reaching for Mary.

I know Father grieved for Milton and perhaps it was partly to relieve his pain that he threw himself so completely into his work. By day he would man the fancy wares shop, although he spent much of this time jotting down notes for the *Empire* or having discussions with men such as Daniel Deniehy, David Blair and James Harpur – Uncle Charles's brother, who wrote articles for the paper and visited Father during the day and in the evening.

FIFTEEN

John Fairfax came to give his condolences one Sunday afternoon shortly after Milton's death. I had never before met the joint owner of *The Sydney Morning Herald*, but Father had often spoken of him as a gentleman of strong character despite his conservative political views. I remember Mr Fairfax shook Father's hand and bowed gallantly to Mamma and me. I made tea for him and Father because Mamma disappeared into the yard, supposedly to feed the chickens but really, I expect, to hide her tears.

"Well, 'enry," Mr Fairfax said in his gruff Midlands accent. "Warwickshire should be proud of the Sydney newspaper business, with both you and I 'aving 'ailed from its valleys."

My father laughed. "Yes, John. But 'ow did we end up with such different views then?"

"Yes, the *Empire* is not to my taste, that's for sure. The writing is good but not the politics you espouse."

"Well, I would say the same of yours and Kemp's 'erald," Father replied.

I handed them each their tea in our best china and Mr Fairfax winked at me as I escaped to my bedroom. I left the door open so I could hear the rest of their conversation.

"I see you've made the *Empire* into a daily now, 'enry. I suppose that's because our *Sydney Morning 'erald* is a daily, too?" Mr Fairfax continued.

199

"That is one of the reasons, John. There needs to be a foil to your conservative propaganda in town."

Mr Fairfax guffawed and I heard the chink of his cup as it hit the saucer. "I wasn't too thrilled, 'enry, when I 'eard young John McKelly 'ad left our business to work for you," he said.

"I do apologise for that, John, but I needed someone with experience," Father said simply.

"Business is business, I know. But I'd like to make a bit of a gentleman's agreement with you," Mr Fairfax said.

My father's voice sounded suspicious, "Oh yes? And what might that be?"

"I am a religious man, 'enry, and it is against my beliefs to have the paper printed on the Sabbath. Would you agree to not printing the *Empire* on Sundays? We can compete on all other days, but I would like your promise as a Christian man yourself, no doubt, not to 'ave Sunday editions of your paper."

There was a brief pause before Father answered. "That seems fair. I can definitely agree to that, John."

"Charles Kemp and I would also like you to agree to the same price of thruppence per issue and the same demi-broadsheet size for our two newspapers. We think this arrangement would be wise so we don't overwork ourselves trying to outdo one another."

"Mm," Father pondered. "I suppose that is fair. Yes, I will agree to both of those suggestions, too. It will keep our papers on an even footing at least."

The meeting ended soon after this, with Mr Fairfax extending his condolences again and asking Father to convey his best to Mamma. "And thank young Menie for the perfect cup of tea, 'enry. She must be a great 'elp," he said as he left.

One of the reasons Father had begun to make the *Empire* a daily newspaper was to outdo the recently formed weekly *The Press*. He was convinced his political friends, John Dunmore Lang and James Wilshire, had established the paper because they did not believe he was capable of being the spokesman for the liberal cause. I remember Father was very bitter about this. He had campaigned for Mr Wilshire at a by-election in 1850 and even more recently for Mr Lang in the seat of Sydney, which he had won. Mr Lang had presented Father with a gold watch at a formal dinner held to celebrate his victory.

"I wrote some of 'is speeches," Father said to Mamma indignantly while I sat at the table beside him doing arithmetic on a slate. "What a 'umbug to think I can't run a paper for our cause. It is because of my lack of formal education, I think, that 'e insults me so."

Father's decision to compete with *The Press* by increasing publication of the *Empire* proved wise, for *The Press* closed within a year while the *Empire* continued to be Sydney's liberal newspaper.

Father set up an editorial office in the lower floor of our Hunter Street flat, so that our living quarters were greatly reduced, and he hired a clerk and thirty-three compositors to set the type each night. We saw little of Father. Often, he would not join us for dinner but would eat cheese and bread in his small office in the front of the main editorial office, and huge slices of bacon from a side he hung from the ceiling there.

As I lay in bed in the early hours of the morning, my dreams would be interrupted by the endless whirring and clanking of the printing machine downstairs as it rolled off the paper ready for its five o'clock release. Sometimes I'd be woken by the chatter of the compositors or the people waiting outside the shop to grab the first copies hot off the press.

Father even hired a group of men to sail in a small sloop out beyond the harbour to intercept ships arriving from England and gather any British newspapers they brought so that the *Empire* would be the first to relate news of the homeland to an Australian audience. And so, at any hour, a man might arrive at our flat, banging on the door to deliver the British papers. The *Empire* was even the first newspaper to report the discovery of gold around Wellington in western New South Wales.

Father rarely slept now that the newspaper was thriving, and when he did, it was often in the chair at his desk. Even though he was rarely absent from our Hunter Street premises, it was a lonely time for Mamma. She grew heavy in her pregnancy and I spent my afternoons, after completing my lessons, helping her around the flat and with Mary. At twelve years old, I was already a competent cook. I would make flavoursome stews and roasts and even a delicious soufflé from a recipe I had found in a journal.

On a Friday late in October, I arrived home from a trip to the market to find Mamma in bed cradling a fair, blue-eyed baby girl.

"Look at the present we 'ave for you, Menie!" Father exclaimed as I walked through the door. "A little sister, Lily Maria. Your mother 'as done us proud again."

Mamma was flushed in her pleasure. I had not seen her looking so happy since before Milton's death, eight months earlier. I was secretly relieved I hadn't been there for her labouring. Her contractions had started shortly after I'd left and I had dawdled through The Rocks after my purchases, and this had been a quicker labour than before.

Lily was a sweet child. She was never robust like Mary, but was angelically quiet and calm. Her temperament was probably the most like Mamma's of all us children.

It was soon after Lily's birth that Father announced one evening that his nephew Tom Parkes was to sail from England to New South Wales.

"Mamma and I are quite agreed that Tom is going to buy the fancy wares business from me," Father said. I was shocked for I had heard nothing of this arrangement until now.

"But why, Father? How will we live?" I asked.

"You see, Menie, if 'e buys it 'e'll be paying us for the stock and the fixtures. And I won't be so run off my feet with both the shop and the *Empire* to manage," Father explained.

"Yes, Menie. There's no need to worry. It will mean your father has more time to focus on his newspaper and family," Mamma said as she smiled at Father.

I had heard much of 'Young Tom', as Father called him, although there was only about eleven years between them. He was the son of Father's eldest brother, Thomas, who had died when Father was quite young. Tom had been raised alongside my father by my aunts and grandmother. I suppose he and Father had been like brothers. We were expecting his arrival in Sydney sometime in January or February 1852. I remember the time as one of great excitement.

I was manning the fancy wares shop the Saturday afternoon that he arrived. A tall, blond man came lumbering into the shop, dragging a portmanteau behind him. When he saw me, he grinned widely. "Why, you must be young Clarinda," he said.

For a moment I was disgruntled at the forwardness of the man, until I suddenly realised whom he must be. "Cousin Tom? Is it you?" I asked and jumped from my seat behind the counter. "Father, Father!" I called into the flat behind, where Father was furiously writing the first draft of an editorial for Monday's edition of the *Empire*.

"Just a moment, Menie," Father said crossly at the interruption.

"But it's Tom. It's Tom Parkes here in the shop!" I called back and, before I could finish the sentence, Father came barrelling into the shop and grabbed the man by the shoulders.

"Young Tom, is it you?" he said, his voice trembling with emotion. "Oh, Tommy, my lad, it's so good to see you."

The two men hugged each other. I was a little surprised at my father's exuberance at the time, but I understand now how momentous their meeting was. Tom was the only one of his family Father had seen since he had left Birmingham all those years ago.

It was several months later that Father had a letter from Birmingham to say his sister Eliza had died on the very day Tom had arrived. She had contracted pneumonia after a heavy cold and died at home with Aunt Sarah and Aunt Maria by her side.

I remember regular discussions concerning the explorer Ludwig Leichhardt around this time. Back in 1844 he had conducted an expedition to Port Essington in the far north of Australia. He became famous when he returned to Sydney in March 1846. In 1848, Mr Leichhardt set out on another expedition, this time government-funded, intending to reach the far west of Australia. However, he and six other men – including two Aboriginal guides, along with seven horses, twenty mules and fifty bullocks – disappeared. I know that in 1852 the government sent a search party to try to find them, but to this day their remains have never been found. It is thought they perished somewhere in the desert in central Australia.

Father's first attempt to stand for a seat on the Legislative Council was not a success. This was in early 1853 and his defeat at the hands of William Thurlow, a conservative and friend of William Wentworth's, laid him low.

"Do they think I am not good enough to stand for parliament, Clarinda?" I remember him saying to Mamma one night. "Because of my 'umble beginnings?"

"It doesn't matter what they think. It only matters that you are a great and principled man, Henry, and that you would be a brilliant politician," Mamma said.

"I suppose it does matter what *they* think, if *they* are the people who are voting," Father answered and shook his head. I did not often hear my father speak so pessimistically and with such a lack of confidence and I went to sit at his feet and hug his long legs. "Ah, Menie, your father 'as shamed 'imself," he said. "I thought I was better than I am. I must be content to be the editor of a newspaper to support the liberal politicians, and not to flaunt myself as one of them."

"Oh no, Father! You are as good as any of them! I don't think you should give up," I said firmly. "You always tell *me* not to give up."

He laughed lightly. "Oh, Menie, at times you 'ave to accept when something's beyond you, though."

But, as history shows, my father did not, in fact, give up.

Mamma was pregnant again that year. Tom Parkes was living with us, finding his feet in the fancy wares business whose sign had changed from *Henry Parkes* to *Thomas Parkes*. I was now a pimply, gangly, fourteen year old girl. Robert was ten, Mary was five and Lily was not yet two.

I remember I fancied one of the young compositors who worked for father, Charles Belford. He must have been at least five years older than me and I don't think I ever spoke to him except in polite greeting. I was moonstruck by his strong, angular features and the deep green of his eyes. I began to make regular trips to the editorial office just to get a glimpse of this rugged man, using a kiss for Father or a surprise cup of tea or piece of newly baked cake as my excuse. I don't know if Father ever guessed at my infatuation, and I remember it ended because of my horror at Charles Belford's involvement in the compositors' strike, which affected Father so greatly.

Father never told me the details of the court case that resulted from this dispute, but I overheard the distraught conversation between him and his overseer, John McKelly, in early January 1854, when Mamma was due to give birth again any day. The compositors, I knew, were paid according to the number of letters or numbers they set, and it seemed they objected to the extra work and time resulting in reduced pay when they had to set occasional tables, for these – by necessity – had more spaces and fewer letters or numbers than normal type. There was one compositor I'd never liked, called John Bone, who seemed to be the ringleader.

"He's demanding an extra fifty percent, Henry!" I heard Mr McKelly say to Father in his office. "When I was at *The Sydney Morning Herald*, Mr Fairfax refused to pay extra for typesetting in tabular form. That's the precedent. That's what we should stick to."

"You're the one who knows this business, John," Father said. "I'll go by what you say. But perhaps the easiest way to resolve this is simply to stop using tables at all. We can present the information in another way. I'll suggest this to the men now."

I heard Father's deep, booming voice from the main editorial office a few minutes later. "You know I treat you men fairly, but, as Mr McKelly says, we need to follow the precedent 'ere. I am 'appy for the *Empire* not to use tabular form if it is to cause conflict. Alternatively, this could be resolved by a meeting of all in the trade so that we can be in agreement with the other papers."

Later, I went down to the editorial office and was surprised to see only around half of the usual compositors were there and that among the missing men was my beloved Charles Belford.

"Where are all the men, Father? What has happened?" I asked.

Father rubbed his eyes and sighed. "The others are refusing to work, Menie," he said, shaking his head. "They refuse to work unless I pay them extra for setting tabular form. I even agreed to not use any tables, but they ignored me. I spoke quite firmly to them saying they were acting like 'ighwaymen and that it was attempted robbery. But even George Dick, whom I employed as a favour to 'is sister when 'e wasn't even fully trained as a compositor, 'as walked off the job. 'E said 'e 'ad no choice when the others 'ad agreed."

The following night, several of father's journalist friends came to help the compositors who had stayed on the job so that the *Empire* could still roll off the press by five o'clock in the morning. I had planned to help in any way I could, but that night Mamma went into labour.

It was a terrible night. It must have been a nightmare for Father. I find it incredible, now, that he managed to get the paper out at all. I was too young to go traipsing through the streets at night, so Tom went to fetch the midwife and I stayed with Mamma. I was frightened and unsure of what I should do to help as I watched her tense in pain with each contraction. Mary and Lily were asleep, thankfully, and Robert was helping Father as best he could with the paper downstairs.

I spent the night following the orders of the midwife, heating water and dripping cool water into Mamma's mouth from a cloth, while Father worked furiously downstairs to get the *Empire* printed. Eventually, when the paper had been completed and the delivery boy had collected it, Father came to Mamma's side.

Annie Thomasine Parkes was born the evening before the keys reading *Monday, the 10th of January* dried on the printing press.

I was surprised Mamma agreed to the name Annie for her beautiful, elfin daughter after her earlier assertion that I would never have been called Ann because of her terrible stepmother back in Birmingham. Many years later when I asked her about this, she claimed she had never said such a thing. Memories can fade, I suppose. I wonder now which of us recalled this conversation correctly.

On the day after Annie was born, Father consulted lawyers before laying charges of criminal conspiracy on all seventeen of the compositors who had gone on strike. The committal hearing was held the next day and the men were committed to stand trial before a judge and jury in the New South Wales Criminal Court. I know both John Fairfax and Charles Kemp appeared as witnesses during the trial in February and that, even though *The Sydney Morning Herald* later berated Father for bringing the charges at all, in court both men spoke in favour of Father's actions, although Mr Fairfax did add that he wondered now if the trade should change its position regarding tabular form.

All seventeen of the compositors were convicted and spent varying amounts of time in Darlinghurst Gaol. The longest of these sentences was for John Bone and another man, William Cunningham, who were imprisoned for six weeks. I believe Charles Belford was only gaoled for a night.

I will always be proud that my father paid the bail for two of the compositors when they could not afford it themselves. It shows, I think, this was a matter of principle for him, and that he bore no personal malice towards the men. I was perplexed, however, over the fact Father had fought these men so vehemently, given that he advocated the rights of working-class men. I asked him about this soon after.

"Menie, I agree completely that the men should be paid fairly. But I 'ad to follow the precedent in the trade. If I 'ad not, the other newspaper proprietors would 'ave strung me up. And the compositors knew I was 'appy to 'ave the issue decided by a meeting of the trade. You see, the principle I was fighting for, Menie, was that an employer should not be controlled by the bullying tactics of 'is employees. That, like any man or group of men, I and other employers have rights, too."

"But you were a union member, Father. Isn't being part of a union in effect forcing fairness on an employer?" I persisted.

My father could have reacted angrily, but his voice stayed calm as he explained his reasoning to try and make me understand. "No, Menie. Unions 'elp represent employees' interests. Every man 'as the right to representation. When I was a part of the Birming'am Union we never used tactics of force or bullying. I believe that later, when the Union joined forces with the London Working Men's Association and they called themselves Chartists, intimidation became more common and there were lots of violent riots in Birming'am. I 'ate to think that my own brothers, James and George, might 'ave been a part of them.

"But that was when I 'ad left England. I still believe strongly in the importance of unions and, indeed, I 'ave never objected to my compositors 'aving a union or union meetings. In fact, I 'ave encouraged it. But just as they 'ave rights, so do I and other employers. They were trying to deny my rights unfairly."

My father was always very sure of his own logic and principles. I did not always understand them fully.

SIXTEEN

I wonder sometimes at the reasons for God choosing some of us Parkes children to live, while others he called to his side. How did he pick who would survive through infancy? Surely it wasn't just a meaningless, arbitrary selection. I still find it difficult to understand why my sweet and gentle two year old sister Lily had to die just months after her baby sister Annie was born.

I can still remember Lily's coy smile. One corner of her lip would rise higher than the other and her chubby cheeks would dimple. I would tickle her tummy and blow raspberries there until she pushed me away in a fit of giggles. Lily was Mary's shadow once she could walk, toddling along behind her on wobbling legs. "Mena, Mena," she would call me, once she'd started talking. "Mena kiss."

"Does Lily want a kiss from Mena?" I would tease. "Do you want a kiss from your big sister Mena?"

"Yes, kiss, kiss. Mena kiss."

I would sweep Lily up and peck her soft cheek over and over until she was giggling and wriggling out of my arms.

She had a fever when she died, just as Milton had. Mamma held Lily in her arms throughout each day of that week and I looked after baby Annie. The sense of foreboding I had felt when Mamma had first told me she was pregnant so soon after Milton's death now seemed justified. On the day she died, Lily lay in Mamma's arms, her eyelids fluttering and her cheeks aflame. I tried to feed her little pieces of bread soaked in milk, but she would not swallow my offerings and I had to take them from her mouth to stop her from choking.

When she passed into a deeper unconsciousness, Mamma rocked her gently and cried. Lily's breathing became lighter and then, just as Milton's had done, it stopped. The only sound was Mamma's sobs, until Annie began to howl from the basket beside me and I picked my baby sister up and took her from the room so Mamma could grieve in silence.

I cannot imagine the desperation Mamma must have felt when she thought of the children she had lost: Thomas and Clarinda before me, the first Mary, Milton and now Lily. Father, too, must have felt the pain.

Despite his protestations that he would not run for a seat on the Legislative Council again, Father began campaigning for the seat of Sydney the month after Lily died. I think that embarking on this busy venture helped him deal with his grief, just as he had thrown himself into work at the *Empire* after Milton's death. But it was difficult for Mamma.

Father was away from the flat and his editorial office most days during that month. His election committee, which included Tom Parkes, met each day to campaign at The Royal Exchange in Gresham Street. The seat being contested had been vacated by William Wentworth who had sailed to England in an attempt to have his Constitution Bill passed through parliament there. My father was deeply against this Bill, which included provision for an Upper House with its members appointed by the governor. Father's opponent, Charles Kemp – the recently retired proprietor of *The Sydney Morning Herald* – supported Wentworth's Bill, and this became the linchpin of their debate.

After his long, busy days of campaigning, Father would come home to the editorial office and work through most of the night in order to publish the *Empire* by five o'clock each morning. I don't think he slept more than three hours a night during this time.

I remember the morning in early May when, after Father had won the seat of Sydney by a resounding majority, I found Mamma lying on her bed with her face in her pillow, quietly crying.

"Oh, Mamma, what is the matter?" I asked as I came to her side, but I already knew the answer to my question.

She turned her face towards me, her eyes red and puffy. "It's so many things, Menie. I don't know how I am to continue without Henry."

"But, Mamma, it is not as though Father has died," I said.

"No, no, of course not. It's just we will see him even less now. I feel so alone. I am so desperate, Menie. Annie is still so young and Lily... Lily..." She broke into a fit of sobbing.

I hugged Mamma until she cried herself out.

"I must not let your father or the younger children see me crying like this. I am overreacting. I am sorry, Menie. I must stop my complaining. I am just being silly."

"Oh, Mamma. You are anything but silly," I said and hugged her again.

Father entered into his role on the Legislative Council with fervour. He was now the Honourable Henry Parkes M.C. But with this title came no financial reward. Only cabinet members were paid an income. My father's unceasing energy has often amazed me. During this first office, he attended every council meeting and served on numerous select committees. And still he continued to produce his daily newspaper. We saw him rarely.

I was immensely proud of Father, as was Mamma.

"Who would have thought," she said to me one day as we sat together on stools overlooking our garden plot, scrubbing the potatoes for dinner, "that your father, who was once slaving on the roads and in factories as a boy in England, and who came to Australia penniless, would reach such heights!"

She wrote to her brother in England to tell him the news so that Father's achievement could be conveyed to her own father. She read to me part of Uncle John Varney's reply.

"'Father and Stepmamma were surprised, as I am. Father said to send his congratulations.'" Mamma folded the letter and said, "I wonder, Menie, if my father regrets his lack of belief in Henry now. I wonder if he feels guilty that he disowned me over his false assessment of your father. But I am being unchristian." She shook her head. "No matter how much he has hurt me, my father is an old man. I would not want him to feel guilt and regret for his actions now. Perhaps I shouldn't have written to John about this at all."

"I don't think that is unchristian of you, Mamma," I said. "It simply shows you were justified in marrying Father."

I know Father wrote immediately to Aunt Sarah and Aunt Maria to tell them the news so they could tell his ailing father. We heard later that his father, Thomas Parkes, died on the 18th of September of that year, so I'm sure my own father was relieved he had not hesitated in sending the news.

Mamma cried when she heard of her father-in-law's death. "Oh, Menie, Robert, I wish you could have met your grandfather," she said as we sat in the yard with the chooks pecking about our feet while Mary bounced a ball and Annie slept contentedly in Mamma's arms. "He was a good man."

"Was he anything like Father?" Robert asked.

Mamma paused for a moment. "He looked like your father, yes. He was tall like Henry, too. But his temperament was gentler. He was content to just focus on his garden. Oh, the pleasure he would get from a basketful of beans grown in his plot. He was very kind to me."

"Will Father be sad, do you think, that his father has died?" continued Robert.

"Oh yes, Robert. He is extremely sad. He loved his father dearly."

I can remember a conversation between Robert and Father in late December 1854, when Robert went to visit him in his office and I was dusting the shelves nearby. Robert was very worked up about the Eureka Stockade and Rebellion that had happened on the goldfields at Ballarat in Victoria earlier that month.

"You are all for the working man's rights, Father," Robert said in a high-pitched tone. "Those men were only fighting for their rights. The Victorian Government has threatened to increase the cost of a mining licence to three times the amount they were already having to pay!"

"I couldn't agree with you more, Bob," my father answered. "The Rebellion was entirely the fault of an incompetent government and the failing in duty of the Governor of Victoria, Sir Charles 'otham."

I was surprised at this response, as, no doubt, was Robert, but we did not totally understand what it meant that Father, while a part of the parliament, was in opposition then. I remember thinking how little I appreciated the intricacies of politics.

"There were over twenty men killed, Father," Robert continued, "and others have been charged with treason and something called sedition. It is outrageous, isn't it, Father?"

"The outrage is that Victoria and New South Wales and the other colonies do not 'ave universal suffrage, son," Father said, placing his hand on Robert's shoulder. "That is the real issue. The rebels 'ad no means to oppose the law. The government under the governor was to increase the fees and yet 'ad not been elected by most of the miners. At least 'ere in New South Wales most men 'ave the right to vote. The only way revolution can be prevented, such as 'appened in Ballarat, is through all men 'aving the right to elect their representatives."

On one rare Saturday night when Father was at home and he, Mamma and us children were sitting around the table eating an apple pie I had baked, he surprised us all by saying, "I believe we should think of moving to a more dignified 'ome, Clarinda."

Annie was in a high chair beside me and I blew on small pieces of the steaming pie to cool them before placing them in her mouth and I almost dropped the piece of pie from the spoon as Father spoke.

Mamma looked towards him sharply. "Can we afford to, Henry?"

"I 'ave already spoken to Daniel Cooper, and 'e 'as agreed to give me a mortgage on the *Empire*. It suits 'im as much as me, for 'e knows I will continue to support 'im in the paper to 'elp 'is plans of joining me in the Legislative Council," Father explained and then turned to me, holding his spoonful of pie in the air. "Delicious, Menie. Just delicious."

"But, Henry," Mamma continued, "will we have enough money to pay the rent? How much is it?"

Father glanced at the faces of his family around him. "It is a considerable amount, Clarinda. But I won't discuss details around the children. Others in the Council – Cowper particularly – 'ave suggested that I, as an M.C., live in a more respectable 'ome. I agree with 'im. And I know it would make you 'appy, too, Clarinda."

"Well, yes," she flushed. "You know how cramped we are in this flat, and how much I have longed for a house."

I was overjoyed at the move to the palatial Helene in the bushland of Ryde on the Parramatta River. I had only ever lived in squashed flats in the centre of noisy Sydney, and this great house, with its 160 acres of land, was like a paradise to me. I had my own room on the second floor, which overlooked the wide river, paddocks and distant bush. Father had bought extra furniture to fill the house and I now had a dressing table of my own with side mirrors and brass handles on the curved teak drawers.

Later that year, for my sixteenth birthday, Father bought me a vanity set with a hand mirror, brush and two candlestick holders on a gold-edged tray, each inlaid with a pattern of embroidered roses and forget-me-nots. I had never possessed anything so precious.

On our first day at the new house, after the furniture had been unloaded from the dray by the driver and his man, and our new maid Enid had helped Mamma and me to set the house in order, I went out to explore the acres of land that we now leased. It was a wonder to me that this could all be ours – every tree, every wildflower and every paddock, and the creek that stretched towards the great flowing river. I envisioned days and days of idle wanderings, particularly now that we had a maid who would relieve me of so many of my daily chores. I had not imagined life could ever be so wonderful.

Tom Parkes stayed on in the Hunter Street shop. He was courting a pretty, buxom girl called Annie Moore and they were married the following year. Eventually, he sold the business and moved to Penrith and later to Wollongong. He named two of his eleven children in honour of Father: Henry and Henrietta. Father and he exchanged letters regularly.

Father had always collected rare goods from Asia to sell in the fancy wares shop, and he kept some of these in his study at Helene. He had always been a collector of books when finances permitted and had a reasonable library on the shelves in the study. I think his passion for collections was due to his poverty as a child, when his family could not afford many books or other items.

At Helene, Father also began a collection of birds and animals. He was determined to catch a wallaby in the bushland nearby and would set out every Sunday morning with a huge, unwieldy net. He caught a white cockatoo and two parakeets and kept these in a cage that Davis, the man we hired for labouring tasks, constructed for the purpose. And one day I found a little, helpless, pink, wriggly four-legged creature alone in the bush and I took it home and fed it drops of warm milk from a soaked rag. It proved to be a koala, and Father had another cage built for it. I called her Kitty.

Of course, as Father was away during most weekdays, Mary and I had the job of feeding our new acquisitions, and I can remember spending hours trying to collect enough gum leaves for Kitty before Davis finally decided to build her another tall cage around a eucalypt tree. Eventually, Father was given a wallaby by Robert Jamison, the son of Father's first employer in Australia.

There were also two baby magpies I began to feed regularly. I would hear their chirrups in the mornings and find them in the garden with their bobbing heads and dappled grey wings and I would throw them pieces of bread soaked in milk. Eventually they let me feed them from my hand and, when they had grown, they would serenade me with their warble.

Mamma was happy at Helene. Father would come home on Saturday evenings and stay until late Sunday afternoon each week, before returning on the steam ferry to the *Empire's* new offices in George Street where he had a bed set up on the floor. I think Mamma was thrilled to at last be the mistress of her own house and not just a flat. And while she missed Father during the week, Mamma loved the quiet and expanse of the property after the noisy, cramped quarters we had left behind in central Sydney. During the week, she had her extensive vegetable and flower gardens to tend and her children about her.

My father was in opposition throughout his first term in the Legislative Council. The leader of his liberal party was Charles Cowper, a man Father had worked with in the Anti-transportation League. As with many of

Father's friends and political associates, he and Cowper had a rocky relationship over the years, but at the time of Father's first term, they were great friends.

Charles Cowper came to visit us at Helene for lunch one Sunday. There were frantic preparations at home for this great occasion. Enid cooked a roast duck, butchered that day by Robert from our own flock. Mamma had only recently made my first elegant day dress and I was flushed with excitement as she fastened my new woman's corset. It was to be the first time I would wear a full petticoat and hoop skirt. I can remember that dress distinctly. It was in light blue taffeta with fashionable flounces and cuffed sleeves over lace undersleeves with a matching lace collar at the neck. The crowning touch was a thick sash of deep blue velvet tied in a large bow at the back.

"Menie, you look beautiful," Mamma said as she stepped back to admire me after fastening the last button on the bodice. "You have truly become a striking young lady."

I moved awkwardly through the house, brushing my hooped skirt against the furniture, and Robert laughed when he saw me. "You look ridiculous, Menie," he said, but I ignored his brotherly taunt.

Mr Cowper was a severe-looking, balding man, older than Father. Enid, who was to act as waitress, took his top hat and coat to hang on the hallstand as Father shook his hand and the rest of the family stood stiffly in a single, graduated line from Mamma with Annie in her arms, down to Mary.

Despite his stern looks, Mr Cowper was a mild, friendly man and his eyes twinkled as he bent to kiss my hand. "Miss Parkes," he said. "I am indeed honoured." I blushed furiously.

After lunch, I was permitted to sit in the same room as Mamma, stitching our tapestries quietly, while Father and Mr Cowper drank port and talked of political affairs. The main topic was the disastrous import of Wentworth's Constitution Bill, which was before the House of Lords in England, but they also talked of the exclusiveness of the Australian Club and its squatter patrons, and of their suspicions of the newly arrived Governor of New South Wales, Sir William Denison.

I went to bed that night realising for the first time that Father was truly a man of great importance in New South Wales.

I was overwhelmed with excitement and pride the day Father brought home a copy of the *Empire* containing a poem I had written. It was in June 1855 and below the stanzas Father had written an editor's note:

> *These lines are the production of a young girl sixteen years of age, and are, we believe, a first effort. Though, as a composition, they are strongly marked by the faults of an immature mind, they yet appear to us to evince originality and imaginative power not often found in first verses...*

I was slightly piqued by his critique, but when I read 'The Dream' now I can understand the need for this editor's note. The voice of the poem is definitely young, inexperienced and melodramatic. I will reproduce only some of it here, for it was also overly wordy:

> *I slept, I dreamt,*
> *Wouldst know my thought?—*
> *O, that such dreams*
> *I had but sought!*

> *Me thought I stood by a river bright,*
> *Which wandered far away,*
> *And the sun beamed on with a golden light*
> *Where a lovely island lay.*

> ...

And in it lay a coffin old,
From which a fair girl sprang on shore.

Angelic beauty marked each line
Of that young lovely face;
And small bright wings of a pearl-like hue
Showed her of heavenly race

Beneath the final line was the initials C.S.P. I thought I would burst with excitement when I saw it printed there, in black and white, for all to see.

Mamma, however, was not pleased when I ran into the kitchen to show her. "It will be obvious to anyone who knows us, that this stands for Clarinda Sarah Parkes!" she exclaimed to Father. "They will all know it is Menie! It is not appropriate for a young girl to be voicing such morbid thoughts, or even to be openly published at all, Henry."

It was me who responded. "Why shouldn't I be a published poet, Mamma? I have a mind as clever as most men. I am definitely smarter than Robert!"

Fortunately, Robert was not within hearing.

"That is not the point, Menie," Mamma continued, although she spoke kindly. "It will appear as unfeminine to be putting your thoughts forward in so public a manner, dear."

"Your mother is probably right," Father said. "I 'ave erred in publishing this so publicly. If anything else of yours is to be published, it should be under a pseudonym. Would you approve of that course, Clarinda?"

"Yes. I suppose. But really, Menie, you must not endeavour to outshine all men."

Outwardly, I quietly demurred to Mamma's judgement, but inside I raged against it – something I rarely did with Mamma.

221

When Father bought a horse each for Robert, Mary and me from nearby Eastwood one Sunday, I thought my life could not be any better. I called my horse Othello, after the play I had seen in the Victoria Theatre all those years ago. He was a black hackney colt with a dark, lush main and a white diamond on his forehead. He had an even temperament and I loved Othello because he was my very own.

None of us had ever ridden a horse before. Davis gave us lessons and took care of the horses. Riding a horse was not as easy as I had expected, however, and I was not a natural as Robert proved to be. I persisted, though, and Othello was patient with me so that eventually we were trotting around the paddocks and then eventually to the town of Ryde to collect any groceries Mamma needed.

On most Saturday nights, Enid would go to her home in Kissing Point and I would cook dinner so Mamma and Father could spend time alone sitting on the shady veranda that ran the full length of the house, surveying their expanse of land and talking about the week's happenings. The kitchen was at the back of the house, so all I would hear was the low rumble of Father's voice and sometimes the high peals of Mamma's laughter – she laughed more often during that time.

Mamma became pregnant again later that year. I worried about her age – she was forty-three – and the difficulty of yet another birth. She was so often pregnant that I sometimes wondered at the passion she and Father must have felt for each other. I would never have spoken to her about this, for it was unseemly for a young girl to even display an understanding of the details of such things.

In October 1855, news arrived that Wentworth's Constitution Bill had been passed by the House of Lords. This ensured that the current Legislative Council would be the last. It would be replaced by a two-house parliament based on the Westminster system. There was to be a House of Commons consisting entirely of men appointed by the governor, and a Legislative Assembly comprised of elected members, of whom the majority would be in power and a premier from this majority would be nominated by the governor. Father was adamant that a strong Legislative Assembly was the only way an elitist House of Commons could be kept in check. I fully expected him to stand for a seat in the new Legislative Assembly.

I think everyone in New South Wales was shocked when Father resigned his seat in the still-operating Legislative Council in early December and announced he would not stand for the Assembly. But no one was as shocked as us, his family.

I don't know when Mamma first knew of Father's financial troubles. We children had no idea that all of the luxuries about us and Enid's and Davis's wages were continuing to be paid for entirely on credit, and that Father had taken out a second mortgage on the *Empire* from his once enemy and now friend and ally, James Wilshire. I understand now that Father's decision to resign his seat was due to his need to focus on the newspaper in an attempt to reduce his debts. Mamma might have put pressure on him, too, for she often complained to me of how overworked he was.

"He is one of the only members of the Council who still has to work outside of parliament to earn a living, Menie," Mamma said one Sunday night when Father had returned to his office in central Sydney and we sat together on the veranda. "It is too much for one man to attend parliament and his business. I have told him what I think, but he only listens in silence when I do."

"I suppose it is his dream to be a politician," I answered.

"Surely he can satisfy his dream through the newspaper. His voice and opinions are heard so clearly through it. I fear he will kill himself with the strain."

Mamma's delight at Father's announcement to not stand for the Assembly was short-lived. I know Father was placed under great pressure from his supporters to stand for a seat on the newly formed Legislative Assembly, but I also believe that he could not easily quell his passion for politics, or his ego.

The attorney-general, John Plunkett, a staunch conservative, was to stand for the seat of Sydney. The liberals decided to promote a coalition of four to stand against him: James Wilshire, Robert Campbell, Charles Cowper, and Father was asked to be the fourth. I can only imagine the conversation between Mamma and Father when he told her that he thought of standing. I know that he waivered in his response to his colleagues, but eventually he agreed to stand as one of the 'Bunch' of liberals, as the four men were called.

All four won seats. John Plunkett had only seventeen votes less than James Wilshire and demanded a recount, but he was still defeated. This all happened in March 1856 – the month we won the Crimean War against Russia, and Mamma was due to give birth within a month. I still knew nothing of Father's financial worries and my life at Helene continued comfortably.

Gertrude Amelia Parkes was born on the 13th of April, 1856. Father was still in Sydney that Sunday and so I sent Robert to fetch the midwife from Denistone. I was very fearful for Mamma, but within an hour of the midwife arriving on the back of Robert's horse, little Gertie was born.

"Not another girl!" Robert said when he saw her. "I had hoped for a brother at last!"

Father arrived on the steam ferry two days later, looking grey and tired, but his eyes glowed when he saw his noisy baby girl. "Oh, Clarinda. This one 'as got a set of lungs on 'er!" he said as he bent to kiss Mamma. "I'll 'ave to get 'er into parliament to out-blast the damned Donaldson government."

In fact, the conservative Donaldson Government did not last long and, after a vote of no confidence, Charles Cowper became the second Premier of New South Wales. But he did not give Father a position on his ministry, and that was when their friendship began to fail. I expect Father was quite delighted when Cowper's ministry also fell, despite the conservative government under Henry Watson Parker that replaced it.

SEVENTEEN

It was soon after Gertie was born that I first began becoming dissatisfied with my life at Helene. I suppose I missed the company of others my age, always having only Mamma and the younger children about. Enid was only a little older than me and sometimes I would sit with her in the kitchen as she baked. One day she told me of a dance she had attended the previous Saturday night.

"There were a lot of young men there, and I was almost danced off my feet by so many of them," she said as she kneaded the bread on the floured table. "It was a wonderful night."

"Do you have a beau, Enid?" I asked shyly.

Enid giggled. "You mustn't tell your Mamma, Menie – or your father, of course. But one young farmer, Bill Gresham, walked me home after the dance, and he kissed me when we got to my parents' gate."

"What did it feel like to be kissed?" I asked.

"It made me sort of melt, I suppose. His lips were really soft and he grabbed me hard around the waist and slid his hand down to my bottom." She giggled and blushed. "It felt wonderful, really."

I was jealous of Enid's experience and tried to imagine what being kissed would feel like. But as I rarely met any young men – only those I saw at the shop in Ryde or at church – I knew it was unlikely for me to be kissed like Enid had been.

It was not until late 1856 that I realised Father was in extreme debt. He called Robert and me to sit with Mamma and him on the veranda one Saturday night when the steam of the day was cooling and a light breeze from the river was blowing.

"I need to let you know of some difficulties I am experiencing currently," he began in a softer voice than usual, looking away from us and towards the darkening floorboards. "For some time I 'ave been expecting the *Empire* to start turning a profit, and no doubt it will within about a year, as its subscriptions and readership still rival the *'erald*'s. But, as you know, I took up a mortgage with Daniel Cooper when we first leased this 'ouse, and later I had to take up a second mortgage with James Wilshire to keep things going."

Robert and I sat in hushed silence as our great father continued his confession.

"The problem I am facing is that Daniel Cooper is putting me under a lot of pressure to pay 'is debt since I told 'im last month of my troubles. I am thinking I may 'ave to resign my seat on the Assembly to 'elp put things to rights, and Cooper is demanding I do, so I can focus my energies on the paper."

Mamma glanced towards Robert and me. "It will be for the best, children," she said. "Your father is overworked and that is a part of the problem, I believe. We will have to be more careful with our own expenses, though. Your father will be dismissing Enid and Davis, so you will both have to take on more responsibility around the house, as will I."

"Of course, Mamma, Father," I blurted. "Whatever we can do to help," although I was upset to think of the loss of Enid's companionship.

Robert, only thirteen years old, looked dismayed as Father turned to him. "Bob, during the week when I am away, you will be the man about the 'ouse from now until things are set to rights. I will be depending on you."

"Yes, Father," Robert said but looked away to hide his fright.

Father resigned his seat on the Friday before Christmas. It was to be a frugal festive celebration that year but we were thrilled to have Father to ourselves for a few days. I can remember we played endless games of Housey Housey and even little Annie joined in to play quoits and Blind Man's Bluff. Father was hilarious as the blind man, purposely waving his hands too high when he knew he had stumbled on Mary or Annie.

Father, Robert, Mary and I took long rambling walks together through the bush, and Mamma and Father spent the evenings sitting on the veranda holding hands while they talked.

The year that followed was a difficult one for Father. He continued to work frantically on the *Empire*, even after Daniel Cooper took possession of the George Street building in early March and advertised its equipment for auction. It wasn't until the newspaper's edition of the 11th of March that Father admitted to the public he was in debt. This confession proved to be a redeeming move for a time, for many of the paper's readers insisted on beginning a subscription fund to help Father pay his debts. If it hadn't been for this support, I believe the *Empire* would have gone under before the year was out. It resulted in Father and his creditors all signing an agreement that they would give him five years to pay his debts.

I was horrified at news of the wreck of the *Dunbar* on South Head during its approach to Sydney Harbour in late August. The first that was known of it was a report from a captain of another ship who'd seen parts of the broken ship floating near Sydney Heads as his ship had entered the harbour. And then, bodies and wreckage began washing up on beaches in Middle Harbour and at Watsons Bay. Father reported the wreck in the *Empire* on Saturday the 22nd of August:

> *On reaching the Gap, a horrible scene presented itself: the sea was rolling in, mountains high, dashing on the rocks fragments of wreck, large and small,*

and bodies of men, women, and children, nearly all in a state of nudity...
Upwards of twenty human bodies were counted under the Gap—the waves
dashing them against the rocks and taking them back in their recoil.

It must have been a ghastly sight, and it was still unknown which ship
had been wrecked, for there were around six vessels expected to arrive
from England at the time.

And then, one day soon after, a man looking down towards the
surging waters and the jagged cliffs of the Gap thought he saw movement
on a rock below. It was a miracle. One of the sailors, James Johnson, had
been thrown from the ship as it broke up on the rocks. He later testified
that he had clung perched on a ledge there for almost two days before he
was discovered. He was the sole survivor.

The ship had been approaching the harbour on a stormy night with
low visibility, Mr Johnson reported. The captain had mistaken the jagged
cliffs of the Gap for the harbour entrance and had sailed the ship directly
into the towering rocks. More than a hundred people – men, women and
children – had perished, and the remains of only twenty-two people were
ever recovered. The wife and children of one of Father's former political
colleagues, Daniel Egan, were all killed. Father attended the mass funeral
that was held for the victims in late September.

Mamma took this tragedy greatly to heart. I suppose she and
Father remembered the perils of their own voyage onboard the ship to
Sydney.

"To think they were so close to the end of their journey," she said to
me with tears in her eyes shortly after we heard the news. "All those men,
women and children having travelled so far, to be dashed on the rocks
off Sydney and never to set foot on New South Wales soil. It is a terrible
thing."

Father was always eerily fascinated by shipwrecks. He kept a bound book
of newspaper clippings on these terrible happenings. These included the

amazing report by Alfred Lutwyche of his survival and that of the other 104 passengers and crew after the wreck of the *Meridian* back in 1853. The mainmast, as the ship was breaking up, fell upon the island they had smashed into and provided a bridge across to the land. Those that were able to cross survived on the island for nine days before they were eventually rescued by a whaleboat.

And then there was the horrible report of the fire on board the *Cospatrick* many years later, when two lifeboats were launched and, of these, only one was ever recovered. It was a ghastly discovery when the three men who'd survived the wreckage admitted they, and two others who'd died shortly after their lifeboat was found, had only survived by eating the flesh of the twenty-five other people who'd made it into the lifeboat but had died from hunger or thirst.

Father never described to me much, and Mamma only brief details, of their own journey to Australia on board the *Strathfieldsaye*, but I'm sure they must have been in fear for their lives for much of the voyage. It is such a perilous thing to travel in a clipper from one end of the globe to another. Fortunately, the steamships of today are far safer. Despite my curiosity about foreign lands, I am not sure I would ever be brave enough to venture on such a journey.

I will always remember my family's shock on that Saturday in October 1857 when Father arrived home from Sydney late in the afternoon. We had expected him home later than usual but had not expected him to only just make the last steam ferry following his business meetings that day.

I could tell Mamma was attempting to control her anger when she eventually saw Father approaching on the path leading to the house. But when she saw his face clearly in the light of the setting sun, she gasped and ran to him. "What has happened to you, Henry?" she exclaimed. "Have you been in a fight?"

Father's face was bruised and cut on both sides in at least five places, and his lower lip was red and swollen.

"Now don't fret, Clarinda," he said as he wearily took off his coat in the hallway. "I am all right now, and I 'ave laid criminal charges. I must apologise to you all for my lateness, but my trip to the police station delayed me."

I could not imagine Father in a fist-fight and, despite my fright at his appearance, I admit now that I was slightly amused at the thought of it. I hid my inappropriate response and went to fetch Father's slippers.

"Tell us, Henry, what has happened?" Mamma continued in frantic tones as we sat on the floor around him, looking up into his unfamiliar bruised countenance.

"I suppose it's to be expected that I will rile some people through the paper, Clarinda," he said, his words slurred by his swollen lip. "It was a young man whom I didn't know, but I 'ave since found out is Arthur Ormsby. 'E came upon me in the street and accused me of defaming 'is father. It turns out 'is father is the superintendent of Cockatoo Island Prison, and I published an article written by another of a fight this man's father 'ad witnessed in the gaol and done nothing to stop."

"Who wrote the article, Father? Shouldn't they have been the one assaulted by him?" I asked.

"Oh no, Menie. I cannot divulge my source. That is against an editor's ethics."

"Are you hurting badly, Henry? Is there anything I can do?" Mamma continued.

"Now don't fret, Clarinda. I'm fine," he said. "I was 'elped by a publican from a tavern nearby and several other people. Owen Cara'er 'it Ormsby to stop 'is attack on me."

"Did you hit him, too, Father?" Robert asked with an enthusiasm that clearly meant he hoped Father's answer would be yes.

"No, Robert. I did not!" Father said decisively. "I was on the corner of George and 'unter Streets. I would not 'ave reduced myself to common fighting in front of the people of Sydney."

The case of criminal assault was heard against Arthur Ormsby in the Sydney Quarter Sessions later that month. He was found guilty and committed to six weeks in prison. John West, the editor of Fairfax's *The Sydney Morning Herald*, who openly despised Father, wrote a shameful article the day after the judgment. It offered a reward of fifty guineas *to any spirited young gentleman who would waylay the said Henry Parkes in the public street, and knock him on the head.*

"How could he write such a thing?" Mamma said, dismayed, when Father showed her the paper.

Father simply laughed. "It's not the worst 'e's said regarding me, Clarinda. John West is opposed to me in every way."

"But why does John Fairfax allow him to write such things?"

I wondered this, too.

"I suppose 'e can't control everything 'is editor writes. And while John Fairfax and I respect each other, we are not friends."

My father's incorrigible confidence must have been part of what originally attracted Mamma to him, but it was also the cause of much of her patient suffering. I think Father was encouraged by the public's support of him in maintaining the paper and following his assault, for he again entered the political sphere before the year had ended. He was adamant this was a move he must make in the circumstances set before him.

"I think I'm the only one who can stop Charles Cowper, Clarinda," he said over dinner one Saturday. "I can see now why 'e's known as 'Slippery Charlie'."

"But surely, Henry, it is not wise when Daniel Cooper has made it clear he has not forced the debt partly due to your remaining out of politics!" Mamma was understandably exasperated, I thought.

"I can't just sit back, Clarinda, and let Cowper get 'is Land Bill passed. It goes against everything we've been fighting for all along."

We children sat silently as our parents spoke, slightly surprised at Mamma's feisty response.

"There must be someone else who can fight this, Henry. Why must it always be *you*?"

"Clarinda, it is me who best understands 'ow Cowper works. And this Bill is undemocratic. It supports the squatters in maintaining their large tracts of land. I am the best man to fight 'im on this. I must!"

And so, on the 7th of December, Father led a massive rally in Wynyard Square where he spoke of the rights of working-class men and the betrayal by the Cowper government of these rights. The next day, without any direct campaigning on his part, when Father arrived at the hustings at Parramatta to support John Lucas in gaining the seat of North Riding, this man, amazingly, stood aside and insisted Father stand in his place. It was a remarkable act and one Father claimed he had not expected. I still wonder, though, if it was something that had been previously arranged.

I know Mamma was secretly relieved when Father did not win the seat. He lost it to Thomas Whistler Smith, a man he disliked and scoffed publicly by calling him 'Whistling Smith'. But it was clear to us all by then that Father would not be deterred from his political ambitions.

Later that year, the governor dissolved the Legislative Assembly and an election was called for January 1858. Father again stood for a seat in North Riding, presenting himself as a liberal who supported neither Charles Cowper nor the conservatives. Both he and Whistler Smith won seats. We discovered his victory when Father arrived home that night.

I can remember sitting in the lounge room playing cards with Robert, while Mamma was reading aloud to us from the Book of Deuteronomy when we suddenly heard deep, raucous cheering from the garden. We all ran out to the veranda, including Gertie who waddled unsteadily on her two year old legs, to find Father emerging through the dark in a carriage being pulled by a group of burly local men in rolled up shirtsleeves. Father was laughing and waving his hand above his head in appreciation.

One of the men saw us standing, surprised, on the veranda and called to the others, "It's Mrs Parkes and the Parkes children! Three cheers for Mrs Parkes and her brood!"

I blushed deeply as the men whooped and Father dismounted the carriage to run up the veranda stairs to Mamma and swing her about. Without his having to tell us, we all knew he was again elected to the Legislative Assembly.

I continued to crave a more exciting life and wondered, if I was not to have a suitor, if I should consider using my mind to become financially independent from my family. I could not bear the thought of becoming an old maid within my father's house. While he was in Sydney during the week, I would often write to him, and I can remember writing to him in early 1858 with a proposal to open my own school. I expected Father to react negatively towards this suggestion but I was determined at the time. I ended the letter with this paragraph:

Do not throw this aside as a foolish, girlish idea for really I am in earnest and should feel very, very much happier if I saw any prospect of rendering myself independent, and do not think it would be any sacrifice on my part for I shall feel much gratified if you consent to my plan.

Father's reaction shocked me, for he replied in a letter dispatched on the day he received mine, to suggest that if I was so determined on independence, I should work for him as a journalist, summarising news items and travelling daily on the ferry between Helene and his offices in Sydney. Agreeing would have made me the first female journalist in New South Wales.

I was thrilled at Father's confidence in me, but extremely frightened. It was an overwhelming possibility. Of course, my boring, mundane life would become one of excitement and real responsibility if I was to accept the job. However, I worried terribly I would not be capable of fulfilling Father's belief in me. I spoke to Mamma of it immediately. I was not surprised at her negative response and I think, deep down, I wanted her to disapprove so I could blame her, and not my own cowardice, for not accepting Father's proposal. I wonder now what I might have achieved had I not been so afraid to surmount my inner belief in my female frailty.

As it turned out, Father was not to remain the editor of the *Empire* for much longer. I will never forget the night he returned to Helene unexpectedly and sobbed loudly in Mamma's arms. We children all stood outside their bedroom, listening silently to this terrible, unfamiliar sound from our father.

He had finally succumbed to his heavy debts and was expecting to become bankrupt. As an insolvent, Father would not be allowed to maintain his seat in parliament and so he had decided to close the paper and resign his seat in the Legislative Assembly. Neither of these events were publicly known until the following week when the *Empire* did not appear on news stands in Sydney and Father's resignation was read aloud in parliament. My father was a broken man.

It was probably the worst day of my young life the day we were evicted from Helene. The landlord gave Father only two days to leave our wonderful home because we were behind on the rent. We had nowhere to go. I was surprised at the time at the strength Mamma showed towards this disastrous occurrence. I did not see her shed a single tear as we packed our belongings into a dray, in contrast to my constantly streaming face.

Father went in search of another home and the first person he spoke to, a supporter of his who lived on the property next to us, Thomas Betteridge, offered him the building there that had once served as a coach-house and stables, free of rent. It was to be a basic dwelling.

I shared a room upstairs with my siblings, which had once belonged to a groom, and slept in one big bed head to toe with Robert, Mary and Annie. Mamma and Father slept with Gertrude in the room next door. Downstairs, on the stone floor of the stables, we piled our furniture into corners and set up a desk for Father and a table and chairs for the rest of us. The hearth served as our simple kitchen. We joined our farm animals and horses with Mr Betteridge's, and set the birds, wallaby and Kitty the koala free into the bush.

"Come on now, Menie," Mamma said to me when I burst into tears again at the first sight of our humble new home. "We must be strong for your father. At least we have shelter and beds to sleep in."

I think Mamma did not mind where she lived at that time, so long as Father was around us during the week and not always venturing away into the city.

Annie was a wild sleeper, and it was she who slept opposite me in our four-man bed. I would often be woken by a rough kick in the side as she tossed and turned in the night. I was almost twenty years old and Robert was a lanky sixteen year old. He was mortified at having to share a bed with me and his ten and four year old sisters.

One of Father's strengths, but also – I believe – one of his weaknesses, was his ability to bounce back from disaster. His despair at his downfall was not long-lived, and with his usual self-confidence and vitality, he decided to reinvent himself soon after our move to the coach-house. He decided he was to become a lawyer and began to study in order to enter the Bar. I knew Father to be a great man capable of many tasks, but this choice was one I secretly thought beyond him. Others, however, including Mamma, encouraged him in this pursuit.

Of course, Father still needed to earn a wage and so he approached his long-term rival John Fairfax, who surprisingly hired Father as a freelance journalist, extracting first a promise from him that he would not write in his usual liberal vein. Unknown to Father at the time, I was also attempting a writing career, still determined to become independent. I had begun to write occasional articles for the *Maitland Mercury* and was also penning a series of romantic tales, which I called *Pet Perennials*. I submitted these to John Fairfax and was distraught when he rejected them, but they were later published in the *Australian Home Companion and Band of Hope Journal* under the pseudonym Patty Parsley.

I was shocked when Mamma told me she was pregnant again in early November. She was forty-five years old and greying, and Father now had a shock of grey-peppered hair. I was longing for love, and I thought it almost obscene that Mamma and Father were still intimate. I now laugh at my young self's reaction, but at the time my parents seemed so old to me.

Mamma's pregnancy was a difficult one and I tried to ease her burden of household duties, while still secretly writing when I had the time. I could not write in the room I shared with Robert, Mary and Annie without being detected, so I would often spend time sitting on a tree stump in the bush, composing my stories and articles. I received no payment for the *Pet Perennials* publications, but I was determined to become a successful writer.

I fell in love in 1859. His name was John Owen and I met him when I went to visit our kind landlord, Thomas Betteridge. I would often take

Mr Betteridge a portion of soup or stew that Mamma or I had cooked, as much due to the fondness I had for the gentle widower as for his charity in allowing us to live on his property. As I approached his door on this occasion, I heard an unfamiliar, deep laugh from within and hesitated before reaching for the brass knocker.

"Why, Miss Parkes," Mr Betteridge said as he opened the door. "Come on in. I have another visitor, Mr John Owen. Mr Owen, may I introduce Miss Clarinda Parkes."

I was immediately tongue-tied and light-headed in the handsome young man's presence. He stood from his armchair to greet me, and I was struck by his blue eyes and crooked smile, but also by the breadth of his shoulders in his fashionable sack coat.

"Miss Parkes," he said and reached for my hand, kissing it gallantly.

I blushed and mumbled his name in reply.

"Mr Owen is visiting our neighbourhood from his father's property in Lane Cove. His father is an old friend of mine," Mr Betteridge explained, and then told the handsome man of my origins.

"Henry Parkes's daughter, indeed," Mr Owen said with admiration. "It is an honour." He bowed and kissed my hand again, leaving me speechless.

Mr Betteridge ushered me to a seat and took the steaming pot from me gratefully, vanishing to the kitchen and leaving me alone with Mr Owen.

"So, Miss Parkes, may I call you Clarinda?" he asked boldly.

I managed to stumble out stupidly, "Actually, everyone calls me Menie."

"What a strange name!" he exclaimed. "Can I call you Clarinda, though? It is such a beautiful name." His crooked smile dazzled me again.

"It is my mother's name, Clarinda. I suppose that is why I have a pet name instead," I blurted out.

"Well, Clarinda," John Owen continued, undeterred, "I am in the Ryde area for a week and have no young company such as yourself. Would you object to showing me the local sights? I could meet you in the town one afternoon, perhaps."

I think my shocked silence must have been amusing to John Owen. Eventually, I swallowed and managed a reply. "Why yes, Mr Owen. That would be a pleasure."

"Very well," he said jovially. "What about tomorrow at two?"

I simply nodded in answer before Mr Betteridge returned.

This was a very forward suggestion of John Owen's, and I knew Father and Mamma would not approve of my stepping out with this near-stranger, so I kept him a secret. Father was too busy in his legal studies to notice my more regular absences from the house that week and I made the excuse to Mamma of my taking long walks or rides on the several occasions when I met John Owen in Ryde.

On the day before he was to return to his property, he walked with me through the bush and held my hand before drawing me to him and giving me my first, exquisite kiss.

I only ever saw John Owen one other time after that, around two years later when I happened to meet him on a street in Sydney. By then, I had almost given up on my dream of his appearing unexpectedly at our home one day and proposing to me, and this chance meeting confirmed my suspicions that this was never to be the case.

"Miss Parkes," he said unsmiling and bowed. "I hope you are well."

"Why thank you, Mr Owen. I am." My heart was fluttering uncontrollably at the sight of this longed-for man.

"I am so pleased," he said. And that was all. John Owen bowed again and simply walked away.

My heart broke.

Eighteen

Mamma always blamed Charles Cowper for Father's bankruptcy. She would tell me how, if Mr Cowper had offered Father a cabinet position before the *Empire* went under, he would have had an income to support the business and it would never have failed. I suspect that even if Father had had this income, it would not have been sufficient to satisfy his debts.

Mamma's anger towards 'Slippery Charlie' was definitely one of the reasons she was adamant Father should not take the position of Collector of Customs that Mr Cowper offered him in late 1858, despite the regular pay it would afford.

"I agree with you, Clarinda," I heard Father say to her from their bedroom as I lingered outside on the way to my own shared room. "Charles is trying to buy me off so I can never again be a threat to 'im in parliament. But let's not decide this now. Think it over. Think of the income."

Mamma could be almost as stubborn and proud as Father in some matters, and I knew she would never change her mind on this.

Shortly after Father's troubles became public, he showed me a letter of support and condolence from Mary Windeyer.

"She was an eight year old girl on the *Strathfieldsaye* coming out to New South Wales with 'er family along with Clarinda and me when you were born, Menie. She was Mary Bolton then and 'as recently married the young lawyer William Windeyer. We didn't know 'er well because 'er family were cabin passengers, but she says she and 'er 'usband 'ave been following my career and they are keen to meet me."

A friendship began between William Windeyer and Father after this, mainly through written correspondence but also through Father visiting him to borrow legal books and discuss his progress in his studies for the Bar with his young supporter.

Father also began a regular correspondence with the lawyer John Dunmore Lang, whom Father had forgiven for his earlier lack of confidence in his abilities demonstrated by the creation of the rival and fated liberal newspaper *The Press*, back in 1851, just as he had forgiven James Wilshire.

Father's determination and self-belief are evident in his reaction to a conversation he had with the lawyer William Barker, shortly after he began his legal studies. Apparently, Mr Barker told my father bluntly that he did not think he had the mental qualifications to go to the Bar and he thought if Father attempted it, he would be a complete failure. Father supposedly stormed out of the lawyer's office and walked immediately to a shop selling barristers' wigs imported from England and ordered one on the spot.

It was another legal friend and politician, John Bayley Darvall, who eventually persuaded Father he should give up the law. Whether he had considered it best to dissuade Father through flattery rather than criticism, I do not know, but Father was only convinced when Mr Darvall insisted he not give up on politics and that the colony needed him as a statesman and not a lawyer.

Father's re-found political ambition was hampered by his bankruptcy, and so he tried to hurry his case through the Insolvency Court. The case for his discharge was heard in early June 1859, when Mamma was due to give birth any day. All of Father's creditors agreed to his discharge and to accept a few shillings for each pound owed, except for one – a stationer called Francis McNab. There were rumours that Mr McNab was encouraged by Charles Cowper to push the case against Father in order to delay his return to parliament.

On the 3rd of June, Chief Commissioner Purefoy discharged Father from his bankruptcy, and, with his accustomed vitality, Father planned to begin his campaign to stand for a seat in East Sydney the following day.

It was this same day – Saturday the 4th of June – that Mamma went into labour in the early hours of the morning. Father tried not to show the anxiety he felt when he realised his nomination might be delayed if the baby was not born quickly, but every time I rushed downstairs to boil water for the midwife, I would find him watching the clock in the room that had once been stables. Fortunately, Varney Parkes was born at eight-thirty in the morning, and Father was able to catch the steam ferry into Sydney soon after.

Varney, or Varry as we called him, was a huge baby, with what seemed like an insatiable appetite. Poor Mamma fed him almost hourly for his first month. I was given the task of writing to Uncle John in Birmingham to tell him of the birth and the name Mamma had chosen to give homage to her ageing father, Robert Varney. I am glad I never knew my grandfather, and while this may seem unchristian, I think it is his actions, or lack of, that were truly unchristian.

Even after my grandfather heard of the birth and the name, he did not write to Mamma. The only word she heard from her father was again through Uncle John Varney – and Mamma's terrible stepmother did not even send word through him. Both Robert and Ann Varney died of influenza the following year, and I still cannot understand Mamma's endless days of crying when the letter arrived to tell of her father's death.

Less than a week after Varry was born, Father was again elected to the Legislative Assembly, this time as an independent radical promising to act as watchdog to the Cowper ministry. He secretly hoped 'Slippery Charlie' would award him a cabinet position anyway.

Unfortunately, Father's bankruptcy would continue to haunt him. Despite his employment as a freelance journalist with *The Sydney Morning Herald*, its editor, John West, still held a grudge against Father. I had to hide from Mamma the article he published the day after Father's election, mocking his discharge from bankruptcy by Chief Commissioner Purefoy. Its words were often repeated by others, though, and Mamma heard them eventually: *'In England'*, said a wit, *'insolvents are whitewashed. In New South Wales they are Purefoyed.'*

The week after Father's election, his creditor, Francis McNab, lodged an appeal against Father's discharge in the Supreme Court of New South Wales. The following day, Charles Kemp – Father's previous rival in the newspaper business and in politics – lodged an objection to Father's election on the basis that Mr McNab's appeal ensured he was still, legally, an undischarged bankrupt. It seemed the main concern was that Father had arranged with the bank to honour cheques he had marked before any others, and the marked cheques had not included Mr McNab's.

In September, Father moved us to a small house in Darlinghurst Street in Sydney. I had hoped this return to the city would improve the dullness of my life, but instead I felt even more trapped in the family's affairs, living in a cramped house in the middle of other people's busy, exciting, city lives.

Earlier that same month, Father's discharge from bankruptcy was reversed in the Supreme Court on Mr McNab's appeal. Father was outraged. Fortunately, though, Charles Kemp's objection to Father's election was turned down. It seemed the new Electoral Act did not contain any reference to an undischarged bankrupt not being able to hold a seat in parliament. And so, through what was probably a simple oversight in the drafting of the Act, Father retained his seat.

I became less and less interested in Father's politics at this time. I began to recognise that the endless drama and deceptions he would relate to us consumed him completely – at our expense. Several governments toppled that year, and I began to privately scoff at the instability of parliament and of my father. I thought he was manic with ambition and the determination to be regarded as a man of importance. I knew he loved us but, like many men of his era, I thought he loved himself more.

I will always love my father despite all his faults. He was a great man in so many ways and his achievements for Australia were hugely important. They will affect our country for years to come, I know. But as his daughter, I cannot deny the negative impact his ambition had on his family – on poor Mamma especially.

Father knew we were unhappy living in that small house in the centre of Sydney. The following October we moved again. Our new home, Werrington House, was a two-storey stone building at the foot of the Blue Mountains – thirty-four miles from Sydney – with 460 acres of grass paddocks and bushland. I had accepted by then that my life would continue in its monotonous routine no matter where I lived, and so was thrilled at the space and the comforts of this new home.

I had also told my parents by then of my recent unpaid publications of *Pet Perennials* and another series, *Miss Jesse's Schooldays and What Came of Them*, under the pseudonym of Patty Parsley in the *Australian Home Companion and Band of Hope Journal*. It had been hard to keep my writing a secret when I had nowhere to write outside in the crowded city centre as I had in Ryde. And so I did not keep my next great achievement a secret.

Before we moved to Werrington, I sent the beginning chapters of a novel, *Bitter Sweet—So Is the World*, to John Fairfax. It was the story of two sisters, Madonna and Selena Lea, and their attempts to bring their respective suitor and half-Aboriginal barrister husband to accept the Christian faith. I remember I was so overjoyed when I received a positive reply from Mr Fairfax that I burst into tears and Robert asked me if someone had died. Mr Fairfax was to publish my novel in serial form on the front page of one of his newspapers: *The Sydney Mail*. I was to be paid a small amount for each instalment and would be a published author. Under the pseudonym Ariel, my dull, confined life now, at last, had a purpose.

Over the years, I published many other serial novels and short stories, as well as a few non-fiction texts in *The Sydney Mail*. Only my family and close friends knew I was the author of these works as I wrote under a pseudonym at Mamma's request, but I am still extremely proud of my authorial career. These published works included the serials: *Which Wins? A Tale of Life's Impulses* published between October 1861 and May 1862; *A Lonely Lot* published between July 1863 and February 1864; *Benedicta* published between June and October 1867; *Fallen by the Way* published between July 1871 and January 1872; and *Mrs Ord* published between August and November 1878. I have kept copies of each paper containing them, their close, dark type proof to me of my existence and worth.

It was in *A Lonely Lot* that I openly expressed my thoughts on the oppression of women, which had become my bug-bear. I was not subtle in this: *Men are always selfish*, I wrote. *It is in their nature to be so... They love yonder woman, yes, love her in real, living earnest. And do you know why? They want puddings and pies, no trouble about their buttons, the luxuries of bright eyes and sweet words to welcome them when they return from their employments.*

And then, *What sort of a woman is she who has no domestic tyrant, before whom she can cringe, submit, get her individuality trampled out of her? She is the most unhappy creature in creation.*

I laugh now when I read these words. No wonder Mamma did not want me to put my name to my writing. She would have expected that, if I had, I would never have won a husband. I suspect Father never read these words for, if he had, I am certain he would not have hesitated in telling me of his displeasure at my backhanded criticism.

There was a terrible day in September 1860 when Father was away in the city and we thought little Varry might die. I remember Varry had cried for most of the night and Mamma had sat by his bed, stroking his fair head, her Bible clutched in her other hand. In the morning, his cries stopped and he fell into a lethargy.

"Mamma," I said, bringing a cup of tea to her at his bedside, "you go and sleep for a while. I'll take care of Varry."

Mamma refused. And then she let out a cry as we both stood, horrified, watching Varry's limbs flaying about as he spasmed in the bed, the bedsheets becoming tangled about him.

"Robert!" I called just as the spasm seemed to ease and Varry again fell into a lethargy. "Robert, go and fetch the doctor at once!"

Mamma was crying by then. "I can't bear it, Menie. I can't bear to lose another. I can't bear it if Varry is taken from me, too."

"The doctor will be here soon, Mamma, and all will be fine," I said unconvincingly.

Every fifteen minutes or so, Varry's little body continued to spasm, violently twitching and jerking.

Robert returned about an hour later without the doctor. "He's been away from home since six this morning, Mamma," he said. "I waited for a time, but the doctor didn't come."

"You must go back, Robert," I said firmly. "You must return to the doctor's house and wait for him to come. It is *most* urgent."

That day was endless. I managed to drizzle a few drops of milk mixed with water into Varry's mouth, and he swallowed each unconsciously before another spasm overtook him. Mary tried to ease Mamma to her bed, but she would not be moved. Varry's spasms became less frequent, and then Robert arrived with the doctor at last around eight o'clock that night.

"He is recovering, I feel," the doctor said. "But the boy is exhausted. He should be given brandy to revive him – four drops every hour."

I had not cried all day, but I burst into tears of relief when Varry opened his eyes suddenly a few hours later and asked, in his baby lisp, if he could have some herring paste.

"Of all things!" Mamma laughed through her tears as Mary went to fetch a slice of bread spread with the paste. We all sat around him laughing and crying as he nibbled at the bread. I had not seen Robert cry since he was a young boy, but even he needed a handkerchief to wipe his eyes.

"Oh, Varry, dear. You gave us such a scare," Mamma said, before he fell soundly to sleep in her arms.

Father boarded at a house in the city mid-week for, until the new train line was built, it took him around four hours to reach the city from Werrington by coach via Parramatta, followed by a train trip. I think Mamma was beginning to become more accepting of his absences. She built up a menagerie of farm animals – cows, pigs, geese, chicken and ducks – and she baked bread and churned butter from the cows' milk. The farming life suited Robert, too. He was never one for books or the indoors.

My days were mainly filled with my writing and tutoring Mary, Annie and Gerty – a role I had taken over from Mamma after Varry was born. I had given up on ever marrying, having had the devastating encounter with John Owen the previous year. I thought I would never be kissed again.

My social circle, however, began to grow after our move to Werrington. I began to attend St Stephen's Anglican Church in the nearby town of Penrith. It was there that I met Lizzie Langley – a lively, vivacious girl. We would stroll together along the Nepean River after church, surrounded by the distant hills and farmland.

One Sunday, Lizzie arranged a picnic with her fiancé, Freddy Martin, and his friend Robert Wilshire. I brought my brother Robert with me. We sat on the banks of the river with a view of the palatial stone Dunheved Homestead and its large paddocks full of cattle.

Robert Wilshire was not handsome like John Owen had been, but he had a kind, open face and I warmed to him immediately.

"Miss Langley tells me you are a writer, Miss Parkes," Robert Wilshire said after a time, and took an enormous bite of a steak and chutney sandwich.

I turned to Lizzie abruptly. "Lizzie!" I exclaimed. "You are not to go telling everyone of my hobby."

"It is no hobby, Robert," Lizzie said. "Menie is just being modest. Her story is being published in *The Sydney Mail* each week."

I blushed furiously.

"I don't think you should be embarrassed, Miss Parkes. I think it is a great accomplishment for a young lady," Robert Wilshire said, which made me blush even more. "I would very much like to read it sometime."

Later, my brother Robert and I walked with Robert Wilshire to the great stone gate of the nearby homestead and my heart fluttered as the man's arm continued to brush against mine as he talked. I thought then, that perhaps I wouldn't become an old maid.

On the other hand, my brother Robert was a terrible flirt with any girl, and often walked the pretty Hilda Cooper home behind her parents after church. I suppose Robert was quite good-looking – tall like Father and with Mamma's eyes and he had begun growing a beard.

It was in 1861 that I really accepted Father's nature was to put himself first in all things. I write this now, but at the time I did not complain. Father had been one of the main advocates for the creation of two positions for government Commissioners of Emigration to be employed to go to Britain to encourage and promote migration to Australia. In early May, Father was offered one of these positions by Charles Cowper. At least Father did not accept until he had first spoken to Mamma.

"I will earn an extraordinary salary of £1200, Clarinda. And it will only be for around a year," he almost begged her that Sunday when he had travelled the four hours to Werrington from the city. They were sitting in their bedroom with the door closed but I, having seen Father's distracted expression when he'd arrived home, stood by the door quietly to listen.

"A year, Henry! A whole year! You could leave us for that long!" Mamma's voice was shrill.

"I consider my sisters in this decision, too, Clarinda. Sarah 'as been ill with tuberculosis for some time. I fear that if I don't return to England soon, I will never see 'er again. You know 'ow dear she is to me."

Father must have known that Mamma would sympathise deeply with this. There was silence for a time and then I heard sobbing.

"I love you, Clarinda," Father said. "You know I love you – and the children – but this is a great opportunity. The time will pass quickly when I'm gone."

And so, Mamma agreed. I don't think she really had a choice.

It was only a matter of weeks before Father left us at Werrington. He departed with Robert at dawn to travel by coach to Parramatta from where he would travel on alone. I cannot possibly imagine the desperation Mamma felt. Her eyes were red-rimmed and swollen as we stood by the stagecoach and watched Father climb into the buggy behind Robert. He held his hand out the window and Mamma grabbed it fiercely, cradling it to her cheek as her tears began to pour again.

"God bless you, Clarinda," Father said gently. "God Bless you all, my children."

Mamma said nothing, but as the coach swung away behind its two horses, she seemed to stumble and I grabbed her around the waist to hold her upright. "Mamma, it will all be fine. The time will pass. I am here with you, Mamma dear," I tried to reassure her, but she must have felt totally abandoned.

A letter arrived from Father from Melbourne in late May addressed to Mamma, and she cried as she read it and again later when she read some of it to me.

"'I feel already bitter regret at parting from you and the children, but I am sure it was my duty to leave you under the circumstances'," she read. "The *circumstances*! What does he mean by the circumstances, Menie? I don't understand him at all."

"I suppose he means with the income he will earn, Mamma," I said.

"I told him I would rather live on bread and water than have him accept that earlier position Charles Cowper offered him, so why should this be any different?"

I know that, despite her complaints to me of Father's behaviour, Mamma was always the dutiful wife and had not complained so bitterly to Father himself before he left.

Mamma seemed to overcome her sadness more quickly than I'd expected, though. I think she continued to love Father deeply but I do not think things between them were ever the same again.

Father had employed four servants to support us in his absence: a young maid named Margaret, a nurse for the children named Ida, and two men to help with the property, named White and Wales – the latter of whom proved idle and a mischief-maker. Father had also arranged an account for Mamma to draw on, and for John Fairfax to deposit into it the extra wage Father earned writing articles for *The Sydney Morning Herald* about the state of England as he travelled. But even so, we struggled financially throughout his absence, not least because Father had other debts, which we were to cover on his behalf.

NINETEEN

Mr Betteridge, our previous landlord in the coach-house, came to visit us regularly during Father's absence. I never asked him about his friend's son, John Owen, however. Mr Betteridge suffered from a form of melancholia, I believe. He would write to Mamma of his distress and, always a kind-hearted woman and one who understood the enormity of dark days, she would invite him to stay at Werrington.

Mr Betteridge, such a gentle man, was always a welcome companion. We would go on long, rambling walks into the bushland of the mountains with Mary, and sometimes with Annie trotting along beside, chatting uncontrollably. On one occasion, Mr Betteridge walked all day to Blacktown and back.

"Goodness," I said to him on his return. "Where have you been all this time?"

"I started off on a simple walk, Menie, but then found myself walking to Blacktown," he said. "It does me such good. I feel so much more refreshed and revived when I'm here. It is the change of scenery, I think. Your mother is a very good person."

One time I stayed for several days in Penrith at Dr Haylock and Mrs Haylock's, who were also friends from church. There was to be a presentation of a silver bugle to a local man who had fought in the Crimean War and shown great bravery. A camp had been prepared for about 400 visitors, and others, like myself, stayed with families about the town. The festivities opened with a ball in Regentville House on the banks of the Nepean, the property where Father had first worked on our arrival in Australia. But I was overwhelmed at the thought of attending and did not own a ball gown and so I stayed at the Haylock's that night.

It was during this stay I met Robert Wilshire again. I was shocked to find him much changed. His previous chatty personality and open, honest countenance seemed to have been replaced by a guarded, grave, overly serious one. He came for tea at the Haylock's and the conversation was stiff and awkward, leaving me feeling sad and confused at the alteration. As he left the house, I hurried out to him. I did not want to seem impertinent and I had abruptly given up any hope of a relationship developing between us, but I worried for him.

I touched his arm as he turned towards me. "Mr Wilshire, you seem much changed from our last meeting," I ventured. "Has there been some terrible event to have affected you so greatly?"

Robert Wilshire coughed, I think to hide his embarrassment. "Do not be concerned for me, Miss Parkes," he said stiffly. "I suppose I have simply matured. I now know true responsibility, which I was not aware of before."

I waited for him to expand on this, but he did not, and bowed to me as he left.

Later, I asked Mrs Haylock about Robert Wilshire and was shocked at her reply.

"I believe his sister is expecting a child, Menie. She is not married. The family is terribly shamed and poor Robert has taken it badly."

"How awful!" I said. "Can't his sister marry now? Can't she marry the man she has been intimate with? Surely all would be forgotten if she did."

"I believe he was a scoundrel, Menie, and left for Queensland when he heard of her predicament. Robert's sister has no recourse but to have the baby alone. I think the household is in turmoil, including poor Robert."

I later heard that Robert Wilshire moved away from his father's property, which would also have been his inheritance, to the recently renamed island of Tasmania. I do not know what became of him or of his sister.

I had been surprised when Mamma announced her pregnancy with Varney, but I was even more surprised when, a few months after Father had left, she told me she was certain she was pregnant again.

"Surely it's just the waning of your courses, Mamma," I said in disbelief as I turned and sat beside her on the settee. "You are almost forty-eight years old!"

"No, I don't think it is that, Menie. I know the symptoms of a pregnancy better than most."

I think I laughed sarcastically at this, and then I blurted out, "But when?" before I could catch myself at this indiscretion.

Mamma blushed. "We were not going to see each other for such a long time, Menie. I love your father. You do understand, don't you?"

I was horrified. "Father doesn't even know you are pregnant, does he? You will have to go through this pregnancy without him. Oh, Mamma!"

We both burst into tears.

It was soon after this pregnancy announcement that Varney had his accident. I was sick in bed with a bronchial cough and Mamma sat beside me, reading verses of the Bible aloud to help pass the time. We could hear the children laughing and shouting from the garden and our dog, Sancho, barking wildly at their play. White had strung up a wooden swing from the bough of a eucalypt and Mary, Annie and Gerty were taking it in turns to see who could swing the highest, while Varry called to them from a short distance, "My turn! My turn! Varry wants a turn!"

"You're too small, Varry," I heard Gerty say to him. "You will have to wait till you are as old as me."

Mary scoffed at this older-sister's taunt and scooped Varry up, holding him as she swung. It must have been as she jumped from the swing that it flung back and hit Varry hard in his left temple.

The first I knew of it was Mamma's scream. She threw the Bible onto the bed and ran down the stairs, holding her skirt high and yelling, "Varry! Varry! Is he all right?"

I jumped from my bed and ran to the window to see Robert carrying Varry in his arms with blood streaming from the boy's head. I quickly pulled on my over-gown and ran downstairs in a terrible panic. I found Mamma sitting with Varry in her lap and a huge, jagged cut on his head pouring blood.

"We have killed him! We have killed him!" Annie was saying over and over again.

"Where is Robert?" I asked immediately and Mary told me he had gone for the doctor already.

"Get a cloth, Mary," I said at once. "And boil some water. Quickly!"

"I'm sure his skull is fractured, Menie," Mamma said, crying as she rocked Varry in her arms. But I was sure it wasn't. His eyes were open and looking as lively as ever and he didn't even cry.

I spent the next few hours holding Varry and walking around the room singing to him until Dr Haylock arrived at last. Even as the doctor examined Varry's head and bandaged it tightly, he still did not cry. Varry was always such a brave little boy. Robert carried him to his bed after that and I stood outside the door, listening while he talked to Varry gently. Robert always adored his little brother.

I remember relating Varry's beautiful, precocious nature to Father in a letter later that night. I told him how the boy would say to anyone he met, "My father is gone to England, and he is going to Ireland, and he has got a big beard and when he comes home I am going to pull it."

After his initial letter from Melbourne, we did not hear from Father again for some time. The mail from England was slow and probably disrupted by the War of the Rebellion (later known as the American Civil War), which had begun that year.

At last one afternoon in October, five months after Father had left us, Robert came riding into the yard from one of his regular trips to Penrith waving a stash of letters above his head. "It is Father!" he yelled as he reined in his horse. "Letters from Father!"

Even Mamma, in her pregnant state, ran down the steps towards him. There were letters for each of us, and Mamma took hers to read alone in her bedroom while the rest of us hurried into the lounge room to tear the envelopes open and wildly share snippets with each other.

Father and his fellow Commissioner, William Bede Dalley, had travelled on the steamship the *Great Britain* in first class. It must have been a very different experience to his and Mamma's voyage to Australia in steerage all those years earlier. Father wrote to me of the people they sat with until late in the evening in the dining salon, eating fine food and talking of politics and literature. I felt a little jealous and did not share with Mamma his description of one lady there, a Miss Lynch, who was *tall and of a handsome figure and walks with a most provoking natural grace and demureness.*

Father was unaware of Mamma's pregnancy at the time, and obviously oblivious to our own financial constraints. But I sensed how important this trip back to his homeland was when he wrote: *We are yet nearly eight hundred miles from Liverpool but the feeling of home grows so strong as we near England.*

Mamma spent a long time in her room that afternoon and when she finally emerged I was not surprised to find her red-eyed and distant.

Robert travelled to Penrith and South Creek twice most days. I believed for a time that he was very religious and attending church there, as he told Mamma and me. However, one night he arrived home late and staggered into the lounge room smelling of liquor. Mamma said nothing but I could see from the worry in her eyes that she was aware of his inebriated state. When Robert went to the kitchen, I followed him.

"Where have you been, Robert?" I asked crossly. "Not to church as you claim, I think." Robert grunted at me and gulped down mouthfuls of milk directly from the jug. "I suspect you have been at the Travellers' Rest or South Creek Inn. Am I correct?"

"What is it to you, Menie?" he snapped.

"What is it to *me!*" I was outraged. "Father is away and you are now the man of the house. Mamma depends on you. You cannot go carousing about when we might need you any moment. What if Varry has another accident? Or mother's labour begins early? What are we to do then?"

Robert did not answer; he pushed past me to go upstairs to his room.

A few nights later, when Robert was away from home from midday till midnight, I sat up to wait for him and when he came home at last, I burst into tears. I think he was surprised at my reaction and sat quietly at first while I spoke. "You need to think of Father," I said in a shaking voice, wiping my tears with the back of my hand. "He has placed great trust in you, Robert, so that we might depend on you. We are your responsibility now – Mamma and I and the children. It is your duty to us and to God to support us."

"I'm not shirking my duty, Menie," he said crossly. "I'm just doing what any man has the right to do."

"But, Robert, Mary had to feed the cattle today and do lots of your other jobs. These are your duties. And what if Mamma should have the baby? We would have to go on foot to get the midwife."

"Your horses are here. There's no reason why you or Mary couldn't ride to the midwife," he said.

"You know we find it difficult to catch our horses to ride them if you are not around."

"Well, you'll have to learn how to get them yourselves then, won't you?" Robert said and walked away.

The next morning, I was mortified to hear Robert talking to our man, Wales, about our conversation the night before and about a girl in Penrith. "She's better than Menie *ever* was!" Robert told Wales. "I won't be told by Menie."

I was aghast at the insult, and so ashamed that it should have been shared with Wales. I ran to my room in tears.

It was not until November that we heard from Father of the desperate state in which he found Aunt Sarah when he at last arrived in Birmingham, and of her death soon after in early September.

Mamma cried and cried at the news. "I feel so guilty now, Menie, that I begrudged your father this journey. He would never have forgiven me if he had not been there for Sarah, and I would never have forgiven myself. Sarah loved your father like her own child."

Father had arrived at Aunt Sarah and Aunt Maria's home in central Birmingham to find Aunt Sarah wasted and gaunt. He immediately rented a four-bedroom house further out of town and moved my aunts into it to live with him, and he wrote to Mr Dalley in London to come and join them. He told us that he began his work as Commissioner from there, writing to prominent men around England to arrange lectures on Australia conducted by himself and Mr Dalley, but that he was reluctant to travel

259

at the time for he was certain Aunt Sarah would not last long. And he was right, for she died soon after with Father and Aunt Maria at her side.

He wrote to Mamma, *Next to you and our dear children I have now lost the dearest creature that remained to me on earth.*

I do think it was providence that, after all their years apart, Father was with his favourite sister in her last few weeks of life, and that perhaps we should have been less resentful of his absence.

It was soon after Aunt Sarah's death that Father wrote to me to ask if I would join him in England. I was stunned and angry and dared not even mention this proposal to Mamma. I suppose Father was at last realising the terrible distance between him and us, and longing for company from a family member. I wrote to him that while I would love to go, *If anything goes a little wrong, Mamma gets confused and annoyed and wants me. And for that reason I could not accept your kind offer. It is impossible, just impossible, my place is here at the present.*

Of course, I really meant *his* place was here, with Mamma heavily pregnant and Robert not supporting us as he should. And that Mamma needed me so greatly because of Father's absence. I would not leave her to satisfy his need for companionship.

In December 1861 and January 1862 we suffered through a terrible drought. Most of the waterholes dried up and the ground became a dustbowl. Cattle on nearby properties were dropping dead from hunger and we hand-fed ours religiously. There were fierce fires in January. The heat was unbearable, but our property and that of our neighbouring landlords, the Letherbridges, were spared while others around us were ravished and homesteads burnt down.

Despite our good fortune, there were many anxious days and nights when we watched the glow of fires only a few miles off and swept the ash that fell on our land into great mountainous piles. Robert stayed with us throughout the fires and filled our well with water from the dwindling supply from the nearby creek.

And then at last, on the 18th of January, there was a great torrent of rain. We all ran outside with pots and bowls to collect the welcome downpour and watched, laughing, as our seven geese stood in a row with their necks up and beaks open, swallowing the rain.

I heard the details of Robert's indiscretion from Mrs Letherbridge. She asked me to tea one day and sat tight-lipped for some time before she began. "There are a lot of rumours about your brother, Clarinda," she said, and I flinched at the uncommon use of my real name as well as the realisation of the import of my invitation to visit. "I thought it my duty to tell you, dear. It must be so hard on your dear Mamma."

"But what have you heard, Mrs Letherbridge?" I asked.

"I have heard that Robert is seeing a young Penrith girl. The girl's mother is a terrible woman – a drunkard I've been told. The girl has been raised as a sort of half-servant by a Mrs Clark. She is a giddy, dressy sort of girl, indeed, and Mr Letherbridge said he saw Robert kissing her fully on the mouth in public and..." She coughed uncomfortably before continuing. "And I believe his hand was placed on an inappropriate part of the girl's body, for all to see."

I held back my tears, for I did not want to satisfy Mrs Letherbridge with a dramatic response she could relate as fresh gossip. "I see," I said simply and sipped my tea.

I told Mamma some of this conversation when I got home, but I was careful not to alarm her too greatly in her heavily pregnant state. That night she asked Robert directly about the girl.

I held my breath as Robert turned to her and answered curtly, "You can find out whatever you want to know, Mamma, on the rumour mills." Then he left the room.

The heat of that summer bore heavily on Mamma, who was exhausted in her pregnancy. Finally, on the 7th of February, she went into labour in the early afternoon and Robert was around to fetch the midwife from South Creek.

I sat by my greying Mamma and wiped her brow as she moaned through yet another labour. Just before midnight, Lily Faulconbridge Parkes was born. She was a large baby with a thick head of brown hair and deep blue eyes, and Mamma wept when the midwife laid her on her breast.

We were all delighted after the birth, not least because Mamma's trial was over. Varry loved his little sister. He would stand by her cot, gazing at her lovingly, and say to Mamma, "Where's my sister, a pretty thing? Has her got pretty eyes, eh Ma, and pretty toes? Won't I take her to meet Father? I will, eh Ma?"

Even Robert seemed to soften and ride out to South Creek less often after Lily was born.

Our finances continued to suffer. In March I sold our two pigs to the Letherbridges to make ends meet. And then, when it was proving impossible to satisfy all our bills and Father's ongoing debts, I wrote to John Fairfax to ask his advice. I knew Father still felt a great rivalry towards the newspaper proprietor, but I was desperate and unwilling to worry Mamma too greatly. Mr Fairfax wrote immediately to ask me to visit him at his offices in Sydney, and I set out on the coach to the city soon after.

I had not been to Sydney for some time, and I found it strange – the bustle and fuss and the carriages racing crazily along the streets. Mr Fairfax's office was now on the corner of Pitt and Hunter Streets, and this corner had become known as Fairfax Corner.

He greeted me warmly. "Miss Parkes, it is a pleasure to see you," he said in his familiar Midlands accent, bowing to me as he took my hand.

I was flustered and nervous. "Thank you so much for seeing me, Mr Fairfax. I am aware you are a busy man. I just, with my father away, you know... I just wasn't sure whom else to ask," I faltered.

"Of course, Miss Parkes. Don't worry yourself. And thank you again for your contributions to *The Sydney Mail*. They are very well received, as you would know."

"Thank you, Mr Fairfax," I said as I took the seat he indicated opposite him at his huge teak desk.

I began to relate to him the difficulties we were experiencing, and Mr Fairfax suggested which debts I could put off for a time and which should be paid urgently. I suspect Mr Fairfax must have spoken to one of Father's creditors soon afterwards, for there is no other explanation I can conceive for the lessening of the pressure of that particular creditor's demands.

Later, I wrote to Father to tell him I had sought assistance from Mr Fairfax, and Father was not pleased. I wrote in my reply to him, *I have perhaps not chosen the person you would best like to be consulted, but then you were not here for me to ask.* My barbs were perhaps blunt at times, but I still regard them as justified.

Father's year away proved to be close to two years. He wrote to us about some of the people he met, including the Scottish philosopher Thomas Carlyle, and of his admiration for the man's wife, Jane. I was particularly thrilled when he wrote of meeting Thomas Hughes, the author of *Tom Brown's Schooldays*, and Father related how Mr Hughes read some of my serialised novel, *Bitter Sweet*, and told Father I showed great promise.

I will always remember Mamma's rage when she received a letter from Father around August 1862. I had never seen her in such a state before. She strode angrily about the room, her face red and her eyes wild, screwing the letter into her fist before throwing it on the ground. I did not know what to say, but Gerty, who was sitting by the hearth practising arithmetic on her slate, banged her chalk down and declared, "Mamma, have you gone mad?"

We were all taken aback when Mamma shouted her angry response to the poor girl, "I'm not the one who is *mad*, Gerty! Indeed, perhaps it would help if I were mad, for then I would not feel this so hard! It is your *father* who is perhaps mad!"

I rushed to Mamma and helped her to a chair. "Calm yourself, Mamma. What on earth has Father said?"

"He is saying he will stay in England longer! He has finished his work as Commissioner for Emigration, but he is now wanting to open another shop on his return, and he wants to stay on in England in order to collect goods for the store!"

"Oh," was all I could say in response.

"And can you believe, Menie, he writes that he wants *me* to set up a shop in Sydney for this purpose immediately, and to sell all the books in his library to finance it! Did he forget I have a baby to care for? Did he forget he has left us here to deal with all of this for more than a year already? Is he out of his mind?"

I wonder what Mamma would have said to Father's face if he were there at the time, but, fortunately for him, he did not have to witness her fury.

"Mamma, if anyone is to arrange all of this, it will be me," I said, trying to stay calm, but Mamma's response was immediate.

"No, Menie!" she said, close to frustrated tears. "If anyone is to arrange this, it is your *father*! None of us are to do anything on this matter until he comes home! I am writing to him today to tell him he must come home now! Fetch me my writing case, Annie dear, I will write to him this instant!"

Robert laughed out loud at Mamma's resolute response to our great father, and I placed a fist to my mouth to suppress my own laughter.

Mamma was the dutiful wife to a point, it seemed, but no further. I was proud of her, and extremely surprised.

I didn't read Mamma's letter to Father, but it must have been confronting and insistent, for he sailed on the *Spray of the Ocean* from England within a month of its receipt. He still had plans for a shop, a kind of emporium, and had managed to collect some goods from England before he'd left, and he had employed his sister Maria and another man, William Cooper, to be his English agents in the matter.

Father arrived home on the 23rd of January, 1863, almost a year after Lily's birth. It seemed unreal to see his tall figure dismounting from the coach near Werrington, his hair now almost completely white and his face bearded. We were all a little uncomfortable at the reunion. Mamma waited on the veranda for him to come to her, holding Lily in her arms as they hugged and he kissed Mamma lightly on the mouth.

"Henry, this is your daughter Lily," she said and gave him the baby, almost roughly, whereon Lily immediately began to cry and reach for Mamma.

The driver of the coach unloaded about seven crates of packed goods and White and Wales brought them inside the house as we all poured in after each hugging Father dutifully. Our maid went to get tea, and we sat around the lounge room stiffly while looking wonderingly at this unfamiliar man.

"Well, are you pleased to 'ave me 'ome?" he asked almost indignantly as none of us spoke. "Do you remember your father, Varney?"

Little Varry nodded his head gravely.

"Of course we are thrilled to have you home, Henry. It has been so long," Mamma said.

"And you, Bob? 'Ave you been doing your duty to your mother?" Father asked, knowing full well from our letters that Robert had been negligent at times.

"As much as I've been able, Father," Robert replied.

"Well, Menie, don't be shy around me now. I'm still your same old father."

I forced a laugh and went to sit on the stool by his chair and held his hand.

"I don't like your beard at all," Mamma said and Father looked shocked at her directness before he laughed half-heartedly.

Twenty

Within a few weeks of his return, Father took a lease on a shop in Hunter Street, opposite our last premises there. He wanted his emporium to be a family affair, but Mamma refused to work at the shopfront in the city.

"Now that you are back, Henry, we must dismiss the children's nurse. I will continue to look after the children during the week. There will be no possibility of my working in the city each day," Mamma told him one morning as he sat at the kitchen table, dipping his toast into a runny boiled egg.

Father was exasperated. "You 'ave begged for and wanted my company, Clarinda! But I need to make a living, and I cannot do it from 'ere!" he exclaimed.

Mamma stood firm. I think he was shocked at the hardening in her. And then when he asked me to be his bookkeeper and Robert to work at the shop, we both made excuses.

"I would be no good at bookkeeping, Father. My experiences in financial matters since you've been away have proved that," I tried to explain, and Father huffed and threw his hands in the air.

And then when Robert told him he was setting off up north the next month to work as a jackeroo, Father roared, "What 'as 'appened to you all? I thought I could depend on you!"

Mamma replied steadily, "You can, Henry, as you must know. We were dependable throughout your long absence, and we will continue to be. But I will not leave the children."

And so Father spent his weeks in the city again, and life at Werrington continued on as usual.

Neither Father nor Mamma were happy at Robert's decision to leave us and work as a jackeroo, but he was a man of twenty now. The day he left on the coach, Mamma wept furiously. "My boy! Oh, my boy!" she said, clutching his tall frame to her.

"Come on, Mamma," he said, blushing. "I'll be back soon enough."

I cried, too, for despite his rude behaviour of late, he was still my little brother and I would miss him. My tears were also ones of self-pity.

Robert's leaving again awakened my own desire for independence. I was still writing regularly, but I wanted more to my life than being an older sister caring for her younger siblings. I still did not want to work at the shop with Father, which had moved now to George Street, especially as I found finance a dull pastime. I began to think again of opening a school, but I did not have the money and was unsure how to begin.

I suppose we were all restless at the time, including Father. He began to talk more of politics and parliament once more. I was not surprised when he came home one Saturday to tell us that he was thinking of running for a seat again. Mamma seemed to have gained an independence from Father during his overseas absence that made her more accepting of this proposal than on other occasions.

It was a controversial move, though. Father's good friend John Bayley Darvall, who had helped him in his earlier legal studies, had won a seat in East Maitland, mainly standing on an anti-Cowper ticket. But then, within six weeks of winning the seat, Mr Darvall had accepted the position of attorney-general in Charles Cowper's ministry, a complete reversal of his campaign promises. Father and many others were incensed. So when Father was asked by other liberal supporters to stand against Mr Darvall in the necessary re-election, Father agreed. This was against convention, as Mr Darvall's prior election to the seat would usually not have been contested.

Then began a bitter dispute between Father and his old friend. Mr Darvall played on the stigma of Father's previous bankruptcy and the newspapers were venomous. Father's editorial enemy, John West, wrote sarcastically in *The Sydney Morning Herald*:

> *We can easily imagine what it must have cost a man of such refined sense, open to all the gentler emotions of the poetical mind, to go into opposition to a man like Mr Darvall, who showed him in the darker stages of his career an amount of kindness rarely exampled... How great must be the strength of Mr Parkes's affection for the country to induce him to cast these reminiscences to the wind.*

Mamma's staunch loyalty was kindled by these and similar articles. She became quite determined that Father should win the seat and so she did not object when he set off for a time to campaign in Maitland.

In the end, Father was decisively defeated.

Father's political ambitions were not dashed completely by his loss. He sat for a seat in Braidwood in early 1864, but again he was defeated. And then, at last, he sat for a seat in the south coast town of Kiama in April 1864, and this time he won.

I had been suffering from a severe bronchial cough for a time and I was also, at twenty-five, quite unhappy in my mundane life. I told Mamma of my restlessness and my wish for more excitement and variability. She must have taken my complaints seriously, for Father arranged for me to visit friends of his, Mr and Mrs Vaughan, in their villa in Balmain opposite Sydney Harbour.

I set off on the coach in early September. It was a thrill for me to be the one saying a tearful goodbye to the family this time. I was to stay for a week and enjoy the warmer climate to help relieve my cough.

Mrs Vaughan took me under her wing as soon as I arrived at their isolated Waterview Bay home, Durham Villa. She was an older, rosy-cheeked, childless woman who seemed to crave company and purpose. We spent time sitting together in the sun on their veranda overlooking the water and watching the sailboats tacking about on the picturesque harbour. One day we travelled by coach into the city and visited the Botanic Gardens where I marvelled at the growth of the Moreton Bay figs since my last visit and, once more, sat on the hard sandstone of Mrs Macquarie's Chair.

Sadly, within days of my arrival, my cough had become worse and I was bed-ridden. And so, the remainder of the week was filled with Mrs Vaughan's chatter at my bedside, but no more outings. It was a disappointment.

Once again, we did not know how severely in debt Father had become, this time due to the excessive purchases of Aunt Maria and his other English agent. Mr Cowper must have had some knowledge of Father's financial difficulties, for he offered him the job of Director-General of Prisons in an attempt, we thought, to get Father on-side and reduce the threat of his competition in politics. This position would have given Father a salary, the first in all his years as a Member of Parliament.

Father refused, so Mr Cowper offered him the cabinet position of postmaster general with a salary of £950 instead. Father refused this offer, too. I am sure he wavered in these decisions, but his massive self-belief bolstered him again.

And then, at the end of 1864, when Mr Cowper's government was defeated by a motion that Father had moved, James Martin, a man who had publicly denounced and attacked Father earlier that same year, was appointed as premier. In the confusing dance of politics, Mr Martin asked Father to take the salaried cabinet position of Colonial Secretary. Father accepted. Suddenly, my father, a man who had come to Australia an impoverished ivory turner, now held a position that made him one of the top three men in the New South Wales Government.

It is a strange thing to have a personal relationship with a powerful man. Henry Parkes was still my father, the man who was always to be the standard by which I would judge all men, but also the man I knew to be human – the man I had witnessed at his lowest and weakest. To be so close to a person in power creates a confusion of standards. But it also made me aware of the vulnerability of all people.

Later that year I stayed with the Taylors, supporters of Father's in Kiama. I stayed with them from late December and throughout January 1865. It was the longest I had been away from home and I found that, despite the tea parties and endless invitations, I missed Mamma and the children desperately.

Suddenly, I realised my usual quiet life had some attractions. When I had the opportunity for time alone, I walked along the seaside and to the magnificent Kiama blowhole to watch the water gushing through in a massive spray, and worried about the meaning of my life.

I do not know when Mamma and Father stopped being intimate, but I think it probably began around this time, for Mamma was never pregnant again. Of course, this could have been due to the end of her courses, but, from subsequent events, I believe their intimacy ceased completely at some point.

Father was absent even more regularly now. He travelled inland for a month, to Goulburn, Yass, Queanbeyan, Braidwood, Albury and on to Melbourne and Ballarat in Victoria. It was a dangerous time to travel due to the threat of bushrangers, particularly the notorious Clarke brothers, and Father travelled with his friend Edward Flood and two police troopers, each of the four men armed with two revolving pistols and a revolving rifle. Father had never before shot a gun and I remember one of the police troopers giving him a lesson at our property one afternoon. Fortunately, Father and his companions did not come across any bushrangers during the month of their travel.

Mamma became strangely content in his absence. They wrote to each other regularly and she pottered in the garden and became more active in tutoring the children again. Lily was three years old by then, Varney was six, Gerty was nine, Annie was eleven and Mary was seventeen. Robert had returned from up north to settle in the city and begin work as a bookbinder. I was only four years away from my thirtieth birthday and was completely resigned now to the life of a spinster. I was reasonably content, focusing on my writing and the children, but I wondered what my life would be when they were all grown.

In Father's first year as a cabinet minister, he achieved much-needed social reform. His Juvenile Reformatory Act ensured that young offenders were not imprisoned with older criminals and it implemented a greater focus on reform over punishment. He also introduced legislation to improve the treatment of lunacy and the quality of hospitals.

I remember one Saturday night we all sat on the veranda after supper and Father told us of the terrible conditions he had witnessed at the lunatic asylum at Tarban Creek.

"There were bars over the windows and every door was locked," he said. "It was as if those poor people were in gaol. And there was no garden or place for recreation. The inmates were treated like animals."

"That's terrible, Father!" Annie exclaimed, always the sensitive one. She couldn't even bear to see a chicken killed.

"It was fortunate I met a naval surgeon, Frederick Norton Manning, who was visiting the asylum and we discussed the type of reforms needed.

I'm considering asking 'im to take up the position of superintendent to improve the living conditions there."

After that Father took the initiative to write to Florence Nightingale, the famous nurse of the Crimean War, to ask her to train four nurses in England who could be sent to New South Wales to improve the standard of the hospitals.

Father's greatest accomplishment of that year, though, was the introduction of the Public Schools Act. It introduced a single Council of Education for both public and denominational schools, which was to be responsible for the funding of all schools and the training of teachers. Both the Anglican and Catholic churches were greatly opposed to this legislation for it ensured denominational schools were under stricter government control. But Father was determined that all children had the right to an equal education.

"It is the education of the population that is the linchpin for social reform," he told me. "It is for the good of everyone that all children be given an education."

Father's business continued but he had little to do with its running from when he became a cabinet minister. He left the daily running of the business in the hands of his employees, Alfred Fowler and John Steele, while Aunt Maria and William Cooper continued as his English agents, purchasing and exporting items from there.

One weekend in early 1867, Father came home in a terribly agitated state. I took his coat at the door and, after he had bent to kiss me, he whispered to me gravely, "Oh, Menie, 'ave you 'eard the tragic news? Does your mother know?"

"No, Father, I don't know what you mean."

Father passed his hand across his brow, wearily. "I feel so responsible. This will stay 'eavy on my 'eart, Menie," he said.

"What will, Father? What is wrong?" I asked anxiously.

"I'd formed a group of special constables to try to bring in the bushrangers the Clarke brothers," he explained. "It was my initiative to do this and I didn't go through the usual police channels. I even met the four men who were to form the group, and briefed the 'ead one, John Carroll, on the operation. 'E was a solid, decent man."

"But what has happened?" I was alarmed at Father's shaking voice.

"The Clarke brothers 'ave murdered all four of them. They were each tied to a tree and shot!"

"Oh, Father!" I exclaimed. "How awful!"

"I feel responsible for their deaths, Menie. Four good men – John Carroll, Patrick Kennagh, Eneas McDonnell and John Phegan. They all 'ad families. What will your mother say?"

"It is not your fault, Father!" I said insistently.

I heard Mamma crying in their bedroom when he told her. The Clarke gang were finally caught three months later and hanged on the 25th of June. Father did not attend the hanging.

"I'll never forget the 'anging I saw in London, Menie," he told me later. "I know the Clarke brothers killed those policemen, but I still believe a man can be reformed – even a murderer. That's where education is essential. Those lads 'ad little or no education and therefore nothing to bind them to society."

I was not convinced that the Clarke brothers should not have been hung, but I was proud of Father's strong principles.

It was in January 1868 that the most exciting events of my life occurred. I look back on this time now as if it were a dream, but the newspapers of the time prove that it was not. Prince Alfred, Duke of Edinburgh and the second son of Queen Victoria, was to visit our shores. I knew that, as

Colonial Secretary, Father would meet the Prince, but I had not expected this honour to include myself.

Mamma never liked the attention or the ceremony of public events, but on this occasion Father insisted she should accompany him to Sydney for the festivities. It was decided that Mary, Annie and I should also go to support her. I remember Gerty, only two years younger than Annie, cried when she was told she wasn't to join us and that twelve years old was too young for such an event. I tried to cheer her by assuring her I'd write every day and include every detail, but it must have been a great disappointment to be left behind.

Mamma spent the weeks leading up to the Prince's arrival making dresses for us and herself. I remember she found a dusky green fabric for my dress, and Father gave me a deep jade necklace he'd originally intended to sell at his emporium. Our home buzzed with expectation throughout those weeks.

Finally, word came in late January that the steamer frigate *H.M.S. Galatea*, which the Prince captained, was nearing the coast of New South Wales. Gerty, Varney and Lily were to stay at Werrington in the care of our maid, Margaret; and Mamma, Mary, Annie and I were to catch the coach immediately to Sydney to meet Father.

The Tuesday Prince Alfred arrived was raining heavily. We were on board the steamer the *Auckland* off Bondi Beach with Father and the other members of the cabinet and their families as the massive hull of the *H.M.S. Galatea* passed and our ship led a convoy of vessels behind it through Sydney Heads. I remember I was very queasy with the strong swell, and the view from the porthole was blurred by the rain. I laugh now to think of the constant chatter from Annie in her excitement throughout the journey to Circular Quay and Mamma saying to her, "Take a breath, dear. You'll be exhausted from talking before we even get there."

As the ship came into the harbour, cannons boomed a salute and the Royal Yacht Squadron encircled the ship. We sailed past the great vessel and landed at Circular Quay where a huge white pavilion had been constructed. Unfortunately, due to the rain, the Prince did not come ashore that day and it proved a disappointing anti-climax.

The following day, we waited at the back of the pavilion with the other ministers' families, listening to the crowd's raucous cheers outside as Prince Alfred landed at the quay and my heart fluttered wildly.

Father and the other cabinet members were all dressed in the same uniform they had worn the previous day, which I secretly thought looked ridiculous. They wore blue, gold-braided jackets and trousers with matching cocked hats and swords in sabres at their waists.

The white flap at the entrance to the pavilion was held open by two guards and, suddenly, the Prince walked in alongside our governor, the Earl of Belmore. I was more overwhelmed by Prince Alfred's presence than I had anticipated. We all bowed or curtsied low to the tall, attractive man, and I remember he was far handsomer than I had expected. He had light brown curls and a close-cropped beard, and when he was introduced to Mrs Parkes and her daughters, I saw that his eyes were lively and green like my dress. Then the mayor of Sydney, Charles Moore, addressed the Prince and he and the ministers left the pavilion in a procession of carriages through Sydney to Government House, led by the volunteer fire brigade and escorted by mounted police.

That night, Mamma and Father dined with the Prince and the other ministers and their wives at Government House. I stayed up late in our hotel room, waiting for their return. Mamma came back giggly and elated from the wine she had drunk.

"Well, Menie," Father boomed when he saw me, "your mother 'as been most distinguished tonight. The order of going in to dinner was the

Prince and the Countess of Belmore, followed by the Earl of Belmore and Mrs Parkes!"

"Oh, Mamma!" I squealed and ran to hug her.

"Who would 'ave thought," Father continued, "that your mother would one day dine with Princes and be led by Earls!"

If ever Mamma was melancholy or despondent after this, I would remind her of this night.

Father was the only one of the ministers to be called into the Prince's rooms for a private meeting that day, too. When he returned to the hotel, his eyes shone with elation.

"'E spoke to me for several minutes," he told us as he sat down opposite us on a hotel chair.

"What did you talk about?" Mamma asked excitedly.

"'E told me 'e was thrilled with his reception and very impressed with our 'arbour, and then we briefly discussed the state of politics in New South Wales."

I remember thinking then, who would have thought my father, once a simple ivory turner, would one day chat privately with a Prince!

The other big event we attended was a ceremony in the Domain a few days later. Father rode in a carriage with Sir George Bowen, the visiting Governor of New Zealand, behind the official party on horseback headed by the Prince and Earl Belmore. Mamma, Mary, Annie and I rode in a carriage behind Father's from Government House to the crowded Domain where Prince Alfred inspected the Queen's imperial regiment and the colony's volunteer units.

There were many other events Father attended that week with the Prince, including luncheons and a ball and the opening of the horticultural society's grand exhibition of flowers and plants. But Father was always most thrilled to relate the tour he and Mr Wilkins took the

Prince on through the Fort Street Model School. My sisters, Mamma and I headed home before any of these occasions, however, and I remember I slept with exhaustion on the coach the whole way back to Werrington.

It was a dreadful shock when, a few months after meeting the Prince, we received a letter from Father telling us Prince Alfred, the Duke of Wellington, had been shot. It happened after he returned to Sydney from visits to other colonies, in Clontarf at a picnic to raise money for a sailor's home. Father hadn't been there, but he'd heard details of the event soon after and relayed these in his letter to us.

A shot had rung out from the crowd and the Prince had collapsed. The would-be assassin loomed over the Prince but failed to raise his gun again before he was set upon by the crowd. It was said that he probably would have been strung up there and then if others had not intervened to hurry the man away to a boat.

The Prince was taken immediately to Government House by carriage and the nurses who had been sent from England by Florence Nightingale attended him there. Lucy Osburn, the chief of these ladies and later the superintendent of the Sydney Infirmary, found that the bullet had initially hit the rubber of Prince Alfred's braces before entering his body, which had prevented the wound from becoming life-threatening.

Father, as Colonial Secretary and therefore Minister for Police, went immediately with police officers to search the rooms of two hotels in which the would-be assassin had stayed. They found, amongst other things, gunpowder and nine pages of a diary that appeared to be clear evidence of a Fenian plot.

The shooter was an Irishman, Henry James O'Farrell, and Father interviewed him several times in his cell. He told us later that he found Mr O'Farrell a likeable, intelligent and witty man.

Father believed, though, that Mr O'Farrell was part of a larger Fenian conspiracy. This assertion was later disputed and the cause of much humiliation. Within two hours of Mr O'Farrell's hanging on the 21st of April, 1868, Father was handed, on instructions from the condemned man himself, a confession that claimed he had acted alone and had not been part of a plot.

However, Father was so convinced Mr O'Farrell had been part of a larger organisation and that the confession was designed to protect those others involved that he did not table the confession in parliament. This proved to be a mistake, for, unknown to Father, another copy of the confession had been given to William Bede Dalley – the man who had been Father's fellow Commissioner of Emigration and had travelled to England with him.

Mr Dalley had been one of Mr O'Farrell's defence lawyers at his trial. He gave his copy of the confession to Father's opposition, who read it out in parliament. Father was accused of withholding his copy of the confession in order to save face. I suspect this was indeed the reason for his inaction. But Father was adamant there had been a plot.

"The man told me, even during my first interview with 'im, that 'e was part of a larger group," Father told Mamma and me when he arrived home the following Saturday. "It's there in the record that was taken of my interviews with 'im. Mr O'Farrell didn't even agree with the rest of the group that they should attempt to kill the Prince. But, as 'e said, 'e 'ad sworn an oath to abide by the majority's decision. 'E was actually relieved when 'e 'eard the Prince was recovering. Mr O'Farrell even said to me that 'e didn't think the Prince should travel on to New Zealand because 'e would be in even more danger there from 'is group."

"Why didn't one of the other members attempt the shooting then, if Mr O'Farrell didn't agree with it?" I asked.

Father was abrupt in his answer. "Because they drew lots to decide who would commit the act. O'Farrell even described to me 'ow tense the moment was when the lots were drawn, and 'ow 'e 'ad 'oped it wouldn't be 'im. Even Mr Read, the Principal Warder at the gaol, was able to tell the exact details of 'ow the lots were drawn from 'is conversations with O'Farrell. There were definitely other men involved. 'E told me, also, 'ow one of the other men wanted to set fire to the pavilion when the Citizens' Ball was to take place there that evening because it 'ad been erected in 'onour of British royalty. I am absolutely certain, despite 'is confession, that O'Farrell was part of a larger Fenian organisation."

So convinced was Father of the larger plot that, later, when addressing his constituents in Kiama, he told his audience he could produce clear evidence that Mr O'Farrell had killed before. It seemed Father had decided this was the case from something Mr O'Farrell had written in his diary: *There was a Judas in the twelve – in our band there was a No. 3 as bad, but his horrible death will, I trust, be a warning to traitors.*

But once again, this became the cause of much humiliation for Father. The unproven murder became known as the story of the 'Kiama Ghost' and was the subject of much ridicule in the press and in parliament. Following this, Alexander Macleay demanded a committee look into the question of the Fenian plot, and Father told us the resolutions of this committee were a direct attack on him and he had argued the point until three o'clock in the morning to ensure his counter-resolutions were tabled in place of Mr Macleay's.

No Fenian plot was ever discovered. Prince Albert recovered sufficiently within a week to lay the foundation stone for the Sydney Town Hall before sailing home. There were no more known attacks related to the O'Farrell incident. But, from the time of the shooting until his own death, Premier Martin continued to carry a gun with him for protection against Fenian sympathisers.

TWENTY-ONE

I fell truly, madly in love during that year of 1868. I was almost twenty-nine years old when I first met William Thom. He was forty-four, a Presbyterian minister who had recently arrived in Australia from Scotland.

I had been invited to tea at the Letherbridges' one Monday afternoon. I always felt obliged to attend these gatherings, although I never felt comfortable with Mrs Letherbridge due to her superior, condescending manner towards me. But I will always be thankful I attended her house on that day.

It was not love at first sight. William was never a good-looking man and, already greying and with deep lines in the corners of his eyes, he was closer in age to Mamma and Father than to me. But it was while attempting to talk with his shy, retiring orphaned niece Katie, a girl of fifteen whom he had raised from infancy due to the death of his sister and brother-in-law, that I became aware of his gentle, encouraging manner.

"Have you liked your time in New South Wales, Miss Marshall?" I asked.

The pimply girl barely looked at me as she replied in almost a whisper, "Yes. It's very different to Scotland, though."

I noticed her glance towards her uncle then, and his supportive wink back.

"You must come to visit my family sometime, Miss Marshall. I have a sister around your age, Gerty, who is always keen for company," I ventured.

Katie seemed to blush at the suggestion and began to stammer a reply before William reached for her hand and intervened. "Katie would be delighted to visit you, Miss Parkes," he said. "Wouldn't you, my dear? She is a little nervous," he addressed me, "and, like myself, she finds it difficult to understand some of your accents."

I laughed, for I had had trouble understanding their strong Scottish brogue, too.

"And, Mr Thom," I continued, "you must also come to visit. Father is not home during the week due to commitments in Sydney, but I'm sure Mamma would be pleased to meet you."

And so, William and his niece came to visit us the following week. My feelings for the man were slow to ripen. I had already resigned myself to the life of a spinster, and did not even consider William as a possible suitor for some time. It was, in fact, a shock to me when he first alerted me to his own feelings some months later when we were walking together through the bush at a distance behind Katie and Gerty.

"Miss Parkes," he began. "I have something which I have been... ah... meaning to talk to you about for some time."

"Oh yes, Mr Thom?" I answered brightly. "What might that be?"

Suddenly, William turned towards me and grabbed both of my hands in his. I think I stopped breathing for a minute with the surprise of it. "Miss Parkes," he said, gazing down into my eyes and saying in a rush. "Miss Parkes, are you at all aware of my feelings for you? I know I am an old man in your eyes, but I believe I have deep, sincere feelings towards you."

I pulled my hands from his grasp and said something like, "Mr Thom! This is most alarming! You should not have said such a thing!"

"But, Miss Parkes – Clarinda – it is something which, even if my feelings are not returned, you must know of," he said as I turned away from him rudely due to my extreme embarrassment, and continued to walk. He hurried after me.

"Mr Thom, Katie and Gerty are just ahead of us. This is not the place!" I said crossly and we walked on in silence. But my heart was racing and my mind was in confusion.

It was after this confrontation that I found myself often thinking about the man. He and Katie continued to visit and, despite my discomfort, William did not falter in his conversations with me, although he did not talk of his feelings towards me again. It was not until late that year I realised I was, indeed, in love. Then I faced the predicament of how to tell William, and the fear that his own feelings might have changed during my prevarication. It was on a day in November that I bravely rode into Penrith and knocked on the door of the small house he rented.

William told me later of the complete joy he felt when he saw me standing there. I went to talk, to say the words I had practised, but they stuck in my dry mouth and so all I did was gaze up at him with tears in my eyes and nod violently. William did not hesitate to sweep me up into his arms right there on the street and carry me into his hall where he kissed me deeply.

We were married at Werrington on the 30th of March, 1869. William had accepted a posting as minister to the south coastal town of Pambula, so we moved to a small house there – a distance of over 300 miles from my family home.

Robert was married two months after my wedding. I believe his wife, Mary Ann, had been pregnant at the time, for their daughter was born only six months later – sadly, she didn't survive the year. I didn't attend the wedding for it was held in Sydney. I wasn't to meet Mary Ann for another year.

I was surprised when I received a letter from Father in September telling me he was joining Mr James Martin to oppose the Robertson government. He and Mr Martin had never been friends. And then when the government was dissolved and elections held in November and December of 1869, Father stood for both Kiama and East Sydney and topped the poll in East Sydney. But Charles Cowper, who had been defeated in this same seat, won a seat later that month in the election in Liverpool Plains and, to Father's disgust, formed a government in January, 1870.

William spent many days and sometimes full weeks riding through the rough country of the south coast and further to visit members of his congregation and to deal with parish matters. His parish extended from Cobargo – forty-six miles from Pambula – down to the Victorian border. He ran services in Pambula, Eden and Twofold Bay. It was a huge responsibility. My life was often lonely that year, apart from the quiet company of William's niece, Katie. She was not as shy towards me as she had been when we first met, but she was never much of a conversationalist. We would spend our evenings silently sewing or reading in William's absence. But when William was home, my happiness was limitless.

I remember the first trip I took with William to Eden that year. The countryside is rugged there, but extraordinarily beautiful. We travelled by coach past two wide, glistening lakes with several small green islands, and across a tidal flat at low tide surrounded by mountains of bushland where I saw crabs scurrying into their caves and the winding trails of sea snails and the deep roots of great messes of mangrove trees.

The beach at Pambula was also my frequent haunt. I would walk its sweeping sands barefoot towards the river, always careful my feet should not show beneath my skirt but loving the massage of the sand

and small shells. Sometimes men or boys would be swimming in the waves as I passed, and I wondered how it would feel to dive beneath the salty foam.

I became pregnant soon after our wedding. I was terribly sick in those first months and wondered how Mamma had endured such an ordeal twelve times over. I was so thrilled, though, at this wonderful change in my life – one which only a year before I had thought I would never experience.

Mary came to visit in August. We both cried hopelessly when she arrived at my cottage in Pambula in the carriage William had accompanied her in from the steamer at Merimbula. Mary was now an attractive, dark-haired beauty of twenty-one.

"Oh, Menie, things are so dull at Werrington without you," she told me as we sat on the veranda that evening while William sat inside to write his next sermon. "I feel like such an old thing there. Mamma's gout has been getting worse, too, and I'm forever having to heat a flannel for her to ease it. Really, that seems to be all I do some days."

"Mary, you must not complain of this. Poor Mamma needs your help," I chastised her before asking. "How are the children? Is Gerty behaving? How is Varry doing with his studies?"

"Varry works hard at it, Menie, but he's not very clever," she told me as she swatted a mosquito on her arm. "And he's become ever so timid and shy these days."

"How strange, when he was such a precocious little boy," I said. "Do you remember how he used to fawn over Lily's basket when she was a baby, and talk of her pretty little toes?"

We laughed at the memory.

"And what of Father?" I asked. "I have letters from him regularly, of course, but how are he and Mamma getting on when he is home?"

"They are still great friends, Menie, of course," Mary told me, "but Mamma is still not much interested in Father's politics, unless it is in criticising 'Slippery Charles Cowper'!"

In November, Mamma came to stay for the final month of my pregnancy. I had missed her immensely over the year and was overwhelmed with joy when my gentle Mamma arrived.

"Menie, my dear!" she said as we hugged. "Look at you, all huge with the baby! My dear, how are you feeling? Are you eating well? Let's get you back in your chair."

And so Mamma looked after me throughout late November and early December and helped the midwife during my labour, just as I had for her on occasions, and little Henry Gilbert was born on the 12th of December, 1869.

I was unaware of the difficulties Father's business was experiencing by then. He still had little to do with its running and it seemed the financial difficulties were due mainly to Aunt Maria and his other English agent overspending. I was horrified when I heard by letter in October 1870 that Father had again gone into bankruptcy. His business was ended, and he had resigned his parliamentary seat and withdrawn from the Council of Education. But his constituents in Kiama insisted on putting Father forward for the seat again, saying his bankruptcy was due to his public service and therefore shouldn't disbar him from parliament. And so, two weeks after resigning his seat, Father was again elected.

It was a few days after my Henry's first birthday that the Cowper government failed, and Father's once friend and now great enemy, Charles Cowper, accepted a post to London as Agent-General for New South Wales. He was to be gone from the political scene in New South Wales forever.

At the same time, Father was being criticised venomously in the newspapers for continuing in parliament when still a bankrupt, and he, humiliated and depressed, resigned his seat once more. Mr Forster from *The Sydney Morning Herald* was particularly brutal in his attack on Father. He wrote that Father had displayed:

> *... the same unhappy egotism which has so much impaired his public useful-ness, and which, for ever involving all surrounding objects in an atmosphere of immeasurable self-importance, has so frequently confounded accident with design, distorted party contests into personal grievances, exaggerated solitary insanity into a world-wide conspiracy, and magnified molehills of private or imaginary wrongs into mountains of public criminality.*

I think such a personal attack was disgraceful. I know Father was humiliated by it and that Mamma would have cried bitterly when she read it.

I loved motherhood. Little Henry was a fair, blue-eyed child with big, soft cheeks and a boyish grin. He was quite robust and began to walk at the early age of eleven months, and whenever William came home, he would throw his arms in the air and 'hurrah'. Katie was a great help to me then, cooking the dinner as I nursed Henry or rocked him to sleep in the evenings. And sometimes she and I would take Henry on toddling walks along the beach to collect shells.

I realised I was pregnant again in late 1870 when the sickness came on me. But this burden was minor in comparison to the joy I felt at the thought of another child.

I went home to Werrington with Henry for Christmas that year but William insisted on staying in Pambula to run the Christmas service in the church there. Henry, or Harry as we called him then, was wide-eyed as we travelled on the steamer from Merimbula and into the great city of Sydney. Father met us there and travelled with us to Werrington.

"So this is my grandson," he said proudly when he first sighted Harry in the blue shirt I had made especially for the occasion. "My name sake, young 'enry."

I had not seen Father since I had left Werrington in April the year before. I was shocked to see his hair was now completely white. He laughed when Harry pulled on his great beard.

"How have you been, Father?" I asked him anxiously, aware of his recent political misfortunes.

He surprised me with his jocular response. "Never been better, Menie," he said. "I'm writing for a range of newspapers from morning till night, and I am relieved to be out of the public eye."

I still wonder at my father's constant ability to bounce back from disappointment. That month, Father had been disgusted that his former enemy and recent ally, now Sir Martin, had joined with their previous political enemy, John Robertson, to form government.

"I am surprised, but relieved at your composure, Father," I told him.

"The Robertson-Martin government is the greatest treason of our political 'istory, Menie," he explained decisively. "God be praised I am clear of its tortuous and shameless complications."

I still find it amusing that Father should have been so outraged. He himself had joined with Sir James, once his political enemy, to form government, and later he was to do the same with Mr Robertson.

That Christmas was a wonderful time. Robert and his wife, Mary Ann, whom I had not met before, came home, too, and so all the family – except my William – was there. My Harry was doted on by his aunts and uncles, being the only grandchild, and Father gave him a little shell-brooch that had once been a gift for me – his blue-eyed ocean child. I helped Mamma to cook a great turkey and a deliciously moist plum pudding.

"It's as good as the one we 'ad all those years ago at the Irvine sisters when we were starving in London, Clarinda, do you remember?" Father said after a mouthful of pudding.

"Oh yes, Henry," she said. "And how those old ladies adored you!"

Father got up from his seat at the head of the table and strode over to Mamma to kiss her on the cheek, an event we rarely witnessed those days, and everyone cheered.

TWENTY-TWO

Mamma and the family moved from Werrington in early 1871, mainly due to its rising rent. It must have been a trying time for Mamma. Father had once again reinvented himself and begun work as an agent for the American shipping entrepreneur Mr Heydon Hall, in an attempt to establish a steamship line between Australia and California.

Father travelled regularly in this role to Melbourne, Brisbane, Tasmania and South Australia, and he was away in Melbourne when the family moved. The move was to a small property with an orchard, Landsdowne, three miles from Liverpool and twenty miles from Sydney. I heard from Mary that the move had been on a rainy, blustery day and she and Mamma had worked tirelessly to pack, load and unload the children, furniture, books and Father's ever-growing collection of animals. These now included an antelope, monkeys, squirrels, hedgehogs, an ibis, a wombat, two wallabies and a variety of parrots.

It must have been an absurd sight, with the animals loaded in cages among the furniture on a wagon and the family piled into a dray, trundling over the thirty miles through the rain to their new home.

It was during his employment as a shipping agent that Father ran into an old friend unexpectedly in Melbourne. He wrote to me later of the event and Mamma's delight when he told her:

I was walking down Collins Street when a man walking towards me cried out my name. I did not recognise him at all, until he showed me his cane and asked me if I knew it. Indeed, I did, I said and told him it was my own hand-iwork from when I was a lad. And that was when I realised that here was my old friend from Birmingham and our London days, John Hornblower. I could not believe it. I had not seen him for close on forty years. I hadn't even known he had come to Australia. It turns out that he had moved to Victoria in the '50s, due to the goldrush and had run a newspaper on the goldfields for some time before he began investing in goldmines. He now lives comfortably with his wife in Melbourne.

I had often heard both Father and Mamma talk of their friend John Hornblower, whom they had known so many years ago in Birmingham and London. The coincidence of this meeting on the other side of the globe was, I think, remarkable.

The family did not stay at Landsdowne for long. It was subject to regular flooding so Father bought land a few miles away on rising ground. He called it Canley Vale and had a house built there, Canley Grange, but this also flooded. And then, without first discussing it with Mamma, Father purchased Milton House in Ashfield – only six miles from the centre of Sydney. I never visited any of these homes, but Father described Milton House as palatial with twenty rooms and extensive grounds, including two acres of vines and a hundred orange trees. I wondered how Father had afforded such a grand house, and on inquiring, he wrote to me that John Hurley, a mining speculator and member of Central Cumberland, had raised £1600 to buy the house for him.

My second child, William Stronach Thom, was born on the 5th of July, 1871, and we called him Willie. His middle name was in honour of a cousin of William's back in Scotland. He was born with masses of brown hair and almond-shaped eyes like Father's and Varry's and, thankfully, he was a calm child and slept through the night within his first month. My days were blissful then.

Winters in Pambula were very mild in comparison to my later winters in the Blue Mountains. I only had to light a fire in the early mornings and late evenings, and I continued my regular walks on the beach throughout Willie's early months, carrying him in my arms with Harry toddling beside me. The days rolled into one another easily. I think on those days now with my two young sons as some of the happiest of my life. I felt truly blessed.

Father left the employ of Mr Hall in September 1871, complaining the man did not have the business acumen he had expected and that he had stopped paying Father's wage.

That month also saw the termination of Father's bankruptcy, and I am certain this was also a reason for ending his employment for, once again, Father was able to return to politics. He was determined to end the Martin-Robertson government. He sat for a seat in Mudgee in December 1871 and won decisively.

I know Father's long friendship with William Windeyer had waned at this time. Mr Windeyer was now attorney-general, and had accepted this position as part of the Martin-Robertson government. There is a long list of men who were at times friends of Father's and, at other times, bitter enemies. These included Charles Cowper, of course, and James Martin, but also John Robertson, John Bayley Darvall, William Dalley, Charles Gavan Duffy, James Wilshire and John Dunmore Lang. And then there were always those whom he opposed but nevertheless respected, such as John Fairfax and William Wentworth. William Wentworth died in London in 1872. His body was brought back to Sydney to be buried at his former home of Vaucluse following a state funeral.

I wonder if Father ever regretted the changing allegiances which politics ensured. When he stood for East Sydney in early 1872, he again won decisively and James Martin and William Windeyer both lost their seats. Mr Windeyer retired from politics for a time after this loss and concentrated his efforts on his career as a barrister.

For Father, though, the political dance had now paid off, for he was to become the most powerful politician in New South Wales in May 1872. He formed government then and began his first term as Premier of New South Wales. It is an amazing thing to me that Father, with all his personal struggles in early life, could rise to such heights. And for Mamma it must have been bitter-sweet. While they were still close and wrote to each other regularly throughout the week, Mamma, I know, would have greatly preferred a simple life with a husband by her side over being the wife of the premier.

My life in Pambula was not much altered by this momentous event. I read the newspapers religiously and was always slightly shocked at how regularly Father's name appeared. It was during this ministry that the mail service to England was improved, both by steamers and by a miraculous undersea electric telegraph line. Father also reorganised the government bureaucracy and, while on a trip through New South Wales, the town of Bushman's was renamed Parkes.

I continued to care for Harry and Willie with Katie's help, and for William when he was home. Then a day came in July, shortly after Willie's first birthday, when William returned from two days of travel around his parish and collapsed onto the settee wearily.

"Clarinda," he said, which immediately alerted me to the fact he was about to say something important, for it was only then that he used my formal name. "Clarinda, I am feeling my age greatly. I am wondering if this position is too much for me to continue. I don't think I can keep up all this constant travel."

I hurried to sit on the floor at his feet and laid my head in his lap. "Oh, William, I, too, fear you are burning yourself out," I said. "Is there an alternative?" I felt a slight dread at that moment, so happy was I with my life in Pambula, and I think I held my breath as William replied.

"Yes, there is an alternative, Menie. And that's what I want to talk to you about," he said. "I've been looking into other vacant parishes, and I'm considering a smaller one in less rugged land than here. It is at Ballan in Victoria."

I raised my head from his lap and looked at him hard as I swallowed. "That is so far, William. I will be so far from my family!" I checked myself, for I could see the angst in his eyes and the spreading lines on his tired face. "But of course, that shouldn't be a consideration," I said. "*Not* when it comes to your health, William. I would gladly move to the other side of the globe to ensure your health is maintained."

William kissed me on the lips. "Oh, Menie, thank you. You are my strength."

And so we moved to the small town of Ballan on the main road to Ballarat and forty-nine miles from Melbourne. I did not see any of my family for the rest of that year or the next – not until a visit from Father in August 1874. I missed them terribly.

I was pregnant again in late 1872 and my third son, John Gibson Thom, was born on the 9th of July, 1873, in Ascot Vale near Melbourne, where we lived briefly while we waited for William's posting to Ballan. I continued to love my role as mother. My three precious boys were a wonder to me. But I felt the distance between myself and my family. I so wanted Mamma to see my new baby, and I wrote to her regularly of the happenings of my brood.

William, the children, Katie and I lived in a small residence attached to the church opposite a bend of the Werribee river in Ballan. This town had thrived during the goldrush years as it was near to Ballarat, and it was said there had been much sly-grog selling on the tracks from Ballan that led to the goldfields. I felt a stranger in this town and cocooned myself mainly in my home with my boys and Katie. My only regular visitor was Mrs Elizabeth Bence, whose husband owned a farm nearby. She and her daughter would sometimes come to our small vicarage for morning tea and tell me stories of the locals and the happenings about.

I will always remember the time Elizabeth told me of two locals who had encountered a highwayman on the Islington Estate in July 1874. Mr Densley and Mr Thompson found the ex-prisoner attempting to rob the estate, and they confronted him and shot him. Later, a public subscription was raised to provide Mr Densley with the reward of a gold hunting watch and a purse of sovereigns for his bravery in the act. It was perhaps the most exciting event that had happened in the town – apart from the regular horse racing meetings.

My Aunt Maria, Father's only remaining sister, travelled with her servant girl, Mary Ann, from England to Sydney at the end of 1873 and Father rented her a cottage in Canley Vale. She had suffered financially when Father's business had gone into bankruptcy. I did not meet Aunt Maria for several years but I know, from Mamma's letters, that they became great friends. I was pleased Mamma had another woman to share her senior years.

Father wrote to me often. He told me of the congeniality of his ministers, of his growing friendship with the new governor, Sir Hercules Robinson, and of dinners and picnics with political supporters. It all seemed so foreign and unreal to me, this world of Father's so different from my own.

When he visited me in Ballan in August 1874, I found Father slightly changed in his manner. He had a greater assuredness and seemed to move with purposeful, slow, stately motion, as though every stance was measured. I teased him about it. "Father, I do believe you are acting a part, even with me," I said as he sat himself on our settee with exaggerated movements. "I believe you are acting the role of statesman, Father."

He guffawed and blushed slightly. "Perhaps, Menie. It is not a conscious thing, though. It is simply that I am always in the public eye now. I need to appear as a great politician to all."

He leant down and reached for John to bounce him on his knee. "I will admit," he said after a moment, "I 'ave even attempted to lose my Midlands accent and to pronounce my aitches so I don't seem like a man of low birth. But, after fifty-nine years of mispronunciation, I find it is beyond me."

"Oh, Father," I laughed. "I don't think you need to bother with that. Your accent gives you a connection with the people, with the working-class men, I believe."

"Mm," he said. "Perhaps you are right. Perhaps it doesn't detract from my political persona."

Father's first premiership came to an end in early February 1875, due mainly to the pardon of the notorious gentleman bushranger Frank Gardiner. Mr Gardiner had been arrested in 1864 and, because of his good conduct in prison, two petitions were made for his release. The first one was rejected by the governor, Sir Hercules Robinson, but then when another petition was made soon afterwards, the question of whether the prerogative of pardon was in the governor's sole discretion or whether it should only be exercised on advice from his ministers was raised.

The governor, on advice from Father and his government, agreed to Mr Gardiner's release. But in so doing, Sir Hercules Robinson tabled an official minute that spoke of parliament in unflattering terms. The opposition later moved for censure and Father, being the premier under Sir Hercules Robinson, was forced to resign. His opposition formed the new government under John Robertson.

I was heavily pregnant again when Father's government demised. My fourth son was born on the 8th of March, 1875 and we named the dark-haired boy Norman Parkes Thom. I had my hands full then with four little boys, six years and under. Still, I thrived in my role as mother and carer. Norman was a sturdy, rosy-cheeked baby. I remember that, like Willie, he slept through the night when still quite young, and he was already sitting independently by the time he was four months old.

It was John who became sick first. He had been grumbly and bad-tempered all morning, on that day in August, before I noticed the first red spots on his cheeks and, when I felt his forehead, it was burning with fever. I remember I hurried him off to his bed and told the older boys they must not go near him but, within a day, Harry also had signs of sore, red spots and fever and, by the time a doctor had travelled to us from Ballarat, the other two boys had also begun to show spots. Poor little Norman was only five months old, and he also developed pneumonia, causing us to fear the worst.

I remember sitting by Norman's cot long into the night for that terrible week. I thought of my sisters, the first Mary and Lily who had died, and of my brother, Milton, and I prayed desperately for Norman to be saved.

On the Sunday night, after William had come home from his service, we sat staring into the crib, listening to Norman's ragged breathing. We held our own breaths for a terrible eternity when Norman became silent, waiting for his next intake of breath... it never came.

We buried Norman at the new cemetery in Ballan. He was the first person to be buried there. The distress of my own grieving was so intense that my hair started to turn grey overnight immediately after Norman's death. His loss left an empty ache inside me, which I feel to this day.

Mamma came to visit me soon after Norman's death. It was a long distance for her to travel and I believe it took her three days by train and coach. Dear Mamma, she had aged most terribly since I had last seen her in the Christmas of 1870. She, who had always looked so youthful and, despite so many pregnancies, had maintained a trim, womanly figure for so long, was now so inflicted with gout she looked ancient and quite fat from the swelling. But her voice and her manner were not changed.

We sat for hours together each day, holding hands while we watched Harry, Willie and John play with the beautiful wooden train set she had brought them from Sydney.

"Does the pain of a child's death ever pass, Mamma?" I asked her softly on one occasion.

"Never completely, my dear," she said after a slight hesitation. "They are always a part of you. Even now, Thomas, who was the first of my children to die, thirty-eight years ago, and the first Clarinda, are in my mind daily. It is a terrible burden but one you will learn to bear. I wish I could take the pain from you, Menie."

"Thank you, Mamma. I know you would if you could," I said through my tears.

Mamma stayed with us for a month, reading passages from the Bible to Katie and me daily and helping as much as she could with the boys, although her gout pained her greatly. I felt such a deep, extreme rift when she left. Mamma was the only one of my family who completely knew and understood my pain, although Father and Robert had both lost children, too. However, I believe it is harder for a mother. William grieved greatly, of course, and I often found him with tears in his eyes during that first year after Norman's death. I was pregnant again before the year was out.

We heard later of the death of Charles Cowper in London that same year. Father's great foe was no more. I was surprised at the regret Father expressed to me in a letter when he heard the news. He wrote:

> *Charles Cowper, like myself, will be remembered in history as a great states-man. There were many policies of his with which I did not agree, but despite his nickname of 'Slippery Charlie', I believe he did much that was good for Australia, and worked tirelessly for the principles he espoused.*

I heard nothing from Mamma about the death, but I knew that, despite her resentment towards the man, her Christian faith would have ensured heartfelt prayers on his behalf.

This fifth pregnancy was more difficult than any of my previous ones. None of my pregnancies had been easy, but this time I grew monstrous and by the end of June 1876, I was barely able to stand from a chair and William had to hire a nurse to help me with the children and a maid for the other household tasks.

We discovered the cause of my great weight when my labour continued for another hour after Clarinda Jean Thom was born on the 12th of July, and her twin, Robert Varney Thom, surprised us. I was, of course, delighted to at last have a daughter, but another baby son was a blessing after the loss of Norman. The nurse and maid stayed on following the births and I, while still grieving deeply for my lost son, continued motherhood with renewed gusto.

A few months before the birth of the twins, I had a letter from Father asking my opinion on a subject that gave him a great sense of pride but also considerable discomfort and uncertainty. He wrote:

> *For some days past I have been thinking of asking you in confidence on a matter of some delicacy. About two years ago the Governor of this colony*

asked me if he might recommend me for some distinction from the Crown. I declined to give my consent, intimating that I would never be a party... to any offering of the kind.

This response did not overly surprise me. Father had always been opposed to Imperial honours, the abuse of aristocracy and fought against representation only by people with titles. But by then, many of Father's colleagues were themselves titled, and Father definitely considered himself their equal. His letter continued:

A few days ago, the Governor sent for me and showed me a telegram he had received from the Secretary of State wishing to know whether I would accept a C.M.G. This is a distinction considered much higher than a mere knighthood as it is the first step of a limited Order which admits of very high distinctions (Grand Cross & c) which an Earl or a Marquis would accept and 'deem his dignity increased'. I declined the C.M.G without remark for which the Governor was evidently prepared.

And then, as I continued the letter, I found myself laughing heartily at Father's attempts to justify his changed attitude. He wrote:

The Governor then told me of his despatch to Lord Carnarvon 'strongly urging' that the dignity of K.C.M.G. should be offered me. This distinction, as I suppose you are aware, gives 'Sir' before the name and 'Lady' before that of the wife and a personal decoration in the form of a star to be worn on the breast. The question is, shall I decline it, which will of course shut the door to all such offers.

I am quite content to live and die with the simple name of 'Henry Parkes' and my inclinations and taste are naturally in that direction. There are some solid reasons too on that side, chiefly arising out of my past misfortunes and my present very limited means.

Still, there are reasons on the other side and while I have not sought it,

I have won it by honest and long services. The substantial reasons to accept are:

(1) As the world goes I should be a little more influential with influential people (not, however, with the mass) and if I live longer this might be of advantage to my family.

(2) If I go into office again, it would give me a little better standing in political life for, however we might philosophise, the generality of persons who move in political life think more than they would like to confess of these distinctions.

(3) It would help me in cultivating an acquaintance with men of mark in other parts of the world which has grown to be one of my highest, and, I hope one of my most innocent, pleasures.

In addition to these considerations, I suspect your mother would rather like it.

If I decline, I do not think ten persons in this colony would appreciate my true motives, while others would invent motives to suit their own estimates of my character.

I want you to tell me, Menie, what you think and to tell me without mincing matters. You probably will see the thing in a clearer light than I.

I believe Father had already made up his mind to accept, but he wanted my blessing on the matter to help assuage his own guilty feelings for turning tables. I, personally, thought he deserved and had earned a reward, and certainly Mamma had. So I wrote to him and encouraged him to accept. However, I was not completely without sarcasm in some of my comments:

My dear Father,

I know – and perhaps I understand better than many – your repugnance, expressed many years since, to the acceptance of this title. Still, reading your own arguments, pro and con, I can see that your own mind has come to the same conclusion as mine.

I need not repeat your own reasoning. It seems to me sound. Only perhaps that it might be more strongly stated. Social position has given you power. Title will give you more power. Wealth would give you most power. In your reasoning, you should substitute your use of the word 'influence' for 'power.' Even those who should be above these things will roll the sugary words out, "I called on Lady P", "I had a chat with Sir Henry P."

And why not have the gratification of gratifying Mamma. I can fancy her innocent pride, and pride always sat with an amusing prettiness on Mamma. Don't tell her I said that, now.

So, let men deprecate your acts as they will, here is an answer – The Crown appreciates them.

William joins me in love and kind wishes.

I am, dear father,
Your loving daughter
Menie Thom

As expected, Father accepted and was appointed K.C.M.G, Knight Commander of the Order of St Michael and St George, in May 1877. My parents were now formerly known as Sir Parkes and Lady Parkes. At the same time, John Robertson and John Bayley Darvall were also appointed K.C.M.G.s.

TWENTY-THREE

Father became premier again in March 1877 and smoothed the rift that had arisen between himself and William Windeyer by appointing him attorney-general. This government was only to last until August. And in the June of that year, Father was distressed at the news of the death of his former newspaper rival John Fairfax. I will always remember this man as an honourable, Christian man. I was also greatly grieved at the news.

After Father's defeat, there followed a series of attempted governments – all short-lived. First, Sir Robertson formed government again, followed by attempts by Alexander Stuart, Mr S.C. Brown and Father, but none of them were able to secure the men they needed to form a cabinet. Finally, James Squire Farnell formed a government that lasted for a year, before Father's party joined forces with the party of his previous opposition, Sir Robertson, and Father was elected premier again in December 1878.

However, I was quite uninterested, and almost oblivious, to the political manoeuvrings at the time.

I suffered a terrible tragedy in mid-1877. It was the day of my birthday and, although William was travelling throughout the day, we had planned a celebratory dinner that night. Fanny, our maid, had already begun preparations, and, to this day, the smell of roasting duck reminds me of the horror I felt when I read the fateful telegram.

As I opened it with shaking hands, I was certain it was to bring news of Mamma or Father being ill, or perhaps of Aunt Maria. I think I staggered to a chair when I read it. It was not Mamma or Father or Aunt Maria, but my William who was the subject of this terrible missive. William had been travelling through the small town of Gordon, about eight miles from our home, when his horse had bolted and he was thrown from the buggy. He had been taken to an inn and a doctor called to examine him. He had injuries to his bowel and liver and three broken ribs, one of which was believed to have punctured his lung so that there was internal bleeding.

I think it was Fanny who rode out to William's good friend and banker, David Chisholm, to bring him to our house. I remember I was sitting in a daze with Katie crying beside me when he arrived.

"Mrs Thom," he said gently as he pulled a chair up beside me. Lottie, the nurse, had hurried the children away from me when we first heard news of the accident and Katie retreated to her room when the man arrived, so I was quite alone with Mr Chisholm, and the silence must have been ominous as I continued to stare blankly at the wall. "Mrs Thom, can I offer my services to take you to your husband? I have brought my buggy. You could be there by his side soon," he continued.

I must have nodded or shown my assent in some form, but I do not remember anything of that trip to William's bedside, and I do not think I uttered a word until I was finally with him.

My shock at the sight of William – grey and haggard, his breathing laboured and with a dreadful gurgling noise emanating from his throat – will remain with me forever. He was barely conscious, but I held his hand and talked to him softly throughout the night.

The next morning, Mr Chisholm, the innkeeper and two other men carried William on the bed where he lay, and placed it on straw on a tray buggy. I sat there beside his bed while Mr Chisholm walked the whole eight miles home holding the rein of the horse to make sure there was no jerking or rough movements to disturb William.

I do not think I cried once during those horrendous few weeks. I was so shocked and numb at the desperate thought of my life without William. Mary arrived to help a few days after the accident and she must have been horrified to see my blank, expressionless face. I know there were letters of sympathy and occasional visitors throughout that time but I cannot recall any clear details. Near the end, William's breathing became a ghastly rattling, but when he died, with his hand held tightly in my own, the breathing had calmed and he seemed to slip away without a struggle.

I lost the one great love of my life.

I was now a widow with five children seven years and under, and I soon discovered I was pregnant again. I longed desperately to be near my family. Father had previously had yet another house built, Stonehurst, a holiday cottage on a property he had been granted near Springwood in the Blue Mountains, which he had named Faulconbridge – his mother's maiden name. Father was also having a grander house built on the property, to be called Faulconbridge House, which the family was to eventually move into, and a smaller house for Aunt Maria, called Moseley after the street they had lived on in Birmingham all those years before. And so, I made plans to live nearby.

I moved temporarily into Milton House with Katie and my children. I remember Mary helped me in the difficult task of travelling by dray, six months pregnant and with a loaded wagon along with five young children, over many days from the country of Victoria to Sydney. We stayed at night in inns on the way, and she was a great comfort to me.

When I eventually arrived at Milton House, I felt an enormous wave of relief mixed with terrible regret wash over me at the sight of my family, of Mamma, stiff and awkward from pain as she walked towards me, her arms outstretched, and Father, and Annie and Gerty, both now grown ladies, and Varney, almost twenty years old and tall like Father, and little Lily, who was now a scrawny sixteen year old.

Robert, Mary Ann and their young son were also there for our arrival. And, of course, Aunt Maria, whom I had never met before. I cried and cried as I hugged each of them in turn.

My life was now completely altered. Mary was a dear to me. Each day she would take my children with Katie on rambling walks through the orchards or to a nearby park, and she continued the instruction I had begun with Harry and Willie before William's death. I was able to spend time on my own or with only the twins and John while I grieved and waited for the baby to be born.

Mamma and I spent hours talking in hushed voices. It was during this time that Mamma told me more detail about her early life: of her mother who had died when she was still a child, and her great childhood friend Isabella with whom she still corresponded, and of her father, brother and stepmother, and the most she had ever told me about the journey she and Father had taken on the *Strathfieldsaye*. I was surprised how much she had loved her time onboard, despite the perils and dangers they had experienced.

Then, when Faulconbridge House had been completed, Father arranged for me to take up land in nearby Mount Victoria and to build a little house there, which I called Carlyle. I had my independence but also my family near.

Mary and Mamma helped me, along with the midwife, at the birth of Martha Wilhelmine Thom on the 25th of January, 1878. I was overjoyed to have another little girl, and she was my last link to my wonderful William. Her features were his, too, and I felt a new ache for my loss when I looked on her.

My darling baby Martha died in April when only three months old, following a terrible cough and fever. My anguish at losing William's last child was extreme.

"Oh, Menie, my dear," Mamma soothed while I sobbed into her shoulder beside the body of my little girl where she lay in the bed I had once shared with William. "My darling girl. It is God's way. You must learn to accept this terrible loss, Menie."

But I was inconsolable. Death changes you. The thought that you will never again see, hear or touch a loved one is completely shattering and destroying. Never again would I be with my dear husband on this earth, or my two beloved children, Norman and Martha. I even had thoughts of joining them in heaven. If it hadn't been for my other children, I think I would have lost the will to live at this time. But the responsibility of my other children was, I think, what saved me and forced me to continue with daily routines and life.

Gerty was married that year of 1878 in the newly built Faulconbridge House. Robert Hiscox was a lawyer from Melbourne whom she had met on a visit to friends in Sydney. He was a stocky, ginger-haired man with a great sense of humour, and Gerty, always one for fun, glowed and giggled in his presence. I was thrilled for her, although greatly upset she was to move to Melbourne.

The wedding was a small affair with only the family present at Faulconbridge House – the impressive mansion built on a ridge with extensive verandas overlooking the great countryside towards the flashing light of South Head lighthouse, which had been built after the sinking of the *Dunbar*. Mamma had two maids at the time and they served appetisers and champagne. Gerty looked wonderful in a white, organza dress with her curls cascading under a netted veil. Mamma cried for the entire next day after Gerty and Robert had left for Melbourne.

I found Varney much changed when he visited for the wedding from his lodgings in Penrith. As Mary had suggested in earlier letters and discussions, he had grown into a shy, retiring boy. And now he had developed into a serious fellow whom I rarely saw smiling or laughing. He had boarded at the King's School in Parramatta for a time and was now working in Penrith as a bank clerk. I think it was difficult for both Robert and Varney, as Father's sons, to live up to his high expectations. Later, though, Varney would study architecture and even become postmaster general in the New South Wales Government.

Father's third premiership, which began in December 1878, was to last for over five years. He became Colonial Secretary, and Sir Robertson was to be the President of the Executive Council, while William Windeyer, his friend again, was attorney-general.

Some of the major achievements of this administration included a new Land Act, Election Act, an Act to fund the Sydney International Exhibition of 1879, and a Public Works Act that established an independent Board of Commissioners for the railways, but which retained the government's control of railway extensions. However, in Father's eyes, his greatest achievements were focused on the welfare of children. His State Children's Relief Act 1881 ensured the Randwick Asylum and church orphanages were closed and children fostered out to families instead.

In his speech to move the Bill for the Public Instruction Act 1880, Father said, "By what you do now, you may render a service that will be felt, 'ereafter, in the aspirations of a 'undred thousand 'uman lives – of that unknown multitude arising in our midst who 'ave yet to employ their faculties in moving the machinery of society and who, for good or evil, must connect the present with the future."

The Act established a Department of Public Instruction, made it compulsory for children between the ages of six and fourteen to attend school, created high schools for girls, bursaries for university, made teachers civil servants, reduced the maximum amount of any school fees, enlarged the curriculum to include English and Australian history, and, most significantly – except for specific grants – removed state aid from any school not under the absolute control of the government.

Naturally, there was much opposition to the Act. The Catholic Archbishop Vaughan attacked public schools as providing a 'godless education' and being 'seedplots of future immorality, infidelity and lawlessness'. The attack came not only from church groups, but also from a Public Schools League under the leadership of James Greenwood, who did not think the Act went far enough.

Within the first six years of the Act's existence, 143 public schools were formed along with 194 provisional schools and 101 half-time schools. The number of children now attending school had increased by almost 20,000.

It was in early 1879 that Father became involved in the hunt for the notorious Kelly Gang. The bushrangers – Ned Kelly, Dan Kelly, Joseph Byrne and Stephen Hart – had previously terrorised country towns in Victoria. In late October 1878, they had committed their first known murders when three Victorian policemen were killed at Stringy Bark Creek. And then, in February 1879, the gang visited the town of Jerilderie in New South Wales.

At Jerilderie, the gang locked up two policemen – including the constable – and wore police uniforms to disguise themselves as police reinforcements. They caused much mischief, and even convinced the police constable's wife they were police, persuading her to let Dan Kelly help prepare the court house for the Catholic service. They also had their horses reshod at the expense of the New South Wales police.

Next they held up the Royal Mail Hotel, which held The Bank of New South Wales, stealing a large amount of money and burning loan documents.

Following this, Father – as Colonial Secretary of New South Wales – and Bryan O'Loghlen, the Attorney-General of Victoria, signed a wanted poster under the order of the Governor of New South Wales to demonstrate the united stance of the colonies. The reward was 8,000 pounds for the capture of all, or any, of the Kelly Gang.

Soon after the reward poster was distributed throughout Victoria and New South Wales, my father received a letter from Ned Kelly himself. Father brought the letter home to Faulconbridge House the following Sunday and we all read it with horror and wonder. It was surprisingly well-written, with only a few errors. It read:

March 14, 1879
To Sir Henry Parkes
Premier of N.S.W.

My dear Sir Henry Parkes

I find by the newspapers that you have been very liberal in offering a re-ward for the Kelly Gang or any one of them. Now Sir Henry, the man that takes I, Captain E. Kelly, will have to be a plucky man, for I do not intend to be taken alive. And as I would as soon die in N.S.W as Victoria, I will give you or any other person who wishes to take me a fair chance to try your pluck. I am at present not very far from Bathurst (in fact I have been in the town of Bathurst and has taken a peep at the bank). Now I tell you candidly that I intend to rob Bathurst – and particularly the bank. So now you are warned. Of course I will not say what time I and the gentlemen that follows in my train will visit the City of the plains. But one thing you can count on is that I will pay it a visit. Now Sir Henry, I tell you that highway robbery is

only in its infancy, for the white population is been driven out of the labour
market by an inundation of Mongolians, and when the white man is driv-
en to desperation there will be desperate times. I present my respects to the
Sydney police

Yours E. Kelly

Mamma, of course, had tears in her eyes as she read this frightening missive. "Oh, Henry," she said, "you do not think the Kelly Gang will come after you, do you? Or any of us?"

"They wouldn't dare!" Father boomed, but I could sense his uncertainty despite the bravado.

"It is so personal, though, Henry – addressed directly to you and calling you 'Sir Henry' throughout. He even threatens that he would stand against you if it were you who should try to capture him." Mamma was shaking slightly as she spoke.

"Now, don't worry yourself, Clarinda," Father said. "They live for the approval of the population, this Kelly Gang. They would not dare to 'urt me *or* my family, for fear of the 'atred that would inspire."

Later, I asked Father whether he really did consider himself safe from the gang.

"Well, Menie, I suppose it does shake me up a bit. But it is my duty to stand against these outlaws – it is my role."

"Oh, Father, it is terrible that you should feel in danger, though! Is the loss of your personal safety worth your being such an important public figure?" I asked.

"Yes, Menie. Of course it is worth it! I was once a struggling working man, too. But I did not resort to robbing my fellow man like these men." He rubbed his brow distractedly before continuing. "No, Menie, at much personal expense, I 'ave, instead, become a man who can make a difference. I know that the Kelly Gang – like the Clarke Brothers – 'ave 'ad limited education, and that is what will make the difference to men such as them in the future. They 'ave nothing to tie them to society."

"But they are lost themselves, Father – Ned Kelly, Dan Kelly, Joseph Byrne and Stephen Hart. There is no chance of redeeming them after they killed those policemen in Victoria, I think," I said.

Father shook his head. "No, Menie, I believe anyone can be reformed, given the chance. I may 'ave been the one who signed the reward, as was my duty, and I know, if they are caught, they will probably be 'ung, but my personal beliefs 'old that even men such as the Kelly Gang could be reformed."

I was proud, again, of Father's strong ethics and beliefs, although I did not necessarily agree with them.

Despite the threat contained in Father's letter, the Kelly Gang never robbed the bank in Bathurst. They were eventually defeated in late June 1880. They had held around sixty captives at a hotel in Glenrowan, Victoria, and the police were alerted. It was said that they drank and danced with their captives before a shoot-out began. Joe Byrne was shot and killed first as he sat at the bar drinking whisky. And then, in the early morning, Ned Kelly came out of the hotel wearing an iron helmet and armour that covered his entire body except his legs. It was in the legs that he was shot and brought down. Later, the police set fire to the hotel – once the captives were out – and the charred bodies of Dan Kelly and Steve Hart were later found inside. It was believed that they had shot each other.

Ned Kelly was convicted and charged with murder, assault, theft and armed robbery and was hung on the 11th of November, 1880, at Melbourne Gaol. I know that Father was relieved not to have felt pressure to witness the hanging, as it occurred at such a distance from Sydney.

Caring for my children became even more important to me. With William gone, my children now became my everything. Harry had suffered terribly on his father's death. He had always adored William and he became very morose, while Willie seemed to react to his loss by becoming argumentative. John, Rob and Queenie (which were the names I called Robert and Clarinda), being younger than Harry and Willie, seemed less affected, especially the twins who were only one when William died.

When we moved into Carlyle in Mount Victoria, I sent Harry and Willie to the local public school. I thought this might distract them from their grieving. Harry always did well at school, but for Willie it was a trial. He was like his Uncle Robert, always revelling in the outdoors but stumbling at his studies.

The land around our home was beautiful. I remember a lovely gorge I would take the children to, with a mass of ferns, flowers and goats among the rocks. A brook tumbled through it and in its midst was a great peach tree which, when the peaches were ripe, we would sit under and eat with the juice dripping down our chins. I owned turkeys and hens and later I bought a cow. I employed an old Irishman, Charley, to help tend to the property, and I was proud of my self-sufficiency.

My finances were always a concern, however, and I was often forced to borrow from Father or Varney. At one time I thought of selling firewood in Sydney sourced from the trees around my home, but the expense of the rail and cartage to Sydney proved this would not provide a sufficient return. I often asked Father for advice on these matters, although I was aware of his own business failings, but I felt I had no one else to turn to. I knew flattery was important in dealing with Father, and so, despite my own financial experience during his time overseas many years before, I wrote to him that, *Women are not so trained as to see their own way clearly in even the simplest business arrangements.*

Of course, this was not what I truly believed.

My brother Robert became gravely ill in September 1879. He was diagnosed with Bright's disease – a failure of the kidneys – and the accompanying dropsy. I went to visit him at his home in Surry Hills in Sydney late that year, leaving my children in the care of Mary.

I had not realised how ill Robert was until my visit. I barely recognised my handsome younger brother and gasped involuntarily at the sight of him. He was lying in bed with cushions all around and his face, and the parts of his body I could see, were so swollen he looked about twice his usual size. Father had arranged a nurse for him, and his wife Mary Ann was sitting beside him, wiping his brow. He didn't know it was me at first, I realised, and I asked Mary Ann why he hadn't recognised me as we stood in the kitchen later talking in hushed voices.

"He's going blind, you see, Menie," she said. "It's one of the things that can happen with the disease."

"Oh, Mary Ann, I'm so sorry," I said, the tears falling fast. She seemed to want to talk of his sufferings, perhaps to relieve her own anxiety.

"He has convulsions, too, and there is often blood in his urine. He is in such terrible pain," she said.

I swallowed hard. I could not help thinking, as she talked, of my own agonies over William's death. I did not stay long. I couldn't bear to see Robert this way – the same man whom I remembered as a baby in his perambulator and who had caused us such distress over his wild behaviour as a young man. And he was still a young man – only thirty-six the following month.

Robert died shortly after his birthday. His coffin was brought by train to Faulconbridge. Father had set aside some land for a cemetery, and my brother Robert Sydney Parkes was interred there in January 1880.

Mary Ann, Robert's simple wife, was distraught at his death. I had her stay with me at Carlyle for a time, with her two children – Henry, aged seven and Rebekah, only two years old. I understood her grief and I also thought her not strong enough to cope with her children during this time without some assistance. She died only a few years after Robert, and young Henry and Rebekah moved in with Father and Mamma and my other siblings with whom they both lived until they reached their majorities.

Father's life continued to be quite separate from the rest of the family's. In September 1880, he travelled by train to Melbourne with Sir Hercules Robinson and Lady Robinson. Sir Hercules Robinson was no longer the Governor of New South Wales and had been the Governor of New Zealand in the interim before his recent appointment as Governor of Cape Colony in South Africa. But he visited Australia before taking this post.

It was around this time that I began to feel greater resentment towards Father and, I am ashamed to admit, some growing resentment towards my younger sisters – all but Mary. I suppose I was feeling the pressure and distress of widowhood, along with the burden of young children, despite my adoration of them. But my life had become very limited. I knew this envy was unchristian, and I prayed regularly to the Lord to grant me greater humility, but still it was difficult not to feel some jealousy.

I cried with self-pity over letters from Father about his trip to Melbourne to visit the Melbourne Exhibition and his exuberance over a giant sculpture of himself there. I cried even more bitterly when I read of his visit to Gerty – and to Annie, who was visiting Melbourne at the time.

On leaving Melbourne, Father travelled to Albury where he addressed an audience of around a hundred constituents at a dinner. This was to be the first time in many years he again raised the issue of joining the colonies of Australia into a single nation, a federated Australia.

My darling sister Mary was married in 1881. Her husband, George Murray, was a widower and a wealthy Scottish paper manufacturer with two grown daughters – Isabella (known as Bella) and Mary – and a younger daughter, Georgina (known as Tottie), at school in Scotland.

Mary worried over her closeness in age to her stepdaughters. "They could be my sisters, Menie. I am only thirteen years older than Bella," she said to me on a visit to Carlyle. "And they don't seem to want me around. Bella, particularly, treats me as though I have taken her father from her. But that is the last thing I want to do."

"Of course, Mary, it's not in your nature," I said, patting her hand. "You always think of everyone else and their feelings before your own. If anything, you might be over thinking your stepdaughters' needs. I'm sure they don't dislike you as much as you think. How could they?"

"I suppose you are right, Menie. I hope you are. But George is such a gentle man and his daughters seem to run rings around him."

I laughed. "Don't worry, Mary. You are as gentle a soul as George. His daughters will come to see that and to love you for it, I'm sure."

I missed Mary terribly after her marriage. She lived thirty-three miles away in Liverpool in George's house, Forbesville, and, with my busy commitments due to my children, I did not see her often.

My resentment towards Father and my younger sisters reached its height when, on advice from doctors to take a break, Father and my sister Annie travelled to America, England and Europe at the end of 1881. Father was still premier and offered to stand down from the position, but his government insisted he remain as premier with Sir Robertson as acting premier in his absence. Later, Father would regret agreeing to this course.

But for me, all I could think of was that I had been replaced by Annie. In the past, as the oldest daughter and being so close to Father, it would naturally have been me who would have accompanied him on this amazing trip. Instead, I was left to look after my children and to struggle on financially, and, like Mamma, I felt abandoned.

I will write only the bare minimum of their trip, as it still galls me slightly to think it could have been me experiencing the excitement along with Father. I received regular letters, of course, but I think I screwed each one up in anger after reading it before reaching for my Bible and praying for forgiveness.

Father and Annie sailed from Sydney to San Francisco on the *S.S. Australia* on the 29th of December, 1881. There they went to the theatre and were privately entertained by notable families. Then they travelled to New York in a director's carriage attached to a train. This had been supplied to Father by the American Government. He described it as having a furnished dining room that was heated by steam tubes, with two bedrooms each with a double bed, a dining room, a kitchen and scullery and a first-class cook and waiter. I could not imagine such luxury. During this train trip they stopped at Niagara and Chicago.

In New York, Father and Annie stayed at the Windsor in a suite and met the mayor and members of Congress, and even the new president, General Chester A. Arthur, who had been vice-president to James Garfield before his assassination the previous year. Father described General Arthur as a tall, portly gentleman. He was to meet him again at the White House when they travelled on through Philadelphia to Washington. From there, they travelled to Boston where they visited Cambridge to see Harvard University, and Father sent a letter to the poet Henry Wadsworth Longfellow, requesting an audience. Mr Longfellow replied that he was currently unable to see Father because he was ill, which proved to be true, for he died a few weeks later.

Their American tour complete, Annie and Father travelled on the steamship the *Germanic* to Canada briefly and then on to Liverpool and London. Here, they had dinners with the prime minister, Mr Gladstone, the Earl Granville, the Earl of Carnarvon and met the Prince of Wales who approved of Father's purchase of the painting 'A Jacobite Proclamation' by Andrew Carrick Gow for the Art Gallery of New South Wales.

One outcome of Father's trip that I was pleased to hear of was his meeting with his old friend and then foe, Sir John Bayley Darvall, who had returned to live in London. Their enmity had begun in 1863 when Father had opposed the then Mr Darvall. But now, almost twenty years later, Sir John was old and almost blind, and Father wrote to me of how they had shaken hands heartily and spent several hours talking of old times. Sir John died in December the following year.

Annie and Father went to the Isle of Wight to stay with Father's friend from his previous trip – the poet laureate, Sir Alfred Tennyson, and his wife and son. From there they returned to London and travelled on to Birmingham as guests of the mayor. How strange this must have been for Father, who had left Birmingham almost penniless with Mamma all those years ago and only returned recently to endure the death of his sister Sarah. Even stranger must have been his visit to Stoneleigh, the place of his birth, where he was entertained by Lord Leigh, the son of the previous Lord Leigh who had pushed Father and his family off his land.

Father wrote to me of a visit he had to the home of the philosopher Thomas Carlyle. It read:

The evening meal was of the most frugal – thin cakes, I think of oatmeal, and a cup of richly made tea. After tea, my host sat down on the floor with his back straight up against the wall and his legs stretched out at full length, and, charging and lighting a long white clay pipe, he happily puffed away, stopping at short intervals to talk on all manner of things.

Father began a correspondence with Charles Dickens during this time – the author he so admired for his support of the working-class man – and this correspondence continued for many years. Father also told me of his visit to the house of the politician Richard Cobden and how Mr Cobden persuaded Father that protective tariffs to support even infant industries should not be used. It was Mr Cobden who established Father's strong stance on free trade.

On returning to London, Annie and Father went to Buckingham Palace for the State Ball where they met Queen Victoria. Then they travelled to Belgium and had lunch with the King and Queen at Laeken Palace along with the prime minister, Mr Frère-Orban.

Then, in Berlin, they had lunch with the Crown Prince and Princess, who was Queen Victoria's eldest daughter and sister to Prince Alfred.

Father wrote how they talked about the assassination attempt on her brother, Prince Alfred, in Sydney. "Poor boy!" the Princess said.

They travelled to Potsdam and met Emperor Frederick, before heading to Paris where they dined at the British Embassy and occupied the ambassador's box at the opera. They also met Father's correspondent Florence Nightingale, the manager of nursing from the Crimean War who had sent trained nurses to Sydney on Father's request.

From there, it was back to London and they sailed home from Plymouth – the very town Father and Mamma had sailed from all those years ago on their voyage to Australia – on the *John Elder* on the 1st of July, 1882.

I suspect this trip was the crowning glory of Father's extreme ambition to become a man of importance. Mamma and I discussed this often in his and Annie's absence. I remember, in particular, one conversation we had in Mamma's bedroom where she lay, almost completely bedridden from gout. My children were in the garden playing with Lily and Katie, and I could hear their chatter and yells. It reminded me for a moment of the time Mamma had sat by my bed while my younger brother and sisters played in the garden at Werrington, and little Varney had been hit by the swing. How our lives had changed since then.

"I do not mind, Menie, that I am missing the receptions and dinners and balls with all these famous people," Mamma said. "I do not mind that at all. In fact, it is the last thing I would want to do. The thing I am the most distressed about is that Henry is having the opportunity to see our home, and that I will never see it again. I will never see Birmingham again. I know it is not your father's fault, for how could I have travelled in this state. But I long to see my home once more." She began to cry and rubbed her swollen knuckles distractedly.

"Oh, Mamma, I can't imagine how that must feel." I reached for her hand to stop her rubbing, "But you never know, if your health improves you may be able to travel to England one day."

Mamma grunted. "I am almost seventy years old, my dear. I doubt that will ever happen."

"Father is almost seventy, too, Mamma. Why shouldn't you be able to travel like him?" I said indignantly.

"Because, Menie, he is a man. He has not had to bear twelve children. It is the way of the world. My body is more worn than his, I believe." Her tears had stopped then, and she reached for her Bible to read a passage quietly, her usual resignation returned.

Father and Annie's celebrations did not end on their return to Australia. In Melbourne where they disembarked, they were welcomed by a massive banquet and the Victorian Government placed a train at Father's service to take them to the border of New South Wales. There, another train awaited them and they crossed the Murray River into Albury beneath a triumphal arch. The town was decorated in flags and evergreens and Father was given an address of welcome followed by another when they arrived in Wagga Wagga. And then, when they finally arrived in Sydney, they were greeted by the mayor and 10,000 people and another banquet was held in the Exhibition Building.

We did not see Father or Annie until after these celebrations had ended.

I was at Faulconbridge House with Mamma and Lily when Father and Annie returned. Annie was glowing and radiant and Father arrived buoyant and jubilant in stark contrast to our quiet congratulations. Mamma was always an amazing woman. I did not witness any obvious resentment or chastising from her. It was me who didn't hide my envy well.

"So, your regally celebrated 'usband, father, sister and daughter are 'ome!" Father announced as he walked through the door and took off his top hat. There was no response from us, but Father went to Mamma in her chair and kissed her affectionately on the cheek. "'Ow is my dear wife?" he asked gently.

"Quite well, Henry," she lied. "I am very pleased you have returned."

"Oh, Menie, Lily, you would not believe how we were toasted everywhere we went!" Annie exclaimed.

"I believe we do know, Annie," I said in a steely voice. "For you wrote to us in minute detail of every bow, privilege and courtesy with which you were honoured."

Annie blushed at my barb and Father frowned at me before attempting to break the frosty silence. "And 'ow are the children, Menie?" he asked as the five of them came bowling into the room and into their grandfather's arms.

As the years have passed, my envy towards Annie over this trip has mainly disappeared. I now recognise that this was to be the one great series of events of her life. Annie never married or had children of her own, and later, when Father chose someone else over her to accompany him on a similar trip, her distress was evident, and it was I who comforted her then.

323

TWENTY-FOUR

Father's trip away while remaining premier proved a great error of judgement. He had asked Acting Premier Robertson to keep parliament in recess until his return, which Sir Robertson did, but this meant there was no parliamentary session for eight months. Father's opposition used this lack of government to attack his party, and many of Father's previous supporters, such as George Reid, deplored the inaction during Father's absence and changed their allegiance.

The election the following year was a disaster. Many of Father's allies lost their seats, and Father was unable to retain East Sydney and only gained a parliamentary seat in faraway Tenterfield.

In January 1882 the weather in New South Wales was very hot. It was said that it was the hottest summer we had had for ten years. About a dozen bushfires began in Mt Victoria over the course of ten days. A house was burnt down on the first day of the fires and I kept watch day and night. Then one morning, two great bodies of fire bore down on Carlyle from opposite sides. Harry was thirteen and insisted he help Katie and me to fight the fires but I sent the other children inside the house.

I was terrified. We filled any bucket or pan we could find with water from our tanks and attempted to douse the flames. A group of our neighbours arrived, including the children's schoolmaster, Mr Whithall. I will always be thankful to this man. He organised the other neighbours into groups, beating back and flooding the fire that was raging on one side, and another group doing the same for the other fire. It was a miracle, I think, for not even our fences were burnt.

Rob and Queenie were six years old at the time. They had both started school and Rob did well at his studies. But Queenie was a shy, sensitive child, and so I removed her from school soon after and taught her from home. Nine year old John, however, was the most eager to learn of my children. I had arranged for his older brothers, Harry and Willie, to be tutored in Latin after school and thought John too young, but he begged me to be included and he quickly outshone his older brothers. He was also keen to learn music, and so I began to teach him some simple tunes on my harmonium.

My dear sister Mary had a baby girl in May 1882 whom she called Clarinda, or Inna for short. I went to their home in Liverpool to help with the baby, leaving my children at Faulconbridge for the month with Katie, Lily, Annie and Mamma, and Father when he was home. Varney had become a partner in a firm of architects in Liverpool at the time and so lived with Mary and her new family during the week.

When dinner was served that first evening of my visit in the spacious dining room of Forbesville, I noticed Varney raced to pull out a chair for George Murray's middle daughter, Mary. She was an attractive, petite girl and I watched as Varney sat opposite her and their eyes met across the table for longer than was necessary. I raised my eyebrows at Varney when he turned towards me, and he blushed slightly before returning his attention to Mary Murray. Of course, there was some confusion of names in this household, for both her stepdaughter and my sister shared the same name at the time.

I noticed the next night, as well, that Varney, usually shy and severe in those days, was very talkative. He laughed loudly at the younger Mary's relating of her dog, Milly, chasing a cat about the yard, and he shared with us all a comical description of a client he had met with at his firm that day. "He truly spoke, as the common phrase goes, as though he had a plum in his mouth," he told us of the gentleman. "It was all I could do not to ask him to open his mouth for me to examine it for evidence of the offending fruit."

"You are such a wit, Varney," Mary said, giggling. She turned to me, "Your brother, Menie, has brought so much fun to our household, wouldn't you agree, Bella?"

Her sister nodded lightly.

"Forbesville used to be such a stuffy, boring old place before Varney arrived," Mary continued.

"Come now!" George said to his daughter. "We were all quite content here before Varney came, I believe. Not that you are not most welcome, Varney. But I think you are a bit harsh, Mary, to claim it was dull here with myself and Bella and your stepmother."

Mary laughed. "I suppose I had nothing to compare it to before Varney came to live with us. Now I know things were relatively boring before."

Throughout this conversation, I was not surprised to see Varney blushing with pleasure. It was not surprising, either, when Varney and Mary became engaged soon after and were married at Forbesville on the 10th of March, 1883. Of course, this created an even greater confusion of names, for my sister, formerly Mary Parkes and now Mary Murray, swapped names with her stepdaughter and now sister-in-law as well.

Since his third premiership had begun, Father had been living during the week in a room next to his office in the Colonial Secretary's building on the corner of Bridge and Macquarie Streets in Sydney. He began to spend less and less time at Faulconbridge, often only spending Sundays with us when he went for long walks.

But on visits to Faulconbridge now, Father would sometimes leave on a Saturday and stop at Liverpool to meet the Murrays, where both Varney and our Mary were living, and he would travel with some of them on to Faulconbridge to arrive the following day. And so Sundays became days of great entertainment at Faulconbridge House – sometimes with myself and my five children visiting, and any combination of the Murray clan. I was thrilled to have my sister Mary visiting Faulconbridge House more regularly, and I became quite fond of the younger Mary, who was a bright, energetic girl – much like Gerty – and who seemed to help enliven Varney's personality. Lily, Annie and I never warmed to Bella Murray, though.

"She talks to me as though I have no knowledge of the world," Lily complained one afternoon after the Murrays had returned to Forbesville and I was gathering my children to leave.

"Yes, she is quite condescending," I agreed.

"I believe she thinks every man in the room is appreciating her to the exception of all other ladies," Annie said.

"Well, I suppose they are, Annie. She is quite beautiful," I admitted.

"Even Father is all goggle-eyed towards her, and she's a twenty year old girl, for goodness sake!" Annie said with more intensity.

"Yes, I do not believe she displays much Christian modesty," said Lily.

Father went into opposition in early 1883. The new premier was Alexander Stuart, a Scot and former merchant. I think Father was beginning to lose interest in politics. He told me he found it all quite hopeless. This might have been the reason for his decision to travel once again. We Parkes women were horrified at the companion he chose.

George Murray had given Father introductions to some prominent businessmen in Edinburgh. Father claimed it was for this reason and her need to seek the continental air to ease her asthma, that he was to take

Bella Murray with him. There was a stony silence for a full minute after this announcement to Mamma, myself, Annie and Lily.

And then, Annie burst out, "But what about me, Father? I helped you immensely on your last trip. Why shouldn't it be me who accompanies you?"

"Or me," said Lily. "I am of an age with Bella Murray. And I am your *daughter*. Why would you take *her* instead of *me*?"

Despite their outrage, Father remained calm. "Because, girls, as I 'ave said, I am to go there for connections with Bella's father, and she needs the warmer air to 'elp 'er asthma. Besides, you need to look after your mother. Bella 'as no responsibilities of this sort."

Annie opened her mouth to argue but Mamma hushed her and, in her usual accepting and calm manner, said, "And, girls, Bella will see her sister Georgina, no doubt. She is in Scotland, isn't she, Henry?"

Father seemed to sigh in relief at her support and he smiled warmly towards Mamma. "Yes, my dear. Of course she will visit 'er younger sister there, and 'er aunt and uncle. I am simply to be 'er escort." He turned towards Annie. "You were very 'elpful on my last trip, Annie, as I 'ave often told you. I'm sorry I can't take you or Lily – or Menie, of course – with me. Bella Murray is Mary's stepdaughter, and it is entirely appropriate she should accompany me so she can visit 'er sister."

We were all silenced then.

Once again, I will only describe Father's journey in the barest of detail, for the resentment I felt towards Bella Murray was beyond anything I had ever felt and it still pains me to relate their trip. For Annie, I think, it was worse. She knew what this imposter was to experience on her travels, and she knew the advantages it would give her. For me, I could only dream of what such a voyage might mean.

They set off in July 1883. If it was any consolation to Annie, Father, no longer Premier of New South Wales, was not received officially on this trip. He met with his previous creditor in London, Sir Daniel Cooper, who, as was the case so often with old enemies of Father's, had forgiven him for his previous refusal to stay out of politics. He stayed with Lord Tennyson again on the Isle of Wight, and he and Bella were guests at the wedding of Lord Tennyson's son Hallam at Westminster Abbey.

Father told us that Bella became great friends with Sophia Palmer, whose father, the Earl of Selborne, was a close friend of Lord Tennyson's. They met with Father's previous minister Sir Saul Samuel and with the poet and playwright Robert Browning and the biologist Professor Huxley. I was horrified to hear Bella had tea with my idol: the author Thomas Hughes.

Father rented rooms in Duke Street, Grosvenor Square in London after taking Bella to her sister Tottie, and her Aunt Kate and Uncle Hugh in Edinburgh. Bella stayed on in Edinburgh for a time, and Father, alone in London, wrote insensitively to Annie: *I often wish you were with me. I am often lonely and sometimes I feel a little helpless in London.*

"The nerve of him," Annie raged to me after she had read the words aloud in clipped tones. "How can he rub my distress in my face!"

"I don't think he realises this would upset you, Annie," I said. "I don't believe he would intend to distress you. I can remember he did something similar to me once, when he was first overseas working as an Emigration Agent and he felt lonely and asked if I would travel out to him. I think he simply misses us and does not think of how his words might upset us."

"And why didn't you go to him, Menie?" Annie was shocked at my revelation.

"Because Mamma was in greater need of me than Father. I would never have left her alone to tend to you children."

Bella returned to Father in London and they went sightseeing, to the theatre, to Oxford and to Cambridge. I must admit, after Father had returned, I once came upon one of his letters from Bella during that year when she must have been away from him in Edinburgh, and I read it: *Oh, dear, I do wish I could talk to you. I have so very much I would like to talk to you about. And I am wondering what kind of little animals you are amusing yourself with, now you have not me.*

Their obviously close relationship still rankles me terribly.

Father and Bella left England on the 4th of July, 1884, on a ship he had previously sailed on with Annie – the *Germanic* – and travelled to New York for ten days of sightseeing, including a six-day train trip across the continent to San Francisco before sailing home on the steamship, the *City of Sydney*.

Father did use George Murray's contacts to set up The Australian Investment Company in Edinburgh during his travels, but this did not succeed, and he also became an Australian agent for a time with a London company dealing with engineering goods – Latimer, Clark, Muirhead & Co – but I do not believe he ever actually conducted any business for them, and I know a part of his contract included a clause that he should not enter into politics while in their employ, a promise Father found difficult to keep.

I do not know where Bella was travelling when she heard the tragic news from home. Her sister, Varney's young bride of only five months, Mary Parkes, had died from an unexpected lung haemorrhage in late August. I heard later that she had had a slight cough throughout the day and it was only in the evening she'd noticed the first stains of blood on her handkerchief. Mary and Varney were still living at her father's house, and Varney had called on our sister Mary immediately.

"It was ghastly," she told me several days after the young Mary had died. "George sent for a doctor, but it was as though something had burst within the dear girl, and the amount of blood she coughed up just got larger and larger. George is distraught and poor Varney is a mess. I am so sad for him. She was so good for our Varney. It was as though he was the old happy self he had been as a child once he met Mary."

And indeed, Varney did seem to revert to his sullen, shy, quiet self in the months following Mary's death.

Mamma was completely bedridden by the time Father arrived home from his trip with Bella. Poor Lily and Annie were her main carers. It is sad that neither Lily nor Annie ever married and I wonder if their experience of caring for our ageing Mamma damaged their prospects for marriage or reduced their inclination.

When Father and Bella returned to Sydney on the 29th of August, 1884, George Murray and Varney were at Port Jackson to meet them and take them on to Liverpool. Varney took Bella to her sister's grave at Rookwood the next morning, where I'm sure she wept furiously.

Father returned to Faulconbridge that night. This time I think he expected the icy reception he received. He sat beside Mamma in her bed for over an hour, holding her hand and talking gently in his deep, melodious voice. I suspect his feelings for her, despite his actions, were deeper than hers then. Mamma was so consumed by her pain and had been so consistently disappointed by this man whom she had once loved passionately, that I do not believe even my sweet, gentle Mamma could have maintained a complete love for him.

Father brought Bella to Faulconbridge the following Sunday, along with Varney and our sister Mary. If Father's reception when first at home had been uncomfortable, this was much worse. The resentment Annie, Lily and I felt towards Bella was overwhelming.

Mamma was gracious as always, somehow forcing herself from her bed and asking the maid to bring in tea. "I hope you enjoyed your travels, Isabella," she said, "and we are so sorry for your loss. How is your sister Tottie? And your aunt and uncle?"

Throughout the day, neither Lily nor Annie said a word to the unfortunate Bella. I felt quite sorry for her then, and tried to chat with her along with Mary. I returned to Carlyle that afternoon and only heard a few days later of the confrontation between Bella and Annie.

Bella had found Annie in the kitchen and had asked her directly what she had done to be treated so coldly. Annie told me she had answered in a matter-of-fact tone that Bella had taken our father's love from us. Apparently, Bella had turned to Annie and laughed before almost yelling at her, "I cannot help it that your father likes me! It is quite unjust and unkind of you to hold that against me!"

And Annie had walked away.

We sisters were very shaken and upset when Father and Varney came home one Sunday, only a month after Bella and Father's return and, immediately after stepping inside, Varney smiled in a way I had not seen since his wife's death and announced, "I have the greatest news! Menie, Annie, Lily, come and sit. I think this will surprise you, and I'm sorry if it does. But I have the most wonderful news!"

Father was grinning broadly towards his son as the rest of us sat uncertainly.

"Would you like me to tell them, Varney?" he asked.

"No, no. I must," Varney continued and took a deep breath. "I am to be married again."

Annie and Lily began to clap in excitement, but I was wary, for we knew of no one Varney had been courting and I could sense his nervousness.

"Who is she?" I asked. "We did not know of anyone you were thinking of."

Varney swallowed hard and said, "I am engaged to Bella Murray."

There was a stunned silence and I grasped Annie's hand in warning as she opened her mouth to question Varney in disbelief. Before anyone could say anything, I stammered out my congratulations and stood to hug Varney.

Annie and Lily said nothing.

"Well, that is a surprise," said Mamma when Varney went to her bedroom to relate the news. "I had no idea."

"Yes, Clarinda," Father said jovially, "'e's a sly one, this boy. But she's a fine woman, Bella Murray."

Again, no one commented.

Later, as Annie walked with me, Katie and the children through the front garden of Faulconbridge House to say goodbye, she was more livid than I had ever seen her. "Bella got her hooks into Father, and now that evil girl has got her hooks into our little brother, too! What is she, a witch? Does she concoct love potions?"

"Now, Annie," I tried to calm her, "those are very unchristian things to say. I'm sure Varney is simply in love. Bella is quite like her sister, and so you can see how his love for Mary, now that she is gone, could transfer easily to her sister."

"She is nothing like Mary!" Annie continued. "Mary was fun and witty. Bella is just conniving and manipulative. And she is to become our sister-in-law! And even more ridiculous, Father's daughter-in-law! Poor Varney! Oh, poor Varney, what is to become of him?" she wailed.

The relationship between Bella and Annie only grew worse in the following months. Annie told me in a rush of one bitter meeting between them.

"It was as though Bella was trying to set Lily and me against each other, Menie," she said. "She kept saying Lily was by far the better looking of us two, to which I immediately agreed in order to quell any bad feelings. Then she sneered when I mentioned my friend Lola Clarke. And she told Lily she should not tie her stays so tightly, that this was the reason for her cough and that she had quite an adequate figure without doing so, although she could never match her own thin frame. But the worst was when she said to me 'Your father loves me so much that he has told me he would be glad to die so long as he could do so in my company'! I couldn't believe the nerve of her!"

"Now, Annie, I think Bella is trying to work you up. You should just ignore her. She is teasing you," I said.

"I know you're right. But then I got angry at Varney, too," she said uncomfortably.

"What did you say? You really shouldn't have involved him, Annie."

"I didn't mean to, Menie. It's just that later he said Lily's cough was all down to her tight stays, and so I told him that was rubbish and it was just Bella trying to cause trouble saying such things."

"Oh, Annie. I know it is difficult, but try to make peace with Bella. She is to be our sister-in-law, and not only that, she is Mary's stepdaughter. We mustn't continue to wage war against her."

"I will try," Annie said but I saw her roll her eyes slightly as she looked away.

Bella and Varney were married at Faulconbridge on Christmas Eve of that year. Only Mary and Father attended from our family. Mamma could not rise from her bed, and I made the excuse that John was ill, while Lily and Annie made some other feeble excuse, but really, none of my children were sick, and Lily and Annie spent the day with me at Carlyle, bewailing the disastrous union.

In February, Annie had an awful row with Father over Bella. I think she told him all the things Bella had said and done, and accused him of loving her more than his own daughters. After this fight, Father assured Annie his love for his daughters was so much greater than what he felt for Bella and following this, a semi-peace ensued.

Everyone was so caught up in this family controversy that it largely overshadowed the birth of Mary's second child, George, in October 1884. I did, however, spend time with her in Liverpool in the weeks following the birth, and, of course, saw much of both Bella and Varney there before their marriage. Bella's attitude towards me was one of forbearance, as was mine towards her, for I did not wish to cause Mary distress during the days after the birth of her child.

TWENTY-FIVE

In early 1885, William Bede Dalley, now Father's political enemy, was in the position of acting premier. In February, news arrived in New South Wales that the British Governor of the Sudan, General Charles Gordon, had been killed in Khartoum by Arab forces. General Gordon had acted against the orders of the Gladstone Government to leave Khartoum and had stayed on to personally supervise the evacuation of the Sudan. He was a public hero despite his disobedience.

The news of General Gordon being killed by spears and beheading on the steps of his palace was met with a huge public outcry in Britain and in the colonies.

Mr Dalley acted immediately on the news and, in the absence of both the premier and the treasurer, cabled an offer of military assistance to Britain. Father saw Mr Dalley's action as unjustifiable and an attempt to gain personal glory. He wrote many letters that were published in *The Sydney Morning Herald* denouncing Mr Dalley for his rash offer of military aid. In one he wrote: *However men may delude themselves, this is not patriotism; this is not loyalty; this is not true British sense of duty. It is the cry of 'wolf' when there is no wolf.*

Father had assured me at the time that his opposition towards Mr Dalley would not induce him to re-enter politics but, of course, this proved not to be the case. Father stood for the seat of Argyle – a large area of New South Wales that included towns such as Goulburn, Collector and Marulan. He won and gained yet another seat in parliament.

337

As a result of Father's criticism of Mr Dalley, there followed a terrible attempt to dishonour Father. Premier Alexander Stuart had recovered from his illness and returned to his position. He used the speech Father had made the previous year when he'd resigned his seat at Tenterfield to accuse him of libel against the House. Father had said in his speech that the government had corruptly used railway extensions to buy support for their other policies.

There followed a massive debate centred almost entirely on Father's credibility. Mr Henry Copeland said of Father, "The Honorary Member found that he could not get a majority in the House, and he said to himself 'I have used you as long as I could. I cannot use you any longer, so I will kick you'."

Father's supporters saw Mr Stuart's motion of condemnation against him as an attempt to gag them, and many of these members rose to agree with Father on the corrupt acts of the government. But Mr Stuart's motion of condemnation against Father was passed.

So then, never to be outdone, Father stubbornly challenged his opposition to expel him from parliament and Mr Copeland moved for the expulsion. This motion was defeated, with only two members voting for Father's expulsion. It was a backhanded victory for Father and an embarrassing result for the government.

I felt some of my old pride for my great father on hearing of his triumph in this political battle, and I wrote to him saying, *The very idea of a Minister of the Crown – the first minister – making such an unparalleled attack upon a private member... Why, how they must fear you! And what idiots they are! If you are afraid of a hornet it isn't the wisest act to stick a pin in him!*

Mr Dalley resigned his seat when the parliamentary session ended, as did Mr Stuart due to ill-health, and Sir George Dibbs formed government, although this was only to last for two months before Sir John Robertson stepped in and offered Father a cabinet position. I think Father knew then that his star was rising once more, and he refused the offer. Sir John's government only lasted for just over two months and was replaced by a government under Sir Patrick Jennings.

The mayhem of politics continued.

In early 1885, Katie, my dear companion and niece, married Edward Bucknall: a man she had met while we still lived in Ballan. He was a strong, assertive man who owned farmland in Ballan, and I had been unaware of their regular correspondence which, it turned out, had occurred from the time we'd left Ballan until the steaming summer day when he'd arrived unexpectedly on our doorstep.

"Why, Mr Bucknall," I said in surprise as I answered the door to his large frame and he took his cap from his head. "What are you doing here?"

Katie stepped from the kitchen to stand behind me and I saw Mr Bucknall's eyes dart immediately towards her. Katie, usually so shy, boldly stepped around me to stand infront of the man.

"You know why I'm here, Miss Marshall, don't you?" the man said to her.

"Why yes, Mr Bucknall – Edward – I believe I do," she said.

I still did not fully gather the import of the visit and it was only when Mr Bucknall got down on his knee before Katie that I realised he was to propose, and I turned quickly to retreat discreetly into the kitchen.

After the small wedding, which was held at Carlyle, Katie moved with Mr Bucknall back to Rodborough Vale. I was more distressed than I would have expected at her leaving. Always a quiet girl, I had not realised how much I had relied on her friendship throughout the years of my marriage to William, and the years since his death.

Harry was always a worry to me during this time. I sent him for a while to work unpaid as an aide to Father in an attempt to spur his idle temperament. He was fifteen when he first went to stay with Father in Sydney on a cot-bed in the room beside his office. Father did not write to me of Harry's lethargy and lack of ability, but he talked to me of it on a visit to Faulconbridge.

I was desperate to assist my fatherless eldest son. I wondered if he should sit the Civil Service examination, but I suspected this would be beyond him. I encouraged him to answer advertisements for work, and, eventually, when he was sixteen, Harry gained employment as a shop assistant in the nearby town of Springwood.

I also continued to struggle financially and considered starting a school once more but, again, I realised this would require money at the outset, which I did not have. Father continued to lend me money, although Varney was now less willing, I believe due to Bella's influence. I even attempted to sell Carlyle during this time but had no reasonable offers. I often thought how grieved my dear William would have been if he'd known he'd left his family in such straits. Such a wonderful, generous man. How different my life and the lives of my children would have been if he had lived.

Father held the seat of St Leonards when he began his fourth administration as premier in January 1887 following the resignation of Sir Patrick Jennings. Father had attacked the former premier venomously throughout 1886 on his protectionist policies. Not only was Father premier again but he now held a clear majority on his free trade platform.

Father had a cabinet salary once more, although his financial difficulties continued. I must admit to being the cause of some of these difficulties, for he continued to lend me money and took over the liability of a debt I had incurred over the years due to the need to feed and furnish my family.

But Father's expensive tastes were also to blame. He was always a collector, but his passion became an obsession as his public life developed.

He had massive collections of books, art, furniture, unique artefacts and animals. In fact, in 1883, Father had reluctantly auctioned over 350 items from his collections in order to retain his solvency. These had included paintings by Picchi, Martens, Poussin and the valuable Giacomelli painting 'Christopher Columbus Sighting the Continent of America', which I had always loved because of the shaded background figures of two sailors hoisting the sails. He also auctioned several mosaics, a bust of Shakespeare, a marble dining room table, other furnishings and many books.

But in 1887, Father was unable to overcome his difficulties through a single auction. Instead, he assigned his estate for the benefit of his creditors to a solicitor and two bank managers. He was not legally a bankrupt but the results were the same. The beautiful Faulconbridge House was part of the assignment. Mamma, now so ill, Annie, Lily and Robert's children were forced to move in September 1887 into a rented house, Hampton Villa, in Balmain, Sydney, where, at least, Father joined them more regularly.

I was left in Mount Victoria. Mary was now the closest to me, but still not close enough to visit regularly, and Varney and Bella had moved to Ashfield in Sydney the year before with their one year old daughter, Mary Cameron Parkes, named for their deceased sister and wife.

Once again, Father was away when the move occurred so that, with my help during the packing, Annie and Lily arranged the entire move. Fortunately, Father's creditors agreed to allow Aunt Maria to remain in her cottage, Moseley, on the Faulconbridge land as long as Father continued to pay her rent.

Shortly after the assignment of Faulconbridge, I was forced to sell Carlyle due to my own mounting debt and also due to my wish to have family nearby. The children and I moved to a rented cottage, Fayre Cotte, in Five Dock, Sydney. At least I now lived only five miles from Mamma, Annie and Lily, and I loved the ferry ride between Five Dock and Balmain.

In late 1887, Father's opposition claimed he should not be allowed to retain his seat now that he was an 'insolvent debtor'. Chief among his attackers was John McElhone and Sir George Dibbs. Father ended their chiding by immediately resigning his seat in St Leonards. But, nominated for this same seat, he was re-elected in 1888, unopposed.

In January, 1888, Father was awarded the Imperial Grand Cross, an honour that no other Australian minister had received. This time, he did not consult me on my opinion as to whether he should accept. He told me again he would gladly have lived and died as simple 'Henry Parkes', but I know he was delighted at his elevation in status. Father was now to be known as Sir Henry Parkes, Grand Commander of the Order of St Michael and of St George, abbreviated to G.C.M.G.

This honour was probably bestowed on Father partly due to the centennial celebrations that took place that same month of January 1888. I remember a conversation I had with Rob when I was standing in the huge crowd with my children at the opening of Queen's Square and the unveiling of the newly mounted statue of Queen Victoria.

"Why is it the centenary?" he asked. "Australia is older than a hundred years, isn't it? This country has been here for longer than that."

"It is a hundred years since British settlement, dear," I explained in hushed tones.

"Oh," he said and was silent in thought for a time. "So the Aborigines have been here for a lot longer than us then, haven't they?" he said eventually.

"Yes, darling, a lot longer." I tried to hide my impatience.

"They wouldn't like us celebrating this, would they, Mum?" he continued.

"No, probably not, dear." I tried to quiet him by turning to Queenie and straightening her bonnet.

"So, Mum," Rob continued, unperturbed, "we sort of took their country, didn't we?"

"I suppose we did in a way, Rob. But let's not talk of that now."

"That would be why I don't see any Aboriginal people here celebrating with us then."

Fortunately, this was the final word on the subject that day from my thoughtful, little man.

Later, the thought of Rob's comments about the Aboriginals plagued me. Their presence in my world caused me disturbance – one I often ignored but which was there, nevertheless. The Aboriginal people were like a subset to our white lives, hovering around the fringes of our world. When I saw Father several days after the celebrations, I asked him if he felt there should have been something in the celebrations to acknowledge the Aboriginal people. They were a topic we rarely discussed.

Father rubbed his brow before he answered. "If we 'ad included them, Menie, we would only 'ave been reminding them that we 'ad robbed them of their land."

His statement startled me. "Robbed is a harsh word, Father," I said. "Do you *really* think it is seen in this way?"

"No, Menie, I do not think many see it that way, or choose to ignore the reality, anyway. But what else could it be? They 'ad lived here for thousands of years before Captain Cook landed 'ere. Yes, our intentions 'ave been good. We 'ave tried to civilise them, unsuccessfully in many cases. And if it 'adn't been us who took their country, it would 'ave been the French, or the Spanish. But it 'as turned out to be like a robbery."

"We have tried to help them, though, Father. We have tried to civilise and educate the Aboriginals. It is *they* who have often resisted." I was indignant now, guilt pressing on me like an unnatural and unwelcome visitor.

"Yes, yes," he said wearily. "I do not know what the answer is to the problem of the Aboriginal population. I believe they 'ave been corrupted by our presence."

"*Corrupted*, Father? How could they be corrupted by us when we have offered them Christianity and education?" I admit that I was trying to convince myself as much as Father in my strong words.

"Maybe corrupted is too forceful a word, yes. But I don't think we 'ave necessarily 'elped them," he said.

To this day, this discussion still bothers my Christian sensibilities.

The Queen Victoria Statue had originally been unveiled at the Sydney Exhibition in 1879, but for the centenary celebrations it had been placed on a new pedestal outside St James Church, which made it stand around twenty-two feet high. When the governor pulled the gold cord to release its covering, there was a distinct gasp throughout the crowd as the statue of Queen Victoria towered over us with its elaborately decorated gown and the orb and spectre held in her hands. The place where it stood was to be known as Queen's Square.

We also went to the celebrations to witness the opening of Father's creation: Centennial Park. There were thousands of people in the still boggy grounds and I could barely see Father as he planted the second tree, following the planting of the first by Lady Carrington – the governor's wife.

Father gave his speech using a great megaphone: "In the course of the next few years, this park will be converted into a place of beauty and joy forever. It will be yours and so long as the land shall last it will be for you... It is emphatically the people's park and you must always take as much interest in it as if by your own 'ands you 'ad planted the flowers."

There was a citizens' banquet that night, too, which I did not attend, and Father's government also distributed 3000 gifts of parcels of food to the poor.

I had never had a lot to do with Aunt Maria. I had always been so busy with my children and had been in Ballan when she'd first arrived in Australia but, before I left Carlyle, I went with Queenie to visit my frail, almost-blind aunt. Queenie and I sat with her in her simple lounge room.

"Your father was always so intelligent, Menie," she told me. "'E took after our dear Mam. Did you know she 'ad never learnt to read or write, but she could recite 'ole parts of *Robinson Crusoe* word for word?"

"Father had told me that," I said.

"Your Aunt Sarah doted on your father, as we all did. I miss my sisters terribly, Menie – your aunts Sarah and Eliza. You must always treasure your sisters," she continued.

"Yes, Aunt Maria, I will."

"How I wish I had sisters," Queenie said, overcoming her usual shyness before this kind, elderly woman.

"Yes, they are a blessing," Aunt Maria said. "I remember the first Christmas your Mamma spent with us, Menie. We lived in a three-bedroom terrace 'ouse on Moseley Street in Birming'am then, and your father and Mamma brought branches of 'olly and ivy to decorate it. It was a wonderful day, and your Mamma so pretty, and all the family there – even young Tom."

"Mamma and Father were very much in love, weren't they, Aunt Maria?" I asked.

"Oh yes, Menie, *so* in love. I don't think I've ever seen two people more in love than Clarinda and 'enry were," she answered immediately.

It made me so sad to think my parents' passion for each other had been largely consumed over the years, and I wished I had known them when they were first in love as Aunt Maria had.

Mamma was now suffering not only from chronic gout, but also from kidney disease and a weak heart. I went to visit her as often as I could. On my visit on the first day of February in 1888, she seemed very weak.

"Oh, Mamma dear," I said, clutching her hand. "I think I should let you rest."

She smiled weakly, her face puffy and terribly lined from age and pain.

"My Menie, what a wonderful daughter you have been to me," she said with effort, and the feeling this might be our final parting overcame me so that I began to cry. "Don't cry, Menie dear. I am not saying goodbye. Only that I wanted to tell you that you have been not just a daughter to me, but a great friend, too. I have been blessed to have you as my daughter, darling. So blessed."

Mamma died the next morning, the 2nd of February, 1888. Lady Clarinda Parkes (nee Varney) died with Annie and Lily by her side just before six o'clock following a night when Father had stayed in the city. He rushed to her side when my sisters sent for him urgently. But Mamma had quietly passed just minutes before he'd arrived.

In *The Sydney Morning Herald* the following day, Mamma's obituary was lengthy. But the part that reflected Mamma's true nature read: *She was an unpretending single-minded woman, with no ambition beyond performing her daily duties as wife and mother, living to the last under the influence of her earliest Christian lessons.*

I do not believe I will ever know another person as good as Mamma.

She was buried in Faulconbridge alongside Robert. Father's creditors had allowed us to retain the cemetery Father had set aside there. I know Father later planted trees around her grave in honour of Mamma.

Even to this day I have vivid dreams of Mamma and, when I think of her, I can picture her in detail still, and hear her voice as clearly as though she were with me. Mamma had such an impact on my life that while I live, her memory will always live on in me.

Twenty-Six

Bella and Varney had another daughter, Isabella Cameron Parkes, soon after Mamma's death, but the poor mite died shortly before her first birthday. They had moved, once more, to a property near Liverpool called Bonnyrigg and I never met little Isabella. Varney was in the Legislative Council by then and I suspect he was away from home regularly, just as Father had often been, so it must have been a comfort to Bella to live close to her father and Mary.

What I must now relate is perhaps one of the most devastating events of my life. It did not hold the agonising pain of a death, but the pain it held was one that destroyed a part of me and of my understanding of the world – as though it chipped away a piece of me and left me not entirely whole.

It was only a year since Mamma's death, and Father had continued to live with Annie and Lily at the house in Balmain – along with my niece, Robert's daughter, Rebekah. I continued to visit them regularly, travelling on the ferry around the beautiful Sydney Harbour. I remember it was a Wednesday in early February that I went to visit my sisters, taking a cake with me. Fortunately, Queenie wasn't with me, having decided to go with a friend to the Art Gallery instead, and so did not witness the scene.

349

I remember as I rapped the brass knocker I was admiring the vibrant yellow roses climbing along their fence and thinking I would pick some to take home to Five Dock to brighten my dark kitchen.

I was surprised when it was Father who answered the door. "Father!" I said. "What a pleasant surprise. I thought you would be at your office."

I went to push past him into the hallway but he moved to gently bar my way. It was then that I noticed his grave look and an unusual blush spreading across his whiskered cheeks.

"Why, what is it, Father?" I asked, confused. "Has something happened? Where are Annie and Lily?"

A young boy of about four years old with a mop of brown curls came racing past Father's long legs. "Papa," the boy said. "Papa, Mamma won't let me have another piece of cake."

The world stood still. I remember gazing wonderingly into Father's face for what felt like an eternity. It was as though this man before me was not my father, as though he was someone I did not know.

"*Father*," I stammered. "What is the meaning of this?"

The boy recognised my angry tone and began to cry.

"Menie, I 'ad meant to visit you this afternoon to explain the circumstances," Father said in his sonorous, commanding voice.

"Is this boy yours, Father? Is he your *son*?"

"Yes, Menie," Father answered plainly. "'E is your 'alf-brother, Sydney."

"And who..." I yelled there on the front doorstep. "Who might his *mother* be?"

"Now calm yourself, Menie," Father said but still did not move into the house, despite the people who must have heard me from the street. "'Is mother is my new wife, Menie. I married again just two days ago."

I think my jaw fell open and tears of shock immediately stung my eyes.

"What do you mean, Father? You have remarried only a year after Mamma's death? You have married the whore who bore you this bastard?" My words were harsh but not, I think, unfair, considering my tremendous shock.

A raven-haired lady appeared behind Father holding a baby of around eight months in her arms. I was visibly shaking. "Hello, Menie," she said, her voice shaking, too. "I have heard so much about you."

"I have heard *nothing* of you!" I yelled and Father wiped my spit from his face.

"Come in, Menie," he said. "I am sorry this 'as come as such a shock to you. I 'ad wanted to tell you before, and I 'ad not expected you would find out in such a stressful, unexpected manner."

I followed Father and his bride blindly into the lounge room, but I refused to sit when he offered me a chair. There was no sign of Annie or Lily, or indeed of Rebekah. When I saw another boy of around two years old crawling around the floor by the woman's feet, I huffed volubly.

"Menie," Father continued in a tone he might use towards a child who'd failed to understand. "Your mother and I were not intimate for many years, as you probably were aware. I always loved 'er dearly, and I mourn 'er death greatly."

"Yes, I see you must, Father, considering you have had yet another child since her death," I said sarcastically, flicking my hand towards the baby. "Did Mamma know of this? Surely she did not! It would have broken her heart! It was broken already by you, I suppose!"

"Your mother did not know of Eleanor, no. I knew it would pain 'er to know. But I believe she suspected I 'ad a mistress. It is not uncommon, Menie."

"That does not make it right!" I shouted. "Look at you – a man in his seventies with this woman of, what, early thirties? It is *obscene!*" I turned and stormed towards the door calling back to Father, "Where are Annie and Lily? Where have they gone to mourn your disgrace?"

He came behind me. "Annie and Lily are staying with their friend, Jane, in 'ampton Street along with Rebekah."

"Did you kick them out? Did you kick your own daughters out of your house so you could live here with your bastard family?" I continued to yell, despite the people passing close by on the footpath outside.

"No, Menie. Of course not. I would never do such a thing. They decided to leave themselves on the morning of our wedding, when I told them I was to remarry."

"You are a disgrace!" I bellowed at him.

As I turned again, I was shaking so violently I dropped the basket with the cake I had brought and Father bent to pick it up for me, but I slapped his hand away before slamming the door. I had never shouted at Father before. But neither had I ever hated him so passionately.

It was even more galling then to have to hear the full story from Bella, sent specifically by Varney to visit Annie, Lily and me at their friend's house in Hampton Street several days later in an attempt to pacify us. Of course, Bella revelled in our distress.

"I am so sorry you had not known of your half-brothers and sister," she said as she sat between us, perched on a chair in the small parlour. "Varney, being your father's son, had known of them before, of course. You have a right to know the details now."

"So you, too, have known of Father's mistress since before *us*?" Annie asked indignantly.

"Yes, I suppose I have known for some time," Bella answered immediately.

"How long has the relationship been going on, Bella?" I asked. "Do you know that too?"

"Well, yes," Bella tried to sound uncomfortable at her response, but she could not disguise the merriment dancing in her eyes. "I believe they met at the Melbourne Exhibition in 1880, and that Eleanor Dixon moved to Sydney in early 1881 with their first son, who died soon after she arrived here."

"As far back as 1880!" Annie exclaimed. "And an earlier child, too? This is beyond belief," she continued, turning indignantly to Lily and me.

"Yes, I'm afraid so, Annie. There was also a daughter born in 1882 who also died," Bella continued with barely a breath.

"Oh, this is *terrible!*" Lily said and began to cry, but I was too angry and shocked to cry.

"So she has been his mistress for nine years – a full eight years before poor Mamma died!" I declared.

"Well yes, Menie. But don't be so angry with me," Bella said peevishly. "I am just telling you the circumstances."

"That means she was already his mistress before you went overseas with Father, Bella. Even before you had married Varney! Did *you* know of this before any of us, even Varney?" Annie almost yelled.

"Oh no," Bella responded immediately. "I had no idea before he told Varney of it after Sydney was born – the eldest boy – not long after our marriage."

"And he has had five children to this woman," I continued, trying to fathom this terrible reality.

"And two of them died, but we have three step-siblings!" Annie said.

"Yes," said Bella simply. "Sydney is four, Kenilworth is two..."

"This is just too much," I interrupted, shaking my head. "And what of the baby?"

"She is named Aurora," Bella said.

"Do they go by the name of Parkes, too?" Lily asked through her tears.

"Yes, I believe they do. And, of course, Eleanor is now married to your father, so she is now Lady Parkes."

"Is there no *shame* in the woman?" I asked, horrified.

"I think, Menie, you will like Eleanor – or Nellie as your father calls her – when you get to know her," Bella offered.

"As you obviously do, Bella. I suppose Varney does, too?" Annie scoffed.

"Well, yes. She is very good for your father," Bella said.

"Honestly, at his age! He'll end up having a heart attack carrying on with a young woman. I had known him to be a selfish man, but this is the worst of his egotistical, self-centred behaviour!" Annie yelled before storming from the room.

"I am sorry, Menie and Lily, that this has pained you so," Bella said as the door slammed behind Annie.

"No, Bella," I said firmly. "I don't believe you are."

Despite our fury towards Father and jealousy of Eleanor, all three of us daughters relied heavily on him. It would not have helped his financial difficulties that not only was he supporting Annie, Lily, me, my children, Robert's daughter and his son – until recently – and Aunt Maria, but that he had been supporting his mistress and her children for many years, too.

But Annie, Lily and I would be close to destitute without Father's assistance, so we had to swallow our pride and attempt to accept the situation. I was proud of the letter I wrote to Father several days later, though:

My dear Father,

Taken by surprise the other day in meeting Lady Parkes, yourself, and your young children, when I expected only to find my poor sisters, I am glad to think that I acted exactly as, after grave consideration, I think I ought to have acted. But you must nevertheless permit me to say once and for all that I look upon your marriage as the most sorrowfully disastrous mistake of your whole life,—one that practically pushes out from you into alienation the children of a wife of over fifty years, and alas! one that will lower you terribly in the estimation of all right-hearted people.

I have had to screw up my courage to say this much; and now, I solemnly promise that none of the alienation shall come from me. I will try to induce my stricken sisters to bear the blow, which gets all its bitterness from the hand that strikes it, with submission and patience, and I will be a true friend to the young creature who will have, I fear, a sore burden of her own to bear. If I can I will love her as a younger sister. Anyway, she shall have full respect from me, for my father's sake.

In return I entreat you, in the future be pitiful and tender towards Annie and Lily who bear so much for your sake, in whose hearts will be an ever-open, ever-tortured wound. That I can speak thus, and act thus, and yet remember my loving, tender, gentle-souled mother, must at last prove to you how much I love my father.

I will formally call upon Lady Parkes at the proper time and thereafter I trust she will allow me to retain as much as possible of my familiar footing in your home.

Your loving daughter,
Clarinda Thom

I did go and visit Lady Nellie Parkes the following week, but Annie and Lily refused to accompany me. I sat awkwardly with her in the lounge room where I had regularly sat with my sisters before, comfortable then in each other's company. Nellie was about twenty years younger than me and, despite my resentment, I did find myself feeling sorry for this youthful stepmother of mine.

"Do you prefer the weather in Sydney to that in Melbourne?" I asked her.

"Oh yes," she answered nervously. "Sydney is so much warmer and a wonderful city."

"Melbourne is also a city with much beauty," I said.

"Oh yes, indeed," Nellie answered briefly and lowered her eyes from mine as she sipped her tea.

"You must meet my children sometime, Nellie. Can I call you Nellie? It would seem strange to call you stepmamma, don't you think?" I asked sarcastically.

"Of course, Menie. You must call me Nellie as your father does. And yes, I would be extremely happy to meet your children. You must bring them here to meet my own," she said, warming slightly at my suggestion.

"Only my three youngest are still at home, of course," I continued. "John who is sixteen, and the twins, Rob and Queenie, who are thirteen."

"Hardly children then, are they, Menie?" she replied.

"Well no. Not like your own. I suppose your young tribe are my children's aunts and uncles, aren't they?"

Poor Lady Parkes, she choked on her tea then, and I left soon after.

Father later rented a house in Albion Street, Annandale, for Annie, Lily and Rebekah to move into. I know that neither Annie nor Lily ever came to visit Lady Parkes.

The public reaction to Father's marriage was largely one of hilarity. Numerous cartoons and articles appeared in the newspapers and magazines, one of them comparing his marriage to a woman forty years his junior to the Seasons statues Father had commissioned in the Botanic Gardens a few years earlier. The picture showed Father as the statue of Winter arm in arm with Lady Parkes as Summer. Another series of sketches was entitled 'Love's Old Dream – Parkes' Coalition'.

Father's marriage to his former mistress also caused issues in the social circle he mixed in as a politician. Nellie was not included with Father amongst the list of guests invited to the Government House Queen's Birthday dinner, and Father refused to attend. He told me he wrote in his refusal: *I owe it to my wife... not to enter the door that is closed against her.*

Nellie and Father's third son, Henry Charles Parkes, was born only three months after Bella gave birth to another boy, Murray Parkes. Again another strange relation was formed, with the slightly older Murray being the nephew of the other Parkes baby, Henry.

Sir George Dibbs had been premier during the January and February when Father had remarried, but Father was asked to form government again in early March 1889. This was to be his fifth premiership.

It was during this premiership that his dream of federation of the Australian colonies was to ripen. An earlier Federal Council had been formed by many of the other colonies, but Father did not think the power of this Council was sufficient to create the union of the colonies and, I suspect, he wanted to lead the movement himself. And so Father took the matter of federation into the public forum.

His famous Tenterfield address on the 24th of October, 1889 was made in the simple building of the School of Arts there by the light of kerosene lamps. It was an auspicious occasion and it created history.

"The great question ... was," Father said there in the eerily stretching shadows, "whether the time 'ad not now come for the creation on this Australian continent of an Australian Government as distinct from the local governments now in existence."

Father was attacked by Protectionists on the issue of tariffs between the colonies being problematic to a federal Australia, but Father, who believed in free trade, nevertheless thought this issue was irrelevant to the greater issue of federation. In a later speech at Leichhardt on the 22nd of November, he explained this in these words: "We should not allow the shadow of the fiscal question to project its outlines on this greatest of all questions – the creation of an Australian people under one national flag, and with one national name throughout the world."

Father continued to claim the need for federation during numerous speeches he made around the country in late 1889 and early 1890, including in Albury, Hillgrove, Berrima and Broken Hill. It became a movement of the people.

In February 1890, Father and other representatives from the six colonies and New Zealand met in Melbourne to discuss the question of federation. This was followed by the great National Convention in Sydney in March 1891. Father was elected president of this important event and a Bill to Constitute the Commonwealth of Australia was accepted. It was proposed that each government was to discuss the resolutions of the Bill before it was endorsed.

However, Father's great ambition of federation was, cruelly, not to be fulfilled during his lifetime. It was hampered by members of the newly formed Labor Party in New South Wales who pushed for social legislation to take precedence within parliament over the Constitutional Bill. Before Father could push for its debate, his administration had failed in October 1891. This was to be Father's last premiership.

More than a year before Father's final government ended, he broke his leg badly in two places. He and Lady Parkes had taken the ferry from Balmain to Darling Harbour and there taken a cab to travel into the city. On George Street, the horse had shied and the cab, hitting the curb, had turned over throwing the driver, Father and Nellie out onto the street. The driver suffered injuries to his head and hips. Nellie was unhurt but shaken. Father's fibula and tibia bones were broken in his right leg.

I went to visit him a few days after the accident and found him grey and morose, lying in bed with his leg in plaster and raised on a pillow.

"Oh, Menie, the pain!" he said as soon as he saw me at his bedroom door and before I could even make it to his side to kiss him. "It is as though I am being stretched on a rack!"

"Oh, Father, it cannot be as bad as all that," I said unkindly.

"It is indeed, Menie. I believe the ache of broken bones must be the worst pain ever to exist," he continued childishly.

"I do not believe anything could be as painful as childbirth, Father – Mamma went through that twelve times. You will have to be brave and bear this, too. And think of what happened to my dear William in a similar accident. You are lucky to have survived," I said.

Father's accident occurred in May, and he was not to return to parliament until late August. He had attempted to master the use of crutches but found himself too heavy and awkward for the task, and so he had a policeman carry him into Parliament House each day.

1890 also saw the great strike of workers, which came to a crisis point on the 19th of September. Father was at home when violence erupted at Circular Quay. Nine wagons with special constables and mounted troopers had begun to unload wool, which they had brought from Darling Harbour to the stores at Circular Quay and the strikers had reacted to this usurpation of their stand by rioting and throwing metal at some of the constables.

One of Father's ministers, Mr McMillan, attempted to circumvent Father's direct orders not to bring in the military to quell the unionists. Father heard of Mr McMillan's plans and managed to stop him before any direct action was taken. Father wrote immediately to Mr McMillan to say that *the Government cannot defend the interests of one class to the neglect of another, whether employers or workmen, but must always act in an unpartisan manner.*

Father won much support from workers and the union movement over his stance in this matter.

Harry did not continue to work at the shop at Springwood now that we had moved to Sydney. He became idle once more. He reminded me a lot of his Uncle Robert then, in his irresponsible younger days. My younger sons had all found work, even Rob.

"You are almost a grown man, Harry," I complained to him one day as he lay in his bed late into the morning. "You cannot sit around every day doing nothing. We could do with the money, too, if you were to get a job."

"Yes, Mum, I am almost a grown man and I can decide for myself what I'll do each day. I don't need you nagging at me incessantly," he said crossly.

"I am your mother, Harry. You have no right to talk to me like that!" I do not think my attitude was unreasonable, but it was shortly after this that Harry told me he was going to travel up north to find work and would send some of his wage home each month.

"But you would find work as easily here in Sydney, Harry!" I was dismayed at the thought of losing my eldest son. "There is no need to travel into the country."

"As you have said to me on many occasions, Mum, I am almost a grown man. I need to have some independence. I'm sorry, Mum, I do love you, but I can't stay here with you forever."

I was devastated at the time. I suppose, not having William to rely on all those years, I had leant heavily on Harry for support. I felt desperate at the thought of one of my children going out into the world alone.

Harry did find work. He worked as a sawyer in Forster for a time and then continued to travel through the North Coast districts, working in sawmills and cattle stations and driving steam trains for a while. He wrote occasionally, and sent money when he could. He returned to us, brown and rugged and grown into a man. It was soon after this that he entered a cadetship as a draughtsman with the New South Wales Public Works. I was so proud of him then. I suppose his independent wanderings up north ended up helping him find his way. Willie gained employment as an engineer and surveyor on the railways soon after, and Rob was to become a fettler on the railways at Berowra. John, always the clever one, later moved to Melbourne and worked his way towards manager of a business there.

I am ashamed, though, to write about the pregnancy of a girl of Harry's acquaintance and of the birth of her daughter, Dorothy Macdonald Barnes, on the 17th of April, 1891. I was shocked when Harry arrived at my door that same afternoon the baby was born carrying a tiny, wrinkled new born in his arms.

"What is this, Harry?" I asked, dismayed and puzzled at the sight of him with an infant.

"Mum, I did not know where else to go," Harry said.

"Whose baby is that?" I asked, still confused at the scene before me.

"It is mine, I suppose, Mum, and also Millie Barnes's, who has died just after giving birth to her today. Millie has no family living, so I had no one else to bring the baby to," he explained, lowering his eyes from my shocked gaze.

"I see," I said coldly at first, so surprised was I that this baby should belong to my unmarried son. But as the poor little baby began to howl, I took her from Harry's arms automatically. Once I had calmed the baby and myself, I realised immediately that the only option was for me to adopt the tiny girl.

Dorothy has proved to be a great blessing to me throughout the years since my forced motherhood at the age of fifty-two. She is a dear, gentle soul. While I am her grandmother, she is like a daughter to me still.

Aunt Maria died in early October 1891, only weeks before Father's government ended. She was buried in a separate plot at the cemetery at Faulconbridge where Robert and Mamma's graves also lay. Father was greatly distressed by the death of Maria, his last surviving sister.

"So many deaths," he said to me at the graveside as we stood looking towards the white headstones of Mamma and Robert beside the freshly turned grave of Aunt Maria. "It is hard to get used to, Menie. We have suffered through *so* many deaths." He sobbed into his hands as I reached up to place my hand on his shoulder.

I felt this weight greatly, too – and still do. So many people I have loved have left me, even Father is gone now. So much suffering in a lifetime, so much loss. I don't think I have ever been the same person since my dear William's death, and I think all of the deaths before and after his have had a cumulative affect on my happiness.

When Father's government failed, he gave up his leadership of the opposition and sat on the crossbench. He told me he was exhausted and did not have the fight within him anymore. I still thought he would bounce back in his usual way, but subsequent events suggest that, perhaps, there was some truth in his lack of resilience then.

He was horrified, however, when the party chose George Reid, the man Father had called the arch-enemy of federalism, as the new leader. Mr Reid would later win the premiership in August 1894, and his government was to remain in power for five years. But Father would never work for him. In a speech in 1895, Father said, "I 'ave said I will serve with none, I will accept service from none, who will not place the flag of federation above all other questions whatever."

This was when Father changed allegiances completely and regularly voted with the protectionists over Mr Reid's free trade party because, as he said, he believed in federation above free trade or any fiscal policy. Mr Reid would later claim to be in support of federation himself.

Once again, Bella and Varney had a son, John Macmillan Parkes, who was born within ten weeks of his uncle's birth. Nellie's fourth son, Cobden Parkes, was born on the 2nd of August, 1892, and named for the great philosopher whom Father had met. Sadly, John was only to live for a short time and died from a chest infection in late 1893.

Bella and Varney were to have another son later, however, Norman Parkes, in early 1894. It pained me greatly when I heard the name they had chosen, for it reminded me acutely of my own Norman who had died so many years before.

At the end of 1892, Father and Nellie had to leave Hampton Villa in Balmain due to unpaid rent. A supporter of federation and estate agent, Donald McCormack, offered Father the smaller and less costly home of Kenilworth in Annandale – the same suburb Annie and Lily lived in. They were uncomfortable at the closeness of their dwellings.

Annie related to me a surprise meeting between herself and Nellie one day. "I had just collected the groceries and was walking back home when I saw a lady pushing a perambulator on the path opposite," she told me. "I noticed the lady particularly because the deep red of her hat made her black hair striking in the sunlight. She saw me looking towards her before I realised who she was and, before I could do another thing, Nellie Parkes had come rushing across the road with the perambulator before her and she called out to me, 'Annie, Annie, is that you?'

"I stood quite still and held my breath for a minute. Nellie was quite flushed and this only made her look more beautiful with the red of her cheeks. 'Hello, Annie,' she said to me. 'I am so delighted to see you. Your father misses you terribly, you know.' I didn't speak. I know you think me ungracious, Menie, but I was so overwhelmed. I really didn't know what to say."

"I do understand, Annie," I said and reached for her hand, "but she is Father's wife now. There is nothing that can be changed. I think it is better to try to forget the disgrace of it."

"No, Menie," Annie said firmly. "I cannot. I cannot for Mamma's sake."

"So what happened then, Annie?" I asked to try to calm her.

"She continued to talk. She showed me the new baby – Cobden, I believe. He is quite like Father, actually. And then I spoke for the first time and said a simple 'Goodbye' before I proceeded up the street."

"Oh, Annie," I said. "It must be very hard for the poor girl. I do think you are being a little unfair."

"I do not agree, Menie. All those times Mamma was so sick and pining for Father, and Lily and I were by her side thinking it was his work that kept him away, but where was he? He was with his mistress and their children. He was with his other family. I can never forgive him, and I can *definitely* never forgive Nellie."

TWENTY-SEVEN

Father attempted to destroy Mr Reid's government by joining with his old enemy Sir George Dibbs in 1894. This proved unsuccessful, and then he stood directly against Mr Reid in 1895, but Father was again defeated. At the time, he was going through yet another personal tragedy.

Nellie was dying of uterine cancer. She was only thirty-eight years old. I went to visit them at Kenilworth in early July and found Nellie gaunt and pale, barely able to raise her head from the pillow, and Father, too, looking greatly aged. I sat beside Nellie's bed and held her frail hand in mine. I felt a strange connection then to this young woman whom I had so chastised and resented in the past, and she smiled at me weakly between fitful dozes. She died on the 16th of July and Father, at the age of eighty, was left a widower again, with five young children to care for.

Annie and Lily showed their devotion and acceptance of their duty towards Father, despite their previous refusal to even enter the same house as Nellie. They immediately moved in with him again to care for him and his children – their stepbrothers and stepsister. I had thought of moving in with Father after Nellie's death, but Kenilworth would have been too small for six children, with my adopted Dorothy included, as well as my niece – Robert's daughter, Rebekah – and Queenie and Rob, who still lived with me at the time. I was secretly relieved I should not have to live with my ageing father.

I suffered my own horrendous tragedy in late 1895. My dear, hopeless, eldest son, Harry, drowned in the surf at Narrabeen Beach. He had married a girl he had met at a dance the previous year, Blanche Folkard, and she related how he had set out early in the morning for a swim with her brother. The two had become caught in a strong current and the other man had not fought against it as Harry had, and so had been able to wait until the last of the terrible drag of the waves and swim safely to shore. Poor Harry had panicked, I suppose, and been pulled under as he struggled. He had long loved to swim in the waves. His love of the beach probably began with his childhood in Pambula.

His body was discovered on the northern edge of Narrabeen shore – almost a week after he had gone missing in the surf. When his distraught wife told me at his funeral that Harry's body had been found dismembered, I vomited violently into the bushes of the church. I could not imagine my Harry in that coffin so broken and incomplete. My darling boy whose head I had cradled in my arms as a child and kissed his soft cheeks before bed. Gone now, gone forever.

He was twenty-six years old. I felt an awful emptiness and a sorrow for my poor son, which left me with an even stronger sense of the futility of life. I could not understand why he had been taken from me, too. I tried to reconcile this desperation with my Christian beliefs, but even now, I find it impossible to fathom why he should have died. My adoption of Harry's young daughter, Dorothy, now seemed as though it had been inevitable. Dear Harry, his had not been a happy life, and I mourned greatly for him and the content, younger child he had been before his father's death.

I believe I had been largely numb since my darling William's death all those years ago, and that each subsequent death had affected me greatly. And that these tragedies had sent me into a lethargy of emotion towards many events that I would previously have found unbearable. This must be the case, for when Father shamed us yet again shortly before Harry's drowning, I did not feel it as strongly as I had on his marriage to Nellie.

Father married a third time on the 24th of October, 1895. This time his bride was a girl of only twenty-three who had been Nellie's personal maid and had resided with them for several years.

It was Annie who told me of the news when she came to visit me in tears shortly after she, Lily and Rebekah had again moved out of Father's house and into another rented house in Annandale. I think I sat stony-faced as she told me of Father's latest indiscretion.

"You will not believe it," Annie declared after I had sat her in a chair by the window and made her a cup of tea. "Father has married Julia Lynch – Nellie's maid – the Irish girl with the dark hair and eyes."

"I see," I said wearily, wiping my hand across my brow. I think Annie was surprised at my lack of emotion. The disgrace was, again, difficult to bear. But I think this second blow was numbed by the first and so I did not rail against this marriage in the way I had his marriage to Nellie.

"Are you not shocked, Menie? Can you think of anything that could excuse this?" Annie said.

"Annie, I think I am immune to being shocked these days. It all seems so senseless," I replied.

"Oh, Menie, you cannot take this so calmly. Surely you want to rant and rave like Lily and I! It is beyond *believing!*" Annie said in a frantic tone.

"Yes, Annie. But it would not do any good to rant, I suppose," I said. "Oh, Annie, I am so sorry for you and Lily. After all you have done for him."

My sympathy seemed to appease Annie slightly and her voice became shrill as she told me, "Father said to me, Menie, that I must not oppose this. He told me icily he must be free to do as seems best for the prolongation of his life and his personal comfort. Those were his very words, Menie, as though he were giving a speech in parliament."

"Oh, Annie, I am so very sorry for you and Lily," I said again.

"It is Lily I feel the most sorry for, Menie. She is not yet thirty. She might have had a chance of marriage once her duties to Father had ended, but now, with the shame of this, I doubt she will ever marry, just like me."

"Oh, Annie. Father is an old man. And what can we do? If it is done, it is done, I suppose," I said.

I went to visit Father and the new Lady Parkes soon after their marriage. Father looked older and more worn than I had ever seen him, and the contrast between him and the fresh, rosy-cheeked face of his new wife was extreme.

"Thank you for coming, Menie," Father said as we sat formerly in the parlour, sipping tea.

"Yes, Menie, I do appreciate your visiting me," said Julia in almost a whisper as she glanced towards me nervously. "I *can* call you Menie, can't I?" she blurted out.

"Of course," I said, smiling stiffly towards her. "Can I call you Julia?"

She nodded furiously.

"I can be open with you, Menie, can't I?" Father said.

"Yes, Father. I hope you always have been and always will be." I looked into his familiar eyes with wonder and curiosity, the same almond-shaped eyes I had always loved. The same man I had always thought I understood.

"I know, Menie, that you did not approve of my marriage to Nellie, but she was a good woman and I loved 'er, as I loved your mother." Father's voice quavered slightly as he spoke, something that was a rare occurrence.

I swallowed hard to hide my own emotion. "That is long past, Father. We do not need to speak of that. I know Nellie proved a good wife and mother, and her death has been devastating to you."

"And, Menie, she 'as left me with five young children. You cannot imagine the responsibility I feel for them."

"I can imagine they are a burden to you, Father. But Annie and Lily have helped you with their care since Nellie died," I said with more passion than I intended.

"Yes, Menie, but Julia 'as cared for the children since their birth. She is like a mother to them," Father said.

I glanced at Julia and she met my eyes. "I do love them as my own, Menie," she said firmly. "And I swore to Nellie, I swore I would marry your father and raise the children as my own."

"Is that true?" I asked, searching the young woman's face, hoping to find some reasonable excuse for Father's latest indiscretion.

"Yes, as she was dying, I willingly swore to do so."

"Did you know of this, too, Father?" I turned to him.

"Yes, Menie, I swore to Nellie I would marry Julia, too," he replied.

I think I smiled then. I was so desperate that Father's shameful act could be explained. I so wanted to see in him again the father I had worshipped and adored – the great man who had filled me with pride.

"And, Menie, I esteem your father greatly," Julia said, smiling shyly towards him. "He is a wonderful man and he has achieved so much, and he is full of compassion. And I love the children, just as I loved Nellie."

I began to cry with a confused mixture of grief and relief and Julia reached for my hand affectionately, thinking I understood their union.

The newspapers had a ball ridiculing father on this third marriage to a girl almost sixty years his junior. *The Bulletin* displayed a cartoon showing father shaking hands with a young boy with the caption from the boy reading, *Oh why did you get married again so soon, Father Parkes?* and Father replying, *Ah, my dear little boy, at eighty, one cannot afford to wait.*

Father not only remarried but also attempted to win yet another seat in parliament. In February 1896, he stood for the seat of Waverley. His new wife, Lady Julia Parkes, stood beside him on the platforms when he spoke to the crowds. I was proud but also slightly embarrassed and wary of this attempt of my elderly father to reassert himself in the political field. The newspapers were not sympathetic, either. *The Bulletin* published a cartoon of Father playing a one-stringed harp entitled 'The Harp that Once'. Father was soundly defeated.

It causes me deep regret to think of Father's public persona in his final years. He had achieved so much of importance and had been such a great man. I wish I could now delete the events of those last years that detracted from his achievements. I hope in the future, as time blurs the details, he will be remembered for the great statesman he was. But for Mamma's sake, too, I wanted to relate this story of their lives, of their love, their endurance and their determination.

Shortly after Father's loss in the seat of Waverley came his final defeat. This man, my father, was, it seems, defeated in life. Father developed pneumonia in early April. He lost his remarkable power of speech on the 25th of April.

I went to visit him that afternoon and was shocked at Father's silence and lack of awareness of his surroundings. He seemed to stare into my face as though he did not recognise who or what I was. That such a great man could be brought so low caused an ache within me that burned like a physical wound.

Father died two days later at four o'clock in the morning on the 27th of April, 1896, with his third wife, Lady Julia Parkes, by his side. She had sent word to Annie and Lily, and they arrived at Father's home only minutes after he had passed. His fight, his ambition, his struggle, was over.

My father, Henry Parkes, was no more.

I will end this memoir here, at the point of Father's death. His funeral was a private affair, but crowds of people lined the streets to view his coffin as it was carried by dray to the station. The shopfronts were closed in his honour and the bells of St Philip's Church rang out for him. He was buried beside Mamma in the grave at Faulconbridge, and Annie later wrote, *They who trod life's thorny path together for fifty-two years now lie side by side at rest for evermore. None can divide them now. May their good deeds only be remembered.*

I will always love them, my parents, Clarinda and Henry.

POSTSCRIPT

The Commonwealth of Australia was proclaimed on the 1st of January, 1901, in the public area that Henry Parkes had opened on Australia's centenary, Centennial Park. Sir Edmund Barton was sworn in as Australia's first prime minister. During his speech, Sir Barton said: "To Sir Henry Parkes is due the fruition of the struggle to unite the colonies which has been today so happily brought about. He had the vision of the future rather than of the immediate present which distinguishes the statesman from the party politician."

Sir Edmund Barton later named Sir Henry Parkes the Father of Federation.

The Australian Constitution was based largely on the Bill drafted by the participants of the National Convention in 1891 including Sir Henry Parkes. It is disappointing, however, that the Aboriginal peoples of Australia were not fully recognised in this Bill or in the Constitution and that the full right to vote was only given to Aboriginal people in the 1960s. Universal suffrage, it seems, did not mean all people during this era!

Henry Parkes was a member of sixteen New South Wales parliaments. His political career spanned forty-one years, including almost twelve years as premier.

Henry had other books of poems published other than those mentioned in this book. They include 'Murmurs of the Stream' in 1862, 'Studies in Rhyme' in 1870, 'The Beauteous Terrorist and Other Poems' in 1885, 'Fragmentary Thoughts' in 1886 and 'Sonnets and Other Verse' in 1895.

Henry and Nellie's five children were cared for by Lady Julia Parkes following his death. The youngest, Cobden Parkes, became Government Architect.

George Reid, the premier at the time of Henry Parkes's death, and someone whom Henry had derided, came to visit him on his deathbed and the two men made amends. Henry said after Mr Reid's visit: "I am glad I saw 'im. I 'ave misunderstood 'im."

Menie Thom died in October 1915. She was survived by her sisters: Mary, Annie, Gerty and Lily; her brother: Varney; and her remaining children: William, John, Clarinda and Robert; and her adopted daughter: Dorothy.

Clarinda and Henry Parkes were my great-great grandparents. Varney and Isabella Parkes were my great-grandparents, and Murray Parkes and his wife, Ida, were my grandparents.

Author's Note

This book is one of fiction, but based on the real lives of my great-great grandparents. In writing it, I have attempted to stay true to the known facts while still imagining and creating the personalities of the characters – their thoughts and actions – and the world they lived in.

I am indebted to several historians for the facts upon which my novel is loosely based. Chief amongst them is A.W. Martin through his work *Henry Parkes: A Biography* (Melbourne University Press, 1980), and his edited collection *Letters from Menie: Sir Henry Parkes and his Daughter* (Melbourne University Press, 1983). A full list of sources can be viewed in the bibliography, but I would also like to mention, in particular, my reliance on the texts by Robert Travers and Stephen Dando-Collins.

I am also greatly appreciative of my correspondence with and the information and detail provided by another of Clarinda and Henry's great-great grandchildren, and Menie Thom's great-grandson, Ian Thom. My interest in the lives of my Parkes ancestors was, of course, first sparked by stories from my mother, Anne Willetts (nee Parkes), and I was also greatly encouraged by my father, Haydn Willetts.

The intricacies of what is fact and what fiction is difficult to unravel now that the book is finished, for in writing this I became so engrossed in the story and my characters that they came alive to me, and much which is not based on fact now feels like truth to me. However, I will endeavour to unravel the tangled thread of fact and fiction.

Part I: Birmingham

All of the Parkes and Varney family members are based on true people. Many peripheral characters were also based on true people, including John Hornblower, Thomas Attwood and other Union leaders; the man Henry was apprenticed to, John Holding; the Reverend John Angell James; and Henry's Latin teacher at the Birmingham Mechanics' Institute, Toulmin Smith.

Fictitious characters included Isabella Parry and her father; Clarinda's tutor; Betty the maid; and the Miss Hamilton whom Martha Parkes is said to have served in her earlier years. I needed to create this character to explain Martha's remarkable ability to recite whole tracts of *Robinson Crusoe* despite never having learnt to read or write. This is believed to be a true fact.

The births and deaths of Clarinda and Henry's first two children are based on fact, as are the births and sometimes deaths of other Parkes children later in the book.

Real places in Birmingham at the time included the Parkes's home on Moseley Street and John Holding's shop on the same street; Henry's first shop on Bradford Street; Carr's Lane Chapel; Lombard Street Chapel; St Bartholomew's Anglican Church in Edgbaston where Henry and Clarinda were married; and St Philip's Church where Clarinda's mother and the babies, Thomas and Clarinda, are buried. Other places that were a part of Birmingham at the time included the Bull Ring; the

Lichfield Street Workhouse; Spring Gardens; the Botanic Gardens; and Vauxhall Gardens. Many of these places I discovered through Wikipedia.

The story of Henry's early life, lack of formal education and his entry into the workforce at a young age are based on fact, as is Thomas Parkes's time in debtors' prison. Also, it has been noted that Henry always had trouble saying his 'h's' and maintained his Midlands accent throughout his life.

Robert Varney did not approve of Henry as a suitor for Clarinda and he never spoke to his daughter again after she married him. It is also believed to be true that Clarinda's stepmother was cruel towards her and this, and her father's disapproval of Henry, were the reasons Clarinda moved out of her family home into a bedsit in Cheapside. This information has been gleaned mainly from other historians' accounts and from family stories.

It is known that Thomas Parkes was ill at various points throughout this time, but the collapse described at his garden plot is fictitious.

Henry did attend speeches by great men of the era such as the abolitionist George Thompson. He was also a member of the Birmingham Political Union and attended the massive meeting on Newhall Hill in 1832 that led to the Reform Act. His friend, John Hornblower, was probably a member of the London Working Man's Association and attended the National Chartist Convention. I do not know if he witnessed the fire in the Royal Exchange in London, or if Clarinda and Henry watched the first steam train between Manchester and Birmingham in 1837, but these events did happen.

The letters between Clarinda and Henry during their courtship are fictitious, as are the letters between Henry and John Hornblower. The poem contained in a letter to Clarinda was one written by Henry, as was the stanza on the Coronation of Queen Victoria. The lullaby Clarinda sings, however, is one I found on Wikipedia.

Part II: London

Clarinda and Henry did travel to London on a steam train without glass in the windows and were rained and hailed upon. This information is known due to a letter from Henry to his sister Sarah, as is the event of the double expense of a luggage handler when they first arrived in London and of John Hornblower arranging their accommodation in a garret room at Hatton Garden. The Irvine sisters were real people – although I invented their first names.

It is known that Clarinda and Henry visited Buckingham Palace, as Clarinda wrote in a letter: *I have seen the fine park and the Quens [sic] palace ... I like not the grandure [sic] and misery of this great Place I Picture [sic] to myself more beauty and happiness even on the wide wide Ocian [sic].*

It is also known through letters from Henry that he struggled to find work in London and his first job in London was making twine boxes, and that he and Clarinda were close to starving on Christmas day and the Irvine sisters gave them each a glass of wine and a piece of pudding.

Letters also reveal that Sarah, Henry's sister, visited Robert Varney and begged him for some kind words for Clarinda before she sailed to Australia, and that he reluctantly gave Sarah a sovereign to send to her.

Henry later showed he did not agree with the punishment of hanging when he refused to view the hangings of the Clarke brothers and of

Henry James O'Farrell, but I do not know if he ever witnessed a hanging. The hanging described in this section of the book is fictitious, although this was around the time of the last hangings in England.

Many of the letters from Henry in this part are authentic, although at times I have deleted parts of letters or joined parts together in order to further the story or not get bogged down in detail.

Part III: On Board the Strathfieldsaye

Much of the story based on the ship, the *Strathfieldsaye*, is fictitious or based on accounts from other emigrants who sailed from England to Australia during the 1800s. A list of the journals I read in order to gather this information is listed in the bibliography.

There are few personal records of Clarinda and Henry's journey apart from some letters from Henry to his family during their time on board before leaving the coast of England. From these it is known the *Strathfieldsaye* did have separate holds for men and women in steerage, Henry found many of his fellow passengers uncouth, a few men disembarked the ship at Plymouth and did not re-embark, and that one male passenger disappeared from the ship in Plymouth leaving his clothes and possessions behind.

I used the passenger list for the journey, which I obtained through ship records online, to invent the characters Mary Reardon and Sarah Crump, using the names of real people who sailed on the ship. Other passengers and crew are fictitious.

Clarinda did give birth to Menie Thom (nee Parkes) on board the ship, off the coast of New South Wales, and with only the assistance of some of the other women on board. It is not known why the ship's surgeon did not attend the birth and so I invented his drunkenness as a reason. I did not use the name of the real ship's surgeon as I thought this might be insulting to any of his ancestors.

There was a family named Higginbottom on board the ship but I do not know if a child of theirs died. I know from other accounts that many children and other passengers often died during the arduous journey to Australia and so I invented this occurrence on Clarinda and Henry's voyage. I also invented the death of the ship's apprentice Jimmy based on accounts of similar deaths from some of the journals I read.

Part IV: Memoir of Menie Thom (Nee Parkes)
Throughout Part IV I used the names of real politicians and friends of Henry's and attempted to capture their personalities based on accounts from other historians. People such as Menie's 'uncles', Charles Harpur and William Duncan, and politicians, such as William Wentworth and Charles Cowper, were real people. John Fairfax is the ancestor of the current *The Sydney Morning Herald* Fairfax family and did have a respectful relationship with Henry despite their opposing views, and Menie did ask for his advice on financial matters when Henry was overseas.

I am indebted to Grace Karskens's work *The Colony: A History of Early Sydney* (Allen & Unwin, 2009) for her descriptions of early Sydney, the social and political climate, and the local Aboriginal people. Rickety Dicky, Mahroot, Cora Gooseberry and her sons were all real people.

As mentioned before, the births and deaths of the Parkes children are based on fact, as are the deaths of the Parkes and Varney family members back in England, and the births and deaths of the Thom family members. Tom Parkes and Maria Parkes did travel to Australia as described in the book.

Author's Note

Much of Menie's childhood memories are fictitious, although those involving Henry's career as a newspaper proprietor and a politician are based on fact, as are details of his bankruptcies and being 'Purefoyed'; the enmity of *The Sydney Morning Herald* editor, John West; the strike of Henry's compositors and the resulting court case along with the birth of Annie that night; Henry's being hit by Arthur Ormsby; and his travels overseas, including the people he met and befriended there. However, much of the reactions of Menie, Clarinda and the rest of the family are imaginary or based on family stories, although it is known from letters that Henry's daughters were not enamoured with Isabella Murray, and that Clarinda did insist on Henry returning from England when he had been away for almost two years. Also true are details of legislation that Henry introduced, including the Public Schools Act and his reforms of institutions such as asylums and hospitals following his request to Florence Nightingale. He continued a correspondence with her.

All of the names of homes where the Parkes and the Thom families lived are real. Henry's obsession with collections, including collections of animals, are true and described by other historians as well as being supported by the lists of items in auction catalogues.

I do not know if Henry was fascinated by shipwrecks, but his report on the sinking of the *Dunbar* is one I found on Wikipedia, and details of other shipwrecks mentioned were found in Rob Mundle's book *Under Full Sail* (ABC Books, 2016).

All letters between Henry and Menie are real, although at times I have used parts of letters and joined letters. These letters include the ones concerning Henry's knighthood and the letter from Menie relating her shock at his marriage to Eleanor. Henry and Menie's poems are real, including 'The Dream' and its publication in the *Empire* along with the editor's note, and Clarinda's adverse reaction. Menie also wrote the serials *Pet Perennials* and *Miss Jesse's Schooldays and What Came of Them*, as well as the novel *Bittersweet*. It is believed the other novels listed were written by her under pseudonyms, Ariel being one of these pseudonyms, as discovered by the research of James Cleary and Catriona Mills listed in the bibliography.

Other events based on fact, mainly found in Menie's letters to Henry or in accounts of other historians, include Varney's sickness and his accident with a swing; Henry's wish to stay on longer in England on his trip as a Commissioner and Clarinda's opposition; Robert's adolescent rebellion; the deaths of four policemen at the hands of the Clarke brothers and Henry's involvement; the visit of Prince Alfred, Duke of Edinburgh; the Parkes family's involvement in the celebrations; the subsequent attempted assassination; Henry's involvement in the question of whether it was due to a Fenian plot, which is a question not resolved to this day; and the letter Henry received from Ned Kelly.

Menie did have feelings for a man named John Owen as she told Henry of him in a letter, although the circumstances of this relationship are unknown. Other real characters included Mr Betteridge, Lizzie Langley, the Letherbridges, the Taylors and the Vaughans. Menie does mention a Robert Wilshire in a letter whom she found much changed, but the circumstances of this change are unknown and therefore my explanation is fictional. Mary Windeyer was on the ship with Henry and Clarinda and Henry did later have a friendship with her and her husband, William Windeyer. It is true that Henry ran into his old friend John Hornblower in Melbourne, and his travels and friendship with Isabella Murray did create much opposition between her and the Parkes daughters, especially Annie.

One fact I found very difficult to explain was Menie's adoption of Dorothy. Dorothy's full parentage is unknown, as are the reasons for Menie's willingness to adopt her. I created the story of Menie's son Harry having fathered Dorothy to Millie Barnes. In fact, it is known that Dorothy's real mother was Mary Ellen Barnes, who was married and had eleven children before Dorothy's birth. Ian Thom provided me with this information from family research, but due to the questions surrounding Dorothy's full parentage, I decided to make my explanation completely fictional so as not to offend any living descendants.

ABOUT THE AUTHOR

Catherine Blake is a great-great granddaughter of Clarinda and Henry Parkes. She grew up in Sydney and studied a combined degree in Arts and Law at the University of New South Wales with a major in history and a minor in English. Catherine worked as a lawyer in Sydney and Wagga Wagga before moving to Canberra and studying a diploma of primary school teaching while her children were young. She has been a teacher in the public school system of the Australian Capital Territory for over a decade. Her passion for teaching and writing was inspired by an amazing second grade teacher, Mrs Clear, at Eastwood Public School, Sydney. Catherine is married to Simon, and has three adult children: Steph, Ellie and Josh.

APPENDIX

Photographs edited by Honor Luckhurst

Portraits of Henry and Clarinda
(Courtesy of Ian Thom)

Henry and Clarinda
(Courtesy of Helen and Peter Webber)

Menie Thom (nee Parkes)
(Courtesy of Ian Thom)

Annie Parkes
(Courtesy of Helen and
Peter Webber)

Lily Parkes
(Courtesy of Helen and
Peter Webber)

Varney Parkes
(Courtesy of Helen and
Peter Webber)

Bella Parkes (nee Murray)
(Courtesy of Helen and
Peter Webber)

Mary Murray (nee Parkes)   Mary Parkes (nee Murray)
(Courtesy of Helen and   (Courtesy of Helen and
Peter Webber)   Peter Webber)

BIBLIOGRAPHY

1. Barnard, Edwin, *Capturing Time: Panoramas of Old Australia* (Canberra, National Library of Australia, 2012).

2. Bavin, Sir Thomas, *Sir Henry Parkes – His Life and Work* (Sydney, Angus & Robertson, 1941).

3. Blair, David, *Henry Parkes in 1850* (Sydney, Centennial Magazine, 5 April 1889).

4. Campbell, Keith, *Henry Parkes's Utopia* (Kulnara, Lynwood Press, 1994).

5. Cleary, James and Mills, Catriona, '"Ariel" and Australian Nineteenth-Century Serial Fiction: A Case of Mistaken Attribution' (Griffith University, Script & Print: bulletin of the Bibliographical Society of Australia & New Zealand, Vol 34, Issue 3, 2010).

6. Clendinnen, Inga, *Dancing with Strangers* (Melbourne, Text Publishing, 2003).

7. Dando-Collins, Stephen, *Sir Henry Parkes: The Australian Colossus* (Sydney, Random House, 2013).

8. Facey, A.B., *A Fortunate Life* (Melbourne, Penguin, 1981).

9. Hirst, John, *Australian History in 7 Questions* (Melbourne, Black Inc, 2014).

10. Hirst, John, *Freedom on the Fatal Shore: Australia's First Colony* (Melbourne, Black Inc, 2008).

11. Hughes, Robert, *The Fatal Shore* (London, Vintage Books, 2003).

12. Karskens, Grace, *The Colony: A History of Early Sydney* (Sydney, Allen & Unwin, 2009).

13. Lord, Gabrielle, *Whipping Boy* (Sydney, Hachette, 1992).

14. Lyne, Charles E., *Life of Sir Henry Parkes, G.C.M.G., Australian Statesman* (Sydney, George Robertson, 1896).

15. Martin, A.W., *Henry Parkes: A Biography* (Melbourne, Melbourne University Press, 1980).

16. Martin, A.W. (editor), *Letters from Menie: Sir Henry Parkes and His Daughter* (Melbourne, Melbourne University Press, 1983).

17. McCullough, Colleen, *Morgan's Run* (London, Random House, 2001).

18. McLauren, M.D. *Sir Henry: A Biographical Sketch of Sir Henry Parkes, G.C.M.G* (Sydney, Whitcombe & Tombs, 1946).

19. Mundle, Rob, *Under Full Sail* (Sydney, Harper Collins Publishers, 2016).

20. Norton, James, *The Condition of the Colony of NSW* (Reading & Wellbank, 1860).

21. Painter, W.F.W., *Sir Henry Parkes – Founder of Australian Federation: A Short Biography* (Sydney, W.F.W. Painter, 197?).

22. Parkes, Henry, *Australian Views of England* (Sydney, Macmillan & Co, 1869).

23. Parkes, Henry, *An Emigrant's Home Letters* (Sydney, Angus & Robertson, 1896).

24. Parkes, Henry, *Fifty Years of Australian History* (London, Longmans Green & Co, 1892).

25. Parkes, Henry, *Fragmentary Thoughts* (Sydney, Samuel E. Lees, 1889).

26. Parkes, Henry, *Murmurs of the Stream* (Sydney, James W. Waugh, 1862).

27. Parkes, Henry, *Sonnets and Other Verse* (London, Kegan, Paul, Trench, Trubner & Co, 1895).

28. Parkes, Henry, *Speeches* (Melbourne, George Robertson, 1876).

29. Parkes, Henry, *Studies in Rhyme* (Sydney, J. Ferguson, 1870).

30. Parkes, Henry, *The Australian Federation Speech of Sir Henry Parkes, Delivered in the Legislative Assembly, 7 May 1890* (Sydney, Charles Potter, Government Printer, 1890).

31. Parkes, Henry, *The Beauteous Terrorist and other poems* (Melbourne, George Robertson, 1885).

32. Parkes, Henry, *The Case of the Prisoner Gardiner: The Prerogative of Pardon: A Chapter of History* (Melbourne, George Robertson, 1876).

33. Parkes, Henry, *The Federal Government of Australasia Speeches, November 1889 – May 1890* (Sydney, Turner & Henderson, 1890).

34. Parkes, Henry, *The O'Farrell Papers* (Sydney, John Ferguson, 1868).

35. Parkes, Henry, *The Policy and Conduct of the Reid Ministry* (Sydney, Turner & Henderson, 1895).

36. Parkes, Henry, *The Union of the Colonies: Speeches Delivered in the Legislative Assembly of NSW, May 16 – 23, 1895* (Sydney, Turner & Henderson, 1895).

37. Rodd, L.C., *Great People in Australian History: Henry Parkes* (London, Longmans, Green & Co, 1965).

38. Russell, Roslyn, *High Seas and High Teas: Voyaging to Australia* (Canberra, National Library of Australia, 2016).

39. Spaull, G.T., *The Educational Aims and Work of Sir Henry Parkes* (Sydney, William Applegate Gullick, Government Printer, 1920).

40. Smith, Thomas, *The Political Lion and the Social Lamb* (Sydney, Andrew & Wall, 1894).

41. Travis, Robert, *The Grand Old Man of Australian Politics: The Life and Times of Sir Henry Parkes* (Sydney, Kangaroo Press, 1992).

42. Walsh, James H., *Early Ballan* (Ballan, Victoria, The Ballan Times, 1917).

Unpublished Journals and Articles

43. Gedge, Edith S., *Journal of Edith Gedge*, MS 9054 (1888 – 1889).

44. Gratton, Annie, *Diary, June 5 – September 18, 1858*, MS 3304 (1858).

45. Gregg, John, *Journal of the Most Interesting Events of and the Employment of Time of Your Humble Servant J. Gregg, Carpenter*, MS 2749 (1862).

46. Parkes, Henry, *Australia and the Imperial Connection*, (1884).

47. Parkes, Henry, *The Protectionists of NSW* (1889).

48. Pegler, Edwin S., *Log Book and Diary of Edwin S. Pegler During His Voyage to Australia*, MS 3128 (1852).

49. Scammell, Luther, *A Voyage to Australia in the Barque 'William Wilson': From the Diary of Luther Scammell 1849*.

50. Shaw, Samuel, *An Account of a Voyage to Australia in a Sailing Ship in the Years 1877 – 78*, MS 2829 (1878).

51. Robinson, John, *John Robinson's Voyage from England to Van-die-mans Land – New South Wales*, MS 1845 (1838).

52. Tarry, Joseph, *A Voyage to Australia in 1853: The Diary of Joseph Tarry* (1853).

Catalogues and Collections

53. Wikipedia.

54. Ship records – *The Strathfieldsaye*- NRS5316/4_4784/Strathfieldsaye_27 July 1839/.

55. Sir Henry Parkes Newspaper Cuttings 1880 – 1891.

56. Collection of Unpublished Papers for Sir H. Parkes – forwarded to London, 24 March 1882, for information of Henry Parkes.

57. Catalogue of Sir Henry Parkes: Rare and Very Scarce Works of Art (Bradley, Newton & Lamb, Auctioneers, 1883).

58. Art Treasures, Catalogue of Sir Henry Parkes, K.C.M.G. – Auctioneers Bradley, Newton & Lamb, 1883.

59. Book of Newspaper Cuttings on Australian Federation kept by Sir Henry Parkes, 1890.

60. Draft of a Bill to Constitute the Commonwealth of Australia (George Stephen Chapman, Acting Government Printer, 1891).

61. Catalogue of the Library and Furniture of the Hon. Sir Henry Parkes, G.C.M.G. Removed from his residence "Kenilworth" (Cunningham & Co Printers, Sydney, 1896).

62. Estate of the late Sir Henry Parkes – Catalogue of the Books, Paintings, Engravings, Bronzes, Antique Furniture (Cunningham & Co, Sydney, 1896).

63. Interstate Estate of the late Sir Henry Parkes, G.C.M.G – Catalogue (Cunningham & Co Printers, Sydney, 1896).

64. The British Newspaper Archive.

Lightning Source UK Ltd.
Milton Keynes UK
UKHW04f0835080818
326932UK00001B/134/P